Allen's third volume of extraordinary short stories reaches new heights of rarity and wonder . . . Without a wrong note, all the stories in this anthology admirably fulfill Allen's promise of "beauty and strangeness."

— *Publishers Weekly*, **Starred Review**

Allen continues to assemble some of the most adventurous, beauteous, and just plain weird stuff our current crop of speculative authors are capable of producing.

— *Strange Horizons*

## PRAISE FOR
# CLOCKWORK PHOENIX 2
## more tales of beauty and strangeness

Allen finds his groove for this second annual anthology of weird stories, selecting 16 wonderfully evocative, well-written tales . . . Each story fits neatly alongside the next, and the diversity of topics, perspectives and authors makes this cosmopolitan anthology a winner.

— *Publishers Weekly*, **Starred Review**

Original tales by some of fantasy's most imaginative voices . . . each chosen for their unique perspective and stylistic grace.

— *Library Journal*

## PRAISE FOR
# CLOCKWORK PHOENIX
## tales of beauty and strangeness

Author and editor Allen (*Mythic*) has compiled a neatly packaged set of short stories that flow cleverly and seamlessly from one inspiration to another . . . Lush descriptions and exotic imagery startle, engross, chill and electrify the reader, and all 19 stories have a strong and delicious taste of weird.

— *Publishers Weekly*

Established writers and new names all are in good form here . . . A series of great promise.

— *Locus*

# CLOCKWORK PHOENIX ⑤

# Also by Mike Allen

# CLOCKWORK
# PHOENIX

# Edited by Mike Allen

**Mythic Delirium**
**BOOKS**

mythicdelirium.com

## CLOCKWORK PHOENIX 5
*Edited by Mike Allen*

ISBN-10: 0-9889124-7-3
ISBN-13: 978-0-9889124-7-2

FIRST EDITION
Trade Paperback Edition
April 5, 2016

Published by Mythic Delirium Books
3514 Signal Hill Ave. NW
Roanoke VA 24017
www.mythicdelirium.com

Printed in the United States of America

Our gratitude goes out to the following who because of their generosity are from now on designated as supporters of Mythic Delirium Books: Saira Ali, Cora Anderson, Anonymous, Patricia M. Cryan, Steve Dempsey, Oz Drummond, Patrick Dugan, Matthew Farrer, C. R. Fowler, Mary J. Lewis, Paul T. Muse, Jr., Shyam Nunley, Finny Pendragon, Kenneth Schneyer, and Delia Sherman.

*In honor of*
*Elizabeth Campbell*

*In memory of*
*Tanith Lee*

# CONTENTS

# INTRODUCTION

## *Mike Allen*

And ashes coalesce into interlocked gears once more, and those gears start to turn, spreading razor-edged pinions to carry the re-formed phoenix aloft.

It soars over glittering plains of ice white as death, then underneath, through blue deeps to the beautiful cities built of bone. Deeper still, through the bottom of the world and out of the mirror's dividing plane, into the terraced gardens reflected on the other side. It hovers to observe ethereal dances performed by rulers and their courts, with soul-destroying intrigues concealed in every graceful maneuver.

Then it rises into a different sky, wind revolving around it in ever-quickening circles, surrounded by other winged beings, some living, some dead, before it beats the thinning air with its gold and iridescent feathers and departs the worldly altogether. It pauses at a vantage outside the cosmic sphere, one that allows it to spy into scenes ranging through multiple times and impossible places. It chooses a destination, prepares to descend.

It's wonderful to meld again with my beloved creation and savor another flight, this one perhaps the most ambitious of all.

I write this introduction in a state of awe.

I'm in awe at the stunning generosity of friends, fans, colleagues, and Kickstarter backers that made it possible for me to assemble the largest, most elaborate installment yet in my imprint's flagship anthology series.

I'm in awe at the talent on display in these pages, and that I have the honor of being the first to showcase these stories.

For any reader who might be new to *Clockwork Phoenix*, the project began eight years ago, intended as a home for works that defy genre boundaries, that stretch the imagination, that experiment with methods of storytelling yet tell stories of heartfelt impact. The name is not truly meant to describe a fantastic creature, but rather to present a striking juxtaposition not unlike "exquisite corpse." (Interestingly, the term seems to have slunk into the zeitgeist, with actual drawings of clockwork phoenixes proliferating on the Internet.)

Other anthologies at the time, such as *Interfictions*, *The New Weird*, *Feeling Very Strange: The Slipstream Anthology*, and *Paper Cities: An Anthology of Urban Fantasy*, explored themes and techniques similar to those that interested me, but did so with the intent to define the sorts of stories they contained. I wanted to create a book that would partake of the same beautiful weirdness without making any sort of academic statement about it.

In fact, I was so determined to let readers glean their own way through the stories I picked that in the first three volumes, I wrote introductions that were essentially enigmatic prose poems, as in the opening paragraphs above, and hid what few guideposts I was willing to offer within my bios at the very back of the books.

I abandoned that tradition with *Clockwork Phoenix 4*.

The first three books were released by another publisher, who became unable to continue the series due to financial woes. In 2012, two years after the appearance of *Clockwork Phoenix 3*, I chose to wade into the waters of crowdfunding to revive the series under my own imprint. The campaign to fund *Clockwork Phoenix 4* was a resounding success, and when I wrote the introduction to that book, I chose to speak plainly about my aims as one way of acknowledging that the book's existence was a community effort.

As with the previous three volumes, the stories in *Clockwork Phoenix 4* were reprinted in *Year's Best* anthologies and nominated for awards, and, more broadly, the positive fallout from the book laid a foundation for other books, other projects.

When I chose to ask for funds for *Clockwork Phoenix 5*, the book in your hands, it wasn't in order to bring the series back from the dead but, if you'll forgive me for hammering home the metaphor, to see how far a new volume could fly.

I can't fully describe how gratifying it was to see writers and readers speak out to advocate for this book and the series as a whole, how even though they perhaps could not wholly explain what made these books so special, there was nonetheless a certain je ne sais quoi they regarded with fondness and hoped to see continue.

I certainly can't fully convey how grateful I am to the hundreds who gave time, creative effort, and money in order to bring about more of our je ne sais quoi.

What follows is what all that generosity has wrought: twenty stories by twenty-one authors, 96,000 words of fiction, the biggest *Clockwork Phoenix* there has ever been.

Let's capture a current of air in the curve of our wings and be on our way. We need no more force to lift us than the teasing exhale of a breeze . . .

# THE WIND AT HIS BACK

## *Jason Kimble*

Benito nudged Breezy from a trot to a canter, hoping to earn the horse her name, but the air of the scalding day didn't want to move. The length of late-day shadows would have been a nice reprieve, except that there wasn't anything along the road home to cast a decent shadow in the first place.

It had been like this for nearly a week. No breeze. No rain. Days so hot they seemed downright angry, squeezing all the water out of a body as soon as the sun caught sight of you. It felt like walking outside was asking the world to crush you as brutal as any storm might. Benito was all knots and nerves, and too exhausted to fight either one.

The long ride home was a fresh misery. As he nudged his Stetson up and wiped his brow with a handkerchief soaked through and starting to stink, Benito itched to wrangle. It wouldn't be anything to reach out, snag a bit of wind, and turn it on himself to cut through the burn of the sun beating down.

But it wouldn't just be a breeze, and he knew it. Touch the wind, and he was touching all the wild up inside it. Or the wild caged up in himself. It was hard to tell the difference when you were wrangling.

"Benito Guzman Aguilar!"

Benito started at the sound of his name. He turned to find Casey, blocky hands on his hips, staring up cockeyed from the side of the road.

"Now I know you weren't going to be the sort who rides right by his husband without so much as a hello," Casey chided, crossing out of the knee-

14

high corn. He wiped the dirt from his face with his unworn work shirt before stuffing it into the back of his trousers. Benito pushed the memories of dread back where they belonged and gave his own crooked smile. There wasn't much that ended a dark mood better than watching Casey wipe down after a long day in the sun.

Benito was about to banter back when he found himself under one of those long shadows he'd been hoping for earlier. Except the closest tree was the Seeder grove at least a mile back. He spun in his saddle, hand snapping for his pistol.

The Mestrovich girl jumped back with a squeak and dropped the gnarled tree stump she'd been carrying. Breezy reared up at the massive thud and dust cloud, but she was solid, and it only took a quick pull on the reins to steady her.

"Careful sneaking up on a body, Sarah," Benito said, fighting to slow the pounding of blood in his ears even as he stroked Breezy's neck.

"Sorry, sheriff," Sarah returned shakily. At nearly ten feet tall—one shy of having a foot for each year on her—the girl was already a mountain. Still, those saucer-plate-wide blue eyes worked as well for the giant child as they did any of her human schoolmates.

He'd almost drawn down on the girl. Scared her as well as if he had. Her fear, her hurt right now was Benito's fault. But he'd given that up, promised it away. No more hurting. No more children crying and screaming and begging for their parents. The pounding surged back up in his ears. It was hard to breathe. If he just grabbed a little wind it would be easier, surely. The howl would drown the pain or drown him in pain, and maybe it didn't matter which.

"Don't listen to him anyhow, Sarah," Casey offered, his light tone bringing Benito back like always. Benito breathed air that wasn't touched by any of the anger and fear and panic. He shoved those things away. Locked himself off from them. From the world. Focused on Casey's tanned, callused hand on his knee. Breathed again.

Casey moved his hand to rub Breezy on the nose as he crossed the road to the girl. "Any sheriff that lets a giant sneak up on him deserves himself a start, don't you think?" he said.

Sarah giggled. "I reckon so," she said. Her smile was the last of what Benito needed to seal off the rough parts of the world. His ragged breath steadied as Casey patted the young girl's hand. Casey gave Benito a wink. No harm done.

"Natalia has family from back east coming in a few days," Casey explained. "I offered to watch little Sarah for the day so she could get her house in order without any other distractions."

"I pulled the stump all by myself!" Sarah announced, moving close to show Benito the mass of gnarled and torn roots. He had to crane his neck up even from Breezy's back to give the girl an encouraging smile.

"Yes, you finally got the last of the hickory you knocked over last winter," Casey quipped. The young giant blushed. Casey waved it off before Sarah could get herself worked up again. "You've been a big help, little one," he offered. "Now I think it's about time you hurried home for supper, don't you? Just drop the stump in the wagon before you go so I can get it back to the house."

Sarah kicked up dust as she sprinted to the wagon. She chucked the stump into the back. The struts squealed in protest, but the giant girl had already turned about and was barreling home fast as her oversized legs could take her.

"Just don't crush the corn on your way!" Casey yelled after her, but Benito doubted Sarah could hear him over the thunder of her own feet on the ground.

"You want one now, don't you?" Benito said with a smirk, jabbing his thumb at the retreating child.

"Bite your tongue and swallow it," Casey returned, smacking Benito's shin playfully. "If we get our own, we can't send her home."

Benito nodded, letting somberness fall into his features. "That's the second one today almost set me off," he admitted quietly. At Casey's look, he added, "Mei Wu."

"What bit her this time?" Casey asked with mild amusement.

"Joint snake," Benito answered, Casey's smile pulling out the glib. "Fool girl's bound and determined to prove herself braver than those Knox twins. She cut the thing in half when the boys went running, but didn't know that's no more than a nuisance to their kind. Snake joined back up when she wasn't looking. If I hadn't been riding by . . ."

Benito felt the slight throb of his pulse at his temples and shook his head. That hurt wasn't him. "Yuna got her fixed up," he said, forcing a smile.

"That's why we love our Doc Hayashi. And you?" Casey asked, green eyes pinning him.

"I'm fine," Benito said, swatting at the worry in the air with one hand.

At Casey's tug, Benito swooped his leg over Breezy's back. He landed with an easy bend in his knees right in front of Casey, whose sandy brown beard split with a grin. Casey used his shirt to wipe the sweat off his brow again. Benito grabbed the other end. He pulled Casey close, lacing his fingers in the wet small of his husband's bare back, then kissed him. Snake bites and guilt-panic and troubling heat waves fell off the wagon of Benito's mind as beards skritched along lips. Casey smelled like loam and prairie grass after a storm.

Casey squirmed away with a chuckle. He tapped Benito's badge with one finger. "That gets a might warm when you've been in the sun too long," he said, brushing his thumb through the soft hair of the matching spot on his own bare chest.

"Well, then, I expect we best get out of the sun," Benito said. His cheeks warmed as a wry smile crept its way onto Casey's face.

The waning sunlight spun with dust and smelled of the stew simmering downstairs. Benito lay beside Casey on the bed. He ran his hand down Casey's back, lingering at a spot near his waist. There Casey's skin quickly faded from the reddish tan that almost matched Benito's own to the naturally pale skin which hid away from the sun under his trousers.

Casey squirmed. "That tickles," he said, batting the hand away with a wide grin. "And none of what you just did lets you out of your turn getting supper ready," he added, rolling onto his side. He propped himself up on one elbow.

Benito chuckled, then slid out of bed. "I *am* getting peckish." He grabbed his trousers from the nearby stool. He'd only pulled one of the braces up on his shoulder when the light dimmed and the rattling at the window drew him over.

Outside, the wind had picked up. Clouds bled gray and churned in the sky. It was the kind of thing that used to happen when Benito lost control. The nagging tug at the top of his throat said this wasn't natural, either.

He flinched as Casey's arms snaked around his middle from behind. The familiar, itchy bristle of Casey's chin on his right shoulder, though, calmed the roiling in the back of his head.

"Haven't seen it turn to storm this fast in a while," Casey whispered. Benito leaned his head to rest on Casey's crown. They both looked out at the grass and dust riled up and flying about. Benito closed his eyes a moment. He breathed in Casey's after-storm smell mixed with his own musk. A moment this soft and warm would have been ripped up and torn to ribbons by the Pac he'd been. Benito breathed them both in again, held the scent until he was sure he'd washed that life back down and locked it up tight, then sighed.

"I should start on the johnnycakes," he whispered, kissing the top of Casey's head.

"Don't know why you haven't already," Casey jibed, sliding around front and kissing Benito properly. He smacked Benito's behind as the sheriff crossed the loft along the worn-smooth path in the floorboards.

Benito had just dropped the johnnycakes into the pan when the bang came at the door. He jumped, knots clenching tight in his shoulders. "You expecting anyone?" he called up.

His sandy-haired other half popped a head and broad shoulders out from the loft. "No more than usual, sheriff," Casey quipped.

Benito sighed. Casey was right, of course. Unexpected visits almost always wound up being for Benito in his official capacity.

He opened the door to see the back of a lanky man. The visitor watched the storm threatening to come in. His dark hair was damp with sweat where it slipped out from under a beaten-up Stetson. Point of fact, most of what he wore, from the shirt to the chaps, was tattered, faded, and worn. Loose fit, too, like there used to be more of him. Benito cleared his throat, and the man turned back with a face as haggard as his clothes. His sunken, scruffy cheeks wrinkled sideways as he grinned.

"Benny!" he said. It wasn't until he heard the name that Benito recognized the man holding out a big-knuckled hand.

"Pete?" he asked. A rush of cold ran down his back.

Pete grabbed Benito's hand where it hung at his side. Clapped his other hand on top and shook, hard and desperate. Benito tried not to stare, and failed miserably.

He flinched back to himself when his shirt whipped over his head. He pulled it off and spun around, where a barefoot and half-dressed Casey clambered down the ladder, Benito's Stetson on his head.

"I was right?" Casey asked with his canary-eating grin. He hooked Benito's gun belt from the back of a chair and scooped up his sheriff's star from the table.

Pete cleared his throat and broke the handshake.

"I . . . yeah. Official business," Benito said. He pushed Pete back outside. Pete didn't object when the door half-closed in his face.

Casey sighed as Benito slid his shirt on and buttoned it up. Benito gritted his teeth, willing his fingers steady.

"I'll try not to eat all the stew," Casey said. "But no promises on the johnnycakes." He handed Benito the gun belt and pinned the star in place himself. Then he flipped the hat off his own head and rolled it to sit on Benito's with a flourish. He frowned when he caught Benito's look. "Is everything—?"

"I'm fine," Benito said. Casey's lips thinned, his eyes searching.

"Just hate having supper spoiled. This might take awhile," Benito said, feeling warmth in his cheeks.

Casey didn't hide the worry in his face, which twisted Benito's insides, but he also didn't press. "Gets too late, you bunk with Yuna," Casey said. "Natalia says she heard whimpuses droning the other night. I'd rather they spin themselves hungry and you come home later but safe.

"Besides, I reckon Yuna might have leftovers from feeding Jenny," Casey added, winking away what Benito wasn't saying. Jenny, Yuna's jackalope, ate whiskey-soaked oats. Casey obviously thought Benito would use this as an excuse to grab a drink with the doc, then.

Benito gave his own nervous chuckle and let that lie between them.

"Be safe, Ben," Casey said.

"Only if there's no better options," Benito returned out of habit.

Benito curled up inside Casey's kiss, away from the noise and grit and stench of the world for just a breath or two longer. Then Casey stepped back and looked behind Benito, green eyes bright.

"Well, look at that. The storm cleared right up for you," he said.

"So this is a fine little situation you got for yourself, Benny," Pete said lightly.

They'd ridden toward town slowly, and hadn't said a word. Looked back and forth, sure. One or the other had opened his jaw to talk, but nothing broke through the thick, heavy air hanging between them. It wasn't until they were passing by the fence of the Seeder grove that Pete finally managed to speak. There always was something about the tinpots' fruit trees that made things a little easier.

"Why now, Pete?" Benito said. A little easier wasn't easy. He didn't have it in him to talk small.

"Can't an old buddy look up his partner from back in the day and—?" The lie died on Pete's lips as soon as he caught Benito's glare. It was hard to read his expression in the deep shadows of sunset, but the quiet told a story all its own. They went back to not talking again for a giant's step, nothing but the clop of hooves on the hard-packed road and the soft rustle of leaves as they passed through the grove.

"It's been tough, Benny," Pete said, slouching in his saddle. Benito pulled Breezy up short. Pete followed suit with his slope-backed mare. Pete's hangdog look was all the longer for the evening closing in around it.

"I went back," Pete muttered. The chill from before came back, only this time it didn't run down Benito's back. It grabbed hold. He thought it might tear his frozen spine out whole.

Benito swung down off Breezy, let her reins go. She was good enough not to wander off on her own. "To them? The Pacs?"

Pete swung down from his own horse, kept hold of her reins. "Benny, you don't miss it? We were kings of everything. We wrangled *twisters*, for Chrissakes. Grabbed something that could rip a house apart easy as eating breakfast, and we made it *ours*. Dammit, I just . . . ." He ran one big-knuckled hand through his oily hair and bit his lip.

"You told them I was alive, too," Benito said, the truth pounding in his ears.

The wind picked up as Pete started shuffling from one foot to the other. "You know I'm not a good liar, Benny. And they're our brothers, you know? You don't just turn your back on—"

"You won't take me back."

"Benny," Pete begged. He took two gangly steps to close the distance between them. The whistle in the wind rose in pitch.

"No."

Pete grabbed Benito's shirt in his stringy hands. A handful of smaller apples fell off the nearest trees when a gust hit them.

"They won't let me back in without I bring you," he whispered. His breath was a mix of whiskey and salted pork. Benito batted Pete's hands aside.

In the fading light, Benito saw Pete's face go hard and mean, his eyes flare wild. The wind whipped around them, dust starting to spin in the center of the road. Benito swore under his breath. It was his turn to grab Pete by the shirtfront. That wasn't all he grabbed. He reached out from his soul and grabbed the wind. He felt his blood throbbing in his temples, felt everything he ever resented well up and scream in his ears. He threw all of that against Pete's will.

There was a loud thump. The road dust flew into the air like someone had thrown a bag of feed down. Then the wind was gone.

"I *worked* for this life, Pete," Benito growled, shoving Pete away from him. Pete started to rush him again. This time Benito had his pistol out. The other man stumbled to a stop with a grunt. Benito forced himself to hold the gun steady, breathe deep. Took in the scent of apples and berries. Pushed the rage and the malice and the screams of children down, back where he kept them locked away.

Pete was wiping the heavy sweat from his face by the time Benito felt himself again. He took two steps toward Pete, slow and calm. When Pete opened his mouth to talk, Benito cut him off.

"I never forgot how it was," Benito said, flat and even. "Don't imagine I ever will, Pete. It sounds like maybe *you're* forgetting a thing or two about what we saw, about why we left in the first place.

"You think this is fine and easy? Maybe it is, but none of it was easy to come by. I'm not giving it up. Not for you," Benito said, swinging back up onto Breezy. He kept the gun on Pete as he nudged the horse to turn. "And sure as seven hells not for Pacos Bill's lapdogs."

"They'll come for you," Pete said, grabbing his own horse, working to calm it down in the face of the sudden squall that had come and gone. "The code's the law."

"*I'm* the law here, Pete McSwain," Benito said. "And I'm telling you: find your way out of town tomorrow before I decide we're all better off with you stewing in my jail."

He didn't wait for Pete to answer. Instead, Benito flicked Breezy's reins. She trotted for Yuna's place just outside town. Casey knew him a bit too well: right about now, he really could use that drink.

"This was the one you left the Battle of Big Bones with?" Yuna asked, locking him in place with her dark eyes. She poured Benito a refill from her side of the table. Benito swirled the rotgut around. It made a tiny whirlpool in his glass. He set the glass back down and nodded.

"That day . . . God, Yuna. All that time I thought we were right, you know? Wasn't a way for us to be wrong. And, yeah, we were mean and ornery, but you wrangle twisters and save who knows how many towns, and . . ." Benito got lost in the fading whirlpool of his drink.

"If you're saving the world, maybe it's worth a few folks having to suffer for it," the doctor finished for him. She swirled her own drink before taking a draw of it. This wasn't a new conversation. Especially when they'd been drinking.

"You're a good woman, Yuna," Benito assured her.

"And you're a good man, Nito," she said with a dry smile. "But that doesn't mean we don't both have plenty of not-good to make up for." She raised her glass and one of her thin eyebrows. Benito nodded and raised his own. They clinked in the middle of Yuna's small kitchen table, managing not to add too much to the liquor already sloshed there, before both Benito and Yuna knocked back their glasses.

"Thought I was done ruining lives when I left the Pacs, but then I see Pete, and I've done it again."

Yuna made a sound somewhere between a sigh and a snort and grabbed up the glasses.

"Seems to me Pete made plenty of bad decisions all on his own," she said. She held the nearly empty bottle over the glasses and looked to Benito. He nodded. Yuna poured one last glug in each and slid Benito's back to him.

"He left 'cause of me," Benito said.

"He left 'cause he had the good sense to listen," Yuna shot back. "Pacos Bill wasn't in his right mind trying to flatten a town for not jumping into a fight between giants and men who throw twisters."

Benito sighed. "A fight we started," he muttered. He leaned back and rubbed his eyes but couldn't get the burning out of them.

"Not you, Nito," Yuna said.

"Pacs."

"Which you aren't anymore."

Benito raised his glass and forced what he hoped was a convincing smile. "To not being a Pac."

Yuna smiled back. She clinked her glass against his. "To deciding to be good people."

The next morning seemed much brighter than the one before. Benito wasn't sure that was a good thing as he squinted against it in the thrum of last night's drinking. Thankfully, Breezy knew her way home. He didn't have to open his eyes overmuch while he worked his way back to normal.

An apple from the Seeder grove helped. Benito was an extra bit grateful as he threw its seeds wide and called out, *"Jonni grow!"*

Bless the tinpots, Benito's headache was mostly memory as Breezy trotted through the half-grown corn. He thought the headache might be coming back at first, but realized the new pounding was Sarah Mestrovich running her way toward him.

"Morning, sheriff!" Sarah beamed. At his raised eyebrow, she said, "Ma wanted to thank Mr. Lawrence for letting me come over yesterday." The giant girl held up a large pie tin. "Rhubarb."

"That's neighborly of her," Benito said. He waved Sarah to walk alongside him. She had little trouble matching the horse's trot with her own lengthy stride.

"It's his favorite, isn't it?" she asked as the top of the house peeked over the horizon.

"Both of ours," Benito assured her with a smile. The smile fell as he saw Sarah's eyes widen. Benito turned his gaze back to the road and pulled Breezy up short.

He could see the front of the house now, where the door wasn't just open. It was shattered, boards thrown about like twigs.

"Sheriff?"

"Stay here, Sarah, you hear me?" he said, drawing his pistol and darting his eyes about. "You see any trouble, you run the other way."

He didn't wait for an answer. He could barely hear anything, anyway, his heart slamming in his ears. He smacked Breezy on her haunch and set her galloping. Pulled her up short and jumped off at a run before he got to the front door.

"Casey?" he called out, trying to see into the black hole torn from the front of the house. It was too bright outside. All he saw was dark. "Casey, I need you to tell me you're—"

"Your little farm dandy's fine," Pete's voice answered. Casey came stumbling into the light. There was a nasty gash dried black on his right temple. He favored his left leg. But he was alive. Benito suddenly realized how long it had been since he'd taken a breath.

Pete stepped out from around back. One hand held the rope he'd used to tie up Casey's hands behind him. The other held a pistol to Casey's temple.

Benito raised his own gun. His jaw ached from clenching.

"Thought it was you coming back from Yuna's," Casey said. His voice carried a raspy edge.

"It's fine, sweet; we'll—"

"Shut up!" Pete said, cocking the pistol. "You'll shut up, both of you, 'cause no one needs to hear this twisted little homebody playacting you're doing."

"Pete . . ."

"I told him, Benny," Pete said, a crooked grin falling on his face. "Told him you're going back."

"And I told you I'm *not* going back," Benito said, though he'd stopped looking at Pete halfway through his rant. He watched Casey, saw the furrow in his brow shallow out, his shoulders relax just a touch. "I have a home here."

"Not anymore," Pete growled, pulling Benito's attention again. "Storm smashed it. Sad thing, that. You should look into getting some Pacs to protect you out here. This time, you're lucky your man is just a little scratched up. Way I hear it, they aren't always right about lightning. Sometimes it hits three or four times. Gets right homey in one spot. Keeps coming back again and again until there's nobody in its way anymore."

Bits of dust flew about as the wind started picking up.

"Put your gun down, Benny."

"Pete, be reasonable about—"

"Gun. Down!" Pete yelled, pressing the barrel of his pistol to Casey's cheek. Casey flinched while the storm gathered. Grit and twigs and splinters rose up in the not-so-lazy circles of wind.

Benito held his hands up slowly. He made sure Pete could see the gun, could see him stooping down to place it, uncocked, at his feet.

"Kick it here."

Benito looked to Casey, who nodded. Benito kicked his gun across the way, the handle skidding to a stop at Casey's feet.

"See? That wasn't so hard," Pete said. He shoved Casey to the ground and pointed the pistol at Benito. Benito held his Stetson in place with one hand. The day wasn't nearly as bright anymore, but the wind and debris made him squint the same as he had earlier in the morning.

"You're coming back with me now, and you get to leave your little honey alive, or I make sure you have nothing left to stay for, you hear me?" Pete screamed, stepping toward Benito as bits of board joined the dust cloud spinning up nearby.

"Pete, just . . . calm down," Benito said, holding his hands up where Pete could keep an eye on them. "We can talk about this like civilized—"

"No!" Pete yelled, bringing his other knobby-knuckled hand to wrap around the pistol's handle. "I am all done talking!"

Benito flinched as the gunshot rang out. He only felt grit whipping up against his cheeks.

Pete's eyes glazed over, and he sank to the ground.

"No, you're just all done," Casey said as he lowered Benito's pistol. He held the loose rope in his other hand and gave a weak smile. "He was as bad at tying knots as you were when we first met."

Benito closed in on him in an instant, one arm sweeping around Casey's waist. He tangled his other hand in tousled, sandy brown hair, then kissed Casey like a drowning man finally making it to the surface.

He felt Casey tense and broke the kiss. Benito clung to him while biting his own lip. "Casey, I'm sorry I never—"

"Ben," Casey interrupted, pointing skyward.

"Dammit," Benito said. He looked where Casey pointed, through the spinning dust and debris. From the green-purple sky, a funnel grew downward only a dozen giant steps away.

"I thought when I—"

"Doesn't work like that," Benito said. He had to yell over the howling. "Once you call up a twister, it doesn't go down again until it runs itself out," He glanced back at Casey's eyes, needing to see what he looked like there even as he dreaded it. "Or until someone goes in there and *puts* it down."

Benito kept watching, wondering if the tension he could feel in Casey's back was fear of the storm or of him, if the shadow behind his eyes was the both of them going dark.

Then the shadow wasn't behind Casey's eyes, but on his face. Benito spun around as one of the barn doors flew straight for them. Before he could do anything else, though, Sarah Mestrovich blocked out the sight of the door. She hugged both men to her. Benito felt a shudder go through her as he heard the crash and splinter of wood.

"Are you both all right?" Sarah asked as she let the men go.

"Are *we* all right?" Casey asked.

Sarah shrugged. "Giants are tougher than regular folk our size," she said, then winced. "Well, maybe it did sting a little."

"I told you to run *away* from trouble, young lady," Benito said, recovering. He grabbed both Casey and Sarah by the hands. "Scolding later. Sarah, take Mr. Lawrence and find cover."

"Ben?" Casey asked. Benito put Casey's hand in Sarah's larger one.

"This thing's still growing," Benito said, pointing to where the twister had finally touched down. It zigzagged its way forward. "It won't stop here. Might not stop until it goes all the way through town. We can't wait for it to wear itself out."

Casey paused just a moment, looking between Benito and the storm, then nodded. "Be safe, Ben," he said.

"Only if there's no better options."

Benito couldn't feel the pounding of giant feet as Sarah and Casey ran for cover behind him. Breezy, having more sense than most folks, followed the pair. The rumbling twister screeched and howled and pitched a fit. Benito wondered just how much of what was pent up inside Pete had fed this thing.

There wasn't time to care. Benito ran forward, felt the wind catch his feet out from under him. He rode the gust up into the bloody middle of the twister.

Twisters didn't talk, but Benito could feel it throwing out spite and challenge all the same.

*I can throw a steer clear across the county,* howled the rage and venom. *Rip a homestead from the ground without even trying,* came with hate and a boil in the blood. *Why should I listen to a little bit of nothing like you?*

The way they taught a Pac to answer was to reach into a twister's heart. Dig in. Give back as much nasty rage as the twister had until it was whimpering and begging to be told which way to go. You beat a twister by showing it you were ten times meaner and stronger than it was. You beat a monster by showing it you were a worse one.

Benito reached down into those nasty places he'd shut away from his life, felt the blood pounding in his temples, the rage burning in his throat, the screams bouncing in his ears.

Then he caught sight of Sarah and Casey—or shadows he thought were them. It was hard to see much of anything from here. He wobbled inside. There was another rumble and howl as the twister threw something heavy at him.

Benito barely managed to bend out of the way as Pete's body flew past. He remembered Mei Wu from yesterday. Wouldn't she be laughing an *I told you so* at him for turning his back on a monster that wasn't dead after all his preaching at her?

He felt an odd shudder in the wind. It wasn't the same as grabbing a twister by the reins, but it also wasn't the beast bucking him off. He'd never felt it before, but he thought, for just a minute, he felt jealousy out of the storm.

*I don't have to be meaner and nastier than you,* Benito pushed back with a smile. *I don't need any of that, because all you have is the next few minutes. You have however little time you can snag to tear things apart, and then you're gone.*

After, there would still be the stubborn refusal of a little girl to let a snake bite scare her off, the sweet juice from a Seeder apple, the proud voice of a slightly tipsy jackalope. There would still be a giant child's oversized grin of pride and the warmth of rotgut and straight talk. There would be the smell of loam and prairie grass after a storm.

The wind began to collapse below Benito, and he rode it downward, smooth and careful. By the time his boots touched the ground, there was nothing left but a soft breeze.

Casey and Sarah moved back into the open cautiously. At a wave from Benito, the pair ran to join him. Casey all but knocked Benito over as he wrapped his arms around Benito's waist, but he held back from a kiss, eyes searching for something in Benito's face.

Benito smiled. Casey returned it, pulling Benito close for a hug filled with desperation and relief. Benito breathed him deep as the sky washed itself clean of the sickly colors of the storm.

"I have never seen anything like that," Sarah said as the pair broke their embrace. "You have to teach me how to do it."

Benito had the briefest flash of the rage and bile that would bubble up on Pacos Bill's face if someone taught a giant, of all people, how to wrangle. He bit down on a chuckle.

"We'll see," was all he said.

"Ben?" Casey asked. "Are you all right?" He took Benito's face in his strong hands.

"I'm fi—" Benito started, then stopped. "I'm tired," he said instead, "and sore. A little queasy. I know we have to talk, and I want to. I really do, but right now, sweetie, right now all I want is you, and a cool bath, and a piece of rhubarb pie."

A soft breeze played in Benito's hair. It carried the pungent scent of horseflesh and the jangle of Sarah's nervous giggle. The sun stung the back of his neck. Casey's lips tasted of dust and grit and the slight tang of sweat as Benito kissed him gently and let the world melt into them for however many breaths it could last.

# THE FALL SHALL FURTHER THE FLIGHT IN ME

## *Rachael K. Jones*

There are things that fly and things that fall. You must remember this distinction, because they are not the same.

Devils are flying things that learn to fall. Lovers are falling things that learn to fly. Do not confuse them.

Saints do not fly, precisely, although they may seem to as they bear our prayers up the sky. They merely learn not to fall. It takes long years of repentance to master this art, and even then, some saints fall anyway, like my mother did.

I repented of my first sin at the age of eight. I do not remember the reason, but I recall the lonely, still hours in the garden, kneeling among the wild onions, the sun's heat my only company, and warm blood beneath the rose stems wound round and round my wrists. High above the willows, my grandmother cut a dark shape from the sky as slowly she raised a naked foot for the next step.

Even then, I dreaded the day I would climb the air to take her place. I feared it more than falling. From the time her feet left the ground, years before my birth, no one had spoken a word to her, lest they cause her to sin and fall. I couldn't fathom a life spent with only the darting chimney swifts for company, and seeds for food.

I prayed I might be spared, but there was no saint to carry the prayer upwards, save for me, and my time of ascent drew near. If I did not go, who would walk to Heaven to ask for rain?

One evening, as I peeled rose stems from my stinging legs, I looked up at the darkling sky and saw a dazzling thing, neither bird nor saint, plummeting toward my garden.

I magine a star falling to Earth.
   From a distance, it appears to fly across the dark shell of the atmosphere. If you are too close—if it is falling straight toward you—it seems fixed like a star whose inner fire is growing brighter and brighter until the illusion breaks, and the heat is upon you, and the light, and the sound, and then the collision, flesh on stone, flesh on bone.
   Imagine finding it was not a star at all.

A *taxonomy of flight:*
   Flying things stay aloft in different ways. There are gliders, floaters, and Mab-like things that catch and ride atoms of air. Certain fish glide by leaping with kitelike fins, while spiders make silken parasols and float like balloons. Still others fly on deep, booming music loud enough to stop your heart. These include shooting stars. Some eschew music and ride on light and heat, like the falcons who soar on the ever-changing thermal winds near Heaven.
   Some things only appear to fly, like the sun and moon, which are actually falling like arrows away from the universe's birthplace, toward some unknown thing. In the same way, given enough distance, raindrops would become racing comets with tails of ice.

F alling is not always *failing*.

S he was not like any angel I ever imagined, but I knew her nature by her wings. She had six: two on her left ankle, one on her right, one sweeping down from each collarbone, and one sticking straight out from her back like a stabbing knife. Her feathers glistened, dark as the night sky, black to my brown. Blood slicked her limbs, congealing into black scabs. Jagged white bones protruded from the wreck of her skin. She had too many wounds to count, too many sharp bones for one body. They reminded me of prickles on a plucked hen.
   When I bent to pick her up, I found her unbearably light. I almost lost her to a snatching breeze. She had all the substance of a dead leaf.

A *taxonomy of falling:*
   There is only one way to fall: *toward* something.
   A goal. A destination. *A stopping point.*

\* \* \*

Imagine a place where falling is not the law, a realm cloudy with sky-people as they sail from island to island in the buoyant air. They are wings all over, too many to count. Whichever direction they throw themselves, they soar like dandelion puffs on an eternal wind.

Far below, they see the earth swimming in orange and green and blue. It haunts their legends. They call it Paradise and believe their spirits go there in death (never their bodies, whose skeletons are too light and angled to obey gravity). But no one ever goes there. No one *falls* to earth, except through a special act, a miracle, and no one ever quite gets there.

Their hatchlings have dreams of plummeting like rockets toward the fast-approaching earth, wings outstretched to embrace it, their fearless faces burning with the anticipation of impact. Other times, they dream of falling in slow motion, oaring toward the ground in desperate strokes, as if all the forces of physics conspired to keep them apart.

Only their saints and heroes fall to Earth. It is the mark of a holy woman to attempt it. Among them there are ascetics, mad devoted ones with their sights set on Paradise who spend their lives studying the art. The best among them, pious Icarus-saints, will bring the Earth so close that its scourging, purifying pressure rakes against their scalps before flight yanks them back to the sky.

I thought the angel a strange omen in my time of cleansing. I feared someone would discover her, so I locked her in my hut. No one disturbs a holy woman purifying herself for the ascent, but once a week, my mother would bring me seedcakes and roses and a little news from the greater world. I intercepted her when she limped up the path on her crooked cane, and I heard the news she brought. The drought had grown worse, spread to the lake country where the wheat fields wilted from thirst. The clouds roiled and flickered but did not weep.

The people prayed for rain from Heaven. Someone must take those prayers upward. Me.

After my mother left, I salved the angel's wounds with a paste of crushed rose petals. "What is your message?" I asked, because angels always bring messages. It is what they exist for. Perhaps I needn't make the ascent, or carry prayers on sinless feet up the darkling sky.

But she did not wake for two days and nights. On the morning of the third day, she opened her eyes. "Ananda," she said in a voice like birdsong. How did she know my name?

"I am here," I told her.

She sat up, shedding all the bedclothes except a sheet. She gawked at the laundry line strung between the rafters. She dug her toes into the dirt floor. A large pink snail on the windowsill made her laugh outright, a sound I hadn't heard since my first repentance. Winged things stirred in my heart and fluttered inside my throat, and I laughed too. Then the angel marveled at *me*.

She traced the tiny muscles that joined my neck to my collarbone, pausing in the hollow that held my drumming pulse before continuing along my shoulder. But when she reached the thorny stems of my repentance twisted around my arm, the swollen black scabs, her eyebrows knit together. Her fingers gently picked apart the thorns. I struggled not to gasp or flinch. I bit my lip and focused on the angel instead—her trembling black wings, the sheet that draped her body, and beneath that, rose petals stuck to her skin where I had treated her wounds. She gathered some loose petals and pressed them against my bleeding arm. The warmth of her touch spread through my shoulder and down into my belly. My mind tumbled like swifts in a gale. I thought I should pull away, but it was already too late.

"Are you an angel, then?" I asked, swallowing back the frantic wings beating in my throat.

"I thought perhaps thou wert," she said. I floated on those rounded syllables and leaned into her breath, her arms, her wings, her everything. My world's center shifted, and I fell toward it.

Then she kissed me.

Falling is a kind of attraction—it is clasping gravity to your breast. This is why we fall in love, not fly in it.

It took me a week to purge the sin of her kiss, rose stems wrapping my arms and legs. Holy women mustn't love. The sin would weigh me down on the ascent so I would die before I reached Heaven.

It took a long time to ascend.

Love made my mother fall, so hard and fast her body never fully healed from the impact. A fallen saint is worst of all, for she drags the prayers of others to Earth with her. Now I must be holy in her stead.

I locked the hut's door and slept under the open sky, but the chirping swifts in the eaves kept me awake.

"Hello?" said a voice behind the door. "Art thou well?" Six wings thumped against oak rafters. "Art thou there? Is it thee that is in't? I am after falling with an urgent message. Wilt thou open the door?"

\* \* \*

It took my grandmother forty years to ascend. When I was little, I would watch her on clear days high above the tree line, receding by inches as the sin sloughed off until she was light enough to take the next step.

The chimney swifts fed her on seeds carried from my family's garden. Poppy and parsley, mostly, and rose hips in the winter. We would lay out sweetened seedcakes on holy days as a special treat, and the birds would swoop low and bear them up. Seeds are the only food a holy woman should eat. Anything else is weight.

One day, while pruning roses, I shaded my face but couldn't see her anymore. I ran for my mother and brother, but their eyes could not find her either. No one knew how long she had been gone. She had disappeared like a steady star which quietly shuts its eye in the night, unmarked and unmourned.

The forty-year drought broke a week later.

She was the last saint to make the journey in living memory. Now all their prayers weighed me down.

Fall is both a season and an action. So is spring.

To spring is to act against entropy, but it is not true flight; it's just another kind of falling. The darling buds of May belong to the Earth, not the sky. But you can find them in the sky-people's gardens anyway, because the chimney swifts bring them seeds.

"Now then. Thine Paradise here, it does not be what I am expecting to find, sure," she said through the door, voice so low and close I thought she must be leaning cheek to cheek with me through the wood.

"Well, what *did* you expect?" I asked, because I was lonely and bored from long hours of repentance.

"Gods and gardens. Whole cities of earth-walkers."

"Well, we do have cities. Just not here," I said. "I have to live alone because I'm holy."

"With our holy women, so they do, too."

"Do I disappoint you?" I asked.

"Well, thou dost not, precisely. Only, to be sure . . ." Her flapping wings stuttered to a standstill. "Thou dost not seem so happy as I expected thou wouldst."

The chimney swift spends its whole life in the air, and comes to Earth only to build a nest from things caught in the wind, joined together with its own saliva. It sleeps on the wing, drifting in a torpor as it rests.

It dreams, perhaps, of falling.

A swift isn't sure what would happen if it ever stilled its wings. Perhaps, like certain sharks, it would die if it stopped. Perhaps it would transcend its own nature, become a mad bird-saint hell-bent on betrothing Heaven to Earth.

We chatted through the door whenever I wasn't purifying or repenting. I could feel myself growing lighter each day, light enough, perhaps, to bear the prayers. My mother had begun her ascent at a younger age than mine.

"Are you hungry?" I would ask the angel. "Do you need anything?"

We shared the seedcakes beneath the gap under the door one bite at a time. When they ran out, I dug up wild onions in the garden, and we ate those. That repentance was easy. Harder, though, to repent of *her*.

"What hath the name of thee?" she asked me.

"You know that. You said it once. Ananda, same as my grandmother." It was an odd question. "What is yours?"

"Sano." Dark, clawed fingers curled under the doorframe like inchworms. "Ananda, I've a message for thee."

"No. Please, not yet." An angel without a message would have to leave me. I wanted to unlock the door, but I was afraid.

The holy women in the sky practice the art of falling in ascending stages. First, an acolyte meditates until she can command each wing still. This is done in utter silence and isolation, for her wings never rest in life, and it takes immense self-control.

Next, she suspends herself over the void and stills her wings, one after another after another, as many as she can stand. Usually the first wing will flutter again before she gets through even the first dozen. It's easiest to start with the wings of the feet, but these are also the most impatient, and won't pause long.

When all her wings stop, she will slowly begin to descend. It can take years to fall. If she loses concentration for even a moment, she will jerk upward like a kite in a strong draft, borne up all the way to the cloud-cities, and will have to fall again from the beginning.

As they fall, the swifts bring them fruits from the earth to weigh them down. Holy women should only eat earth-food. Even the acolytes cultivate gardens from the seeds the birds bring. In this manner, the flying peoples' gardens have become the wildest and most variable in the world.

Occasionally, their gardens sprout roses by mistake.

\* \* \*

It grew harder to stay grounded. I filled my pockets with rocks to hide my lightness from my mother when she limped up the path that week.

"Aren't you going to invite me in?" she asked, craning her neck toward my hut. It was a long walk from the village, especially for a lame woman, and we were accustomed to taking rose hip tea for refreshment. It was threatening to rain.

"We might disturb the nesting swifts," I said. "I'll prepare tea in the garden."

I struggled to sit down. I had grown so light already, the ground shrank from my touch. My skin itched. Already prayers flocked to me, clamping to my skin like mosquitoes, opening the scabs left by the rose thorns. I scratched running sores beneath my sleeves.

"It's nearly summer." My mother poured herself a cup of tea. "I began my ascent in summer, you know." It happened before my birth. My grandmother took to the air the next day, even before she knew if her daughter would survive her injuries.

"Mm-hm." A prayer floated on my tea's amber surface, its ten black legs floundering for purchase, its proboscis extended. I tried to sip around it.

"It's a good season for it, don't you think? Weather's nice. Plenty of seeds to eat. I remember seeing the garden in summer from high over the trees, everything green and growing and the roses in bloom."

"Yes, it's very nice," I agreed. Over my mother's head, I caught a flash of wings in my hut's upper window.

"And of course, the rain would be most welcome right now, during the growing season."

"What rain?" I slapped three biting prayers roosting on my hand.

She fixed me with a piercing look. "What do you *mean*, 'what rain'?"

"Right. I'm sorry. I forgot," I admitted. My hand trembled, and tea splashed from my cup. When I bent to pour myself more, rocks clicked in my pockets and a trickle of pebbles bounced around my feet.

My mother gaped at them. "What's this?" She grabbed my arm, and more stones spilled, and without their weight my feet left the ground instantly like terrified sparrows. "You—you've been stalling! How long have you been ready?"

"You don't understand." I tried to pull away, but how did one gain traction, treading on air?

Her fingers dug like claws into my wrist. "Oh, Daughter. Oh, you mustn't do this. Have you learned nothing from me?"

The prayers buzzed and nipped at my face. My feet dug into air. She was only one lame old woman, and somehow I yanked away, stumbled several steps higher. I floated level with the high windows. Inside, wings fluttered in the rafters. I pounded on the glass. "Sano!"

"Ananda!" she yelled back, voice muffled through the glass.

"Who are you hiding in there?" my mother demanded. She tried the door, but it was locked. Sano's flapping grew more frantic.

I skipped across air over the hut, but did not know how to descend. I had so little sin left. Every step carried me a little higher. I knelt over the roof and dipped a hand downward until my fingertips just brushed the straw.

The prayers swarmed in my eyes, and I swatted at them, casting for something to weigh me down, anything to bring me near her. A chimney swift hovered near my shoulder, its tiny vestigial talons almost invisible against its underside. Down in my empty pocket, I fished out a little brass key—the one that unlocked the door.

*Down you go now. Down the chimney, little swift.*

Thunder rolled, but it did not rain.

There is another way the holy women of the sky can learn to fall. It is not artful. It is not celebrated, or even condoned. But it is very, very swift.

If a woman wants to reach the ground in a hurry, meditation will not do. But there is no faster way to still one's wings than to tear them off. As many as you can reach.

One's errand would have to be very urgent to attempt such a thing.

She had changed during her time in the hut. I'd expected her wounds to heal over, but instead bones had grown like shoots from the many, many holes. Some had even sprouted a fuzzy black down. They all flapped at once. I could just make out Sano's body at the center of the scintillating sphere as she stepped into the yard. Her feet no longer touched ground. She must have been lighter than me, judging from the speed of her ascent.

"Ananda!" she cried out. "'Tis myself that is ascending now!"

I grabbed at a wing-bone as she rose past me. It cut me like a blade, but I pulled her close, clasped her through the beating flurry until her wings embraced me back. One by one, they ceased their frenetic flapping and rested against me. Slowly we descended, together heavy enough to fall.

"Don't let go," Sano said.

"I won't."

The saints of Earth leave the ground in search of Heaven. They step on water and ascend the air. Falling is an art reserved for demons.

What if, when the saint reached Heaven, the angels were amazed? If the saint explained Earth wasn't Heaven at all, but only another destination? If the saint's coming caused a great debate among the people of innumerable wings? If their priestesses called it blasphemy, but their people, raised on falling dreams, saw a way to Paradise?

What if lightning were not a natural phenomenon, but the war machines of furious angels, weapons against a schism?

My grandmother had reached Heaven after all. "It was years ago, and thy grandmother ascending in our midst, so confused," said Sano. "And asking wouldn't we take the prayers from her, but we could not, to be sure. We are not gods or angels." Our toes touched my hut's roof. We hugged tighter, afraid to lose each other. "We do not send the rain. We only go to war."

"Why did you come here?" I asked her.

"Because she said they would have sent another like her, and another, and another, until someone showed them their errors. Our priestesses, the rumors they quelled this time, and my people they convinced thy saint was mad. But if another saint of Earth arrives in our city, it will be war for certain. It needs to end."

"Will you toss aside the prayers of others so easily?" asked my mother. "Oh, you will fall too, and then what will we do?" She knelt among the roses, cane in lap, cheeks wet with tears. Pity pricked my heart. My whole life I had been intended to carry their prayers to Heaven. It had been no different for my mother, only no messenger came in time to save her from a wasted life, a pointless fall.

I clutched Sano tighter. "I am sorry, Mother. I won't be like Grandmother. I can't."

Sano whispered in my ear. "Let go, and trust me."

I let go of her waist. The moment we lost contact, her wings fluttered, and she rose like a kite. My own lightness bore me up alongside her. Afraid, I clutched at her, and Sano gave me her hand. It felt cool and clawed and secure in my palm. Hand in hand, we shot straight as arrows toward the mountains, neither falling nor flying as long as we touched.

There is another way to fall: toward *someone*.

My Love and I have become flying, falling things. We have no need of a Paradise above or below. We are not saints or demons. We are fallen women. We are broken angels. We have an embrace that anchors, a kiss that soars, and a love that balances entropy.

We sow our garden from seeds the swifts bring us, and whatever grows, we eat with thanks. We dine on plums and parsley and rose petal tea.

One evening late in the fall, when leaves paint the ground in sunset colors, Sano points upward and shouts my name. High above, a dark speck floats down from the clouds: an old woman descending step by careful step.

# THE PERFECT HAPPY FAMILY

## *Patricia Russo*

Mathie was a little girl who thought everything smelled like candy. The old woman who kept mumbling that she needed to sew her buttons always sat next to Mathie when the group took a rest, and slept beside her when they found a place to camp for a night or a month. Leyis, the boy who insisted that his jar used to be able to speak loudly before it was broken during a raid on his settlement by the Rat Folk, but which now could only whisper half-words, teased Mathie by saying the old woman was her grandmother. Soon enough, they were all calling the old woman Grandmother. She didn't seem to mind or, in truth, even notice.

"Be careful. They might start calling you Daddy," Ketter said to Ched. That night they were camped by a river. The children had collected several armloads of firewood, and Ched had gotten a fire started with one of the bits of old tech he carried in his pockets. Ched carried nothing else—no backpack, no satchel, no bedroll. He liked to say he had no baggage, especially when he got fed up with the bitching and groaning from the skull in the sack Ketter hauled around. The sack was full of bones as well, almost a complete skeleton, but it was only the skull that grumbled and bemoaned its fate.

"They can call me whatever they like," Ched said. "Names mean nothing. Ask your friend the skull. It can't even remember what its name used to be."

"He's not my friend. He's my responsibility."

"You don't even know if it is a he."

"Whatever. When I was lost in the dry lands, dying of desiccation, the skull showed me the path to the crystal lake. I could not be so ungrateful as to leave it behind. He or she used to be a person, just like any of us. Its spirit is bound to its bones, and I promised to help free it."

"We know," Ched said. "You've told us the story at least ten times."

The sack began to rattle. The first few times this had happened, the clattering of dry bones had frightened the children, but now they both called, "Let Uncle Skull come out."

"It could be Aunt Skull," Ched said.

"My jar says it's Uncle Skull," Leyis said.

"I need to sew my buttons," Grandmother mumbled. Nobody knew why she kept saying this. She wore a long smock-like dress without any buttons at all, a shawl, and rubber boots.

"I need to see if I can catch us something to eat," Ched said. "I don't know if there are fish in that river, but there are certainly frogs. I can hear them."

"There are fish and frogs and water spinach," Mathie said. "I can smell them. They smell like caramel and peppermints and licorice."

Ketter unlaced the top of the sack and rummaged around for a moment before pulling out the skull. "Woe is me," the skull said as soon as it was out of the sack. "My spirit is bound to my bones, and it will never be released until every one of my bones has saved a life."

"We know," Ched said. "Do we have to hear it every single time?"

"I don't think he can help it," Ketter said. "It's probably part of the curse. Uncle Skull, in the dry lands I collected all your bones, remember? We gave your finger bones and toe bones to the green ants to build fortifications against the vermilion spiders, so we've made a start."

"Use my ribs to make a net to catch fish. Sharpen my wrist bones and use them as spearpoints to skewer frogs."

"And how is that saving lives?" Ched asked.

"Feeding us saves our lives," Ketter retorted. "I believe that's what Uncle Skull means."

"I need to sew my buttons," Grandmother cried, rocking back and forth. Mathie put her arms around the old woman.

"It would be nice if she stopped saying that," Ched muttered.

Leyis whispered to his jar, then put his ear to the crack that ran from its rim to its base. He shook his head. "Great-Uncle Jar doesn't know why Grandmother needs to sew buttons."

"Now there's a surprise," Ched said. "The broken prophetic jar can't read an old woman's broken mind. And you can call one your great-uncle and the other your grandmother all you like, but they will both still be broken."

"Why are you so prickly?" Ketter asked. "You're the one who gathered us from every corner of the six-sided world."

"Hardly that. I came across you on my way to the City of New Unity City, that's all. Lost children, a demented old woman, a man with a sack of bones—if I'd left you where I found you, you'd all be dead by now. Except for Uncle Skull, who is already dead. Oh, and the jar, which was never alive."

"Why do you want to go to the City of New Unity City? Which is a stupid name for a city, by the way."

"I didn't name it. I'm traveling there because I want to live in a civilized place, with streetcars and electric lights, running water and regular garbage pickups. These wastelands and wildernesses are not for me."

"You were born in one of these wastelands and wildernesses," Ketter said.

"I was not. I angered a Misfortune Teller—an error of youth—and she banished me for a period of seven times seven years."

Leyis said, "Daddy Ched, Great-Uncle Jar says you have softened the curse on yourself. Now the banishment will end in three times three years."

"How did he do that?" Ketter asked.

"By consenting."

"I don't understand," Ketter said.

The boy shrugged. "Neither do I. What does consenting mean?"

"Ask your jar. If it can really talk, it should be able to tell you," Ched said. "I'm going to the river. Mathie, would you give me a brand from the fire to light my way?"

"Yes, Daddy," she said.

Uncle Skull said, "Take my marrow for bait."

"Your marrow is dry as dust, useless for bait. But give me your strongest leg bone, and I will use it as a club to whack the fish on the head."

"Thank you, Daddy," Uncle Skull said.

"How are you going to catch the fish?" asked Ketter.

"I have my ways."

"You were not born in the City of New Unity City."

"No, but I was born in a city."

"I don't think the City of New Unity City exists."

"It does," Mathie said, bringing Ched a torch of resin wood. "I have smelled it in my dreams. It smells like honeydrops and chocolate."

"I doubt that," Ched muttered.

Ketter pulled a long leg bone out of his sack and passed it to Ched.

"I need to sew my buttons," said Grandmother.

Ched rolled his eyes. "Why don't the rest of you try to do something about that while I'm gone?"

"Like what?" Ketter asked.

"Since two of our party are known to lie under curses, I wouldn't be terribly shocked to discover Grandmother suffered under one, too. It may be that she can free herself through sewing buttons."

"How do we find buttons?" Ketter asked.

"I've heard buttons can be made of bone."

Uncle Skull let out a howl that filled the night, reached up to the sky, and bounced back off the clouds. Ketter cried out in trepidation, but Leyis and Mathie laughed. Ched strode toward the river, leg bone in one hand, torch in the other, without glancing back.

"Mother Ketter," Mathie said, "don't be afraid. Look at Grandmother. She is smiling."

"Mother? I can't be your mother. I am a man."

Leyis pressed his ear to his jar. Looking up, he said, "You can if you consent. What does consent mean, anyway?"

Uncle Skull said, "Mother Ketter, to save a mind is as worthy as to save a life. Give Grandmother some of my small bones."

"But how is she to make buttons? How is she to sew them?"

"She will use stones to shape the bones, and splinters from my thin arm bones to fashion needles; she can bore holes in the needles with either bone or stone. As for thread, you can unravel my sack."

"Uncle Skull's bones smell like fruit jellies," Mathie said.

Leyis said, "Great-Uncle Jar says that if Grandmother sews enough buttons to bring her spirit back to herself, then Daddy's banishment will be reduced to one year and one day. By that time, we have found the City of New Unity City."

"And what will we do there, if such a place exists?"

"Don't you know?" Mathie asked. "You and Daddy will get a house. Brother Leyis and I will live with you until we are grown. Grandmother will live with us until she dies, and Great-Uncle Jar will live with us, too. Uncle Skull may have found release by then. If he hasn't, then he will live with us until he does."

"Mother," Uncle Skull said, "please consent."

"I owe you my life," Ketter said. "If you wish me to give your bones to Grandmother, then I will."

He opened the top of the sack wider and foraged around inside until he came up with a handful of small vertebrae and ankle bones. Then he brought them to Grandmother and laid them in her lap. She patted his cheeks and drew him closer to kiss his forehead. Mathie and Leyis went to look for stones that could be used for shaping and drilling.

"Do not stray too far from the fire," Ketter called.

"We won't, Mother."

"Unravel my sack," Uncle Skull said. "Wind the thread around a sturdy stick."

"I have no knife to unpick the first thread."

"Use one of my teeth, Mother."

By the time Ched returned from the river, his torch burnt out and Uncle Skull's leg bone split into four lengths, three of them thrust through several small fish, and the last bearing four fat frogs, Grandmother was busily rubbing bone with stone, Ketter was winding thread on a stick, and Leyis and Mathie were playing at thumb-wrestling.

"Daddy!" Mathie called.

"Daddy!" Leyis shouted. "It will be only a year and a day now!"

"Cook these," Ched said, handing them the fish and the frogs. He looked at Grandmother. Then he looked at Ketter. "What's been going on?"

"Grandmother is making buttons. I am collecting thread so she can sew them when they are made. Leyis's jar told him your banishment will be reduced even further once Grandmother has sewn enough buttons to call herself back to herself."

"Anything else?"

"I think you can guess."

Ched sat down near the fire, but not too near. "A year and a day, Mother? And then we will all enter the City of New Unity City, and live happily ever after?"

"I don't know about the happily ever after part, but basically, yes. If you consent."

"How could I not?" Ched looked around. "Mother, father, grandmother, great-uncle, uncle, sister, brother. It looks like everybody's pretty happy already. All right, maybe not the jar. It's still broken."

"Possibly someone in the City of New Unity City will be able to mend it."

"Possibly. Or perhaps a cousin or grandfather we meet along the way will know how to do it. What do you think, Uncle Skull?"

"I think nothing is impossible."

"Nothing?"

"I lay in the dry lands for more than a century before Mother found me. Mother was on the point of death when he stumbled across my bones. Grandmother is piecing her mind back together, button by button. The children were wandering lost and starving when you found them, and look at them now. And you have mitigated your banishment from forty-nine years to a year and a day. If all these things could come to pass, who can say what else may be in store for us?"

Ched sighed. "True enough, but I have to say I never planned on being a father."

"You think I planned on being a mother?" Ketter said. "And don't say they're only names. These names bind us."

"I know." Ched looked at Mathie and Leyis. "Children, be careful. Don't stand too close to the fire when you're roasting those fish."

"We're being careful, Daddy," Leyis said.

And Mathie said, "I'm roasting a frog. It smells like cinnamon and starlight."

Great-Uncle Jar let out a soft whistle, and Grandmother looked up from her button-making and whispered, "Starlight tastes like candy."

# THE MIRROR-CITY

## *Marie Brennan*

The sun's right eye gazed down upon La Specchia, and its left eye gazed back a thousandfold, unblinking. Clouds and high winds had blinded those thousand reflected eyes for weeks, ever since the death of the city's ruler, but now the canals and lagoons lay flat and quiet, not a ripple disturbing their mirrored surfaces. The skies were always clear and the winds still when a Giovane met his bride.

Cloth shrouded every reflective surface but the water. In the palazzi of the rich, sumptuous silk brocade had been hung over the expensive glass windows, inside and out. Mirrors stood draped as if awaiting the tailor's measuring tape. Vessels of gold and silver were bundled and tucked away into cabinets, where no trailing edge could slip free and reveal a gleaming curve. Ladies and lords alike put away their jewels, adorning themselves instead with colorful embroidery, silk threads knotted into intricate lace. Even the floors were strewn with fine dust, lest their polished surfaces show too much.

In the houses of their lessers, plainer fabrics sufficed, and the precautions needed were fewer. In the houses of the poor, no draping was needed at all, for they had nothing so fine as to give a reflection.

Except for eyes. Every citizen of La Specchia, from the heights of the palazzi to the depths of the gutters, went about with gaze downcast. For the eyes, they said, were the mirrors of the soul.

\* \* \*

One might almost have thought La Specchia a deserted city, haunted only by banners and bunting, the curtains draping the windows of glass. Here and there, though, the occasional figure moved. A servant sent on business his lady insisted could not wait. Merchants whose decorations were not yet hung, hurrying to complete their preparations before the city's heart resumed its beat. Death had stopped the blood of life and trade, but soon it would flow once more.

Guards, dressed for today in leather armor and armed with staves, patrolled to ensure no one went too near the water.

The patrols were hardly needed. There were a hundred stories of what would happen if someone chanced to see their reflection too soon on this day, and few of them ended well. The pragmatic tales said the guards would promptly beat the offender to death—if he was lucky. If he was not, then he would die much more slowly, in the dungeons of La Specchia. The sinister tales said the unfortunate soul would lose his mind, or drown, or fall dead of no visible cause. Most foretold doom for the city, and credited past calamities—earthquakes, plagues, destructive storms—to the errant eyes of some careless resident.

Only one story ended well. It was to avoid this fate that Mafeo slipped down an empty street, all but pressing his chest to the wall.

Early in his journey, he had not held back. The front of his doublet bore scuffs and the dangling threads of an absent button, torn off when it caught in the crack of a post. But scraping down the front of a shop like that had made noise, and caught the attention of the shopkeeper inside. The man came out to harangue him, and Mafeo ran—*ran*, as if this were an ordinary day and he could step where he liked without fear. He almost collided with a parapet overlooking a canal before he realized the danger. After that he kept his distance from water and wall alike, to the spaces where an overhanging eave would have sheltered him from rain, on a day when the sky above did not blaze a pure, unsullied blue.

But there were precious few places one could go in La Specchia without risking the water. It surrounded him on all sides, cut across his path without warning. He knew the great canals of the city, but not the backwaters, and time and again what he thought was a sheltered alley dropped down to meet a muddy ditch, or arched over in a narrow footbridge he dared not cross.

And so Mafeo became lost.

He blamed that shopkeeper, and himself for rousing the man's anger to begin with. Had he not fled, he would have found and crossed the Ponte Cieco long since. There was no safety on the other side, but at least he would be farther from danger. Now he did not even know in which direction the bridge lay. The sun offered no guidance, for it stood almost at its highest station: the hour drew near.

He should have taken flight days ago. Mafeo was a young man, seventeen years of age; he should have known—*had* known—that he might be chosen. But the possibility was a distant one, so small as to be laughable.

Until the city's ruler died and the moon waned dark, and the youth of the city, every man and maid in their seventeenth year, crafted lantern boats from paper and set them adrift on the lagoon. Mafeo had done it a dozen times before, to celebrate the new year. As they grew older, he and his friends placed bets, competing to see whose boat would float the farthest before it sank. It never occurred to him, in his ambition and naïvete, that on this occasion he should craft his vessel with less care than usual.

Maybe it wouldn't have mattered. The priests and priestesses said it was an omen, fate, the mirror's will. Perhaps even his worst effort would have stayed whole, carried out to sea by its own reflection.

No vessel would carry him to safety now. But perhaps if he hid, that would be enough. Once night had fallen . . .

No. Mafeo heard voices, the tramp of feet. The entire thing had been madness from the start, doomed to failure. The guards had only to ask at the three bridges: the Ponte di Mani, the Ponte di Ambra, and the Ponte Cieco. Few enough people were about, and most of those known to one another; even with gazes downcast, someone would have noticed Mafeo passing by. If he had not crossed any of the great bridges, then he must still be in the heart of La Specchia. From there, they had only to search.

The sounds echoed off the walls and the ever-present water. He could not tell where the guards were, which way to go to avoid them. Mafeo chose his turns at random, pace quickening until he was almost running. Water seemed to be everywhere. Here a gutter; there a silenced fountain, its basin still full. Someone shouted, and he spooked like a cat in the opposite direction.

And there, ahead of him, was the Ponte Cieco.

It rose in geometric perfection, the straight ramp of its central stairs flanked on either side by shops that blocked the view of the canal. These were arrayed in splendor, for soon enough the streets would be filled with all the people of La Specchia, from the eldest to the babes in arms, each one hoping to see good fortune in the water. But that time had not yet come, and for now the bridge held a scant handful of merchants, startled into looking up as Mafeo ran toward them.

If he could clear the bridge's crest before the guards came within sight . . .

The comandante was no fool. He'd sent his men to patrol the streets, yes—but he had left others behind to block Mafeo's escape.

Even four were enough to cordon off the bottom of the stairs, forming a line close enough that they were sure to catch him if he tried to rush through. From behind Mafeo, more shouts: he needed no glance over his shoulder to tell him that other men were rushing into position, denying his retreat.

They would not kill him. And Mafeo did not want to die. He only wanted to save La Specchia from disaster—the disaster *he* would surely bring, weak and unready as he was. Which meant that only one path remained to him.

Mafeo darted left. It was a risk: the outer stairs of the Ponte Cieco were narrower, scarcely wide enough to let three men pass between shops and parapet. If they tried to stop him—and they would—then either he or the guard would run a great risk of looking upon the water. His only hope was that the guard's fear of the consequences would overcome his determination to do his duty, and in that lapse, Mafeo might slip through.

That guard's devotion never came to the test. As Mafeo ran through the portico at the bridge's crest, he collided with a shopkeeper curious to see what the noise was about.

Mafeo and shopkeeper both went sprawling. Only a quick thrust of Mafeo's hands kept him from cracking his head against the stone balusters of the parapet—and then he looked down, through the gap, and he saw the canal below.

Another face gazed back at him.

The reflection should have been dim and muddied. The waters of La Specchia, no matter how still, were not clean; they should not have been able to produce so clear an image, its colors so bright. But today was the day the Giovane met his bride, and Mafeo, in his attempt to flee that duty, had brought himself to it just the same.

It was a face he had glimpsed a hundred times before, but rarely looked upon directly. Why should he look? Only after his lantern boat floated blazing out to sea had Mafeo been named the Giovane; only then did his reflection matter, the Giovane of La Specchia's mirror-city. Her hair was darker, her chin more fierce. She dressed in clothes not much different from the servant's robe he had stolen stole before he fled the palazzo, as if she were born to a lower station than he.

Mafeo had, without realizing it, climbed to his feet and leaned over the parapet. Below him she did the same, echoing his actions in perfect synchrony.

Had she, too, been fleeing through the streets of her home?

They said the citizens of the mirror-city had their own lives; only in the waters of La Specchia's many canals did they reflect their counterparts above. The family she hailed from was not his, and her thoughts today were not his, either. She was as alien to him as the sun: sometimes visible, sometimes not, but never within reach. Mafeo wondered what had brought her there—what events had drawn her away from the Ponte di Mani, where five hundred years of tradition dictated they should meet.

Whatever the answer, it changed nothing. The sun stood high overhead, and here, with only a dozen guards and a handful of shopkeepers to watch, the Giovane would be wed.

Mafeo climbed atop the parapet. No one stepped forward to help him; no one would risk seeing their own mirror-city echo in the waters below. Not until the ceremony was done. As a boy, Mafeo used to believe that whoever first looked in the water on this day would take the Giovane's place. It seemed a grand thing back then. Then he became the Giovane, and it did not seem grand at all—to know that the well-being of La Specchia would rest upon his shoulders, a burden he could not possibly bear.

Until now. Until he stood balanced on the parapet's thin edge, meeting the gaze of the young lady below him, the two drawn together like magnets seeking their mates. He did not know how he would find the strength to do what he must, what his predecessors had done, day and night without respite, from now until he died.

He knew only that he longed to be complete.

Mafeo spread his arms—she did the same—and as one they fell.

The Perfette rose from the water to the sound of bells. All over La Specchia they rang, above and below . . . and e knew it was illusion, that one was above and one below, one the truth and the other mere reflection.

But all of La Specchia rejoiced, for it had a ruler, and the two halves were whole once more.

There should have been robes waiting to receive em on the bank of the canal. There should have been a triumphant parade, an honor guard a thousand strong, priests and priestesses to bless the perfection formed by the unification of the two Giovani. Instead there was a wall covered in the slick growth of weeds, a challenge to the Perfette's grip. E shed the waterlogged clothing that weighed em down, and climbed the wall naked. On the pathway above people were beginning to emerge from their houses, eager to greet their counterparts in the mirror-city. But on this pathway they stopped, gaping, and knelt when they saw their neighbors doing the same—for the Perfette stood before them, dripping with the waters purified by eir marriage, male and female melded into a single harmonious whole.

As La Specchia was whole. Once again trade would flow, the two faces of the city brought together as before. The crowded warehouses would throw open their doors, every lack answered by abundance from the other side. The two realms would prosper, their ruler the gate through which everything passed, the point upon which the city's peace and prosperity balanced. It was a burden too great for one alone to bear . . . and so Giovane wed Giovane, and in completion found strength.

Soon enough the Perfette was gone, whisked away by guards to eir palazzo, with only a damp patch on the stone to mark where e had stood. But the memory lingered. When the citizens rose from their knees and flocked to the canals to greet their reflections, to celebrate the beginning of a new reign and the renewal of La Specchia's unity, each of them studied well the face in the waters below: women gazing down at men, poor reflected by rich. If they leaped into the canal now, they would only get wet; the moment of transformation had passed. But when they returned to their homes and uncovered their windows, brought out once more their copper pots and silver spoons, they studied their faces in the polished surfaces and remembered perfection.

# THE FINCH'S WEDDING AND THE HIVE THAT SINGS

## Benjanun Sriduangkaew

When the frozen tide sweeps in allusions red as pomegranate seeds, it also brings the oxblood contrails of Fallbright Choir, their canticles making a prayer flag of the sky. Ystravet observes through the part of her trapped in frost and reads their intent in the hull of Fallbright Envoi, the spilled ghosts and void steps of its navigation.

One Envoi and three lesser Cantos, in katabasis: descending, they find perches and berths in a monastery glacier, each ship unspooling pathways for their judges and commanders, assassins and foot soldiers. They walk as though on surface tension, every pace a sanctified action; under the Song all land is holy, an expression of the eternal symphony. Each quark is a note, each composition of baryon or meson a stanza.

This is not written anywhere. As much else with the great symphony, the fact is simply known to the skin much as the heat of the sun, the pangs of hunger, the threshold of pain.

The monastery gives Fallbright welcome within the heart of its glacier, and the heart of the monastery is a map. Here the Cotillion—territories brought into the Song—is shown in real time, its boundaries snapping and stretching as stars are lost, worlds forfeited, asteroid belts absorbed, and planets conquered.

The Finch oracle is flensed down to essential bone and skin, wracked and cadaverous. Clerics and novices bow as she walks over the map, the fall of her

49

bare feet casting ripples over the cusp of borders, momentarily disrupting the vectors of veilships in skirmish.

"Commander Anjalin Vihokrasi, the Ghazal of Five Victories." The Finch shakes as she makes her greetings, though her eyes are calm. "Her entourage, the aubade of Fallbright. As you achieve your fullness at dawn, so we receive you now in the hour of our morning. I am Ystravet Dal, the Finch of this monastery."

They touch their wrists, Anjalin's thick-boned and circled by iron, Ystravet's bird-thin and torqued by velvet. They twine their fingers, Anjalin's callused by knife hilts and triggers, Ystravet's shrunken with cold and ailment. They share a tisane of coruscating heat.

Anjalin's officers unpack cyclical snake-lyres, a violin with strings of frozen mercury, and a quartet of automatons with fluted hands and parrot throats. The Finch's treasury is piled high with similar gifts from other choirs, but she does not say so.

Offerings made, lesser personnel retreat. The hall seals behind them, doors clicking like beaks, windows shutting like claws. Oracle and commander are left to the map.

Absent an audience, Ystravet sits, careless and cross-legged, on the edge of a solar system being shredded to shadow-dust. "I'm surprised to see you here, Commander. Fallbright was busy with Hamalyon, last I heard."

"I've left that in the capable hands of our serenade officers." Hamalyon is no challenge, as most such things are no challenge. Worlds and nations are to the choirs as ripe fruit on the grass: soft and burst-sweet, effortless to pulp. "It's another operation that I would like your advice on."

Ystravet motions with a palsied hand. "You only have to point."

"It's not on this map."

"Then I can be of no help."

Anjalin undoes the pinions of her armor, tugs apart the rutilated ribcage that shields her torso. She draws forth a length of coordinates bleeding ochre fumes. When it settles on the floor, that section of map blanks out, taken over by a gray ruinscape.

The Finch runs a tongue along the cracked parchment of her lips. "That is a world under Hegemonic rule."

"So it is." The commander's face shows bird-blank.

"What would you do with it?"

"What does any choir commander do, Revered? I am trained to one purpose. My skill set is particular." Anjalin holds up her hand, talon-gauntleted, hooked tips shedding icy light. "Therakesorn is a wasteland. What material wealth it had has long been stripped; what intellectual riches it possessed have long been exported. The Hegemony has been on the brink of giving it up. The expenses of administering it have outgrown the gains."

"Having it torn out of their grasp and dropping it as a matter of good economic sense are two different things, Commander." Ystravet passes her hand over the ruinscape, spanning the view outward: stretches of barren fields between flower-cities, arched gates, and spider-bridges that connect nothing. "Your family was from Therakesorn. You've risen far."

Anjalin's mouth is a scimitar curve. "Before the Song, all bow alike: each heart a verse, each throat a mouthpiece for the infinite meter. No matter my birth, I'm the equal of anyone in the choirs. Isn't that right?"

The Finch sips from her cup of steam and liquid fire. It ignites her briefly from within, stilling the tremors. "Have you considered asking your ancestral land if they *want* to be liberated from Hegemonic rule? I say this out of theoretical interest. I'm not going to participate."

"If I asked, they'd say no."

"Presumptuous of you to emancipate them by force, then."

"You know why they would refuse. Hegemonic sync has brainwashed them; they would know no other answer, wish for nothing but what they're *told* to want." The commander inhales. Composes herself, line by line. "They don't know themselves. I do."

"I'm sure," the Finch murmurs, and sweeps her cup over Therakesorn. The Cotillion map returns: binary stars in close orbit, several fission shadows away from a cannibal event. "But that much is beside the point, Commander. I will not do what you ask."

Anjalin takes the last of her fruit, latches her armor back in place. It melds onto her frame, seamless. "I hear there will be a wedding here."

"A time for casting fortunes, yes, and interpreting the eternal verses. So nuptials and war unite." Ystravet shudders, pierced by chill. When she speaks again, her voice is rimed by sickness, though as before her expression is serene. "Springrise and Autumnsigh will send their commanders, or at least a delegate of judges. No monastic marriage is ever short on guests. I try to keep it discreet, but the new always leaks, even as far as the Hamalyon frontier."

"Whose marriage will it be?"

"Mine," says the Finch. "You're invited, for I can hardly keep you out."

Under the Song there are no dynasties, and monarchies have been buried in history so distant they may well be apocryphal. But fables of such concepts endure on Therakesorn, and Anjalin imagines the conjugal preparations of those alien creatures—queens and empresses—could hardly compete with those of the Finch and her intended.

Within these quarters all labor is taken up by human hands. Novices in umbral robes lead obsidian peacocks on silver thread, arrange them in ebb and flow, fall and rise, the trajectory of power and catalyst. Priests trained to cloistered life rather than military duty move in vestments of ivory and pearl, admitting no choir colors. They lay down fiberglass pennants and put up lily mosaics that reflect the map and erase soldier presence. Even when Anjalin has taken off her armor, she doesn't appear in the lily panels. A glass of polar liquor or slice of rime-bear held in her hand would float in those reflections as though levitating.

She keeps an eye out for the Finch's betrothed, who to her exists as a voice at prayer—mezzo-soprano—and not much else. Her senior-most judge reports a glimpse of marble vestment weighted down like roofs, of flanks like arched gates and throat like stone column. Her assassins are more specific: curls of hair the color of jungle jade, an origin in the fallen monastery of the Cormorant. Little by little they construct this person, a house of hearsay, an edifice of impressions.

Delegates from Autumnsigh and Springrise arrive, then Galetide: all three choirs greater than Fallbright, led by commanders of longer battle records and finer birth than Anjalin's. Few children of Hegemonic refugees ascend through the ranks as she has. They regard her with bemused wariness, a touch of condescension.

Inevitably they ask her, "What was it like being a child in those godless bounds? Is it true they brainwash you? Can you truly understand the tenets of Song?"

To which she answers, "It was a childhood like any other. Outsiders believe *we* sacrifice infants on Song altars, and that is to my knowledge untrue. I understand the vast music as well as you, for within it we are equal in our insignificance; on that scale, our individual spirits hardly matter, and that's a sacred certitude which I hope you will not contest."

Sometimes the questions are less frank, sometimes more, but she hasn't achieved her station without weathering worse. Finding tolerable company in Judge Lisvade of Galetide, she asks the senior officer for advice on dress, hair, and presentability. "I've never attended a monastic wedding," she confesses over a small breakfast shared among her, Lisvade, and a Springrise soldier. "And dress is everything."

"You aren't wrong," Lisvade says, mock solemnly. "You might think we have better things to worry about than who wears what to a prestige event, but when so many choirs gather in one place—well, we're going to be an embarrassment to ourselves, not that anyone will have the self-awareness for shame. Imagine the laypeople seeing the lot of us squabbling over who's wearing the fanciest skirt."

"Someday one of the birds will append this to the Eight Facets of Virtue: *Dress with the opulence of fifty worlds upon you; let the devotee spare neither expense nor good taste.*" The Springrise soldier taps their plate with a two-tined fork. "Not that you'll have trouble achieving that particular virtue, hmm, Lisvade?"

Lisvade commits no opinion, merely gives one of eir black-lacquer smiles, a flash of tongue the color of bluebells. "Commander. Have you thought of matrimonial presents?"

"Yes." Anjalin doesn't admit that she has noted the Finch's indifference to the customary offerings of exotic instruments. Presents, too, will be gladiatorial: choir against choir, gift against gift. "Galetide's will be peerless, I expect."

Ey flick their hand. "Oh, splendid it will certainly be. Hard to match in scope, that's how we do things: never halfway. Our commanders neglected to consult me, however, and that's *slightly* insulting, seeing Ystravet is one of my wives."

"She is?" Anjalin was under the impression oracles, holiest of holy, could only join in matrimony with other priests. Never soldiers. "Is her intended— will that be your spouse as well?"

"No. We married before she became the Finch, so our wedlock has been annulled unless I abandon military duty and turn monastic. We remain partnered in all but name, though. As for her betrothed, we haven't been introduced." This is said with no rancor, matter-of-fact. "Though knowing Ystravet, it's not going to be a contralto; she can't stand those. Bass is right out."

A countertenor herself, Anjalin doesn't pass remark; everyone has their preferences, and choir commanders do more fighting than singing in any case. "Were it up to you, Galetide's gift would have been different, then."

"Drastically." Ey sketches in the air: hematite feet crusted in amber pollen. "It would have been nice to give her something she likes, and I can't do that without upsetting my commander. Politics are *absolutely* tiring, don't you think? So the gift—let's say a fruitful apiary. A vice of Ystravet's. She can't resist it."

And if Anjalin knows few things beyond the theater of war and the anatomy of strategy—engine specifications like ribs, logistics like vertebrae— she knows apiaries. Not as a beekeeper might, but she knows them with the visceral certainty of prions twining and synapses firing the syntax of *remember*. Thoraxes copper-red and amaranth, wings like platinum filigree. The hives of Therakesorn produce the best; nowhere else is honey so bright from seasons of fierce sun, so gravid with spice.

Her afternoon she spends in communication with her serenade counterpart, immersed in Fallbright's internal weave: she is a mote among helixes of light, a verse in the lyrics of her choir. The elation filling her and telling her heart she's been born for this is an illusion, a drug, to draw her deep into duty, to ensnare so this becomes the entirety of her life and thought. Each time withdrawing from the weave becomes a fraction harder. An exercise of will.

Hamalyon frontier. Five concurrent battles, but the one that summons her takes place between luminous shadows of blue giants and asteroid ash. The throne-spires of the Hamalyon armada fly clad in palinopsiac coronas, their eclipse-guns black with furled charge.

Through the weave a battlefield looks slightly different to each commander, adapting to personal parameters, and to Anjalin it is a vast flower forever caught between blossom and decay. Concentric rings of rotating petal-teeth so ripe they are on the cusp of dissolution. Anthers tipped in tapered tusks, sepals sheathed in frictionless frames. To most the virtualization seems nonsensical, but to her they map perfectly to combat, distilled to moments of wither and bloom.

A Hamalyon throne-spire operates on human minds hung on the trellis of drive and engine-parts, twined to the lattice of artillery targeting and potential-lash. Throne-spires require less than twenty to crew, and entire armadas can fight—and win—with personnel of under a thousand. Even at peak efficiency Cantos need fifty, Envois a hundred fifty.

But the Cotillion has that many, and more. To secure a vast and wealthy territory that might otherwise fall to the Hegemony, the choirs can spare a great deal.

Anjalin doesn't take charge; her serenade counterpart is more than competent. Throne-spires meet Fallbright in sunrise surges and probability whips. The maws of Envois unhinge wide and swallow eclipse fire. Fleeter, smaller Cantos slice into wall formations, ballistic storms ripping through Hamalyon interceptors.

It ends quickly. These always do. As the throne-spires collapse, she catches a skein of signal, Hamalyon frequency. A plea for mercy, a call for help, inarticulate rage from minds incandescent from machine-merge. One of those, or all of them.

She is no sadist, does not rejoice in final words from the dying. They rarely vary, in any case. Anjalin ignores the signal and disengages from the weave.

The arctic ranges around the Finch monastery are not home to bees, not even the subspecies that build their hives in the parabolas of space-time, sipping nectar from event horizons lined up like piano keys. The glaciers are too cold for the bees of summer and grass, and not cold enough for the other sort. Three months until the nuptials begin, a short time to prepare an apiary by any metric. In the end, Anjalin enlists one of her contralto judges, a former agriculturist.

"You've set yourself quite the task, Commander," says the judge needlessly. Sarasad has been with the choir longer than she, and not always at peace with her advancement. For the most part, he puts Fallbright before personal grudge. "But to be sure, it will exceed all other presents, unless Lisvade of Galetide means to sabotage us."

"I don't think ey intends that."

He blinks slowly, though he has sufficient control of his facial topography to not show outright contempt. "Your military finesse has never been in question."

She cocks her head. "Flattered."

"In personal combat you are more than capable." Sarasad gestures with a hand braceleted in inertial coils. "When it comes to navigating the labyrinth of intrigue and etiquette, Commander . . ."

"I'm hopelessly incompetent because I was born outside the Song?"

"What I meant to say was that you are too trusting. Galetide isn't one of our rivals—we're far beneath them—but it's the habit of the powerful to toy with and ruin the lesser."

Anjalin smiles with cremation warmth. "I will overlook the irony of you, or any of us, declaring that. I don't believe Lisvade is an embodiment of virtue and charity. Neither is ey petty. So let's say we trust my sense of discernment for a day and go through with the bees."

Sarasad makes no further remark. "I recommend hybrids. You will prefer ones that produce honey?"

"We can't engineer or breed something from scratch in ninety days, can we?"

"There's a lunar hive-cluster two transfers away. They are entirely silent, and what they yield is more liquid-metallic hydrogen than honey. You have your work cut out for you, but these hives are constituted from recombinatorial logic. Highly adaptive, receptive to splicing."

Two transfers. She would be away at least a month. "We depart in five hours. I leave the team selection to you."

They take a Canto and an attendant tetrameter, cochlea hulls unmooring in a flare of hymns and glacial crust. Anjalin spends most of the initial transfer in dreamless rest, gathering her strength. Sometimes she starts awake to a frigid hand on her arm, but her room is empty, her bed containing only herself. Still, a coat of rime clings to the edge of her mattress, crackling as it falls apart. Icicles glow in the dark, gossamer lace across the frame of her window.

Second transfer, she contacts the Finch.

Ystravet is reclining on a divan, swathed in thermal layers. Her intended sits close by, a crescent shadow flat in profile, two-dimensional. "Commander," Ystravet says, eyes shut. "What is it?"

"When we landed on the monastery, I observed a statue of ice on the roof. It was remarkably lifelike, detailed, if archaic in form and material. Can I assume there might be a reason I've been seeing parts of it onboard?"

"Ah. That'd be when we shared our drink—a glitch contagion. Not to worry; it will pass." A hand of smoke and shimmering shade closes over Ystravet's. She returns the contact, skin and nails sinking into penumbra. "I committed an infraction, and as a condition to assuming my office, one of my neurals was sensory-linked to that statue. So a part of me always experiences the ice. I could get rid of it, but that would forfeit my post."

"That seems unnecessarily harsh as punishment." Anjalin absently brushes snow off her shoulder. "The office of the Finch can't be worth so much. I can tell it's slowly killing you."

"Put yourself in my place. Do you value your own rank so little? If all your life you've directed yourself to it, shaped yourself for this one path, made its pulse your own, and primed your breath to match its pace; if you do this until your life becomes *this* one trajectory, with a single, inevitable destination—would you surrender it so easily?"

"I take your point. How long before this—have you chosen a successor?"

"Referred hypothermia. I've held up well but not for much longer. An inventive way to go." Ystravet clenches her fingers to still the trembling. "As for successors, we oracles do it differently than in the army. We cultivate our candidate for leadership, ensure they are well-versed in the verities of birds, and the holy lottery secretly marks them years in advance. When a present oracle falls, they step up. Last season the Crow heir became the Wren; the Wren's candidate assumed office of the Dove. I myself was from the monastery of the Shrike. So it goes, our leadership rotating as the seasons do. Difficult to predict or corrupt, in theory. When it manifests, the lottery's spectacular. All light."

Anjalin tightens her thermal. Her body temperature has dropped two degrees off default. "Does Lisvade of Galetide know about your condition?"

The intended issues a noise less than sigh, fraction-wind whispering across the link between monastery and Canto.

"I'll take that as a no."

The Finch starts to answer, dissolves into a coughing fit. "It was good of you to call, Commander." She gathers her breath. "My betrothed would like to consult with you."

Anjalin glances at the form slipping in and out of view, ranging the light spectrum. "I'm here to serve."

The link shifts, folding into a private channel; the betrothed comes into focus. "Commander Anjalin?" The voice is that mezzo-soprano she heard before, and if it is less powerful speaking than singing, still it is nova-bright.

Anjalin is choir-trained and so can stand against it, but a temple supplicant would have been brought weeping to their knees. "I have a favor to ask."

"I will listen. How may I address you?"

"That doesn't matter, not until the ceremony—at the moment I barely exist, being more function than person." The crescent form swells, traveling from inverted light to ultraviolet edge. "The downside of marrying the great: you're reduced to an appendage, and even if they are perfectly good, you are still a possession. I adore Ystravet, but sometimes it chafes. Perhaps I should have courted her before she became oracle, but that wouldn't have deterred her from this office. Nothing could: not me, not even Lisvade . . . the Galetide judge being whom I wish to discuss."

Anjalin doesn't allow herself the luxury of astonishment. She's hardly a marriage counselor. "If you feel less than delighted with eir arrangement with the Finch, I fear I'm not the right person to talk to."

Another shift, this time to infrared. "Not so. Judge Lisvade—ey's a most elegant person. Worldly, charming, and kind. The last is a quality not often seen in one of eir rank, and I've long wished to make eir acquaintance."

"Oh." She can't rein in her incredulity this time. "You've broached this with the Finch?"

"She finds it amusing I haven't worked up the courage to approach em myself, as wooing a choir officer isn't prohibited to me. Won't endear me to traditionalists, but being born to the Cormorant, I was never going to be a favorite. It will work out quite well; my courtship of Lisvade would let em and Ystravet spend more time together, so this isn't entirely a selfish request." More quietly, "And there are few years of joy left to Ystravet."

"I'm not schooled in matchmaking." Or much else outside the bounds of tactical treatises, the making and maintaining of supply chains, probability flux, and terrain. "To the judge I'm barely more than a stranger."

"Ey's taken a liking to you. All I want is a chance. I am no fool, Commander; all the choirs will try to sway my spouse to interpret the Song in their favor. At the moment, Ystravet is inclined to interpret nothing at all, save minor clauses to make some bureaucratic procedures less painful."

The rest needs not be said. A gift, however unique or a proxy of affection from Lisvade, will not suffice to persuade the Finch. "I can make an effort."

"I will ask for no more."

Anjalin cuts contact as the transfer ends. Another finger of cold runs down her spine, but she pays it no heed. Where she is going, there will be much worse to face.

* * *

The moon is not so much home to the hives as made of it: over the cycles of breeding and internecine fighting, lunar surface has been chipped away and remade in hexagons. Birthing chambers are ordered by propriety, larvae raised according to their destiny—to fight, to work, to rule. Swarm cycles bring war and shatter hives in patterns of accretion bloom, but sometimes a peaceable generation veers instead for the nearest sun, there to weave orbit-hives and turn their wings to solar sails, their thoraxes to plasma chassis.

On arriving, there is no space to land; tetrameter crafts fold into the Canto's hull, detached wings returning to their joints. Anjalin and her soldiers step out clad in beaked filters and pinion sheaths. Their sidearms are individual and particular, adhering to no stricture or standard. For herself, Anjalin carries a gun whose metal spurns light and whose chamber croons annihilation. The corkscrew knife at her hip bears the promise of polynomial wounds.

They find an entrance. Their feet are firm: the moon—or the hive-nexus—exerts its own gravity, gives anchor.

The Shemronn Silk-Orbit had possession of the moon once, a palimpsest colony winding through the lunar body like fabric ligaments through a doll, and those remain even now within the bee-built tunnels. Kites bear scenes from Shemronn epics, taut from their memory of marking the boundaries of corporate concerns. Compound scarves swaddle eggs the size of toddlers; cryogenic silk hangs in tassels, beaded with hydrogen. Some queens lay textiles instead of eggs; adopting the habits of Shemronn silk worms, the judge says, citing it as evidence of the species's flexibility.

Anjalin has her doubt, but no better options to offer. She does keep an eye over her shoulder; an expedition like this would be the ideal place to attempt her removal, and though she's left the choice of personnel to Sarasad, she's worked hard to build loyalty amongst the aubade. At least two present here, an assassin and a tactical advisor, would see Sarasad downed in Anjalin's defense.

The bees are not sapient, it is said, though there are primitive couplets written in ultraviolet ink across the walls, reports of battles between generations and instructions for the next swarm. "What happens," Anjalin wonders aloud, "if we leave a baby here?"

Sarasad holds up a hand gloved in waveform generators. Sonar canaries undulate forth and bring back negative space, a spatial feedback that lets them navigate the hive. Visual feelers would have stirred sleeping queens. "It's not impossible that introducing a primate might change them, but I'd say their combinatorial threshold doesn't stretch that far. Or the Shemronn colonists would have already been incorporated into their . . . configuration."

Deeper into the tunnels they silence their communications. The bees are sensitive, quick to hear pulses of data being exchanged, sampling the crevices between sentence and intent the way connoisseurs taste varieties of honey that come in the liquid green of fresh photosynthesis, the fused crimson of red dwarfs, the colorless silicate of bullets. Anjalin avoids the hunters and workers. To meet one detachment is to meet the entire hive, alarm rippling over the strings of shared awareness. While her Canto can bombard the entire moon to grit and salt, she'd prefer to be aboard her ship rather than inside the target.

Sarasad cross-maps the hive's structure to similar clusters: as a species, bees are unvarying in their design. He finds, unerringly, the chamber where spare queens are kept.

Bioluminescence creases in the folds of ancient skirts, brims in the cups of cracked eggs, and capillarizes the angular walls. Nested in the jaw of sharp geometry is a newly hatched queen, proboscis like lacquered teak, jeweled eyes the size of Anjalin's fist.

They assemble the cage, shaking containment gossamer over a scaffolding of flexsheet and contradiction mesh. Anjalin kneels by the judge as he peels off membrane and nutrient tubes that attach to the queen's proboscis.

A spasm of wings, a quiver of antennae. The queen wakes.

The response is immediate, a quake of vibration tectonic-deep, sound of wings against wings and bright-banded bodies sweeping through tunnels.

Anjalin's first shot obliterates, turns a tide of thoraxes and stingers to carapace shrapnel and hemolymph. "How do we fertilize the queen when we get back?" she asks, calm, contacting the tetrameter crafts. Small and surgical would be best, not the full destructive might of a Canto. "Do we have to capture a drone as well?"

"We fertilize her with possibility. I asked a former colleague to send a few drones from other subtypes." Sarasad levels his pistol but refrains from firing. He studies the indigo stains of bee fluids clinically. "By the time we're back at the monastery, those should have arrived, the Song willing. Were my opinion solicited, I'd say this acquisition is the easy part. The actual breeding and maintaining will be much more complicated."

"Duly noted," she says, and directs the tetrameter to fire.

They leave the moon chipped and blistered, a segment-wound hemorrhaging fabric and hexagon intestines. The hive, Sarasad assures Anjalin, will rebuild and repair. She stifles her absurd guilt; like any choir commander, she's orchestrated carnage on a far greater scale, draining the heat of planet cores, erasing entire nations. Allowing her conscience to be pricked by taking out some bees is hardly proportionate.

Within the cage, the queen spends most of its time asleep. On the rare occasion that it rouses to feed, Anjalin fancies that those immense eyes are watching and appraising her, though all studies and treatises indicate these creatures are mindless. The queen has not yet matured; full-grown, it will be nearly half Anjalin's weight, three-quarters her height. Enormous, and when something reaches that mass, it is difficult not to ascribe it a little intelligence. Like domestic pets or young children.

They clear a hall on Fallbright Envoi while Judge Sarasad selects drones sourced from twenty subspecies, former inhabitants of volcanoes and dead oceans, broods that construct their hives from ground fog and blasted glass. Anjalin never suspects the drones of sentience: they are truly blank of thought and memory, receptacles for hive routines. They will have to be induced to mate with the lunar queen, but that is easy to arrange, a matter of chemicals.

Anjalin issues invitations to Lisvade and Ystravet's betrothed.

Lisvade comes first, arrayed in Galetide plumage and claws. "Apologies." Ey motions at emself, self-deprecating. "Boarding another choir's Envoi, I *have* to puff up and overdress. My superiors wouldn't have let me out without the pomp."

"Understandable. What do you think?"

The judge peers through the observation lens. "More flowers?" A laugh. "I only know what Ystravet likes, not how to achieve it. It looks to be coming along well, so I leave it in your hands. And I'm glad. She needs more things that are good for her heart, even if it comes with obligations."

It is three days before the intended comes aboard, wrapped in billowing haze. The ensemble leaves their hair visible, alike to snake vines in hue and thickness, braids that stir and purr liturgies.

They bow to the judge. "Judge Lisvade of Galetide. It thrills and honors me to make your acquaintance."

Ey returns the curtsy. "My pleasure, though I'm at a loss as to how to properly address you."

"I can't speak my name or title." The intended pulls a sheaf of scattered light over their hand, perhaps scribbles down a sign, a sentence. "Will this do?"

Too collected for surprise, Lisvade doesn't quite widen eir eyes. Ey takes the glimmering hand briefly, a brush over sacred matter. "Then I'm doubly graced by your presence. Shall we look at the queen?"

Over the weeks the queen grows fast, its colors deepening. Blue bands on thorax, lightning veins on wings, and frost-coated antennae. This last prompts Anjalin to ask Sarasad, "Is *that* normal?" To which he answers, easily, "It'll integrate into an arctic ecosystem."

When the first batch hatches, Lisvade and the betrothed are there to watch. When the larvae pupate, Ystravet's intended is the first to give touch.

Bare hands for once—sculpted palms and tapered fingers that can't help but captivate, all the more for being the only part of them broadcast in the clear. Workers alight on their wrists, bangles of furred bodies and snowflake-motif wings, and leave spots of rime like gifts.

Betrothed and judge don't appear to converse much, save perhaps on a private channel, but Anjalin hears no complaint and assumes the bride contented enough. Piously, Sarasad has engineered the new brood to produce according to hymns, and Ystravet's betrothed takes delight in singing the workers to honey like quicksilver and rose gold, honey like larimar and the glow of blue giants. Judge Lisvade never fails to attend and listen.

Anjalin will have her cast of fortune, her bid for Therakesorn. Even the sound of buzzing and the waft of sweetness—homesick-making both—pale beside that.

The hive solidifies around the queen, a nimbus of frost radiating into chambers for storing, birthing, hibernating, and data ingestion. Inexorably, it also traps its ruler. Anjalin decides not to draw comparison between brood and monastery.

The wedding closes in, and the hive approaches completion. Drawing perhaps on inherited memory, it takes on the appearance of ghost nebulae, in visuals if not in temperature, verdigris frost and silver lace; without music, the workers fall back on the habit of converting sugared water and peach liquor to metallic hydrogen. Sarasad and Anjalin take turns guiding them with liturgical praise and the occasional secular aria. She introduces him to music from Therakesorn—more cymbals and stringed instruments than vocals, but she focuses on the ballads. He goes along grudgingly at first, obeying her out of obligation to protocol. Later she catches him rendering the haunted verses and eight-ten meter on his own. More choir-orthodox than she likes, not that she is going to criticize. She teaches one of the ballads to the betrothed as well, who—charmed—spins it into a weave of their own design boasting a novelty of pitch Anjalin attributes to Cormorant idiosyncrasies.

The date arrives. Anjalin prepares for it as she would for battle; the intended must be doing likewise. *Even if they're perfectly good, you're still a possession.* Anjalin can't imagine what that is like. Though Fallbright has etched its ownership onto her soul, her relationship to it isn't quite the same. Of all people, she understands that distinction.

By the nuptial day, the glacier has gone from cabochon to faceted with Cantos from six choirs; the greater Envois have lifted off to orbit, too immense to be borne by arctic shore or the dreams of deep-sea ice. Anjalin's entourage is the smallest at the reception. It seems the other choirs have taken their troops off duty just to attend this, pausing invasions and halting skirmishes. So much rides on a monastic wedding, and no choir would spare expense or officers. Were such events more frequent, Anjalin thinks, the choirs would find hardly any time to wage genocide.

The first gift is an engine of halo blades and seismic wheels; expanded, it will integrate into the monastery as a defense strong enough to hold off Cantos. Ystravet Dal acknowledges the practical use of this and accepts the engine with a token of grace: a tail feather, chiseled from glister ivory.

The second is a lepidoptery of monarch masks and moth mantles, sicklewing gloom and tortoiseshell veils—evidently meant for the intended. Ystravet rewards the tribute with a bird's tongue, shaped of fine scrimshaw.

Through all this the betrothed is silent behind the Finch, contained within a pennant that radiates colorless chill. More reserved than ever, as though the weight of ceremony has drowned their voice.

Then it is Fallbright's turn. Anjalin advances and removes the containment web from her offering.

This split-off chamber, housing a cadre of hunters and workers, doesn't possess the grandeur of the hive entire. Still it demands attention, holds the gaze fast. A glory of rime and hydrogen chiffon done in the best, most jealously guarded Shemronn embroidery. A low buzz primed to a Therakesorn ballad metered in Fallbright symphony.

"This hive has been bred to Song guidance." Anjalin stands before Ystravet, hands clasped behind her. "They make honey in flavor, texture, and color according to music of the holy. So we have proven that even brute animals may be brought into the eternal harmony, taught to give tribute in what form they may." Dogma for the audience's benefit; let Sarasad never complain again of her lack of formal manners.

The apiary fragment doesn't match the flair of the lepidoptery or the puissance of the engine, and to any other bird-oracle, it would have been so humble as to cause umbrage. Ystravet straightens slightly, her gaze sharpening with interest. "A demonstration, Commander? It should be quite the way to open the feast."

Anjalin gestures her assent, and as though this is a stage and all of them yoked to a script, the intended glides forward.

The bathyal depth of their bridal garb gashes open, a wave of vituperative cold and voice. The same ballad Anjalin taught them, filigreed in Cormorant mezzo-soprano: liquid sunlight peering through threshing black. The first stanza reels the bees in, workers and hunters circling in mesmerized orbit. The third and fourth loosen them into a corkscrew spiral, blue-banded, lightning-winged.

The fifth stanza crests. The bees hover in coiled tension.

Anjalin's breath snags. She reaches for her pistol. Knows she will be too slow after all.

The hunters are almost quiet under the ballad's climax. They are exact as they would never have been on their own, animal instinct leashed by human intent: all precision.

Ystravet stiffens, doubles over without noise. Her betrothed, still singing, follows and catches her. Or perhaps to use her as a shield when the guns come out. Anjalin does not toggle the safety off, but points hers all the same. In this moment it is important to fulfill a specific function, if only in appearance.

"She lives!" The intended is a flux of sun-struck sea and abyssal dusk; the hunters lie about them, dead and spent, dusted in snow. "She's more alive than she has been for years."

Understanding crystallizes. Anjalin lowers her gun and negotiates her way past other choir commanders, past Judge Lisvade who stands feet apart and weapon leveled at the intended's throat. Eir face is hard and ashen, jaw a concrete line.

"May I verify that?" Anjalin says to the rapid-fire shift between ocean colors as gently as she knows how. At a nod she kneels and pulls Ystravet to her, puts her finger on the Finch's arm where the bees stung. No inflammation. A scan informs her Ystravet is in perfect health. Entirely too perfect. There was never apid venom dispensed, only a surgical severing of a neural link.

"Ystravet Dal is well," she says loudly, voice trained to carry like anyone else's. "Her vitals are pristine, and her neural signs couldn't be finer."

The phase-shift in expressions—the intake of breath—tells her who knows of Ystravet's condition and who doesn't. Lisvade sags in relief, uncomprehending.

"Then," a Springrise officer says, "she is no longer the Finch."

"She is not." The veil of frigid water falls, sluicing away. For the first time, the betrothed is bare to sight, attired only in a thin robe. Anticlimactic in their plainness: the jungle-green hair, the sharp bones, the ordinary tears on ordinary cheeks. Anything but anticlimactic in what crawls on their skin. "But I am. As Cormorant candidate to succeed the Finch, I'm ready to assume my post."

The lottery shudders along their arched flanks, their columnal throat. It writhes in splats of light, resolves to the lexicon of bird-oracles. Anjalin can't decipher all. Still, she's learned enough to know that the betrothed speaks true, despite the Cormorant being institutionally extinct. This she does not say aloud—best to see how matters turn first. Instead she murmurs, "Is this claim disputable?"

It is not; all know this. Before an ecclesiastic court the claim will be needled and picked at, perhaps the length of rule cast in question. But the office itself will stand uncontested.

Ystravet Dal, now only that—not the Finch nor conjoined to a statue of ice—stirs in Anjalin's arms. Skin still ravaged and too close to bone, but that will change in time; that will heal.

Looking up, Anjalin holds her wrist out to the intended. "Commander Anjalin Vihokrasi, representing Fallbright aubade, offers you greetings."

"Indresha Suleiha." The betrothed touches a salt-damp wrist to Anjalin's. "As the Finch of this monastery, I give you welcome."

The rites proceed and conclude; by the end of it, Indresha and Ystravet are joined in matrimony, and the rest of the commanders give Indresha their courtesy—if some are more grudging than others, they know better than to show it. Dessert comes in the form of honeycombs glittering like citrines and the promise of sunlight long unseen, and cups of honey freshly sung into the color of new frost on seafoam.

After, they gather in the apiary: the new Finch and their new wife, two Fallbright officers, a bewildered judge from Galetide. The hive smells of industry and ozone, underlaid with passion fruit and wisteria nectar. Workers go about their routine; hunters perch, stingers sheathed, and through their eyes the queen observes. A payload of insectoid attention.

Anjalin doesn't ask Sarasad if he played a part: without his help, Indresha couldn't have achieved this. He bides at her side, impassive. Some of the bees alight on him, turning his shoulders to wintry slopes.

"You will have what you want, Commander." Ystravet sits straight, her hands at rest; if her cheeks are not yet flushed with health, there is more color in them than before, more clarity in her eyes. They turn to Indresha and Lisvade standing within the hive's embrace, heads close together. Lisvade seems torn between fury and relief. "And so, I suppose, do those two."

"While you are, for the first time in decades, not dying. That is something, Revered, and Indresha surely did it for love of you."

"Did they?" Without the annihilating cold, Ystravet's lips are deep bronze and thin, nearly disappearing into her expression. "They would have succeeded me, with full rights, in a handful of years. A part of me will always wonder: did Indresha get impatient? This way, of course, they can have Lisvade, too—now that I'm no longer oracle, I can reinstate my marriage with em. But perhaps I need to stop thinking as the Finch. The post that I was. The post I'd have died to keep. You, I expect, have no intention of changing."

Anjalin lets that pass. "Could Indresha be ousted?"

"No. Even if this is brought before a court, their jury will be other oracles, and none of us likes choir interference in matters of succession. The lottery is sacrosanct." Ystravet takes her cup of honey, dips a finger in, and gives an experimental lick. "It's been awhile since I could taste anything properly.

Being part statue kills your palate sure as anesthesia. Once, I would have said Indresha incapable of such a play, but earnest affection can be a formidable force, and they've always closely studied the bylaws of birds. They will do well as my successor."

The commander gazes into the honeyed depths of her flute, where residual music swirls like shifting cartography, plotting the change in national boundaries, reflecting victory and loss. "When I have what I want and my work there finished, perhaps my course will be amenable to a new direction. Until then—"

"Until then you will not bend." The former Finch lifts her cup to Anjalin. "Of all people, I won't criticize. When I was younger, perhaps I strived as idealistically—but that was long ago. Shall we join them? It's time."

Lisvade and Indresha stand hand in hand, waiting for their third. The ground ripples, sinusoid, monastic heart-map blooming through hive frost. A shift, a murmur, and the view brightens with spider bridges and flower-cities, where orchid temples and hydrangea libraries rise from porphyry fields: Therakesorn. Above that, the Song gleams absolute, ever-living, all-encompassing.

Anjalin's pulse quickens. Their privacy is at an end: a broadcast channel blooms for the new verses, the cast of fortune. The choirs watch.

The Finch begins the Psalm of Verity, matching their voice to the Song as only an oracle may. It is schooled; it is practiced. Ystravet has taught her betrothed well, chiseling them for this post.

Indresha's voice rises and the Song speaks.

# SQUEEZE

### *Rob Cameron*

Gone: two stolen "I messed with Texas" shot glasses, photos of us at your niece's graduation, seashells you found in the middle of that parking lot in Great Neck, my empty Red Hot Chili Peppers CD cases, your panties under my bed. High on grief after your funeral, I took everything imbued with your essence and shattered it against the wall or burned it like witches at the stake while the smoke detector screeched in short bursts.

I stopped speaking to people. In the morning I would dress myself, chin to chest, fumbling with buttons, head bowed like the lilies on your casket, and take the 7 train from Times Square to where you used to live in that ancient duplex on the corner of Cherry Avenue in Flushing, last stop. That's where we had chilled on your landlord's bleached porch swing with our feet up, drinking Red Stag whiskey in every kind of weather. That's where, in your own quiet way, you had tried to prepare me for the inevitable.

Since you weren't there anymore, there was no reason to get off the train. So I'd wait for it to fill with bodies and ferry me back to Manhattan. Unable to move forward or go back, this became my life for maybe a hundred years (time moves differently on the 7). Passing under the lethean waters of the East River eroded my memory until I couldn't remember your face or the smell of your hair. Terrified, I listened for your voice, but it was lost in the dull roar of rush hour.

\* \* \*

One morning, as the train emerged at Vernon Boulevard in Queens, a stinging sensation struck the crown of my head, forcing my starving mind to aggressively adhere to the smallest, most perfect details which, while still of no interest to me, now could not be ignored.

At Queensboro Plaza, light traveled broken paths through the scratched, stained window and became prismatic, oscillating streamers of blue, purple, and gold. Bruised tangerines scattered through space like cooling stars born from the bursting scarlet plastic bag of an elderly Chinese couple at Roosevelt, bloodying the air with their tart flavor. Squat graffitied rooftops were a fast-moving dream coming into focus while neck muscles tensed against the subtle pull of gravity as the train came to a full and complete stop at Junction Boulevard.

The platform was crowded. Plump Ecuadorian children played soccer as their parents pressed shoulder to moist shoulder for position by my train car door, weighed down by toddlers, baby carriages, and carts. The doors shushed open and all of Queens flooded in, eager to escape the sharp briars of a New York summer. Everyone had an unhealthy metallic sheen to them, beaded with mini vernal pools. The sudden influx of heat and mass made my teeth ache with stomach-turning vertigo. As my vision doubled, a little ghost boy slipped under the turnstile and appeared on the train.

The doors chimed, shushed together, and we moved. The MTA kept the cars cold enough to retard the ammonia-producing chemistry of so many bodies. The chilled spot I heard you're supposed to feel around poltergeists didn't even register.

The ghost child blinked in and out of existence. Every time he reappeared, I had to remember him all over again, like catching the tail of a fleeing dream. At first I would be watching a square of light crinkle and color like tinfoil as it drifted through the car. Then a child would cry, and the light became the boy, going through people's bags or sitting on old women's laps.

He pulled the pacifiers from beautiful sleeping brown babies and tried to lift them from their seats. He finger-painted messages from the dead into the grime on the window. Sometimes he used his face. He danced around the pole singing at the top of his lungs, which sounded like the screech of the train wheels going around a turn at incautious speed.

It's easier to imagine the ghosts of men than "ghost children." The two words in juxtaposition cry out for a comma between them or a period, a division of ideas in the same way there should be a barrier between life and death. That lack of imagination is why people don't see him.

In the same way, it is difficult for a young child to understand death. So sometimes they do not die.

Although calling it a child might be misleading. The ghost looked right at me, one eye glaring white, while the other was a hole, impossibly deep. But I was not afraid.

I wondered why I could see him when nobody else could. Then I remembered near-death experiences can shift your perspective. Losing you had almost killed me.

The ghost child climbed up next to some woman, knelt backward on the bench, and looked out the window while babbling. The woman had one arm. The other was gone at the elbow. I'd noticed her in the same way I noticed anyone on the subway. There was a process: awareness, speculation, judgment, and ignorance.

Awareness: She was tall and brittle, skin made of a dark, distinctly nonnative graphite; her eyes were chips of tarnished bronze. I could tell she'd been more colorful once. Recent fossils show dinosaurs had feathers. There were imprints in the stone. Feathers meant color. She was like that—imprinted.

Speculation: I imagined her homeland was once a happy place where everyone sang everything everywhere they went. It was Eden, it was Zamunda, it was *The Lion King*, but with Real People. Then disaster struck. She'd escaped on a boat that was over capacity. It tipped, and she swam to shore through the floating bodies of loved ones and strangers. She'd survived and now rode my 7 train to the last stop.

Judgment: I didn't like her because she would take up two seats; because she wasn't big enough or crazy enough to deserve two seats; because I looked at her and thought, *Bomber*. "Nigeria is experiencing a rash—a rash!—of female bombers," said some CNN breaking news update somewhere.

Because she wasn't you.

Ignorance: After a while, she became background, and my eyes passed over her, flattening her like the ads for 1-800 immigrant legal services I didn't need, surgical body hacks I couldn't afford, and postcard-sized notes stuck in the seams of the subway maps, warning of a wrathful second coming of Jesus I didn't believe in.

I'm sure everybody noticed me in the same way.

All of a sudden, the woman slid over and made room for the ghost child. He turned, sat, and took her hand, or where her ghost limb would have been. She squeezed her other fist, but you could imagine.

A small sound escaped from both her and my opened lips, and her body, which had been a desert, briefly flooded with color. She looked through me, eyes glistening with tears that welled but did not fall, and before I could blink them away, my vision blurred, too.

I realized we had been on the same commute now for years. She'd been squeezing her fist just like this every evening at exactly this time between

Junction and Flushing. Of course she'd always been able see him. I wondered what else she had lost along with her arm. I wondered what else she could see. Maybe it was a trick of my peripheral vision, but for a moment she and the ghost child shared an unmistakable resemblance.

I suddenly found that I'd walked through the crowded train and was standing in front of her.

"I see him, too," I said.

"The boy?" she asked, her voice carving out each syllable with precision.

"I thought I was the only one," we said at the same time.

"Is he your son?"

I could tell she wanted to say yes. "I don't know what he is."

We stood together in awkward silence, neither of us used to talking, while the train pulled into Flushing and emptied.

"This is my stop," she said, walking past me. Then she turned back at the door. "How sad is it that we need the dead to connect to the living?" Which is something you would have said.

The ghost boy was gone, too, and I sat alone in my train car.

But then it began to fill back up with people. Tomorrow we will talk again. If not tomorrow, then the next day. It will be another great adventure, like loving you, which was the same as facing death.

# A GUIDE TO BIRDS BY SONG
# (AFTER DEATH)

### *A. C. Wise*

Instead of a suicide note, Dana's lover left her a typewriter.

Not an apology, not an explanation. Just a ream of blank pages and the waiting keys.

When she closes her eyes, Dana sees Katrin falling. Fourteen floors. The rush of wind. Pavement and broken bits of sunlight casting shadows under the pedestrians below.

She picks at the edges of the scene. Her fingertips hunt threads, any narrative she can hold on to in order to make sense of the world without Katrin in it. The beauty of flight. The turned wing of a bird, arched open to the blue of the sky, sunlight streaming through each crystalline feather.

Dana wipes at her face with the back of her hand and touches a single key. Lightning streams through her veins, and she gasps. There, just beneath the keys, is a pulse, a wingbeat, the drum of frantic bird's heart spelling out words she can almost understand. Katrin is there, her story tucked into the blank pages waiting to be filled.

If she wants a reason, a story to take the place of her sorrow, she'll have to write her own.

And so . . .

Dana drove into the desert, leaving the hot, crowded city for the hot nothingness of sand and sun. She drove until the car ran out of gas. She walked, lugging Katrin's typewriter, until her legs gave out.

Where she stopped, a church made from the bones of a whale rose out of the sands. Open jaws whispered sanctuary. Dana crawled inside, and the ribs arched over her, sheltering her.

She curled against the ivory while her body curled protectively around the typewriter. Whale bone and woman flesh, both enclosing a space of absence, the ghost Dana had come to pull from under her skin.

It was there, typing in the desert, writing her lover's suicide note, that Dana met the angel.

ↄ

*Sparrow: She's a psychopomp carrying your lover's soul. Her song tastes like the first moment you saw your lover in that little café. You almost choked on your coffee. That is love, the beginning seeded with the end. That is the sparrow's song.*

ↄ

Gabrielle sets the typed page on the desk amidst the halo of empty bottles, empty coffee cups, and empty cigarette packs. Only the ashtray is full. She's started looking at the objects, and the typewriter in their midst, as artifacts.

She's an archaeologist, peeling back the layers of Dana's manuscript, trying to understand her. The pages pile ritually beside the typewriter each evening and vanish by morning. Dana never speaks of them, and Gabrielle has learned better than to ask. The secret of her lover lies in these pages; it's up to her to unearth it.

She doesn't understand anything about Dana. She's still trying to piece together the shape of her life from before Dana appeared, seemingly falling out of the sky to occupy a hole Gabrielle hadn't realized was there. Until Dana filled it.

The moment of impact: when Gabrielle looked up in the café and saw Dana standing in the door. Sunlight caught in her dyed-black hair. It washed the meaning from her tattoos, leaving only the impression of ink on skin. The weight of sorrow was palpable around her. It made Gabrielle catch her breath, almost choke on her coffee. From that moment, she wanted to understand Dana. She's been trying ever since.

Dana doesn't make it easy on her. Every time Gabrielle looks, the story changes. Last time, Dana took the typewriter to a cliff and wrote on pages warped by the sea while a storm crackled along the horizon. The time before, it was a subterranean cave, and Dana wrote her lover's death by the glow of luminescent mushrooms.

Gabrielle asked about it only once, her chin nestled against Dana's shoulder, her arm around Dana's waist. "What are you writing?" she'd asked.

"A ghost story."

"Like around a campfire?"

"Sort of. Except it's about the way absence reshapes the world around it. Like the impression left behind on the pillow when you lift your head."

At the sound of a key in the door, Gabrielle starts. She shifts the notebook to cover the pages, but the door never opens. Only her imagination, her guilt manifesting in an auditory hallucination. Dana never told Gabrielle she couldn't read the pages, but she never invited her to read them, either.

Gabrielle drains her wine and moves from the desk. She pours another glass, and one for Dana, leaving it on the counter. She loses herself in dinner preparation, not thinking about Dana, not thinking about the manuscript.

Fingers brush the back of Gabrielle's neck, and she jumps. Dana must have slipped in while Gabrielle wasn't looking. Must have called Gabrielle's name, and she didn't hear. Gabrielle brings plates to the table. The untouched wineglass remains on the counter; her own is stained with imprints of her lipstick.

As she eats, Gabrielle is careful not to ask about the manuscript. She doesn't even glance toward the desk or the typewriter. The sun sets, and shadows creep over the litter of bottles and coffee cups. Gabrielle talks about the museum and the new wing they're building. Once it's done, the ornithology collection—Gabrielle's collection—will fill the space.

After dinner, Gabrielle does the dishes, sliding everything into the soapy water, keeping only her wineglass. She hears the rattle of pills in their little plastic container and tenses, waiting for a sharp comment: *See? I'm taking my medicine like a good girl.*

But nothing comes. They aren't going to fight. Gabrielle breathes out. Either the pills are working, or the manuscript is.

There's a murmur, so soft Gabrielle doesn't catch the words, but it's Dana's voice. It's accompanied by the tap of fingers against Gabrielle's hip. Gabrielle's eyes snap open. Cooling water drips from her hands. She withdraws them, drying them, and in her haste her elbow catches the wineglass balanced precariously on the edge of the counter.

"Damn it!"

She crouches, shaking unaccountably as she sweeps broken glass into her bare palms. It slices her, and she hisses surprise, letting the pieces tumble back to the floor. Drops of blood tap-tap-tap the blond wood.

But Dana's fingers are on her shoulder, pulling her away. She lets the glass scatter, brushes off her palms and stands. Her cheeks are wet. Steam from the dishwater? She doesn't dare wipe them for fear of tiny grains of broken glass still clinging to her skin. She breathes out, closing her eyes again and surrendering to the moment, even though the trembling hasn't stopped.

Gabrielle lets her lover fold around her. Breath stirs against her throat. Lips follow breath, tracing over Gabrielle's skin. The hand on Gabrielle's waist brings the heat of the desert sun.

She keeps her eyes closed. Her fingers fumble at buttons. She presses her palm to the ribbed fabric underneath, remembering too late the smear of blood she'll leave behind.

The cloth's texture writes itself on Gabrielle's skin. She nearly trips up the steps to the half-floor holding the bed. The aerie—Dana's word for it. If she keeps her eyes closed, nothing can spoil this moment. She doesn't need to see Dana's face; the fingers, sure on Gabrielle's skin, are enough.

This. Here. Now. It's good. Better than it's been in a long time. Maybe she shouldn't. . . . But it's so good, and it's been so long.

Pleasure builds like a rush of wind, like the ground rising to meet her.

Impact.

Gabrielle's eyes fly open, her head jerking toward the window. The ghost-impression of wings lingers on the glass. The violence jolts, a moment too late; a shock of another kind is already running through her, a gasp slipping free as she comes.

❧

*Mourning Dove: She's deceptive. You think there is only one layer to her sorrow, the weeping sound she makes as though her heart is broken. But there is also the whistle of her wings as she takes flight. It is the sound of rushing air. It is the last sound your lover heard as she fell.*

❧

There's a smudge of blood on the window where the bird struck the glass last night. Gabrielle notices it as she's rinsing the cup from her morning tea. The memory of impact jars her, and she catches her breath. She glances toward the aerie before remembering she woke up alone.

Sometime in the night, she heard the distinct clack of keys. But her limbs stayed heavy, trapping her in the bed, and sleep dragged her back down. The second time, her sleep was deep enough that she never heard Dana leave.

Gabrielle pulls cleaning supplies from under the sink and climbs onto the counter. The window is stiff with years of paint and humidity, but Gabrielle gets it open. Balancing precariously, she reaches out as far as she can.

Her muscles are pleasantly sore, her skin raw and tingling. She hasn't showered yet, putting it off for as long as possible. It's silly, a teenage thing, like when she was in high school and bought the same kind of perfume as the girl she had a crush on. Not so she could wear it, but so she could spray in on her pillowcase before going to sleep each night.

She wants to hold on to the scent of Dana, pressed into her skin. She cherishes the faint nail marks left on her body. Distracted, Gabrielle slips. Her arms pinwheel a moment, trying to catch herself on the window frame. She misses. Her cheek strikes the counter on the way down, and stars pop, bright, behind her eyes.

Dazed, she lies on the floor, staring at the ceiling. When she turns her head, a stray page lies inches from her face. She must have knocked it over when she fell. Sitting up, she reaches for it, but pauses.

There's something missing. No shards of glass, no blood. She broke her wineglass last night, didn't she? She cut herself. Gabrielle turns her hands over, examining them, but her fingertips are clean. She pushes her sleeves back to look at her arms. The marks Dana left, the secret language of love bites and scratches, is gone. Gabrielle presses a hand to her forehead, blinking against sudden dizziness. When she looks up again, even the blood on the window is gone.

☙

*Mockingbird: She is a trickster, an illusionist. After death she has the ability not only to recreate common sounds—the neighbor's cat, a car alarm—but sounds specific to you: the catch of your lover's breath, her footsteps on the stairs, her voice. This is not cruelty; your reaction to the mockingbird is your responsibility alone.*

☙

It was there, typing in the desert, writing her lover's suicide note, that Dana met the angel.

Sunrise found her chilled, her back against a curve of whalebone. Pages lay wedged beneath the typewriter, sand clogged between its keys. There were feathers, too.

One from a gull, miles from any shore. Another, jammed beneath the space bar, bright canary. Parrot. Pigeon. Crow. But the keys still worked, responding with letters instead of a flock of birds. Typing eased the ache in her fingers, so Dana didn't stop until a shadow fell across her.

At first she mistook it for a massive vulture. But when she shaded her eyes, she saw it was a woman, not a bird. Or it was both.

The angel's toes curled around the whale cathedral's arched ceiling as she peered between the slats of its ribs. Everything about her was pale—hair, lips, even her nipples. Only her eyes were dark, black all the way to the edges. Her shoulders, when she flexed them, made a sound like settling wings.

The angel opened her mouth, and Dana waited to hear Katrin's voice. Instead, the angel let out a piercing cry. Sunlight caught the fine crystalline feathers covering her body. When the angel leaped into the sky, Dana scrambled to follow.

❧

*Storm Petrel: Her song is a rush, a voice too eager to get the words out, afraid of losing ground. It tumbles like gravity until it hits the right tempo, then it becomes the sound of a record scratch, long and drawn-out. It is the sound of your first fight with your lover—vinyl pulled from beneath the needle, then shattered against the wall.*

❧

There's a bird in the apartment. Gabrielle drops her keys, startled at the unmistakable whir of trapped wings. She reaches for the light, heart hammering, but the sound doesn't come again. Nothing. The apartment is empty. The window above the sink is closed.

Gabrielle pours wine to calm her nerves. What would make her think a bird had gotten in?

Dana's desk is immaculate. All the bottles and cups gone, loose pages stashed out of sight. The typewriter gleams in the late-afternoon light. Gabrielle runs a finger over its keys, resisting the impulse to check between them for feathers.

She opens her laptop and searches for "whale bones in the desert." Her stomach twists, and she almost closes the tab before scanning the results. Images appear—bones laid flat, broken, scarcely recognizable as whales. What did she expect? An actual cathedral entered through propped-open jaws, a vaulted arch of ribs leading to the altar of the tail?

She shuts the laptop before she can search for Katrin's name. Katrin existed. Dana loved her. And she fell. That's all.

To distract herself, Gabrielle pulls the proofs for the museum's latest catalog from her work bag, pages filled with beautiful hand-drawn illustrations showing details of wings, feathers, beaks, claws. Mockingbird. Mourning dove. Sparrow.

When a subtle ache starts behind her eyes, she sets the pages aside, glancing at the door. Dana should be home by now. Gabrielle moves to the desk, presses a hand flat against the stacked manuscript, fingers itching to rifle through the pages.

*A ghost story is about absence, the way something that isn't there shapes what's left behind.*

The spaces between the words. The spaces around them. Maybe that's where Gabrielle should be looking for her answers. If she traced the emptiness on each page, would it reveal the shape of Dana's heart, the shape of Katrin?

Gabrielle fans the pages, but doesn't lift them. In all her writing and rewriting, what is it Dana isn't saying about Katrin? What is the absence hiding?

Falling. The beauty of flight. It's almost romantic. A loveliness covering something ugly, harsh, something Dana can't bring herself to write. Bloody water filling the tub, dripping on the tiles, wet ropes of hair and cooling flesh starting to soften around hard bones. Maybe her dead lover's name wasn't even Katrin.

For a moment, Gabrielle feels it, the ghost winding between the words, pressing up, pressing back against her palm. It's almost a heartbeat, tapping out words, a name. She yanks her hand back. A shadow darts past, wittering overhead. The rustle of feathers. The panicked flight of wings.

∾

*There is an uncanniness to all birds' voices. Sometimes there are words just on the edge of hearing. They say* me, too *or* help me. *Sometimes they say their names, the ones we've given them—chickadee, chick-a-dee-dee-dee. Sometimes it sounds like they're saying the name of someone you should know, someone you can't quite remember. (The human mind is designed to seek patterns, to find meaning where there is none.) After death, birds' voices become clearer. You'll wish you could put things back the way they were, when you didn't understand them.*

∾

Dana came home from the desert with the angel on her back. In her apartment, it perched in the aerie, watching her. She tried to reread the pages she'd banged out until her fingers ached, fighting stiff keys clogged with feathers and sand. But they'd turned ancient, gone the ivory of bleached bone, the ink paled to brown like dried blood. Illegible.

Panic. The sensation of wings. Tiny claws scratching at her skin from the inside out. A thousand birds trapped between her bones.

With her eyes closed, she pressed a hand to her chest. Through cloth and skin she felt the faint tap-tap of a beak, Morse code answering her pain. *K-A-*

*T-R-I-N.* Her pulse drummed a response: *I'm here.* The words echoed, written featherlight against her palm. When she opened her eyes, she found the angel waiting with her arms open.

ભ

*Evening Grosbeak: She is a multiplicity. Instead of one voice in her song, there are many, each clamoring over the other. Each one a lie. Each one the truth.*

ભ

Gabrielle half-wakes, struggling to come up the rest of the way. A weight crouches at the end of the bed. Her eyes won't open. Her limbs won't move. She wants to sit up, but the sheets hold her down.

There's a rustle of pages like wings.

Her eyes snap open. She's lying on her side, facing Dana's naked back. She can't tell if Dana is breathing. Everything is indistinct. She's seeing the room through a fog; the space is wrong. She wants to reach for her lover, but can't.

Her eyes snap open. She is alone. But footsteps climb toward her. She can't see. Can't wake up. Can't get away.

Her eyes snap open. Dana's naked back faces her, furrows scored deep into the skin, welling with fresh blood. It drips tap-tap-tap on the floor. Blood soaks the sheets. Everywhere. Tap-tap-tap on the window. The moment of impact shocking her awake.

Her eyes snap open. A weight crouches at the end of the bed. She can't see it properly, but she knows it's the angel, the one who followed her lover home from the desert. Feathers brush her skin. A cold hand reaches for hers.

Her eyes won't open. Hands strike the pillow around her. The terrible sounds of impact. The promise of violence never delivered. Close, but never touching. They create a rush of air, a sound. They draw closer, but not close enough.

Gabrielle sheds dream after dream. Fighting to wake up for good. Her throat is raw with every word she fails to scream. It tastes of blood.

She is falling.

Sunlight knifes her awake with a ragged gasp. A sound like dying, which turns into a choking cough. Gabrielle claws at her throat and the sheets until the sensation passes, then draws in a lungful of air.

For a moment she can't orient herself, can't trust that she's finally awake. Then she manages to roll over. The imprint of Dana's head haunts her pillow, but Gabrielle is alone. She kicks the covers away. Pages fresh from the typewriter scatter like feathers.

She snatches them up, scanning.

There are words scribbled in the margins, curled around the text, filling the blank spaces and defining them. Notes on birdsong in her handwriting.

No. It must be a trick. She couldn't have written them. Didn't write them. She's being haunted.

Gabrielle tosses the pages away from her, but it isn't enough. She scrambles after them, tearing and tearing and tearing, scattering them from the aerie like snow.

*❧*

*Calliope Hummingbird: In life, her song is called bickering. In death, she is silent. You find yourself wishing she would speak again, even to argue. Even to weep or scream. But she only looks at you with bright eyes, withholding judgment, withholding forgiveness, withholding her song.*

*❧*

Fucking the angel is nothing like Dana expected. It was . . . it is . . . It is moments threaded along a string, constantly picked apart and woven together again. It is. It was. It will be.

The angel's talons rake her back, her thighs, her arms. Let out her blood.

The angel takes her hand, leads her to the aerie.

"I'm not ready for this. Katrin . . ."

The angel's eyes are black all the way to the edges. Her pulse drums *K-A-T-R-I-N*. Dana's answers: *I'm here.*

Dana's fingers tangle in feathers, pulling the angel down and into her, harder and deeper. The angel's beak is between her legs, and she is coming. Oh, God, she is coming, and nothing has ever felt this good.

Blood soaks the sheets, hotter than tears. Tap-tap-tap, hitting the floor. She cries out, choking on her lover's name, and all that comes is a sob.

Her fingers are in ~~Dana's~~ Katrin's hair. Wet ropes tangled from bathwater grown cold.

Gabrielle's fingers are in Dana's hair, on her wrist. So much blood. Shaking her. Holding her down, keeping her from flying.

She . . . No. Dana. *Dana* brought the angel back from the desert. Dana holds Katrin, soothes the goose-pimpled flesh where the pinfeathers have torn free. Gathering bloody feathers and keeping them from scattering in the wind. She will hold on until the shaking stops. She will never let go.

Fucking the angel is . . .

Gabrielle tears the pages until there is nothing left. Only blood and feathers covering the bed.

She pulls the angel into her. Deeper. Harder. She comes.

And she is all alone.

*Loon: There is much debate over her song. Is she laughing or crying? Is it a lonely sound or an invitation to join in her joke? Do you think death will make it easier to tell?*

Gabrielle opens the apartment door to birdsong. A robin, a pigeon, a thrush. A high, nattering yell, and one that sounds like a question asked over and over again. A macaw, an owl, a peacock's scream. She drops her keys, throwing her arms up to cover her eyes as wings rush overhead.

When she lowers her arms, her iPod glows at her from the docking station, a single word scrolling across the screen: BIRDSONG.

Her fingers shake as she turns the player off. The cacophony stops.

"Dana? Hello?"

The silence is thick, a presence filling every corner of the room.

"Dana?"

Part of her knows there won't be an answer, but she wants one, needs one so badly it hurts. She needs something to still the flutter of her pulse, so close beneath the surface of her skin. The pills by the sink aren't cutting it anymore. That's why she stopped taking them. That's why . . .

She closes the door, sets her keys down. The window over the sink is open. There's a smear of blood on the glass, almost like a fingerprint.

A breeze rustles the papers on Dana's desk, peeling them from their neat pile and scattering them around the room. Gabrielle's head throbs, the edges of a migraine coming on.

She reaches for the pill bottle, knocks it over.

Bending, she picks up a fallen page instead. It's blank. She picks up another. Blank. All of them.

A shape of absence. The words picked apart too often, unraveling. One tug and the whole story comes undone.

Wind rattles the single page left in the typewriter, demanding her attention. Blank, too.

Feathers roll through the room. No, not feathers, paper, torn to shreds. There's a scrap lodged between the typewriter keys. She digs, trying to reach it, but her fingers are too large and the space too small. The keys clatter, a staccato pulse, Morse code, the rattle of wings. An apology. A confession. A ghost story. Each key strike echoes the frantic, trapped beating of her heart. Begin again.

She waits for the door to open, the sound of Dana coming home to prove her wrong. But the only answer in the silence is the frantic scrabble of the typewriter and the shiver-hum of wings.

Words crowd the blank spaces of the page, responding to the strike of her fingers. She shakes. Tears roll down her cheeks. Haunted.

Instead of a suicide note, Gabrielle's lover left her a typewriter.

# THE SORCERER OF ETAH

## *Gray Rinehart*

The birds returned early, as if the breath of a storm god chased them up from the south. Isi sniffed the gentle wind as he watched the little auks; it was all wrong.

The serfaq flew in by the hundreds, by the thousands, a month early—the days were short, the twilights long, the nights dwindling but still dark. The rookeries were packed with snow and ice, and the birds flapped and screeched and fought over the few clear spots on the cliffs. They were almost as thick and loud now as they would be when the little ones fledged, before they flew south again.

Isi's sledge coasted as the dogs raised an outcry at the birds. They flew crazily, as if they were drunk, and some wheeled in close enough that Isi could almost have snared them without a net. He'd netted five hundred a day during the hunt last summer, many of which were safely cached inside sealskins back at Siorapaluk, slowly fermenting into slimy, delicious kiviaq.

Isi pondered the wheeling birds. *When I get to Etah, I will ask the sorcerer what this means.*

He whipped the dogs back to their task and the sledge moved forward again.

His full name was Isigippoq, but everyone called him Isi—the eye. Villagers bragged that he could see a bear's black eye a mile away in thick snow fog, but he was not so boastful. Half a mile, maybe. Some thought he was an angakkoq because of his eyes, but he was no sorcerer. Sorcerers controlled their magic; Isi did not know how his vision worked, except that it seemed sometimes to pull distant objects toward him and render them as clear as if they were close enough to touch. But he didn't need any special sight to observe these serfaq, or any special knowledge to know that they should not have flown back so early in the year.

*Yes, old Anoraa will know what this means.*

Isi gloried in the cold spring day as he sledged over the ice pack with the casual familiarity of having done it a dozen times before. The sun, slanting in over his shoulders, cast the ice in distinct patterns that he read and understood at a glance. The ridges and icy terrain reformed year after year and, scoured in distinct patterns by wind off the ice cap, presented ever-new and ever-changing pathways. But the mountain that held back the ice cap did not change, and Isi knew every peak and promontory and could pinpoint his location from any of them.

This trip, however, was no simple hunting expedition, no family migration. Ukutseq, the head man of Siorapaluk, had sent Isi out alone to deliver the newly made amulet to Etah's sorcerer. Isi had not seen the amulet; he knew not what power it held or even if it was bone or stone. It lay hidden inside a soft leather pouch half the size of his head, sewn from the skin of a single hare. Elaborate seal's-blood designs decorated the pouch, which was heavier than a fox and crinkled from the grass cushion that protected its cargo.

He was now three days out of the village, having stayed last night at the tiny camp of Neqi. It would take him two more days to reach Etah. After he delivered the mysterious bundle, he thought he might stay a week or two to hunt. Even if he stayed three weeks, he should still be able to journey back south to the pretty little sandy beach that was Siorapaluk before the sea ice started to thin out. That was when the first serfaq should have returned—not in the thousands or even the hundreds, but perhaps by the score as their pathfinders made their way back to the brightening world.

In the cliffs to his right, the serfaq struggled over the few clear nesting spots, but they seemed not to know what they were doing. And—

A figure stood at the top of the cliff: a woman, by the cut of her anorak. She pulled back her hood, and her long, dark, stringy hair flailed in the breeze.

The breeze stank.

Not the usual stink that Isi got behind the dogs—their dung and piss in bits and droplets in his face as they ran in front of the sledge—but a rotten stench, worse than the opened stomach of a narwhal. The smell dripped from the air like blubber dripping as it rendered, and he knew who the woman was.

*Mother? Not possible. . . .*

Isi reached up with his left hand to his own amulet—a walrus tusk hung on a leather cord—and called the animal's strength into him.

The wind changed subtly—a faint brush along his eyebrows and lashes, a droop in the woman's wild hair—and all the squawking serfaq went silent. Even the dogs hushed and slowed to a trot, and Isi did not bother to whip them. He checked his harpoon and his sharp iron savik as he studied the snowpack, especially the thick ice to the west. No bears, for which he was grateful; the abundance of seal this year meant there had been more bears than usual. No hunters, no other activity at all. He looked back up the cliff—

—and the woman was gone.

Isi dragged his right foot and brought the sledge to a stop. One of the dogs whimpered, and they all cowered onto the snow, but other than the traces creaking and the runners grinding a little as the sledge settled on the snow top, everything was silent as death. Even the birds had landed, anywhere they could, and the sky was darkening as if a storm was coming—but the only clouds were tight on the western horizon and blurred the distinction between ice and sky.

*The sun*. . . . Something was happening to the sun. The moon slid over its face, and the day darkened.

*Seqineq pulavoq.*

Isi didn't often concern himself with the moon. Aningaaq's phases and its coming and going were of interest primarily to the head man Ukutseq, who timed the hunts by its cycles and through the long dark counted how long until the sun would rise again. But now Isi watched, fascinated, the dogs' leather traces still held tight in his right hand but almost forgotten.

Gloom settled over him, but he was more interested in the ridges—mountains?—he saw on the backlit edge of the moon. Its face was blank as it moved over the sun, and yet it wasn't. . . . His vision pulled Aningaaq toward him until Isi saw faint blue-white blemishes, like pores or wounds. The deeper dark areas that he thought of as the moon's birthmarks stood out the way a raven stood out against the night sky.

Then the sun was a thin ring, and the day was cold and the wind even fouler than before.

And then Aningaaq moved on, uncovering Seqineq's face. The day brightened, slowly.

Isi blinked. His eyes hurt from the fetid wind, so he held them closed. The afterimage of the hidden-and-reappearing sun played on the insides of his eyelids. Gradually, the birds raised their voices, but they were muted, as if half of them had disappeared. His lead dog barked, followed by another, and then they growled and grew silent again.

When he opened his eyes, the woman sat on the sledge.

Her figure was indistinct—no, everything was indistinct. He looked at the mountain, his hands, the dogs, and everything looked as if he saw it through a thick sheet of glacial ice. He stooped down, dug up a handful of snow, and held it to his eyes. It did not help.

The woman laughed at him, and her breath was more horrible than the wind. Her breath *was* the foul wind, rotten beyond comprehension. The dogs whimpered and the birds began flying away south, back where they should have stayed.

If he did not look straight at her, he saw her more clearly—and wished he didn't. What little hair she had was long, matted together, and as ragged as her torn and filthy clothes. The skin on her fingers clung to the bones, but looked thin, dry, and cracked into strips like the dog's traces. Her eyes glazed over with milky white film. Her face was dark brown, in places almost black with frostbite, and sunken into hollows around her jaw and temples. The few teeth in her foul mouth were ground down, as all women's teeth got from chewing fox and rabbit hides to soften them, but the stumps were black with rot. And the smell radiated from her, the odor of decay and death.

In all that, she was unmistakably his anaana.

But she could not be. Three years earlier his mother had graciously fallen off the sledge during a trip from Siorapaluk to Savigssivik. An ancient and bitter woman, she had terrorized their village for so long that no one had mourned her—neither neighbors nor family. They simply thanked her for removing her burdensome hostility from their lives, and tried to forget her.

Isi guessed her spirit was angry enough that even the animals avoided her; otherwise, she would have been eaten by now, her bones scoured by the winds off the ice cap. She might be disappointed that none of the village newborns had been given her name, so her spirit could live again in them, but who wanted to put up with another Alianakuluk, another "little misfortune"?

Nothing to do but ask, so he did. "Why are you here, arnaqquassaaq?"

If she was offended at being called a hag, she did not show it. Isi looked at her without looking, turning his head slightly to catch her from each side of his blurred central vision, but she barely moved. She chuckled, low and rotten.

Isi said, louder, "Why are you here, anaana?"

She focused her dead eyes on him. Her ulcerous tongue wetted her lips, and in a voice like the slow scraping of a dull savik over driftwood she said, "To sit with you while you die."

"I'm not dying," he said.

"You're always dying. Everything is always dying." She took a slow breath with a sound like sucking marrow from a bone. "'You live, you suffer, and you die,'" she quoted.

It was a truth Isi's father had taught him, as all fathers taught their sons. But Isi did not relent. "The first part of that is, 'You live,'" he said. "And I am still alive."

"Even so. But you are not Isigippoq anymore, are you? What will you do now, Isiluppoq?"

Isi turned away, looking askance at everything and seeing none of it clearly. She was right: his fine eyes were ruined. The dogs were dark shapes on the snow, still whimpering, and the few auks still flying nearby may as well have been drifting pieces of soot.

His undead mother laughed. "If you return to Siorapaluk, they will turn you out. Try your luck at Qaanaaq or Qeqertaq, the same. If you make it down to Uummannaq, they will chase you over the bay to Pituffik."

*Where the dogs are tied up, indeed.*

He knew what she said was true: if he could not hunt anymore, every village would shun him. But Isi would not easily accept that fate. He must be able to do something.

"Perhaps," she said, "you could set your face toward Savigssivik, and you can fall off the sledge on your way."

Yes, the crone would be pleased to see him do so, but he would not follow her example. Not yet. No—there was one thing at least he could do, and that was to finish the task Ukutseq had set him. He would continue north to Etah, find the angakkoq, and deliver the amulet. After that, who could say?

"Shut up, dead woman," he said. "I am not going back to Siorapaluk."

Her leathery eyelids narrowed over her dead white eyes. She bared her rotten teeth and growled, deeper and longer than a bear.

"Fall off the sledge again, old hag," Isi said. He snapped his whip over the dogs' heads, ordered them up and forward again.

His mother—the grotesque corpse of his mother—stepped lightly from the sledge and stood to the side as he passed her. Isi did not look back. Within two lengths of the dogs' traces the air cleared, as if he came out of a fogbank of decay. Isi breathed deep the sweet, clean air.

Then he choked as the foulness returned, and her voice sounded so close she might be sitting on his shoulder.

"Keep a close watch, oh Isi. You might see your death coming."

It was going to take longer than two more days to get to Etah. Isi trusted his dogs. He cracked the whip, and they did not disappoint him. But he did not trust himself.

As they detoured around icebergs frozen in the pack and crevasses formed in the frozen sea, he constantly feared losing his way. He could no longer see the mountain features that had so reliably guided him in years past. He marked the angle of the sun as much by its warmth as by sighting it, and often by the shadows he sensed more than saw from the corners of his eyes. But in front of him he saw little of value or of note. It was as if he lay under the water, looking at images moving above the surface.

He gauged his speed by the feel of the sledge and the motion of the sun. Just before the sun set, as its light diffused through the clouds and made his task all the harder, the dogs stopped at the edge of another crevasse. Isi walked along it, to the right, toward the land and the mountain and the great ice, measuring its width and testing the strength of the edges with the shaft of his harpoon. It took him longer than ever to find a passage. He tried to force all his anger into his muscles as he pushed the sledge to the narrowest spot and bridged the crevasse with it. He tested its stability and then stood on it while he tossed the dogs across, one by one. Again on his way in the twilight, he drove the pack east to find a place to camp. The dogs barked their encouragement to one another; they knew the long day was coming to an end, and there would be meat and rest for them.

Isi found a suitable place near but not under the mountain, lest an unstable piece of ice fall on his tent or on the dogs. He staked the dogs away from the sledge; by feel he cut hunks of walrus and gave them out according to the pack hierarchy. He ate some himself as he worked, sucking on the frozen meat until it softened enough to chew.

He pitched the tent over the sledge as much by feel as by his damaged sight; it took far longer than it should have. He started a piece of peat burning for warmth and finally tumbled, exhausted, onto the skin-covered sledge. It creaked under him. Outside the tent one of the dogs growled in its sleep, but the only other sound was the steady breeze off the ice cap.

He might have slept, but wasn't sure: one moment he noticed his fatigue and the breeze, the next he noticed the stink.

"You'll never make it," said his mother-who-refused-to-die.

"Shut up, old woman. Dead woman."

He hated the rattling sound of her laugh almost as much as the hollow scrape of her speech. "If I am dead, and you are talking with me, does that mean you are dead, too?"

"No," he said. He drew his savik slowly from its sheath. "By the bear in the sky and his brother on the ice, I live."

"We shall see," she said.

He stabbed at where the voice came from, but his savik cut only the foul air. Her laughter rose to a crescendo and then faded, replaced by wind and more wind.

The tent shuddered. Frozen pellets driven off the ice cap struck it with magnificent force and turned the skin sides into drums. The rhythm beat into Isi's ears, and his heart raced to catch up with it. The flap blew open and storm-driven snow flew inside.

Isi crept outside, into the stinging twilight. The wind smelled like a butchered walrus's guts; the ice that blew into his mouth tasted charnel. It had to be the old woman's doing.

Low to the ground, he worked his way around the tent, checking its moorings. He listened for the dogs but heard neither barks nor whimpers; they should all be safe under protective blankets of snow by now. By the time he reached the flap again, ice coated his eyebrows and mustache, and his hood was frozen to his ears. He slipped inside and fought to tie the flap shut.

Before he could get it tied, the dogs started barking. The sound barely penetrated the wind, which stung Isi again when he stepped outside.

A tremendous growl answered the dogs, and even with his broken eyes Isi saw the great bear—so white it nearly glowed in the storm—rear up on its hind legs as the lead dog sprang at it. The bear batted the dog away as easily as Isi might smack his own head, and charged at the tent. The other dogs broke loose from their stakes and leapt at the bear—from its right, as their instinct taught them—but this bear hit them as easily with its right paw as with its left.

Isi knew that was wrong, too, but his knowledge didn't matter: his remaining dogs, all four of them, were flung aside one by one by this colossal ambidextrous bear.

He dove into the tent to retrieve his harpoon.

As his fingers closed around the shaft, the tent ripped open with a sound like drops of fat sizzling as they fall into a fire. The bear lunged past the torn skins and landed on the side of the sledge. The sledge cracked and skittered sideways, spilling Isi's belongings and tangling in the tent.

Isi jabbed at the beast with his harpoon. The bear slapped the weapon away with its left paw, then swept Isi's chest with its right. Isi gasped as its claws tore through his thick jacket and ripped into his muscles. The claws caught the thong holding his amulet; it snapped as easily as breaking a bird's breastbone and flung Isi's walrus tusk out into the storm and ice.

Isi backed up a step and tried to raise his harpoon, but he slipped to one knee, suddenly weak. The harpoon felt heavy and started to fall from his grip. Without his amulet, he no longer had the walrus's strength.

The bear rose up to its full height and bellowed foul breath into the storm.

Isi looked at it askance and saw, at the clear edge of his vision, not the huge bear, but his mother's shriveled form. His thoughts jerked forward in short bursts, as a child chases after a fleeing hare. How could his mother transform into a bear, unless she had learned some sorcery? Could her dead self have become an angakkoq? More likely she was an ilissitoq—she had been awful enough in life to be an evil spirit in death. But if she was a full angakkoq, the only wound that would kill her would be to her throat.

Isi gripped the harpoon and readied for the false creature's attack. But its triumphant roar became a scream of pain as Isi's lead dog jumped from beside the tangled tent and bit the bear's flank. The dog struck and dropped away, unsteady and favoring one front paw, then sprang again at the bear's back. The bear spun toward this new attacker.

Isi charged. His feet moved sluggishly, as if his boots were blocks of ice, but he closed the distance and struck just under the beast's ribcage. The bear's right paw swung back and caught Isi a glancing blow that knocked him off his feet. He landed hard beside the sledge.

Isi drew a sharp, painful breath as he watched the bear finally strike the dog a horrible blow that stove in its side. Isi felt his chest where the bear's claws had torn him and wished for his walrus amulet to strengthen him—and remembered the amulet meant for the angakkoq of Etah.

He dug through the skins and goods around him as the snarling bear approached, and came up with the leather amulet bag. He gasped as he picked it up, not from the pain that wrenched his smashed side but from surprise. Three or four of the stitches on the amulet bag had popped, either from the bear jumping on the sledge or Isi pulling too roughly at the pouch, and some of the cushioning grass poked through. But with the grass came light—glowing white, whiter than the brightest snowbank under the harshest summer sun.

Power flowed into Isi. He surged to his feet, the bag heavy in his left hand, his savik in his right. He held the glowing opening in the bag toward the awful bear and the creature stopped, growled loudly, and shuffled its feet as if unsure whether to advance or retreat. Its black eye clouded over with the same milky glow Isi had seen in his mother's corpse-eyes.

Isi rushed forward, thrust the sun-bright talisman up and followed with his knife. The bear's glazed white eyes reflected the incredible light until it closed them in apparent pain. Isi slashed at the creature's throat, and though he barely nicked it the bear turned aside, screamed a woman's scream, and disappeared. The storm and the foul air disappeared with it.

Isi stood alone on the ice field, surrounded by debris.

He sat on his ruined sledge and lamented. The whalebone runners he had fashioned, the precious scraps of driftwood he had retrieved from the sea, lovingly laced together and kept strong and in good repair for so many years, now broken by a bear spirit that turned out to be his own dead mother; all five of his dogs dead; his chest torn and ribs likely broken; and for what? To keep him from getting to Etah? To divert him from delivering the amulet?

The amulet bag in his hand glowed more softly now. Its light faded as fast as the day brightened around him, until it was just a torn leather bag.

* * *

Isi sat on the sledge until the sun cleared the mountain behind him, the leather bag with the amulet cold and heavy in his hand.

Gradually it occurred to him that real bears might find him, enticed by the dogs' blood if not his own. He should start moving.

But which way? Back to Neqi, the tiny camp where he stayed two nights ago? Or onward to Etah, where the angakkoq waited for the amulet hidden in its leather pouch?

Neqi was closer, but Etah must still be his goal.

It took Isi until the sun reached its zenith to refit the unbroken pieces of his old sledge into a miniature version to pull behind him. He loaded it with everything he could salvage: walrus meat, some of the better skins, peat to burn, the precious stalks of dry grass in their fox-skin pouch. As he moved, his ribs rubbed their broken ends together inside his chest; the pain tormented him with everything he picked up, every knot he tied, every breath. The shaft of his harpoon was undamaged, and he fitted a new head onto it; the other had apparently disappeared with the bear-creature. He never found his walrus tusk.

Rather than lay it on the little sledge, he fashioned a sling to carry the amulet bag close to him.

Before he set out, Isi replaced the insulating grass in the bottom of his boots. He placed a last stalk in his mouth, crossways, to protect his lips from frostbite, and started north.

That night, Isi sheltered against the mountain, out of the wind. If ice or rocks might bury him, he little cared.

The next day dawned dreary and cold. Isi walked through icy fog, with only the obscured sun to help him keep going in the right direction. As the sun slipped down to the horizon, he found himself in the middle of a snow field adjacent to the mouth of a small glacier. He didn't think a piece would calve off the glacier in the night, but living through another day made him wish for more days still; he was reluctant to take the chance.

Isi tested the snow with his harpoon, and found it a good consistency for an illuliaq. He stood in one spot and scribed a circle around himself with the harpoon, then carefully cut and set the snow blocks in place. He was growing accustomed to doing regular tasks with the limited vision of his new eyes, and though it took him twice as long as it should have he was satisfied with the snow house when he finished.

Isi lay on the skins atop the small snow shelf he'd left for sleeping, when the smell of death returned.

"You should turn back," she said.

Isi picked up the amulet bag, intending to ward her off, but the light coming from it was barely brighter than a seal-oil lamp. Its pale, grey, misty light reflected off the snow domed around him. Isi choked on sudden terror. Had he drained the amulet of its power?

She chuckled, and anger flooded over his fear. "Come closer," he said, "so I can slash your throat again."

"Such disrespect for your mother," she said.

"Such disrespect for your son, witch-woman."

She snarled, more like a fox than a bear. "Why should I respect a no-good who never married?" she said. "Who never gave me grandchildren to carry my name? Who didn't even turn and look when I stepped off the sledge to pee? When I yelled and yelled?"

Isi tried to remember that day. She hadn't yelled. Had she?

Had she never meant to relieve the people of her loathsome presence? That, Isi realized, would be more like her.

She must know she was the reason he hadn't married. When she was alive, no girls considered him because none of them wanted to live in the peat house with her.

After she died in the cold waste—and now Isi imagined he might have heard a voice on the wind that day—his migrations along the coast always seemed contrary to those of any marriageable girls. As for giving her grandchildren, he did not know. He didn't think so. In Qeqertaq, one of the hunters had loaned Isi his wife for a time, because she wanted him, but the baby she bore was her husband's, not Isi's. She said so, and the mother always knew.

The mother always knew—what did his mother know? Had she yelled when she fell off the sledge? Isi forced his mind back to that day, back when all the villages were more prosperous and he himself owned seven dogs. They were on the move, trying to make distance while tiny pellets of ice whistled through the air all around them. She was on the sledge, riding, and Isi had gone forward to jog with the dogs and scout the path. Did he hear a plaintive wail on the wind? He thought not; he thought maybe; he thought so.

Beside him, his corpse-mother laughed her horrid laugh. "Are you suffering enough yet?"

Isi left the past. It did not matter what he heard or didn't hear; what mattered was that his mother was supposed to be dead but apparently was not. He considered her question. If he said yes, it would be like admitting defeat and inviting the release of death. If he said no, it would be like asking for more suffering. The snow house was quiet except for her hideous breathing.

"Are you dead enough yet?" he asked.

His not-dead mother gave a great cackling laugh that filled the illuliaq with her vile breath.

"Not yet, my thankless, far-seeing son. Not yet."

She touched him then, and he tensed, but it was a surprisingly soft, intensely cold caress. He backed up on the sleeping shelf, knocking the amulet bag to the illuliaq's floor.

Her fingers dipped into his oozing wounds and walked their way up his chest, and her naked arm was no longer split and leathery but smooth and supple. Her face was complete, and young, and beautiful; she was naked, as if it was summer, and her breasts were firm and had never felt a baby's mouth.

She leaned in toward him, and the light in the illuliaq grew.

Isi turned his head away, and at the edge of his vision he saw her as she really was—putrid and horrifying.

She clamped her bony fingers on his throat and pushed him back into the snow wall, snarling fetid breath through rotten teeth. His vision wavered, and beneath his mother's dead face he glimpsed another face—an animal face, like a seal's but skinless and with thick, powerful jaws and large, jagged teeth.

Isi groped for the amulet bag, but it was not in reach.

He grasped his savik instead and thrust it up, past her other arm. She leaned her head back, away from the blade, fighting as she continued to choke him, but Isi's arm was stronger and longer than hers. The blade slipped in next to her windpipe, tore through cartilage and gristle, and came out the other side. The meteoric iron, pride of Savigssivik, felt hot in his hands.

His mother—or the thing that looked like his mother—released him and grabbed her own throat, wheezing out horrid breath that could no longer form a scream, and vanished.

Isi sat up and rubbed his own throat. The light from the amulet bag at his feet faded, to yellow, and to grey, and to darkness.

Isi reached Etah three days later. The tiny sledge behind him was piled only with a few worn skins. All the walrus meat was gone; he had eaten it on the run, and to make haste had not even tried to hunt at the seal breathing-holes he passed. He had not slept, for fear that his mother's shade or something worse would visit him. He could barely stand.

But he could see now, after a fashion. His eyesight had not cleared, but the blurred center of his vision seemed smaller and easier to see around.

He swayed but stayed upright at the edge of the ice field before the tiny village, farther than any of the men could hurl a harpoon. He tried to shout, but managed only a whisper. "Anoraa."

"I am here," said a voice beside him.

The old—no, the ancient—sorcerer smiled at Isi. Isi was too tired even to express surprise that the angakkoq had come upon him as swift and silent as the wind.

"You have something for me," Anoraa said.

Isi collapsed to his knees. He unslung the amulet bag and held it out to Anoraa.

Anoraa pushed Isi's arm away. The angakkoq reached in and dug his fingers into Isi's side. Isi gasped as the old man probed his cracked ribs. He wanted to faint, but his body did not permit it.

Anoraa moved his fingers to the bloody gouges on Isi's chest and back to his side, again and again, and each time Isi found it easier to breathe.

Anoraa stepped back. "Rise, he who was once Isigippoq," he said, and pulled Isi to his feet.

Isi stood easily. He was still hungry, still weary, but in much less pain. Slowly he registered what Anoraa had said. "What?"

"You are no longer Isigippoq, at least not fully. But you have seen the truth of the false bear, and the truth of the false witch, and you have it in you to see more fantastic visions yet."

Isi did not question how Anoraa knew what he said; he was the village angakkoq, skilled in such things. But the old man was not finished speaking.

"You do not know who you are, but I do. I thought to name you Takunnippoq, but that only speaks to your past journey. For you now and for the future, I prefer Isigaa."

Isi's fatigue made him slow to understand—"has had a vision" was true enough, but "can see it"? He wasn't sure if he liked the new name, or if he believed it.

Anoraa slapped Isi on the back, and a jolt of pain woke him from considering the name. He was not yet whole, though he felt better than he had in days.

"Come," Anoraa said, "you will share my kiviaq."

Isi's stomach rumbled at the thought of the tasty fermented birds, but the pain that throbbed through him reminded him of his errand. He again held the amulet bag out to Anoraa. "This is for you," he said.

Anoraa's eyes glittered with reflected sunlight. He took the bag, but said nothing when he saw the popped stitches. He drew his savik and slit the remainder of the seam. The crisp grass complained as he withdrew a smooth, polished egg of meteoric iron from its grasp; the egg hung in an intricate woven sling suspended from a thick leather thong. As Isi looked closer, he saw that the amulet was not shaped quite like a bird's egg: it had no pointed end and fat end, but its ends were similarly rounded. Though dark iron, it seemed to glow inside its web. Somehow the shape soothed Isi to look at.

The amulet held Isi's attention, even in the center of his damaged vision, the way a dancing flame enraptures a child. He turned his head a bit to the left, and the amulet's shape sharpened and its color shifted. It may have been a trick of the springtime sunshine, but the smooth edges of the near-ellipsoid metal shone as if it remembered its fiery descent to the earth.

Isi's nose caught a hint of foulness in the air. He looked away from the amulet, first toward the village where three of the hunters were approaching, harpoons in hand, then in a wide circle of sky and ice cap and still-frozen sea.

Anoraa wrinkled his nose. "Tipi," he said.

"Yes," Isi said. "It stinks. It is the same smell. What is it?"

"You know what it is. You know what they are, Isigaa. You can see it."

The memory came to him of that inhuman face behind his mother's dead one, and he did know.

"Yes, Isi. You saw the Tornit's true face."

Isi shivered. The Tornit, the old ones who used to share the world with the people, had been thwarted long ago. They were supposed to be very powerful sorcerers, but the people had chased them away beyond the great ice. Everyone assumed they were gone forever—only stories now, to keep the children close to the houses in the deep winter dark.

"No, Isi, not just stories. They are coming back, and we must be ready. You will—"

Isi looked to the south, and in the center of his blurred vision saw a speck on the ice cap. He turned his head slightly, but it was still a speck.

"Hold this, and *see*," Anoraa said, and placed the iron egg in Isi's hand.

Isi felt the amulet's power again. The speck resolved into his mother's ruined form, and then into a barely human form, huge and malevolent, with strong, twisted limbs and the strange naked animal face. In his long vision, the creature bared great bloody teeth at them. Then the foul wind blew a curtain of ice in front of it, and the Tornit vanished.

Anoraa exhaled a great sudden breath, with the sound of an iceberg calving off the end of a glacier. Isi turned as the Tornit, larger than a bear, roared its foul breath and swung its huge clawed hand at the old angakkoq's head. Anoraa crouched and turned aside and put up one hand which the Tornit grabbed. It lifted the old man up off the ground and shook him. Anoraa's shoulder popped and cracked as the joint shook loose. The sorcerer screamed.

Isi's hand found his savik. The blade seemed so small against such a creature, and his harpoon was on the remains of his sledge. He hesitated for an eyeblink.

The Tornit drew back its left hand to strike Anoraa, and the motion seemed to draw Isi toward it. The amulet in one hand and his savik in the other, he stepped in on its right side and struck the horrible beast in the chest, under the arm that held Anoraa high.

Anoraa fell from its grasp. His hand grabbed Isi's shoulder as if to hold himself up, but Isi felt himself pulled backward. His savik pulled free, and dark red blood spouted from the Tornit's side.

The Tornit's right hand, unburdened of the sorcerer, came down. Its claws ripped through Isi's hood and tore chunks of skin and ear away from his head.

Isi fell, gasping from pain and fatigue and the stink of the thing.

The Tornit spun, and its left hand came a hand's breadth away from destroying Isi's chest.

Isi landed on top of Anoraa. He rolled to his left—the cold snow stung but had no time to numb his mangled face—and came up in a crouch. The Tornit held its side and stepped, snarling, toward the sorcerer.

The first harpoon hit the creature in the leg. The Tornit turned toward the approaching hunters, and the second harpoon passed between it and Isi. The third harpoon hit it in the gut, and it howled in rage.

Wind off the ice cap rose to match the pitch and fury of the Tornit's scream, driving ice crystals that obscured all vision. Isi struggled forward, left hand holding the amulet in front of him. It glowed fiercely now, its light reflected on all sides by the blowing ice until Isi ran into the towering mass of the Tornit. The creature howled in new agony as Isi touched it.

Isi thrust his savik forward, unsure even what part of the creature he was trying to strike.

The blade moved through hair and hide and meat. Isi's hand followed it in, pushing it deeper until the Tornit spun, pulled free, and backhanded Isi into the snow.

The wind shifted and whirled so violently it lifted Isi, tumbled him to the side, and piled a drift behind his back. Then it dissipated, and its fury melted away into the daylight.

The Tornit had disappeared.

Isi's savik was gone. His arm was soaked with gore up to the elbow, as if he had been butchering a walrus and giving the hunters their shares. He still held the iron amulet in his left hand, its power and light fading again.

He pulled himself free of the drifted snow and crawled to Anoraa.

The old sorcerer was half-buried in snow. Isi scooped the snow away, staining it red and scattering sparkling bits across the frozen, blood-soaked ground. Anoraa winced when Isi touched him; he held his left arm tight against his chest.

Isi called to the Etah hunters for help. They stood in a row between him and the village, silent, but did not venture closer.

"Hold this," Isi said, and put the amulet in the sorcerer's hand. He stumbled to his small sledge and stopped to catch his breath. Drops of blood fell from his face onto the piled-up skins.

Isi pulled the sledge to Anoraa's side. The angakkoq groaned as Isi maneuvered him onto the sledge, but he did not cry out.

Anoraa held up the amulet in its woven net. It looked inert, a smooth and shapely lump of iron, but as Isi watched a tiny ripple of light moved across its face. The sorcerer pressed the amulet against his wounded shoulder and covered it there with his palm.

"They will come again, Isi," he said. "We must warn the people. And we must prepare." His eyes closed and he looked as if he would faint. Isi gently propped the old man up so he would not tumble off the sledge. He thought of his mother, and guilt crept over him; he feared her memory would haunt him now, that on long moonless nights every icy breeze would call to him in her voice to turn the sledge around, to come back, come back.

Anoraa opened his eyes and looked straight into Isi's.

"Look forward, Isigaa, not back. See things as they are, not as they appear."

Isi looked back toward the ice cap, but nothing natural or unnatural moved on the white expanse. The wind blew against his face; it stung his wounds, but it was clear and fresh. He wondered how long it would be until the foul wind blew again.

"Take me home, Isi, and share my kiviaq," Anoraa said, and Isi's mouth watered. He turned away from the ice cap.

The angakkoq held out the amulet, which swung on its tether and flickered with light. "And keep this safe for me," he said, "until we need it again."

Isi brought the sorcerer into Etah. The amulet felt warm in his hand.

# THE PRIME IMPORTANCE
# OF A HAPPY NUMBER

## *Sam Fleming*

The world learned a new player had arrived with the Vanishing of Swindon's infamous Magic Roundabout one sunny August Saturday. The Wiltshire and Berkshire Canal, upon which the roundabout had been built, reinstated itself over the course of seventy-nine seconds, replacing England's most ridiculed junction with a seven-metre-wide stretch of churning, foetid, muddy, oily water containing twenty-three surprised frogs and one shocked heron. There were seven fatalities, thirteen seriously injured, and nineteen walking wounded.

It had been months since any decent villainous activity, years since a début. It was trending within the hour: **#goodtrick** and **#uphissleeve**.

The Internet, everyone agreed, could be a cruel place.

Criminal Intelligence relayed a request to Wiltshire Police in a somewhat awkward telephone call, asking them to scan camera footage looking for anyone making "abnormal physical contact with the pavement." Unfortunately, Swindon Town Football Club had been playing Bristol City at home. The pitch was a skimmed stone away from the roundabout. It was impossible to tell if anyone was fondling tarmac in a suspicious manner or merely one of the casualties of too much celebration spilling from the nearby pubs.

Someone leaked the e-mail with predictable results, although even Criminal Intelligence had to admit it was funny.

In a small office in the corner of a building in Edinburgh's Canongate, at the very moment the first frog blinked in amphibian bewilderment, a woman shuddered under the cold, hard, shivering-slick weight of fulfilled prophecy, and bent to her stack of origami paper with renewed focus.

Her name was Audrey.

The following week came the Miniaturisation of the Eiffel Tower for twenty-three hours, twenty-three minutes, and twenty-three seconds. News outlets fed greedily on the bait-ball that was 383 tourists trapped inside an edifice shrunk by a factor of 103 in less time than it had taken the frog to blink. The pictures showed suspicious dark stains glistening under the feet of the structure and seeping into jagged cracks where the ground had given way.

Just as the pundits had worked themselves up into full, frothing moral outrage and were using it as a mêlée weapon, and the French President was preparing his speech, the tourists reappeared at the Louvre, huddled together like a gaggle of geese, unharmed but subdued and suffering from shock. The dark stains had been no more than water from a sudden rainstorm that morning.

They popped back into existence outside the glass pyramid, which sent the conspiracy theorists into a frenzy. The rest of the Internet was content with #happyprime, #pi22decimals, and #definitelyuphissleeve.

Interpol relayed a query to the Direction Centrale de la Police Judiciaire at 11, Rue des Saussaies, Paris; unfortunately, CCTV failed to record anyone massaging the metalwork. Various anti-terrorist networks erupted in a flurry of desperate questions and data analysis, but the only thing they could agree on was that this could not be religious extremism. Magic was involved. Powerful magic. That went hand in hand with megalomania, not ideological fanaticism.

If only they knew.

Audrey looked up when Athelstan brought her a new box of paper and a mug of coffee. She stared right past him, but he was used to that. She did it to everyone.

"Is there anything I can do?" he asked.

"It's starting," she said. "Kenneth said it would. I can't let it play out like last time. I can't."

She slid the box across her desk and split the seal with her thumbnail.

"You'll be all right," Athelstan said, seeing the tremor. "You're ready."

But Audrey had already sunk back down into the dark depths of her focus from where she would not or could not respond.

The mainstream media began making comparisons with the major villains of the last four decades, but only the male ones. Faced with ridicule, commentators observed that all previous supervillains making a spectacular appearance had been men; women tended towards Machiavellian manipulation and subverting traditional male roles in organised crime. This generated yet more arguments, a rash of doxing, and seventeen Kickstarters from both women and men wanting to prove that, with the right training, they could be major supervillains or beat the Mafia Witches at their own game.

#notallwizards happened.

Everyone agreed, should this supervillain turn out to be a woman, then of course she would be treated exactly the same way as all the male supervillains had been.

No one could specify what this was. No one actually knew what had happened to *any* of the supervillains. Apart from the Magpie. Everyone knew what had happened to him. It had been all over the newspapers, because he'd been all over the street.

Certain offices that did not exist sent messages to other offices that did not exist, using couriers who did not exist. Meetings did not take place and were not minuted. While this wasn't happening, the villain—now referred to simply as "the Prime"—Transformed St Peter's Basilica into an aquarium, complete with resident sharks. Nineteen of them, naturally.

Twitter said #jaws and #watnolasers #pewpewpew. The Pope asked the Internet for help in finding the 2,039 lost souls, while marine specialists and UNESCO archaeologists tried to work out how to remove the water and the sharks without damaging anything.

The Corpo della Gendarmeria dello Stato della Città del Vaticano received no request for information. How would they distinguish someone making the necessary contact for magical transformation from the merely devout?

Thus far there had been none of the usual demands: money, land, a private moon base, a place for a secret experiment on the next Mars mission. Talking heads asked the question, "What could someone with that kind of power actually want?" Pop psychologists suggested acceptance, respect, some kind of revenge for having his inner nerd rejected by his mother. The Internet consensus was #becausehecan.

An office marked as a broom cupboard on the third floor of an unremarkable building in London's Docklands dispatched a handwritten note, affixed with a second-class stamp under which were inscribed certain runes, the Royal Mail having proved more reliable than pigeons. It landed, three hours later, on the doormat of a partially reconstructed castle in the wilds of western Sutherland, where a Jack Russell called Spare, in defiance of its magical protection, attacked it.

Spare's owner, Kenneth Mackenzie, was much older than the spry seventy he looked. He retrieved the missive, now damp and smelling of Pedigree

Chum, and took it to his study, where he finished Spare's attempt to open the envelope.

The note was brief and to the point. He spent a few moments staring at his tall, wispy-haired reflection in the window and the unsettled waters of Loch Assynt beyond, aware of the concrete weight settling around his heart.

Kenneth, also known as the Brahan Seer, or Scotland's Nostradamus—although no one had called him that in years, at least not to his face—poured himself a large Talisker. Audrey, her brother, and her parents spiralled around his Sight as they had done for the best part of two hundred years, only now it was guilt and regret that brought them, not prophecy. He'd been too old for the front line when somebody young and fresh would be there anyway.

The Sight hadn't told him how young. How fresh.

How desperately close she would come to utter disaster.

He'd promised himself then he would not put her through another major début alone, but his Sight hadn't told him how old and tired he would feel when it happened.

He picked up the phone and dialled a number from memory. Four hundred years really was too old. "Tell Audrey I'll be in this afternoon," he said to Athelstan.

He sipped the Scotch while he composed a reply to the Secret Service, detailing instructions in the neat roundhand he had learned as a boy. He sealed this inside a plain brown envelope, put runes where the stamp would go using a single hair from a weasel's tail and ink made from iron gall, and dropped it off in Lochinver post office on his way.

Mairi, the postmaster, gave him a sympathetic smile. "Have they called you in, then? We were wondering if they might."

"Och, I'm retired," he said. "Have been for years."

The land up there grows canny folk. She wasn't fooled. "You said that last time. Drive safely, a Coinnich."

Speeding up the journey of a man is harder than that of a letter, and there were some aspects of living in the future for which Kenneth lacked all want. Flying was but one of them. It was a good three hours before he reached the office, even taking liberties with physics, the law, and the theoretical top speed of his Austin Healey Frog-Eyed Sprite.

Within two minutes of arrival, he was behind his desk with a pot of tea, a plate of custard creams, and Spare not quite Banished to his basket in the corner.

"Audrey," he said to Athelstan, his secretary. "How is she?" He was almost afraid of asking.

"Origami," said Athelstan. "Seven months now, nonstop. I've never seen anyone develop focus as precise as hers. As long as she has a supply of paper, she's golden. We tried taking it away from her to give her a break, but gave it back when she blew up the coffee machine."

"What did you do about that?"

"What do you think? This place runs on caffeine. We bought a new one. It's much better than the old one. Audrey signed for it."

"Good. Are she and Fiona getting on?"

"Getting there. We're providing counselling. Fiona knows Audrey protected her from much worse. It was just hard for her, coming to terms with the fact her wife is—"

"A counter-villain Thaumaturge."

"It's a bit different from Health and Safety manager, and there's that whole thing of Audrey being Audrey when she's tapping her talent. She'd done a good job of hiding it until the Magpie got too lazy to avoid collateral damage. If he hadn't taken her by surprise, Fiona would still be none the wiser, but you don't really expect to see number three on the supervillain most-wanted list absconding from Jenners with three hostages and a backpack full of diamonds while you're doing your Christmas shopping, do you?"

"Fiona was damn lucky Audrey was there!" Kenneth exclaimed. "As was everyone else, apart from the Magpie and the street cleaners. Would she be happier if Audrey were running the Mafia? Maybe it's time we explained to Fiona what really happened to her wife's family." He scowled for a moment. "Anyway, I'm only here as a distraction."

"Hagakure's Inverse Importance Gambit?"

"Aye. We'll need Matthew and Laura. Neither of them is after, you know . . ."

"Doing an Audrey? No. At this point, I think we can safely say they have neither the talent nor the ambition."

"That's a blessed relief."

A young woman Kenneth vaguely recognised, her smartly tailored tweed suit and rock-hard bun marking her as one of the formidable admin team, entered and flicked on the flatscreen television on the wall with a disapproving expression. She left before Kenneth could say *thank you*.

The screen showed the latest trends, one of which was **#pipipipigeons**. Athelstan watched several of the linked videos, all of which were varyingly short films of various pigeon flocks, mouth moving as if he had something stuck between his front teeth.

"They've used the right ones. The numbers are good," Athelstan said. He would know. He was as talented with numbers as Audrey was with the other.

"Then he should be here soon, unless he's potent enough to fill cathedrals with fish, but his numbers come from Wikipedia."

"If he turns up today, we may have a problem."

"Let's hope he doesn't. Gather the troops."

The Prime arrived the following day. Athelstan fetched him from reception. Kenneth took his place in the conference room, feeling more ancient than ever. The years sat in his bones as if they were petrified wood, and stretched away around him like an endless city inhabited by ghosts and flickering memories. He could think of a thousand things he would rather be doing at that very moment. A thousand thousand.

But some things he couldn't refuse, no matter how old he felt. At least, not more than once, not if he valued sleeping at night. Audrey needed him for the talking, for the distraction. It wasn't a big ask, considering.

Not that she had.

She sat beside him, busy folding paper aeroplanes from a stack of paper taller than her coffee mug. She was thinner than she had been when Kenneth last saw her, pinch-faced and pale, hazel eyes bright with restless exhaustion. She'd hacked at her grey-sprinkled ash-brown hair with a straight razor; it stood up in ragged tufts. Kenneth could see her talent seethe and bubble, barely controlled, held in check by the act of turning paper into darts. It reminded him of the Corryvreckan tidal race, fizzing and churning with the power of a remorseless ocean facing down an uncaring gale at spring tide. Her fingers worked incessantly, quick and nimble, folding each sheet precisely before dropping it on the floor and taking another. She was already ankle deep.

When he touched her arm, she could give him no more than a brief smile before returning her focus to her planes. He could only hope this was a good sign.

Ambrosius Wilt, as he introduced himself over a perfunctory handshake, was tall and gangly, with an unruly crop of ginger hair, freckles, and hands that were far too large. When he sat down after examining the chair for booby traps, the furniture seemed too small for him.

Matt and Laura appeared shortly after, bringing cups and tea and coffee and biscuits before sitting on the side of the table nearest the refreshments.

"This is Audrey," Kenneth said. "She runs things when I'm not around."

Ambrosius made no attempt at hiding his doubt, not even for politeness.

"This is Matt and Laura. They do bits and bobs and such."

Ambrosius nodded, uninterested.

"I'm—"

"I know who you are," Ambrosius said. "You're Kenneth Mackenzie, the Merlin of the North. I've wanted to speak with you for years."

"Does anyone know how to make that paper aeroplane that's made of two hoops joined together?" Audrey asked. There was a moment of silence, then Laura and Matt began chatting about something they'd seen on television.

"I'm flattered, I'm sure," Kenneth said. Audrey dropped her latest paper dart and took another sheet from the pile. "What cause is at you for speaking with me?"

"Everything! How ugly and banal and *stupid* the world has become! How blind its people are. Look at us! We're men of means, you and I. We can do things most people lack the imagination even to contemplate, and what do we do with it?"

"In your case," Kenneth said, "turn cathedrals into shark tanks."

"That was just to get your attention." Ambrosius gave a dismissive wave. "I'd already tried less interesting demonstrations. Everyone thought I was aiming to be the next big thing in street illusion. I was compared to Derren Brown. I was compared"—he leaned forwards, complexion reddening with fury—"to *David Blaine*. I've had an invitation to join the Magic Circle, would you believe?"

Kenneth gestured to Matthew, who poured him a cup of tea. "Did you accept?"

"What? No! Why would I? I don't want to waste my time with pointless tricks and chicanery."

"I see." Kenneth sipped his tea. Matthew and Laura were still quietly discussing the previous night's episode of some Scandinavian crime drama. He gave no impression of minding. "Are you any good at matrix algebra?"

He took a sugar cube from the bowl and tossed it at Ambrosius, who caught and examined it as if it might bite.

"I can manage. I derived your address from the pigeons, didn't I?" Ambrosius pointedly dropped the sugar cube into his coffee.

Laura broke from her conversation and wrote this down.

"What about the chemical formula for hydrocarbon combustion?" Kenneth threw another sugar cube. Ambrosius set it alight, making it explode in a puff of dull orange-black, acrid burnt-caramel smoke.

"Really, though," Audrey said. "Does anyone know how to do that paper plane that's made of hoops?"

Kenneth and his staff ignored her. Despite the intensity in her eyes, Ambrosius took his cue from them. "I don't, no," he said. "Things burn just fine nevertheless."

Laura noted this, too. Kenneth pondered for a few moments. "How do you feel about custard creams?" he asked.

The others fell silent. Even Audrey stopped her incessant origami and listened, as if there were no more important question in the world.

Ambrosius broke the stillness with a single word. "What?"

"For or against?"

"I can't say I've ever thought about it. Against?"

There was a murmur of disappointment. Laura made more notes. Audrey's fist clenched tight around the half-finished dart, crumpling it into a ball. She started a new one.

Kenneth heaved a sigh. "Fetch some more tea, would you, Matthew, please?" he asked. Matthew nodded and left. "Then I'm left with asking you what you want, as if it makes any difference."

Ambrosius rolled his eyes. "At last! I want to prove to you I have what it takes to work for you. Work *with* you. You've seen what I can do. I have the talent and skill, I'm self-motivated and ambitious. With your help, there's no limit to what I could achieve. Global warming? I could fix it. World peace? A bit more training, and there will be no war anywhere ever again."

"All very laudable, I'm sure." Kenneth finished his tea, taking his time, deconstructing a custard cream into two halves and licking the filling away before nibbling on the biscuits with exaggerated enjoyment. Laura drew an exceptional likeness of Spare.

Matthew returned, new cups and a fresh pot on a silver tray. He had almost put it down when Kenneth asked if he'd remembered the biscuits. As he turned, the tray followed a trajectory that should have seen it smack forcefully into Ambrosius's head; instead, it slid off, cups barely rattling.

Ambrosius relaxed, reassured his magical defences operated within what he assumed was Kenneth's domain. He smiled, picked up one of the custard creams, and rubbed it between the fingers and thumb of one hand, as if he were a spoon bender with a piece of cutlery. It Transformed into a chocolate Bourbon.

Audrey lost it. She threw the contents of the sugar bowl at him, one cube at a time, then the bowl, her mug, teaspoon, a cup and saucer. She threw the biscuits, one after the other. No one tried to stop her. She Apported an antique silver pepper pot from who knew where and hurled it at his head.

Ambrosius caught or blocked them, and, making a show of power, Doubled himself. Audrey materialised more objects to throw, faster and faster, eyes flashing like thunderclouds. A potato, a can opener, a wooden spoon, a sealed deck of cards, a bar of soap, a plush penguin, a small statue of an elephant, a milk pan, a stick of butter, the contents of a box of paper clips, a bicycle bell, a small pot of petroleum jelly, a stick of celery, a fish head, a roll of sticky tape, three live mice, and a surprised frog. A cut-glass fruit bowl containing thirteen grapes, three strawberries, and a lemon.

Two sets of hands could catch more, but were much harder to control. As the fruit escaped from the bowl, forming a cascade of berries and citrus, the doppelgänger faltered. The bowl bounced from its fingers, landing a glancing blow on Ambrosius's brow on its way to the floor.

Audrey chucked a desultory ball of crumpled plane, then returned to folding, muttering angrily to herself. Ambrosius, livid, jerked to his feet, preparing to retaliate, but Kenneth held up one hand, indicating he should wait.

"Really," Audrey said. "Does anyone know how to do the plane with the hoops? It's by far the best design. Someone has to know how to do it."

"She's damaged." Kenneth pointed to his own head, painting his face mournful. "There was an incident. Do you remember the Salamander? She took him on all by herself. I should have been there, and I wasn't."

"The Salamander?" Ambrosius eyed Audrey with the kind of expression one might find on a wildlife presenter who has just been told the harmless ground snake he was poking is really a coral snake. "The Thaumaturge who ended him turned a Birmingham multistorey car park into a volcano."

"She's had treatment," Kenneth said. "She was doing her best in a difficult situation. I'm very fond of her and feel somewhat responsible, but she can be a handful on her bad days. I'm sure you understand. If we could show her the making of this paper plane, perhaps she would settle down."

Ambrosius sat, rubbing the bruise on his head, lips pressed together in a thin, tight smile. "Of course." Three sheets of paper slid across the table. The roll of sticky tape levitated from the floor and settled beside them. He began folding. "It is sad when someone without the necessary mental acuity explores the further limits of her—or his—talent and ends up hurt." The 'or his' was added as an afterthought, as if it were implausible. "People need to learn to identify their own limitations. If her brain doesn't work the right way for complex layers of focus and intent, or her psychology isn't suited to large-scale workings, she should have stuck to table magic and tarot cards. Yet this sort of thing happens all too often. While I'm not at all sexist, I have to say, I mostly see it in women. It's the magical equivalent of reverse parking."

Kenneth nodded, hoping Ambrosius hadn't spotted the expression of disbelief on Laura's face. "A terrible tragedy. I suppose a dose of reality is the hardest for swallowing."

"The things that are good for one often taste bad," Ambrosius said. "Here. For you."

He slid the paper plane over to Audrey. It was made of a piece of paper rolled tightly into a tube, joining two other sheets of paper folded into strips and rolled into hoops, one bigger than the other.

"What do you say?" Kenneth asked.

"Thank you," she said meekly, fingertips tracing the folds.

"So," Kenneth said. He put his hands on the table, palms up, arthritic joints curling his fingers toward the ceiling.

Ambrosius did likewise, albeit with straight fingers. "So."

"What did you foresee happening next?"

"I'm not sure what you mean."

"Well, we've established your control over stuff and whatnot—"

"The Warp and the Weft." Ambrosius nodded.

"If you like. We're a bit less formal. We know you don't like custard creams—not quite an unforgivable sin—and can manage a bit of maths, but chemistry isn't your thing."

"I can access the answer to anything, including how to build paper planes and decode ridiculous videos of pigeons, by consulting the Akashic Record."

Laura made a note. It read, *Wikipedia*.

Ambrosius very nearly curled his hands into fists. "I'm not sure how you managed to keep me from finding your location sooner—presumably the same way I prevented you finding me—but I have no need of factual trivia."

"Mmm." Kenneth pursed his lips. "As you say. Now you've demonstrated all of that, what were you for happening next?"

"I thought it would be obvious to a man of your talent."

"Humour me."

"I want to become part of the Great Work and join the Ruling Elite in Manifesting Destiny." Ambrosius was perfectly serious.

Audrey's fingers didn't quite stumble, and no one kicked anyone else under the table.

"Had you considered entering politics?" Kenneth asked, in a tone one might use for suggesting a bathroom colour scheme to an acquaintance obsessed with interior design.

"Politicians are silly little men with no real power, tiny ambition, and no grasp of the whole picture." Ambrosius was working hard to keep his hands still.

"I can't argue with that," Kenneth said.

"I want to be where the real power is. I want you to introduce me to the Great Circle and welcome me with your blessing. I have given ample demonstration of my ability to change the petty, insignificant lives of mortals."

"Aye," Kenneth agreed. He took a breath, lifted his hands from the table, and put them in his lap. "You have."

Audrey flicked the paper plane, eyelids drifting closed. Her shoulders slumped, tension surging from her in a wave that carried the dart, straight and true, aimed right between Ambrosius's eyes. Irritably, he snatched it from the air.

A crackling hiss filled the room with static. Bewildered shock turned his mouth into an O. He blinked like a toad. The others watched in quiet fascination as his skin charred and crisped to black where it touched the plane. He tried to drop it, and his fingers crumbled to fragments and dust, as if they were burnt wood hit with a hammer. The char spread, smog grey and singed barbecue under a coating of orange fading to silver. His jaw worked, trying to speak.

Once it hit his chest, the char accelerated, rippling, audibly fizzing. Within a few moments, his head was no more than ash held together by memory.

Laura threw one of Audrey's paper darts at the remains. The top half crumbled into a drift of powder. His lower legs, untouched, remained upright in front of his chair. Steam drifted from the stumps, carrying the unmistakable smell of roast pork.

"Thank you," Kenneth said.

"Don't mention it." Audrey shrugged. "You called it seven months ago. I do listen, you know."

"And don't take a risk like that again," he continued, stern as a disapproving grandfather. "When that bowl hit him, the last person to touch it was his own double. His defences didn't work because he hit himself. He made the plane for you, but you could have contaminated it when you took it back to charge it."

"I didn't touch the plane," Audrey said, fatigue and indignation giving her voice the texture of crumpled cellophane. "And I spent last night embedding Cremate in every one of those sheets of paper."

Laura hurriedly dropped the piece she'd been folding into a water bomb, as if it might actually explode. "It's all right," Audrey said. "It needs three sheets."

She turned back to Kenneth. "Do you have any idea how long it takes to learn how to manipulate paper mentally while making it *look* like you're holding it with your fingers?" She clenched her fists and glared at him. "Well, do you?"

Kenneth gave her a tight hug. "Seven months," he said. "Nonstop."

"Seven *years*," she corrected him, sniffing. "If you're going to learn restraint, you're best doing it properly."

Spare nosed open the door, tail wagging, and ran under the table. They all watched what was left of Ambrosius's right leg disappear out of the room to the sound of contented growling.

"You don't have to be neuroatypical to work here," Audrey said after a few moments. "But it helps."

---

**Magical Origami @PaperCraneStyle**
MT **@huntingnumbers**: New prime found! bit.ly/1e5WB6L
#newprime #sadnumber

# SOCIAL VISITING

## *Sunil Patel*

The Seven Trials of Shaila Patel—as Shaila dubbed the most epic social visiting excursion she'd ever been on—began when her mom threw open her bedroom door and told her to get ready. "No warning, no explanation!" Shaila texted her friends as she canceled their Sunday plans.

When her mom told her they were visiting seven motels, Shaila grimaced. "Do I have to?"

"Yes, Shaila," her mom said. "Today is special."

But it wasn't. The day played out the same way it had for as long as she could remember. Whether it happened in her own town or when they were in another state, social visiting was the bane of Shaila's existence. They always seemed to do it on the hottest days, too, and it was hotter inside the motels than out. Plus ever since she'd gotten her learner's permit, they forced *her* to drive. Normally she would be excited for the opportunity, but it felt like added punishment to be an agent of her own boredom.

Her parents had a schedule. Flora Motel, Ray Motel, Ranch Motel, Sunrise Motel, Sunset Motel—she could never remember all the names, let alone the names of the people they were visiting, or how they were related to her. Mom's brother's cousin's wife. Mom's mom's sister's husband's sister's son. Dad's college roommate's best friend's wife's brother. These were the tenuous connections that brought her to each Patel-owned motel. One of the places would serve lunch, she hoped. If she was lucky, it would be pizza. Otherwise, vegetables stir-fried and drenched in oil, the Gujarati way.

At each motel, they walked up to the front desk and were let in to the residential area. The masa and/or masi greeted them, and Shaila offered them the obligatory namaste. She took a seat on the couch in the living room. Her parents usually claimed the swing—there was always a swing. Once they were seated, she remained quiet while her parents conversed with the other adults. Often they talked about her, describing her recent accomplishments. Shaila felt like a houseplant they were showing off. A pretty plant, according to many of the aunties. Her dad said she was pretty under the pimples. Her mom said she was pretty *despite* the pimples.

Ranitamasi never mentioned her pimples at all. Shaila found it a small comfort that they visited her first.

"You won a lot of trophies, huh, Shaila?" said Ranitamasi.

"Yeah. First place in science, second place in math." She had been so close at the last competition. Her small comfort faded at the memory.

"You're a very smart girl. Going to be a doctor?" All the aunties and uncles wanted her to be a doctor (or marry a doctor), but she wasn't interested in medicine.

"I don't know," said Shaila, not wanting to have this conversation so soon after her meeting with her guidance counselor, who provided no guidance or counsel when he admitted that although she was a "bright young girl," he didn't know where to apply her "obvious talents." Shaila knew about her obvious talents; it was the not-so-obvious ones she wanted to discover.

"That's okay, child," said Ranitamasi. "It's far too early to choose." She sighed and lowered her voice. "Though not to be chosen."

"Chosen for what?" asked Shaila.

"Chosen for chevdo!" said Ranitamasi as she dashed into the kitchen.

After leaving Ranitamasi's, Shaila knew to expect the same for the rest of the day. The greetings, the awkward conversation, the refreshments. An endless supply of snacks and drinks, from chevdo to falooda. All of this was familiar to her.

That changed at their third stop. As usual, the auntie—whose name Shaila could never remember—brought out chaa. Shaila preferred coffee, which she'd started drinking to feel like a grown-up, but she couldn't deny that chaa smelled wonderful. Her dad had let her try some of his when she was a kid, but the taste hadn't matched the smell. She was never offered any on these trips, however, until now. She stared at the cup.

"Drink your chaa, Shaila," said her mom. She raised her eyebrow slightly in the direction of the auntie.

"That's okay," Shaila said. Though she hadn't chosen a career, she had chosen a caffeinated beverage.

The auntie glanced at her mom. "Manju said . . ."

"I know," said her mom. Her voice became more pleading. "Shaila, it's good, see?" She took a sip of her own chaa, and Shaila felt like a two-year-old even though she was turning sixteen next week.

She hesitated. The auntie said, "Let me bring out the par vadi biscuits! They taste very good with chaa." She exited to the kitchen.

"Shailaja," her mom said, "please drink just a little bit. It's rude not to."

"What's the big deal?"

Her dad responded, "It's no big deal. Think of it as an experiment."

He had a point. It had been years since she'd had any, and her tastes had changed, recalibrated. She ought to try it in the name of science, if only to compare it with coffee.

The auntie returned with a plate full of par vadi biscuits. Shaila did love par vadi biscuits, with their crunchy exterior and chewy center. A few years ago, she'd discovered they were nothing more than Pepperidge Farm puff pastries, stuck in an oven and baked on a cookie sheet. She'd thought they were an Indian delicacy, but they weren't. They sounded special, but they weren't.

The auntie was right, though: they did go well with chaa. She bit into one and took a sip. The bite at the back of her throat was surprisingly satisfying, an acidic kick without the syrupy sweetness of soda. The buttery dough of the biscuit cut the bitterness of the tea. A smile crept upon her face and she tried to hide it.

"See?" said her mom.

Shaila couldn't finish a whole cup of the stuff, though. Just a few courtesy sips, enough to accompany one biscuit. Or two.

Not drinking the whole cup proved to be a good move, as she drank chaa at three more motels. By the end of the day, she'd almost acquired a taste for it.

As the Seven Trials of Shaila Patel came to a close, the faint flavor of ginger lingered in her mouth.

Now here she was again a month later, part of the same routine, though this social visiting trip consisted of only one stop. After offering everyone water—which was offered no matter the temperature but was especially welcome on this hot day—Ranitamasi had taken Shaila's parents shopping for saris and left her alone. Mostly alone. The uncle was running the front desk. Pratik? Pradeep? Just "Uncle" would do. Although her parents had thought she wouldn't be interested in accompanying them, she thought it had to be more interesting than sitting on the swing in front of a soap opera on Zee TV. Ranitamasi had the best swing, ornately decorated with a depiction of a savage battle scene on the back, which was also more interesting than the soap.

Shaila pushed gently with her feet and listened to the swing creak back and forth. It was like a squeaky metronome. She measured time in creaks. One creak, two creak. Three creak, four freak. No, creak. She laughed and then felt self-conscious. Luckily, Uncle hadn't heard her because he was helping a guest. She continued to count the creaks, calmed by the regularity. It reminded her of the wave patterns her math teacher had talked about.

The swing could only entertain her for a few minutes, though. She should have brought her homework. She'd told her parents she had homework, but they'd insisted they wouldn't be long. The soap opera was in Hindi. Even subtitled, it held no interest for her. She didn't see a remote, and besides, these places only got the Indian channels. Shaila contemplated the emptiness and relative silence, the dialogue on TV occasionally punctuated by a bell as a guest came up. It was the same, she thought. Always the same.

She put her feet down and stopped the swing. It wasn't the same. She couldn't deny it any longer. Not after what Divya had said about Ranitamasi and weakening barriers. Shaila would investigate. Propose a hypothesis, collect some data, reach a conclusion. She hypothesized that Divya was telling the truth, even though it made no sense.

Now to look for anything . . . incriminating? She didn't want to snoop, but they *did* leave her all alone here. All alone except for Uncle, and he wasn't paying any attention.

It wasn't snooping if it was for science.

She went into Ranitamasi's bedroom, being careful not to alert Uncle. Ranitamasi had kept the room tidy for her expected guests. Nothing stood out as unusual at first glance, but Shaila doubted what she was looking for would be out in the open. She began with the nightstand and opened drawer after drawer, finding nothing but assorted bracelets on racks and a stash of Cadbury Flakes. She had no luck with the armoire either. If the answer lay in the motel, it wasn't in this room.

As quietly as she could, Shaila examined the other rooms in the residence. In one bedroom she came across the mandir, a miniature temple that housed pictures and figurines, and scanned it for any pictures of Ravana. She didn't think Ranitamasi worshipped the demon king, but she needed something, anything, to go on. She found nothing interesting in the bathroom, the living room, the kitchen.

By that time, Shaila wanted to eat something, but not the sort of thing she always ate on these trips. She spotted a box of Special K on top of the refrigerator and laughed. "Special K" had been Ranitamasi's nickname for Shaila's mom in college. Whether it was meant as a joke, Shaila didn't know, but she had found an appropriate snack.

She grabbed a bowl and spoon and took the box down from the fridge. The box was new; she hoped Ranitamasi wouldn't mind. Shaila opened the box and partially extracted the plastic bag. She seized either side and pulled hard, but it wouldn't give. *Finally*, something unusual, and it was keeping her from eating. Shaila clenched her teeth and pulled again, and the bag opened like a crack tearing the earth asunder.

Being as careful as she was when pouring liquids in the lab, she tilted the box above her bowl and gently tapped it to nudge the cereal out. And then— as had happened last week with that graduated cylinder—her arm jerked suddenly, and the entire contents of the box came pouring out, covering the table in flakes and crumbs.

And one white flower.

"What the hell?" said Shaila.

Despite having been packed in a box of cereal, the flower gleamed, vibrant and fresh. Not a single crumb clung to its pristine petals. She recognized it as a lotus. A lotus that had been inside a *sealed* cereal box. Unless cereal companies had changed their stance on what constituted a prize, she didn't think Kellogg's was responsible.

It was time to call Divya.

Divya's motel had been the fifth stop of the Seven Trials, and Manjumami had presented Shaila with yet another plate of snacks. She couldn't eat any more, but every auntie and uncle insisted on feeding her, even when she told them she was full. When Shaila tried to refuse, her mom gave her The Look and smiled. They could communicate wordlessly quite well after all these years, and Shaila liked to think she was in tune with her mother's thoughts. Like two nights ago, when they shared a look after her dad had gotten some kadhi in his mustache. Or the time Shaila brought home a paper with a big red A+ and knew from the way her mom's mouth curled upward ever so slightly that it was what she'd been waiting for, even though she had never said anything about the previous As. Here, again, Shaila would please her mother and take a few courtesy bites.

"How is school going?" asked Manjumami.

"It's good," said Shaila. "I'm taking chemistry this year, and I really like it."

"That's good," said Manjumami, who had probably never taken chemistry.

Shaila tried to think of something else to say. There was nothing. What could a houseplant add to the conversation?

She looked away from her and there against the wall was a girl who hadn't been there a minute ago.

"Oh, Divya has arrived!" said her dad. "Shaila, you remember Divya, from Columbus."

Columbus. Shaila didn't remember this girl at all. Columbus. Then it came back to her. Manjumami had made them sundaes.

"I was six," she told her dad, not meeting the girl's eyes. An easy feat, since the girl was doing the same, ducking her head so all Shaila could see was her wild, unkempt hair. Shaila let her gaze drop to the girl's body, which her mom would describe as fat—"Divya's gotten fat," she said on the way to the next motel—but Shaila thought was just a bit curvier than her own.

"You had so much fun then!" said her mom. "And now she lives here. Go play with Divya."

Play? Shaila was about to turn sixteen. Her mom hadn't gotten out of the habit of saying it, though. "Go play with So-and-So," she'd say at each visit, and the kid would take Shaila into his or her room and try to entertain her. Watch some cartoons, play a video game, stare at the wall. She liked staring at the wall with Guru. There was no pretending that either one of them wanted to be there. Well, he lived there, so he maybe he did, just not with her.

Divya looked up, expectant. She, too, had a duty to perform, a mother to please. Manjumami gestured toward the back. "Go show her your posters." Divya looked at her mother and shook her head. "Divya," her mother said. Shaila knew that tone of voice.

Divya led her to the bedroom in the back. The walls were covered in prints of skulls and murder scenes and horrors. Shaila recognized some artists' names, like Georgia O'Keeffe, but not others like Remedios Varo and Käthe Kollwitz. The images of death and madness were made even more disturbing by the contrast with the comforter's drab pattern of interlocking shapes.

"So," Shaila said.

Divya said nothing.

"You like art."

Divya said nothing.

"Do you draw?"

Divya said nothing.

"Do you want to just stare at the wall? I'm cool with that. We can just stare at the wall."

Divya said nothing, but a smile flickered, like a burnt-out streetlamp.

They sat on the bed and stared at the wall for several minutes. Shaila listened to the adults talking and laughing in the other room. Probably talking about them.

"I don't draw. My mom does, though." Shaila rummaged through her purse and pulled out a little comic book, handmade from wide-ruled notebook paper folded up and stapled. She showed Divya the cover, with the title *Shaila the Conqueror* in ballpoint pen. "In elementary school I ate lunch alone. Me and my sandwich and apple. It was kind of boring. But then my mom started sticking these in my lunch bag."

Shaila flipped through the pages to show Divya what was inside: stick figures. "She's a terrible artist. Even her stick figures are bad. But see here?" She pointed to a stick figure labeled SHAILA. "That one's me. I could tell because it says so, with an arrow and everything." Divya's smile flickered again, holding for longer this time.

On the last page, Stick Figure Shaila stood triumphant, sword raised high above her head as she looked down at the body of a fallen demon. "She had me fighting demons, I think. Some had a lot of heads, and sometimes she colored them with markers. It was basically the same story every day, but it gave me something to read at lunch."

Divya took the comic from her and thumbed through the pages, intently looking at the crude figures. "How did she know?" she said to herself.

"Know what?" asked Shaila, pleased at getting her to speak.

Divya handed back the comic. She went to the nightstand and opened a drawer, then pulled out a stack of papers. Her medium was ink, like Shaila's mother's, but the figures were far more than mere stick figures. "I drew these," she said as she offered them to Shaila.

Shaila didn't know what to make of them. A speared boar, blood running down its stomach, life fading from its eyes. A young woman dismembered, her limbs strewn around her body. A fearsome lion-headed beast crunching down on a snake. So gory, and so detailed, despite resembling half-formed visions out of a nightmare, barely remembered upon waking up. "These are really good," she said, knowing as much about art as Manjumami knew about chemistry.

She stopped at one drawing. A ten-headed demon, each head crowned, wielding dozens of swords in his many hands. "That's Ravana."

"I see him more than the others."

"You see Ravana?"

"In my dreams."

"All of this . . . you see it in your dreams? That's horrible."

"What's horrible is that it's real." Divya turned her eyes toward a charcoal Kollwitz print, a naked woman embraced by the specter of death. "I wonder if she saw that in a dream," she said softly.

A silence hung between them, finally broken by the sound of Shaila's dad laughing in the living room. Shaila cringed, wanting to console Divya. "They're only stories," she said. "And besides, even if the *Ramayana* really happened, Rama killed Ravana, so he can't be haunting you now."

"Ranitamasi says the barriers are becoming weak. That he's going to break through." Divya's voice quivered on the last two words.

"Divya, are you okay?" Shaila opened herself up to a hug.

But Divya ignored it. "I'm sorry," she said, composing herself. "I don't know if I'm supposed to talk about it with you yet. But your comic made me think of it."

"Did you say Ravana was going to break through? The actual Ravana?"

"I don't want to . . ." Divya pointed to *Shaila the Conqueror.* "Tell me about your comic. Tell me about the girl who defeats the demons."

"I call her 'Stick Figure Shaila,' you know? She's like a cool warrior version of me. I don't think my mom wanted me to go around waving a sword, but . . ." Shaila moved to face Divya. "I'm happy with who I am. I think she is too. But I can't help but think there's a potential me who is better. It's like . . . if you could be a mango lassi, would you?"

Divya blinked. "I don't want to be a drink."

"But if you *had* to be a drink?"

"Then yes."

"If you had the option, though, wouldn't you rather be a *ginger* mango lassi?"

Now Divya smiled. "The same, but better. You're looking for your ginger."

Shaila laughed. "I'm looking for my ginger."

This. This, right here, could be her ginger. A mysterious lotus flower in a cereal box? This was providence. She felt the thrill of discovery. Was this her Alexander Fleming moment, stumbling across the key to a new field? Maybe it was nothing more than a flower with absolutely no electrostatic forces to attract cereal crumbs, but even that was something. She'd never thought she would enjoy contradicting her textbooks so much. As she pulled out her phone to call Divya—her mom had put Divya's number into Shaila's phone in the hopes that they'd become best friends or something—she wondered if she was a different Alexander.

"Divya, come here, I want to see you," Shaila said when Divya answered.

"Hi," Divya said hesitantly. They hadn't spoken since their previous meeting, and she didn't catch Shaila's reference. Shaila decided Divya could be the Watson to her Bell anyway.

"I'm at Ranitamasi's. I was pouring out some cereal when a white lotus flower came out. And it's completely clean. Nothing will stick to it. Strange, right?"

"Hi, Shaila, it's nice to hear from you," said Divya, as if Shaila had greeted her properly.

Shaila took a deep breath. "Sorry. Hi. It's nice to hear from you too. I need your help. Do you know anything about a flower?" She held it in the palm of her hand. Before she could think about it too hard, she made a fist, crushing it. When she opened her hand, the flower unfolded into its original conformation, perfect once again. As she had suspected. It wouldn't have been able to fit in the cereal box otherwise.

"I don't remember any flower. Ranitamasi hasn't mentioned one."

Shaila had hoped Divya would have information for her, but she could still be a resource. "Could you come over? Maybe your mom could give you a ride."

A ride. Of course. Divya had been talking about Ravana and demons, but if they were real, then the gods and goddesses were real too. And they all had their own rides. Ganesha rode a mouse. Durga rode a tiger.

And Saraswati rode a white lotus.

"Eureka," Shaila said to herself.

"What?" asked Divya.

"This has to be related to Saraswati!" Shaila stood up and stuffed the flower in her pocket.

"That does make sense," said Divya.

Still clutching the phone, Shaila dashed over to the bedroom where the mandir was. Sitting on the second shelf was a picture of Saraswati atop a white lotus. Shaila took the flower out of her pocket and placed it front of the picture.

Nothing happened.

"I don't know what to do now," she said. "I put the lotus in front of her."

"Try asking her."

After placing the phone on the bed, Shaila closed her eyes, folded her hands, and bowed to the picture. "Saraswati, please tell me what to do. You're the goddess of wisdom and learning, so help me learn. What is this flower? How does it work?" She opened her eyes.

Nothing happened.

She picked up the phone. "Maybe I didn't pray hard enough."

"Maybe that's not how it works."

"Can you come over? Even if you don't know what it is, I'm all alone here except for Uncle, and it would be fun. Plus it's really hot. I'm alone and it's hot."

"I can be there in—" Divya stopped. Seconds passed. "I can be there in fifteen minutes."

"Great!" said Shaila. "See you then."

She took the flower back to the kitchen and began opening drawers, looking for matches. She needed to do some more experiments.

Fifteen minutes later, the doorbell rang. "I'll get it," Shaila called in Gujarati, not wanting Uncle to interfere. She opened the door and let Divya in. Unlike Shaila, who had been forced to wear "something nice"—a nondescript blouse, not her math/science team shirt covered in physics equations—Divya was dressed comfortably in jeans and a T-shirt with a painting Shaila didn't recognize.

"It's nice to see you again," said Divya.

"Good to see you too," Shaila replied.

"Show me the lotus," said Divya with startling authority.

Shaila led her to the kitchen, where the white lotus sat on the table. "I tried burning it and cutting it with a knife while I waited, but it didn't work."

"Why are you trying to destroy it?"

"I'm not *trying* to destroy it!" said Shaila. "But the fact that I *can't* is pretty weird, okay. And if it connects to what's going on, I want to know what I can."

Divya picked up the white lotus delicately and examined it. "It's beautiful," she whispered. "The curve of the petals, the smoothness . . . it's perfect." She set it back down. "But Ranitamasi never mentioned it to me. I don't know what it does."

"But *she* does. As soon as she gets back, I'm asking her."

Divya looked up. "Why wait?" She strode confidently to the other end of the kitchen. "I've never tried this, but I watched Ranitamasi do it once." Shaila heard her mutter something under her breath: "A day for trying new things, I guess."

"Tried what? Where are you going? Should I bring the lotus?"

"Leave it there," said Divya. Shaila followed her to the laundry room.

Stacks of washers and dryers lined the walls. Divya led her to a dryer in the corner. "This is the one. I saw her use it to talk to someone." She opened the dryer door. "Is there a washer that's done?"

Shaila opened up a washer that wasn't running. It was full of towels. She reached inside and grabbed one.

Divya took it from her and threw it into the dryer. "We should probably fill up the dryer to be safe." Together they filled the dryer with the other damp towels. "And don't forget the dryer sheet."

"Will it help with the magic phone?" asked Shaila.

Divya gave her a confused look. "No, it reduces static cling."

Shaila looked around but couldn't find any dryer sheets. She shrugged, and Divya shrugged back and closed the door. Through the glass all they could see was white fabric.

Divya waved her hand around the glass door in a clockwise direction three times. "I think it was three times," she said. She closed her eyes tightly and pressed the button. The dryer came on with a start, and the towels began tumbling clockwise. "Or maybe it was the other way around . . . ?"

For a few seconds, Shaila and Divya didn't speak, focusing on the mechanical sounds of laundry all around them. The repetitive rotation of the dryer reminded Shaila of the creaking swing, and she began keeping time with it as she stared into the window.

And then the monochrome white shifted into a blur of orange and purple and green. An image formed on the glass, and as it resolved, Shaila recognized rows and rows of saris. "Divya? Is that the sari store? Is the dryer showing us the sari store?"

"That must be where Ranitamasi is. I thought about her as hard as I could before turning it on."

The focus of the image moved downward as if it were a camera, and Shaila saw her mom and Ranitamasi evaluating selections at the counter while her dad looked at something on his phone. Probably checking the news. She knew her mom was picky about her saris, but when the right one struck her, the search was over. Her dad glanced up occasionally, clearly not wanting to become too engrossed in case that moment came.

"Kirti, how much longer?" he called, and Shaila jumped.

"Divya, *I can hear him!*"

Divya shushed her with a finger but looked at Shaila's dad, who didn't react. "Kavimama!" she called, waving. "Kavimama!" He still didn't react. She sighed. "I did it wrong. We can't talk to them."

"Maybe they'll talk about me," said Shaila. Under normal circumstances, she wouldn't approve of spying on her parents, but these were not normal circumstances. It was a *magic dryer.* The mystery of the lotus temporarily receded, replaced by these impossible images.

"Found it!" exclaimed Shaila's mom, holding up a bolt of rich purple and deep yellow fabric.

"Oh, yes, very lush," agreed Ranitamasi.

As her mom began haggling for a better deal, Ranitamasi walked over to her dad. "Any interesting news?"

"Gas prices are going up," he said.

"That's not news, nor interesting," she said with a smile.

Her dad swiped the screen and put the phone in his pocket. "So we're telling her today?"

Shaila clapped her hands together and mouthed, "See?" to Divya. Even though Divya said they couldn't hear her, she didn't want to take any chances.

Ranitamasi nodded. "She's sixteen. It's time."

Shaila had turned sixteen three weeks ago. They had waited long enough to break the news that *magic was real.*

"And you're sure she'll be safe?"

"Do you doubt the power of my chaa, Kavi?" Ranitamasi wiggled her fingers in front of his face, and tiny green sparks came out.

"Whoa," said Shaila, before covering her mouth with her hand. Then she realized what Ranitamasi had said. The chaa kept her safe?

Her dad frowned. "Don't do that in here."

"Do what?" said her mom, walking up with bag in hand. Ranitamasi wiggled her fingers in front of her face; this time the sparks were white and orange. Her mom pumped her fist in the air a couple times and hummed a tune Shaila recognized as her college fight song. Her mom hoped Shaila would have cause to hum it herself one day.

"Allow me my fun," said Ranitamasi. "Ravana will be here before we know it. He's waited for millennia, and we've seen the signs."

Shaila saw Divya tremble slightly at the mention of her drawings. Remembering them, she shuddered too.

Her dad shook his head. "I didn't think it would happen in my lifetime. Or Shaila's lifetime, goddammit."

"*Kavi,*" said her mom.

"Vishnu be damned if he allows Ravana to rise again," seethed her dad. Shaila had never heard him so angry, though he was keeping quiet to avoid disturbing the other customers. "He's not going to kidnap *my* daughter."

"We've made sure of that," said Ranitamasi. "How's Manju doing, by the way?"

Divya perked up at the mention of her mother.

"She's lovely," said Shaila's mom. "She makes the best idli, you know that?"

Ranitamasi smiled. "I know that. You know what's in it, don't you?"

Her mom stared back in shock. "No."

"I hope Shaila ate a lot of it too."

"It's her favorite!" said her dad. Shaila nodded enthusiastically to Divya.

"Good!" said Ranitamasi. "No way she's being kidnapped." Shaila's mom was still staring at her. "Don't worry, the enchantments will have no effect on you, bad or good. They're designed to work on children."

Shaila's dad looked at the floor. "I want her to grow up, Ranita. I want her to be—"

Suddenly the image went fuzzy and the sound became distorted. "What's going on?" demanded Shaila, banging on the metal doorframe to improve the reception.

"Maybe you do need the dryer sheet," said Divya.

Shaila groaned. "What were they talking about, with the chaa and the enchantments? Are they magic-drugging me?"

"It's to protect you," said Divya. "When he comes. You know he likes to kidnap girls."

Shaila remembered the story. Ravana had kidnapped Sita, Rama's wife, and Rama had slain him. Apparently not enough. "But Sita was much older than me."

"We know about her because of the *Ramayana*, but I think there were others. They don't all get stories." Shaila wondered whether she would get a story if Ravana took her.

"What was in the chaa?"

"He won't be able to touch you," promised Divya.

Shaila's voice rose, frantic. "But what if he sends someone else?"

"They're working on modifications to the spell." Divya remained calm, but Shaila sensed some uncertainty.

The window into the sari store returned with a slight buzz. Her parents and Ranitamasi were still talking.

"Different line, honey," said Ranitamasi.

"Yeah, my line's got this," her mom said, and held up her left hand to show off the sixth finger dangling from her thumb.

"It's not the most attractive appendage," noted Ranitamasi.

"Well, it attracted *him*," her mom said, shoving her sixth finger in her dad's direction.

"I was not attracted to your *finger*," said her dad. "Your *figure*, on the other hand . . ."

Shaila buried her face in her hands.

"Quit it, you two, or my fingers will be doing things you won't like." Ranitamasi shook a finger in their direction, but no sparks came out.

"My mother thought it was a sign when I was born."

"Of course she did. Anything abnormal is a sign. We know more about signs now, though, and that isn't one of them. What you've got is an appendix hanging from your thumb, basically useless. I'm surprised you didn't have it removed."

"I'm used to it. It makes me feel different. A bit special."

Shaila braced herself for another cheesy remark from her dad, but Ranitamasi cut him off. "You're special, K."

Her mom looked up with alarm. "You don't think she'll find the lotus, do you?"

Ranitamasi laughed. "Who would look in a cereal box?"

"I would!" Shaila declared with gusto. "Accidentally," she added.

Blue sparks shot out of Divya's fingers and dissipated before they hit the lotus. "Ranitamasi hasn't taught me how to change the color yet. I know they mean something different, but she wants me to 'reach for the colors inside me, for that is where the magic lies.'"

Shaila sat across from her at the kitchen table. She focused intently on the lotus between them and wiggled all her fingers at once. Nothing happened.

"You only use one hand," said Divya.

"I thought I would have twice the shot at success."

"It doesn't work like that."

"How *does* it work?"

Divya sighed. "I don't know."

"Then let me see you do it again." Divya repeated the gesture, and Shaila observed the motions of her fingers. They weren't as erratic as they seemed; it was as if she were playing an invisible piano. Her thumb hardly moved. Shaila asked her to do it one more time, noting which fingers moved when.

Shaila stretched her right hand out toward the lotus. Divya abruptly pushed her chair back and stood up. Shaila laughed. "I'm not going to blow you up or anything."

She wasn't even wearing safety goggles. She *hoped* she wasn't going to blow anything up.

Closing her eyes, she replayed the image of Divya's fingers and moved her fingers in the same way, up and down, up and down, humming the imaginary tune to herself. She expected to feel a surge of power, perhaps heat.

Nothing happened.

She kept her eyes closed for another minute, picturing Stick Figure Shaila and her stick figure sword. She added in sparkles around it because of course it was magic. Her mom would be so proud if she could do what Divya could. She'd be an A+ girl.

When she opened her eyes, Divya had sat back down. "It didn't happen for me at first," she said, not looking at Shaila. "Ranitamasi came and told me the whole story about Ravana and the demons, all sealed in another dimension. She said we were descended from disciples of Saraswati, blessed with special gifts. I didn't believe her, and then she turned my stuffed cow into a frog."

"Not a cow?"

Divya shrugged. "It's Ranitamasi. That's how she is." One year Ranitamasi had given Shaila $27 for her birthday. The other aunties gave her $25 or $51, traditional amounts, but Ranitamasi gave her $27.

"My mom has told me some funny stories from when they were in college. Nothing about turning anything into frogs, though."

"It didn't come easily for me. I had to practice. They said they were telling you today. When you start practicing, I can help you."

"And then we can fight Ravana together," added Shaila, hardly wanting to say the words out loud not only because of their absurdity but also because of their gravity. She hadn't been prepared to believe in demons, let alone fight them.

Shaila heard a car pull up outside. Divya heard it too. "Should we put the lotus back?"

"No," said Shaila. "It's a catalyst. I want to see their reaction."

The front door opened, and Shaila heard the adults enter, chatting about their recent purchases.

"Put the bags in the bedroom," said Ranitamasi. "I'll check on Shaila." Then she stepped into the kitchen. "Divya?" she said. "I didn't see—" Her confusion turned to understanding. She clicked her tongue. "I do see. We'll talk later."

Shaila had cleaned up the cereal, but the white lotus remained on the table. "Look what I found," she said.

Her parents walked in behind Ranitamasi. "Shaila!" said her mom.

Her dad started laughing. "We shouldn't have left her alone here. Divya's been talking, hasn't she?"

Divya crossed her arms, defiant. Shaila crossed her arms, disappointed. Some reaction that was.

Ranitamasi picked up the lotus. "Let's begin then, shall we? I assume Divya has told you all about—" She wiggled the fingers of her other hand in the air, letting out bright white sparks.

"I know Ravana is coming, and we have to fight him, and you've been poisoning my chaa—"

"If we were poisoning you, you'd be far too dead right now. Let's call it an elixir. And it's derived from this very flower. Here, smell it." Ranitamasi held it to Shaila's nose, and Shaila inhaled deeply. "What do you smell?"

It smelled like . . . a flower. She didn't know the right answer. "A flower."

"No questions about flowers to get your science trophy, then." Ranitamasi brought it to her own nose, closed her eyes, and breathed in. "It smells like history," she said. "This flower is thousands of years old."

Thousands of years old? Thousands? It looked like it was gathered this morning. "That's impossible," said Shaila.

"I told you she would say that," said her dad.

Her mom reached into her purse and handed him a five-dollar bill.

Shaila stared at her parents, aghast. "You bet on me?"

"It was his idea," said her mom.

"Ranitamasi," said Divya, getting up from the table, "what does it do?" Shaila got up and stood by her.

"Close your eyes," said Ranitamasi.

Divya closed her eyes. Shaila crossed her arms and took a step back. "Why? What are you going to do?"

"I told you she would do that," said her mom, and her dad handed the bill back.

Ranitamasi grinned. "I am going to show you something that will change how you perceive the world."

Shaila returned her grin. "Divya already did that by turning the dryer into a . . . scryer."

"You *were* watching us," said her mom as she handed the bill to Ranitamasi.

"Close your eyes," repeated Ranitamasi.

Shaila hesitated, afraid not of what would happen but of what she would find out. She hadn't been able to do what Divya could.

"Shaila, beta," her mom said. And that was all it took, that one term of endearment, and Shaila felt like a two-year-old, but she welcomed it. She felt calm, supported, safe.

Shaila closed her eyes.

She felt a light, soft touch on each eyelid.

"You can open your eyes now," said Ranitamasi, and Shaila opened her eyes and yelped.

Ranitamasi was glowing.

Not like a lightbulb. She had a faint yellow aura around her as she bent down to Divya, who glowed lavender, the color shimmering slightly. Shaila looked to her parents, who were not glowing. They had their eyes closed, and Ranitamasi touched their eyelids with the white lotus, then closed her own eyes and did the same.

"Well, now that we're all on the same page."

"Ranitamasi . . ."

"Oh, you think that's weird, look at the wall."

Shaila did.

There was a doorknob. Not a door, just a doorknob protruding from the wall. Shaila closed her eyes tightly and opened them again. It was still there.

"I'll let you do the honors." Ranitamasi extended her arm toward the wall. "Divya, I'm sorry for not bringing you earlier. But we can take care of some business while we're there."

Shaila cautiously approached the doorknob and slowly grasped it, ready to retract her hand if the knob burned or froze her, the two most likely ways a mysterious doorknob could hurt her. It did neither. Steeling herself, she turned the knob, and pushed.

She found herself outside in front of a forest, a dark forest with thick foliage from which no light could escape. She felt no wind; the air was cool on her skin, a welcome change from the oppressive heat of the motel. The grass beneath her bare feet tickled. The sky was a deep pink, with shades of purple in the clouds.

"Welcome to the Land of Eternal Sunset," said Ranitamasi, coming up behind her with her parents and Divya. When they had come through, Ranitamasi kicked the door closed without turning, and the door disappeared, doorknob and all. Shaila gasped. Ranitamasi sighed. "Ah, I've stranded us here forever, how careless of me." Shaila relaxed, her shoulders slumping. "Really, Shaila. Really."

"It's been so long since I've been here," said her mom, looking around with wonder. "Not since I was your age, Shaila." She held her dad's hand tightly.

Her dad simply smiled, looking more at peace than he ever had. "You never told me how beautiful it was, Kirti," he said.

Ranitamasi gazed upon them with amusement, then understanding. "It is a beautiful place. A terrible place, but beautiful."

"Where are we?" asked Shaila.

"The Land of Eternal Sunset," said Ranitamasi. "Weren't you paying attention? You're going to have to keep up; it only gets weirder from here."

"But where is this place? I opened a door in the wall." Today Shaila had spied on her parents with a dryer and discovered an invulnerable flower, but she still couldn't accept interdimensional travel. "You can't do that."

"Throw away your *can'ts* today, child. Today is about *can*." Ranitamasi closed her right hand into a fist, squeezed, and flung her fingers out in the direction of the forest. A rainbow of colors shot out like fireworks, bright against the dull twilight.

Divya whispered to Shaila, "She says things like that all the time." They shared a giggle.

Seconds later, a figure appeared from inside the forest. As it walked closer, Shaila recoiled in horror. The blue-skinned beast, clad in rags, had a mop of green hair that partially obscured its face, which was covered in scabs and boils. A large pink tongue hung out of its mouth, and Shaila could make out two rows of sharp teeth. It swayed back and forth as it walked, groaning with greater intensity each time it pulled itself back to the path.

It stopped in front of Ranitamasi and folded its hands, bowing its head. She did the same.

"Shaila and Divya, meet Bhagho."

"Kem cho," growled the beast in perfect Gujarati.

Divya gasped. "A rakshasa. I've drawn him." She hesitated to approach, simply returning its greeting. Shaila timidly raised a hand and waved.

"Shaila," said her mom. "What do you do?"

She had a suspicion that this demon was her elder. She walked up to it, folded her hands, and bowed. "Namaste." The beast ran its hands over her head in blessing, and she tried not to cringe as she felt its claws in her hair.

Ranitamasi gestured to Divya to move closer. "Don't worry, Bhagho won't hurt you. We're old friends." Divya bowed as well, and Bhagho blessed her.

Divya stepped back to stand by Shaila. "Should we be here, Ranitamasi? Isn't . . . isn't *he* here?"

"Ravana's around. But not close by. Right, Bhagho?" The demon nodded.

Shaila had to admit that Ranitamasi had been right. The way she perceived the world had gone out the window. How did this place exist? "Is this like another dimension?"

Ranitamasi tilted her head. "Kind of. I prefer the word 'realm.' This is where the stories come from. It's where the stories stay." Bhagho growled a word. "Yes," she added. "Trapped."

"But last month things changed." Seven motels in one day. Shaila's parents must have been terrified. They'd wanted to protect her.

"I was drawing him more than I ever had," said Divya. "Sometimes dead girls lay at his feet. Never the same arrangement. Faces up, hands clutching his legs . . . if they still had their . . ." She trailed off.

Ranitamasi nodded grimly. "Ravana has found a conduit, a way to breach the barriers we put up so many thousands of years ago. They're weakening."

"Will I . . . will I have to fight him?" Shaila looked at her mom, her hand clutching the idea of a sword.

"Bhagho, what's the verdict?"

Shaila understood now. That hadn't been a blessing. The creature had been testing them.

It raised one clawed hand and pointed to Divya.

"Good to have that confirmed." Ranitamasi glanced at Shaila, and the demon shook its head.

Shaila released her imaginary sword, letting her hand fall to her side. Like her mom, who wasn't glowing, she had failed the test. After all that had happened today, she had expected the natural conclusion. A not-so-obvious talent that would give her direction. Shaila Patel, teenage scientist/witch. She knew Divya was special. She'd hoped she was special too.

But she was a teenage scientist who knew a witch, and something fell into place. "Divya, your mom doesn't let you drive alone. How did you get here?"

Divya looked at Ranitamasi guiltily. Ranitamasi gave a light laugh. "She's a little too powerful for her own good."

Shaila held a hand in front of her face, turning it from side to side. "So I don't have any magic at all?"

"I didn't tell you this to make you feel bad," said Ranitamasi. "You're a part of this too. You all are. Divya won't be able to do this alone. I need you to be ready to step up."

"But what can I do?" Shaila wanted to replace herself with Stick Figure Shaila.

"You'll think of something," her mom said. "I know you will." She hugged Shaila tightly. "I believe in you," she whispered. And then Shaila understood what those comics had been about. Stick Figure Shaila wasn't the girl her mother wished Shaila was: it was the girl she saw.

She felt a hand on her shoulder. It was the first time Divya had touched her. "I need you to help me figure things out. Like you did with the lotus."

Shaila looked up at the otherworldly sky. How could she be disappointed standing in the realm where her childhood stories were true? She didn't need magic inside her when she'd found so much magic outside her. Ranitamasi had presented her with a whole new world to try to understand, and she would have a scientific objectivity Ranitamasi and Divya wouldn't. Shaila could address questions no one had tried to answer before because they'd never been asked. The promise of knowledge was dizzying.

For some reason, all she could think to say was, "Can we go home? I have a lot of homework to do."

Ranitamasi wouldn't let them leave without feeding them. The laws of hospitality still applied, even if the laws of physics didn't. Shaila accepted her chaa with no complaints and even breathed in the aroma appreciatively. She had never noticed that it smelled less bitter than coffee. Her loyalty was being tested. Despite the strong ginger that attacked the back of her throat, the tea was soothing. Was that the effect of the magic? She would have to compare with a normal cup of chaa as a control.

Later, she thought, glancing at Divya next to her. For now, she appreciated her magic tea.

"Can I have some par vadi biscuits?" she asked. Ranitamasi went to the kitchen and returned with a tray full of them. Shaila had expected her to snap her fingers and make the biscuits appear, but she didn't know how it all worked.

She dipped a biscuit into her chaa, holding it in long enough to soak in some flavor and pulling it out before it became a soggy mess floating in her cup. She took a bite, thinking of Oreos and milk, even though this combination tasted entirely different.

Shaila ate the rest of the biscuit plain, and as she chewed, she realized she was the anti-biscuit. The par vadi biscuit sounded special, but it wasn't. She didn't sound special, but she was. It didn't matter that she had no apparent role in the coming conflict: so few people knew there even *was* a coming conflict. She was always going to be a part of it, and now she could give herself a role.

"Suck it, biscuit," she muttered unintelligibly, her mouth full.

"What did you say?" asked Divya.

"I told the biscuit to suck it," said Shaila.

"I wish I were fighting biscuits instead of demons." Divya smiled at Shaila, a wide, genuine smile this time. "But you can be my sidekick."

Shaila smiled back. "And you can be my lab assistant."

She took a gulp of her chaa, and the ginger burned. She burst out laughing.

Her ginger. It had been there all along.

# THE BOOK OF MAY

## *C. S. E. Cooney and Carlos Hernandez*

**From:** Morgan W. Jamwant <theglatisant81@me.com>
**To:** Harry Najinsky <hn@lnnlawvt.com>
**Date:** January 22, 2015 12:58:59 P.M. EST
**Subject: Death Is the Tree**

Eliazar,

Dude. I wanna be a tree when I die. Make them put me into one of those urn-y things. The biodegradable ones with the seed inside. Go look it up. I swear to God. Gawd. Gerd. Gods. All of em.

I wanted to be oak, 'cause of what you wrote a hundred billion years ago in our high school yearbook. "To Morgan, an Oak amidst the Spruce." But I didn't see oak on the website. Maybe I should go sugar maple instead. I'd be so fabulous in October.

Can you take this seriously? I mean, not too seriously but a little seriously? I'm kind of on a time crunch here, they tell me.

M. W. J.

**From:** Harry Najinsky <hn@lnnlawvt.com>
**To:** Morgan W. Jamwant <theglatisant81@me.com>
**Date:** January 22, 2015 6:07:21 P.M. EST
**Subject: Re: Death Is the Tree**

Hey May,

You know you're the only one who still calls me Eliazar? And it's not like I don't hang out with all our old D&D buddies. It's just that all we play these days are Eurogames, and you don't give yourself cool, vaguely medieval names in Eurogames. Mostly you do math. I guess all that resource management makes them feel adult or productive or something. To me it feels like a job. I miss D&D.

So I googled it. Eco-urn? It doesn't sound like you. It sounds like earthy-crunchy ooey-gooey overpriced bourgeois bullshit. I mean, it's not like we have a choice. We're all recycled eventually. Do you think Nature gives a shit about how we're packaged when we die? She'll eat us any way we come prepared.

But okay, you said take you seriously. So you want to be an oak? I can see that. I see your hair, and I can imagine it defying gravity and tendrilling up toward the sky. I'm imagining each lock crusting over, becoming strike-a-match rough, radiating like a bark-brown crown around your head. Then come the leaves, not slowly like boring normal trees, but in one verdant, fireworks-ical explosion. You'd spontaneously generate a heavy load of acorns, and the squirrels would be so pleased that they'd learn to speak, just so they could sing choir songs of gratitude.

How's that? I was never as good at that shit as you. You were always the roleplayer. I was the rules lawyer. It's why we made such a good team. Well, and you knew the Raise Dead spell, and could bring me back to life every time I miscalculated.

I wish I hadn't said Raise Dead. It's just too painful to contemplate a world where a spell like that could exist. That's the real reason we don't play D&D anymore. Fantasy is hopeful. Fantasy hurts.

You're not a sugar maple. I forbid you from being a maple! Maple trees are all sweet and Canadian and self-sacrificing. "Yes, take my blood, human, and pour it all over your flapjacks. I bleed to make your breakfast slightly more enjoyable." Fuck that. Come back as hemlock or something. The way the world's treated you, you should poison the shit out of anything that messes with you next time around.

—Eliazar (Harry)

❦

From: Morgan W. Jamwant <theglatisant81@me.com>
To: Harry Najinsky <hn@lnnlawvt.com>
Date: January 24, 2015 10:41:36 A.M. EST
Subject: Who the fuck's a name, anyway?

I never liked Harry. I mean . . . *Harry*! Harry was this old guy who used to come into the costume shop. He lived out of his car and smelled like it and had no one but me to talk to. There I was, puffed up on superprivilege and sorry for him and trapped behind a counter. There was *Harry* on the other side looking oh, so sad. Aside from that, *Harry* is so primordial, so hirsute, something you'd have to shave. Not to mention Rowling.

Egad, I can smell him now. I'm tempted to get Tyrell in here to check under my bed for skulkers, except I know the old-man miasma's not real. Yesterday it was citrus . . .

Never mind.

Eliazar is cool. Eliazar can swim a mighty underworld river in full armor and pwn all the Orcs. It's not that I don't like YOU, Harry, although when you're Harry you always sound slightly more worn than when you're Eliazar, whom even the Dungeons Cannot Defeat. I think the dungeons have defeated me, Harry. Eliazar. Harry. You can be Harry today if you want.

You call me May after my favorite month, my parents called me Morgan after their favorite rum, and if I want to call myself a sugar maple, I can damn well be a fucking sugar maple.

Sorry. My head hurts today. Whatever. Whatever, head.

Re: Hemlock. I could dig a hemlock. Like that Neoclassical monologue I used to do from Shadwell's *Lancashire Witches*: "Henbane, Hemlock, Moonwort too, / Wild Fig-Tree, that o'er Tombs does grow . . ."

I know next to nothing about Eurogames. I have forgotten most of what I used to know about D&D. It was the pretending I liked. The pretending out loud. The words that made us disappear, then reappear in another world, this time with spontaneous superpowers and monsters you could see to fight them. I wish I had a Morning Star and my monster here before me. It'd be a Siege Crab, I think.

In theory, I want to go down fighting. In practice, this slow fading is maybe more merciful. And I must say, synesthesia has its own unique brand of charm. And In-Home Hospice > Hospital, that's for damn sure.

Blah blah blah time for nap reset, and GO!

M. W. J.

P. S. Funny you should imagine me with hair "tendrilling" into sky-hungry branches. I still imagine me with hair, too. Sort of like having 140,000 ghost limbs.

*ↄ⌀*

**From:** Harry Najinsky <hn@lnnlawvt.com>
**To:** Morgan W. Jamwant <theglatisant81@me.com>
**Date:** January 24, 2015 7:24:07 P.M. EST
**Subject: Re: Who the fuck's a name, anyway?**

I know I sound tired. But that's only compared to you. I mean, Manic Pixie Dream Girls call you for perkiness tips! No one, anywhere, ever, is less tired than you. Even now.

So I almost don't want to say this. The last thing I want to remind you of right now is memory loss. But healthy people forget things all the time. *The smelly guy's name wasn't Harry.* You started calling him Harry to bug me! His name was Gunnar. And he wasn't a bad guy. He just got stupid around you because he thought you were pretty. When you weren't around he was cool. We talked classic rock and extreme survival. He only lived out of his car because he thought it was stupid to pay for a hotel. Last I heard, he moved back to Wisconsin to take care of his folks. I always liked the name Gunnar.

You asked who (sic) the fuck are names. I have a theory. Names are mechanized robo-suits.

Hear me out! I've heard people say names are masks and names are costumes and a rose by any other name can kiss my ass.

But names don't just paint over nouns. Names come with fuel cells and lasers and flying robot-fists. You jump into a name the same way you jump into a mech: you turn on the power and grab the controls and all of a sudden you can K.O. all the kaiju in Tokyo.

And after writing that, I don't think you're an oak, either. Too monosyllabic. I think we need more options. There's a good tree farm/ bookstore 20 minutes by car. The woman who runs the place is one of the smartest people I've ever met. Did you ever go to Tasseography? Books, trees, and hot-brewed tea. The owner's Lourdes Belen. If she doesn't already know the perfect tree for you to become, I bet she knows the book that can tell us.

—Eliazar the Slightly-Less-Worn-Sounding-I-Hope

☙

**From:** Morgan W. Jamwant <theglatisant81@me.com>
**To:** Harry Najinsky <hn@lnnlawvt.com>
**Date:** January 25, 2015 2:35:23 P.M. EST
**Subject: The State of My Brain Is WORD GAMES**

Harriazar,

You say Lourdes, I say:

LOURDES –> Madonna –> DaVinci –> Woman with Weasel –> Weasel from *Newsies* the Musical –> Young Christian Bale –> *Batman* –> Nolan Movies –> Dark Doomy Downward Spiral of Main Protagonist –> Brain Tumor –> Pain Meds –> Morphine –> Jolie Holland lyrics.

Let me tell you all about that time I sang "Give Me That Old Fashioned Morphine" to one of my nice nurses and made her giggle. She mistook Jolie Holland for Judy Garland, and suddenly we go from Doom to Rainbows in the veriest flicker.

See? I spread my brain before you. Tread softly, because you tread on my brain . . .

Jolie Holland –> Judy Garland –> "Over the Rainbow" –> "Look to the Rainbow" –> Leprechauns –> Green, "verde, que te quiero verde" –> Trees –> What Tree Should I Be? What Tree Will Make a Grave of Me?

Look, we're back to graves again. At least we took the Bifröst to get here, baby. Definitely sparkly. Speaking of sparkly, I ever tell you how sometimes I see lights? Frequently, actually. It's the whole going-blind thing. Not like "I SAW THE LIGHT!" but little lights. They come zooming right at me like I'm walking the double yellow line on a dark country road and every asshole rushing home from work has his brights on.

You say "perkiness tips" and all I got is "perky tits," man. I didn't have those even when I was fifteen and handsome as a Renoir. I admit I'm shallow; I always wanted to play the Manic Pixie Dream Girl, but she's an ingenue, and I've been a character actor since age four. You know who I played in my junior high production of *The Diary of Anne Frank*? Mr. Frank. They sponged on dirt-brown greasepaint for my beard and strapped my 8th-grade boobs with an Ace bandage.

What did I pop open my laptop to say? I had a purpose. Hm. Rereading your previous emaiiiiiiil——ah! Yes.

A. His name was *Gunnar*? Goddamn it, I thought it was Harry. I get dizzy thinking his name was Gunnar. Stupid trick, brain. Harry, really, did I really call him Harry to annoy you? Jeebus, I was cruel in my twenties. Probably jealous. I hated when you talked rock with people. I could never join in. I'm useless after the 60s, and even my 60s repertoire (thanks to the hippies I called parents) is mostly folk stuff and Broadway. Never cool enough for rock music, never sexy enough, never angry enough.

Maybe I'm angry enough now. Take me to a rock concert, Eliazar the Defiler. Take me to tapas. Take me away from here.

B. In other words, yes, please, YES, I would be very pleased to attend Tasseography Books and Trees and Tea with Thee. When can we go? Now? What about now? Come now. Now, now, now. Doooo eeeeet. I may not be here tomorrow.

C. WAS THAT MEAN? It was, wasn't it? Maybe I haven't lost it after all. Good. You always liked when I was a little cruel. But quietly. Like our secret. For your ears only.

M. W. J.

ɞ

**From:** Harry Najinsky <hn@lnnlawvt.com>
**To:** Morgan W. Jamwant <theglatisant81@me.com>
**Date:** January 26, 2015 6:50:17 P.M. EST
**Subject: Re: The State of My Brain Is WORD GAMES**

It's okay, May. Let your mind do its thing. You go fast, and I'll go slow. You do the living. I'll do the remembering.

Today we went to Tasseography to find out what tree you should be. It'd been a long time since I'd been, and I was worried that it wouldn't be wheelchair-accessible. But you told me to, and I quote, "stop being such a prairie dog." Which made no sense to me until I thought about it—prairie dogs spend all day standing just outside their little holes in the ground looking for any excuse to get spooked and hide. They've developed a sophisticated language of chirps and whistles just to tell each other all the things they should be scared of in the world.

It's not much of a life. I shouldn't be such a prairie dog. So we went and I pushed your wheelchair, and we trundled and trampled and popped wheelies and plowed over anything that got in our way.

And it was so nice to see Lourdes Belen again. She hasn't changed since we were teenagers: 300 pounds of smarts and laughter and pure love. She didn't remember me, but she remembered you. She said she was always jealous of your big hands: better for gardening than her stunted little fingers, she said. Then we all started singing "Blister in the Sun" together, and it was weird how well we remembered the lyrics. But I guess that's what they say. Music is the last thing to go.

You rolled around by yourself for awhile. You said you wanted "the silent company of flora." I was watching you, because the worst thing in the world is your seizures, and I was ready to super-jump to you if you had one. But you were fine just then, meandering through the potted young saplings, sniffing and musing like a happy animal.

You were so beautiful I almost broke down. I wouldn't tell you this, but if I'm going to be your memory, I have to record everything, even the things I'd normally hide. I said aloud, "I hate the world." I meant it.

Lourdes was still with me. She put a hand on my shoulder and said, "A lot of people are going to tell you let go of that rage, or you'll never be happy. But rage isn't a balloon you can release and let fly away. It'd be easier to let go of your lungs."

"Then what should I do?" I asked her.

"You should buy a carnivorous plant," she said.

And she introduced me to a species of carnivorous plant called the Cape Sundew. It's a sprawling, spidery plant with purple flowers and red hairs sticking out of its Krazy Straw branches. Each of those million hairs has a drop of "mucilage" (said Lourdes) hanging from it. When a bug lands on the branch, it gets stuck in the mucilage, and the branch curls around it. That's called "thigmotropism" (another magic word from Lourdes).

Lourdes told me to touch a branch with my little finger. When I did, the plant slowly started to wrap itself around it. It took a minute or so. I was reminded of the way babies will latch onto your pinkie. When I finally pulled my finger away it was sticky and buzzing with feeling, simultaneously numb and alive.

That's when I told Lourdes everything. Our lives since high school. How I messed things up between us, how you forgave me and rescued our friendship. Your illness. This stupid useless plan to find the right tree for you to become. "I don't want Morgan to be a tree!" I yelled, and instantly wished I hadn't because I didn't want you to hear me. Quietly to Lourdes I whispered, "I want her to live."

Lourdes frowned, maybe for the first time in her life. She said to me, "Wait here." She came back some minutes later with a packet of seeds. Vintage, from 1899, with a gorgeous Victorian illustration of an elder tree on the front. "Dragon elder," she said, and her smile was back. "For Morgan."

And I said thank you and asked her how much. She said it was a gift. And then she played a Violent Femmes air-guitar solo.

I bought the Cape Sundew and found you holding a wordless congress with the evergreens. "Christmas starts early around here!" you said.

—Harry

ᘒ

**From:** Morgan W. Jamwant <theglatisant81@me.com>
**To:** Harry Najinsky <hn@lnnlawvt.com>
**Date:** January 30, 2015 4:34:15 P.M. EST
**Subject: Calm today. Drifting.**

The seeds glow at night through the paper bag by my bed. Clusters of emeralds disguised as seedpods. They don't talk, but they whisper. Though I shall never grow old, they tell me, I shall be an elder. (Bad pun, emeralds! For shame.) They say that when an elder dies, be it from drought or disease, it becomes a dragon. And dragons never die.

So I promise you, Eliazar, Keeper of Cape Sundew, I promise you I shall live forever and never die. Just like you wanted. I shall live forever and devour death. But first you must plant me.

The flowers of the elder tree are edible. We will practice this most secular transubstantiation together. This is my petal you eat. This is my elderberry wine you drink. Make a pipe from my branches and play me on a windy day. I love the idea of you playing music with my bones.

Lourdes is a mighty sorceress. Did I remember to thank her? Bring her gifts of my body in flowers and in wine. How long does it take an elder tree to grow? Dragon elders grow swiftly, don't they? Dragon elders grow overnight if planted on a hallowed site. You must water me with your tears and ask me any favor. I will speak to you from the tree.

May

&

**From:** Morgan W. Jamwant <theglatisant81@me.com>
**To:** Harry Najinsky <hn@lnnlawvt.com>
**Date:** January 30, 2015 5:21:05 P.M. EST
**Subject: You know what? Screw calm.**

*"No, calm doesn't interest me."* (IMHO, the best line in *The Death of Artemio Cruz*, by Carlos Fuentes. Other than the sex scene.)

Harry, goddamn it, if I had ever been a pretty young actress, I'd've at least gotten to play Antigone, Saint Joan, Electra. Now I'm to be shored up and sacrificed and bricked in, and all I'm saying is that it would've been nice to have gotten some practice in.

Roles I will never get to play, roles that I merited, that were my *right*:

1. Hedda
2. Lady Mac
3. Phaedra
4. La Marquise de Merteuil
5. Medea

&

**May (11:47 P.M.)**
Was there really ever a time we weren't friends? Seems so unlikely as to be mythological. Tell me that story. Don't text back. Write a letter instead. Give me something to hold onto.

eõ

## THE LAW OFFICES OF
# LORIMER, NGUYEN & NAJINSKY
*HELPING YOU KEEP CONTROL OF YOUR GREAT IDEAS SINCE 2011*

North Main Street
Rutland, VT 05701
Tel: (734) 389-7473
E-mail: contact@lnnlawvt.com

February 1, 2015

To the Most Honorable Morgan "May" Jamwant:

We have an old electric typewriter here in the
office, since sometimes we have to fill out legal
forms on triplicate carbon paper. This letter is
being composed on said carbon paper. I will keep
the bottom (pink) copy for my records. The other
two copies are for you.

I know what you're doing. You're making me write
it out. Because this is the last chance for you
to read it. And because I've been a coward all
these years, even though you forgave me. So
be it. I am your memory now. Let this be the
affidavit of how I failed you, and how you would
not let that failure stand, and how we were
reunited.

I was married for eight years to Cathy Berd.
You told me not to marry her because, you said,
Cathy was a soul-eater. You literally said "soul-
eater." You said she would make demands and run
things her way and erase my identity and turn me
into her hunchbacked Igor.

I said I wanted to be her Igor. That it was
nice to feel needed, to be loved. That I didn't

believe in souls, so Cathy would have nothing to eat.

You couldn't stand it. You said you'd stand up at the wedding; no fucking way you'd forever hold your peace. You'd write all the reasons we shouldn't get married on a scroll, and the scroll would be really long, Jack-Kerouac long, because there were a million reasons we shouldn't get married, and it would be obvious to everyone what a huge mistake this marriage would be, and even Cathy, in a weird Shakespearian reversal, would agree, and she and I would part friends and we'd have the reception anyway, just as a celebration of life.

A scroll!

So I uninvited you to the wedding and kicked you out of my life. And everything happened just the way you said. By degrees, I lost my friends and my hobbies. I quit being a public defender and joined a private practice because the family "needed" money. The sex went away four months into our marriage and never came back, but that was okay; there are more important things than sex, right? I loved her. I would do anything for her.

And then she left. She wasn't even having an affair or anything. She was just bored. She'd feel less bored alone, she said. The divorce papers said "irreconcilable differences," and I couldn't help wonder if boredom legally qualified as one.

Over the next two years, I considered killing myself eight different times. The first seven times I was able to talk myself down. The eighth time I called you.

Within five minutes we were fighting over who
would make a better replacement for Satan: Nero,
Erzsébet Báthory, or Jigglypuff.  WHICH OF COURSE
JIGGLYPUFF.

The only one. You're the only person I could have
had a conversation that stupid with. It saved my
life.

With sincerest gratitude,

Harold Najinsky, Esq.

☙

**From:** Morgan W. Jamwant <theglatisant81@me.com>
**To:** Harry Najinsky <hn@lnnlawvt.com>
**Date:** February 2, 2015 4:08:39 A.M. EST
**Subject: Thank you for your letter.**

Oh, Harry. Oh, Eliazar. Thank you. Thank you for this. I've been wanting,
for years, to . . . Well. But you know. You're not the only coward here. It's
just hard. How sometimes conversation stops short of this invisible wall.
And there's no way around, no portcullis, no battering ram, and you
know there's broken glass and barbed wire at the top.

As for Cathy Berd.

Cathy Berd. Cathy Berd. Cathy Berd. No. Nothing. No story. Erased. A
blank space.

Even when I was in the pink perkiness of health I had trouble
remembering names. Most people just pass me by. Maybe that's why
I used to give so many of my friends nicknames. Mnemonics. Anchors.
Little yellow thumbtacks pinning people I liked in place long enough for
me to remember them. But I'd only pin the pretty butterflies. The ones
who caught my eye.

Cathy Berd. Was she your wife? She is nothing now. I cast her and the
scroll of my objections into my private oubliette. Both are rotted away

to shadow. She is banished and devoured and there isn't even a mark on your finger from the wedding ring you wore. Is there.

Now who is the soul-eater?

I'd give this to you if I could, this empty space where Cathy Berd used to be, but you wouldn't have it, would you? You want to remember everything, keep it safe and sound in my Eco-Urn. I don't want to be kept safe beside Cathy Berd. My grave will be roomier without your regrets. Ash and emeralds and elder seeds, yes. Cathy Berd, no. Not that faceless nothing with her Jeanne Toussaint tote and her Armani skinny jeans and her latest Amulette de Cartier.

Maybe I haven't forgotten as much as I pretend.

You say I wanted us all to part as friends? Huh. Could be I did back then. I was younger, more generous; optimism trumped antipathy. Now I wish I could have destroyed her for you.

Do you know how fiercely I missed you? I dreamed about you every night that first year. I avoided whole chunks of city. Those places stained with you, us, whatever, stained, and even my taste buds rebelled at foods we'd eaten together, and I wrote so many e-mails and sent them to nothing, to nobody, to that place Cathy Berd has gone.

What a mess. Better hit SEND before I delete this whole damn thing. I've deleted too much in my life, in all my elaborate games of pretend.

May

ഗ

**From:** Harry Najinsky <hn@lnnlawvt.com>
**To:** Morgan W. Jamwant <theglatisant81@me.com>
**Date:** February 2, 2015 4:40:25 A.M. EST
**Subject: You still don't understand. Thank you for making me write the letter.**

I swear I'm going to number every sentence you write from now on. A little superscripted "15" or "77" or "155." I'm going to catalogue them by theme and make them searchable in a database by keyword. That way when some shitbag nonbeliever 15 years from now says, "Oh, come on, she couldn't have been *that* amazing," I can say "The Book of May, February 2, 2015, 22–23: 'She is banished and devoured and there isn't even a mark on your finger from the wedding ring you wore. Is there.' Those two sentences *defibrillated* me, motherfucker."

Promise me you will never delete anything ever again. Always press SEND to me.

—Eliazar, The One You Named

☏

**Harry (6:44 A.M.)**
What the fuck, May? I just got off the phone with your caretaker. Where are you? No jokes, no Yoda-babble. Tell me!

**May (6:45 A.M.)**
Busy. Talk soon. Maybe.

☏

**From:** Harry Najinsky <hn@lnnlawvt.com>
**To:** Morgan W. Jamwant <theglatisant81@me.com>
**Date:** February 3, 2015 12:58:59 P.M. EST
**Subject: In Which May Gives Harry an Infarction**

You have to understand, May. If you care about me at all, you have to remember. That "Maybe" you texted me? A sword in the chest.

Tyrell said he and the rest of the search party found you in a woods five miles away, drenched and mud-caked. No one can explain how you got there. There were no wheelchair tracks to follow the whole time, even though the ground was wet and soft. They found you in a clearing, seizing in your chair. Your face was streaked with mud and something red that I am praying to the Book of May wasn't blood. But they didn't find any cuts on you.

They were about to rush you to the E.R. when you suddenly stopped convulsing. Your eyes popped open. You smiled. And then you started singing. Do you remember? Tyrell sure does. He sang your song back to me: "Should all my features be forgot, and rot before I die? Yes, let them tumble from my face, if ear or nose or eye." Poor guy thought you were about to go *Poltergeist* on him. He said he took ten craps and ran the other way and let the other nurses bring you back.

So yeah. That's pretty funny, now that I write it out. This is normally the part where I start cracking up at all the shit you pull.

But it's too scary now, too risky. You can't go escaping into the woods. You could easily die. And if you die in the woods alone, how will I ever get your ashes in an Eco-Urn? How will we pull off our miraculous plan to make you an immortal dragon tree?

Please, just call or text me next time before you run off. If you disappeared forever without a trace that would be the end for more than just you.

—Harry

❦

**From:** Morgan W. Jamwant <theglatisant81@me.com>
**To:** Harry Najinsky <hn@lnnlawvt.com>
**Date:** February 4, 2014 11:51:13 A.M. EST
**Subject: You didn't laugh till paragraph three? Harry, you're slipping . . .**

It wasn't blood, it was elderberries. Medea gave them to me. It was awesome; she rolled into my bedroom in a wheelchair pulled by a dragon the color of the sun, and she looked old and bloodstained, and her apron was full of elderberries, and she painted my face with them. I don't know how they got through the door. Dragons are like cats; they sort of slink bonelessly through narrow spaces, then fill a room. It nudged my bed to the middle of the room, and made three complete circles of itself around it. I was so warm I started sweating. The smell was molten glass and ozone. Like when lightning strikes sand.

I told Medea I used to be a redhead too, but I lost all my leaves because I am a tree in winter. She pulled me onto her lap, saying, "Let me teach you how to drive a chariot." I asked if I should take my anti-seizure meds with me, since I'd need them if we were gonna be gone more than three hours, but Medea just rolled her eyes.

Then off we went into the woods together.

I forget how we got out of the room. Medea has WAYS. I thought for two seconds this morning that maybe I hallucinated the whole thing, but I couldn't have gotten out of my house alone. I can't even go to the bathroom alone.

But that wasn't the weirdest thing that happened yesterday. Before Medea showed up, I was vomiting, right, like you do. And I started vomiting elder blossoms. Still gross, but kind of neat. And I showed the Judy Garland nurse, and she said, "Honey, that happens at the end." And when Tyrell came in, he said the last dude he cared for vomited up a whole hibiscus shrub the night before he died, but he'd never seen elder blossoms before.

So apparently people puke flowers when they're about to kick it. As if we needed any more clues.

It was going to be great. It was going to be ritual. I sang all the right songs, Harry. Medea said I could go ahead and skip the gross interim; she'd turn me into a dragon right away if I liked. No muss, no fuss. But it wasn't right, because you weren't there. "I have to wait for Eliazar," I said. "He's writing a book about me." And she shrugged her muddy shoulders and straddled her dragon's neck and flew away into the east.

So. I guess I'll have to do without the ritual and the dancing and the dragons. I'll wait for you, Harry. But it's gonna be soon. Woman cannot live on petal puke alone. Stay over tonight, just in case.

Remember that New Year's Eve you stayed all night? Never did drink so much champagne before or since. You said that if we were both still alive at eighty, we should get married and raise hell in the old people's home. I bit your finger and said my tooth mark was a promise ring. Remember our breath turning silver in the moonlight? That's how I see you now when I close my eyes. Silver-sketched. Embroidered on my eyelids in thread of frost.

Some animals crawl off at the end to die alone. If we can't have dignity, what with all the boredom and bedpans and pills we can't keep down, at least we can be disgusting alone, singing at the top of our lungs.

Medea was pretty cool though.

May

❧

> **May (12:15 P.M.)**
> Sorry about the maybe. Never again. Promise.

> **Harry (1:07 P.M.)**
> Shit. Just got this. I am leaving work right now. I'll sleep on the carpet next to your bed and be there when you wake. I'll stay for as long as you want me there. Don't go anywhere.

❧

**From:** Harry Najinsky <hn@lnnlawvt.com>
**To:** Lourdes Belen <lourdes@bookstreestea.com>
**Date:** February 17, 2015 1:24 P.M. EST
**Subject: <no subject>**

Dear Mrs. Belen,

This is Eliazar Najinsky, but when I visited Tasseography a few weeks ago I was Harry. I'm in the process of legally changing my name. I came with Morgan Jamwant. She was in a wheelchair. I bought a Cape Sundew from you. (It's doing great, by the way.) You gave Morgan a packet of Dragon elder seeds.

I planted them last night with Morgan's remains. Per her wishes, her ashes were placed in an Eco-Urn, along with the seeds. She wanted her new home to be in a woods north of Rutland, but I couldn't bear to have her so far from me. I buried the urn in my backyard.

I did it in the middle of the night, wearing nothing but the paper hospital smock she died in, because she thought it would be funny. She had asked that I water her with tears, but tear ducts just can't produce enough fluid to keep an elder alive. So I did the best I could. I caught most of the tears I've cried since her death in a biodegradable kitchen sponge I bought expressly for that purpose and buried it along with her. Then I got practical and doused the seeds with my thoroughly unsentimental garden hose.

I sat for a long time with my bare ass on the grass, hugging my knees and holding silent vigil for Morgan. When I noticed I was crying I remembered myself and leaned my face over her grave so that my tears would sink into her soil. That might sound like maudlin nonsense to most people, but I thought you'd get it. I cried until I couldn't, then sat for hours watching the newly turned soil do nothing.

Which is what is supposed to happen. It would take months to know if the seeds would take, if there would be any tree at all to help the world remember Morgan. But—oh God—what if no tree emerged? What if Morgan stayed dead forever?

I started tearlessly heaving and barking and swallowing air. I tore that stupid stupid hospital gown off my body. I felt myself becoming deranged.

That's when I noticed that the Dragon elder had broken through the soil.

I took a seat again in the grass. In a half-hour the elder was a sapling, skinny and self-assured. Two hours later she was a young tree. I climbed up her then. I have never climbed a tree naked before and couldn't believe I had denied myself that pleasure up to now. That feeling of union.

The tree grew for the rest of the night. She slowly lifted me toward the sky. I fell asleep on a branch like a leopard and didn't wake up until morning was well underway. Anyone who visited my house would think the tree was half a century old. All the grass in the yard was dead, crisp, brown-black. The shrubs had shriveled. The Dragon elder was fruiting, laden with berries.

I took my breakfast from those berries. They were messy; they painted my face, matted the hair all over my body, turned me purple.

I climbed her for the rest of the morning. I didn't want to get down. I would just live in the tree forever, naked and happy. She would feed me elderberries and flowers, and occasionally I'd catch and eat a bird. I'd eat the insects that lighted on her. Ants would march toward me in sacrifice and become my food.

But then I had to pee, and there was still enough of civilization in me to make me go inside to use the bathroom. I was anxious and impatient the whole time. I couldn't wait to be in the tree again. I swore the next time I would just do my business from a branch.

As I headed back out, almost running, I saw my laptop. I grabbed it. I am now writing you this message from high up in the tree, naked save for elderberry stains. I'm writing you because I know you'll understand. You're so good at life. I've only met you a few times and I know with every ounce of my being that you're one of the kindest and wisest people I've ever encountered. You know what Dragon elder is; that's why you gave the seeds to Morgan. No tree can do what your seeds did. So tell me how all this works. Tell me what happens next. Tell me what to do.

—Eliazar

℃

**From:** Lourdes Belen <lourdes@bookstreestea.com>
**To:** Harry Najinsky <hn@lnnlawvt.com>
**Date:** February 17, 2015 1:54 P.M. EST
**Subject: Re: <no subject>**

Eliazar, I love your new name. It suits you. Eliazar is a name that unlocks potential.

Send me your address. I am coming to you. Don't bother getting dressed unless you're feeling shy. But I don't think you will be. I think you're well beyond the neurosis and nonsense of Original Sin. You stay in the tree, and I'll let myself into the backyard.

It's going to be a few minutes. I need to stop at Saverin's first for supplies. Meat, mostly. A lot of it. It doesn't need to be fresh. It can be scraps; it can be rotting. Trees aren't picky eaters. Volume is the name of the game. You and I are going to spend a lovely afternoon burying rancid meat in the soil. You can reimburse me later.

I'll explain more when I get there. But for now: technically, the Dragon elder isn't a tree. It's what cryptobotanists call a tregg. Think a caterpillar's pupa stage. This one will take 5-6 years. And then the Dragon elder will rend itself in two, and you and Morgan get your wish.

But wishes can be curses. We need to start preparing now. She's going to be newborn-hungry when she emerges. She would eat you quicker than Saturn if you let her. Not to mention all of Rutland County. We will need to lure her into a forested area, far from people, with lots of elk and bears for her to eat. We have to start planning now how we're going to get a half-starved apex predator out of city limits. It will probably involve a trail of meat.

But there's time. For now, stay in the tree. Rest. Sing to her, speak to her. Wrap yourself around her branches. Don't remove splinters; let them dissolve into your body. Eat all the berries you want. I'll be there soon. Sleep and eat and rest and stay with Morgan. And don't forget to talk to her. Nothing will help her grow strong more than your voice.

# THE TIGER'S SILENT ROAR

## *Holly Heisey*

Evin was on his way in from the gardens, taking his usual shortcut through the formal parlor, when he first saw the soul hunter. She stood in her violet aura near the hearth chairs, hair glinting an unnatural silver. Her gaze razored to him with a predator's instinct.

A throat cleared. His father. "Oh, Evin, you are here. This is Mira Tran. Ms. Tran, this is my son, Lord Evin Arduay."

Evin made his bow, and the hunter returned it.

His father continued. "Ms. Tran is a member of Lord Jerain's court—from the inner worlds, you know—and tells me she is a great admirer of the arts. She has expressed interest in seeing your work. She will be staying with us for the next hand of days, I am sure you will be accommodating?"

Evin eyed the hunter. Beyond the silver hair, could he see her second soul?

The hunter's gaze stayed steady on him. "I have seen your works, Lord Evin, and they are much talked about in the courts abroad. I am partial to *The Waterfall* in particular; I have spent many an evening watching the ripple of the glowworms across its branches. But of course that is a recording. My Lord Jerain desired me to come to you and report back if these works are as extraordinary in person as the holographic representations suggest."

Evin saw the earl's aura swimming with murky, distressed blues. His father certainly hadn't invited the hunter.

"I will of course show you my work," he said.

148

And if he didn't think he could see her second soul, could she see his?

His father cleared his throat. "Well, then, we can have dinner, and after dinner Evin will tour you through the gardens. The sculptures are best seen after dark."

"That is true," Evin said.

The hunter nodded, and her gaze settled into that of a predator, waiting.

Evin's jaw clenched, and he swallowed bile. Damn the inner-world nobles and their outsourced souls.

The hunter's face didn't change, but her aura shifted a shade darker. He didn't think she could read his thoughts, but if he could see her aura, she could see his.

May the gods help him this next hand of days.

At dinner, Evin ate because it would have been suspicious not to, and mostly listened to his father and the hunter speak. His father's view on the outsourcing of souls was no secret among the worlds: "They're all on a permanent functional high, and it damn well doesn't improve their judgement."

But the hunter avoided the subject deftly, engaging the earl in this political foray or that economic debate until he began to relax and words flowed more freely. And there was laughter.

Was that also a power of the second-souled?

She was younger than Evin had thought. She spoke with such animation, her eyes blue and vital, yet her aura had settled into a violet-gray and hardly shifted, while his father's reeled through the patterns and colors of his own emotions. And what did Evin's aura show?

When dusk had fallen, Evin found himself on the garden path with the hunter. Glowworms in the bushes and on low-hanging branches lit as the two approached, shifting through green and white and gold. The flagstones were solid and familiar beneath his boots. Deeper, the roots of trees hummed, now and then asserting themselves to push a flagstone upward or a few inches askew. The smell of rich earth held the air, blending with the citrus of the leaves, the pepper of the glowworms, the perfumes of the flowers. Evening mist cooled Evin's face and dampened the chorus of crickets and braying of frogs from the ponds. This was his place, his world, where everything was known, and everything was always changing: growing, living, dying. Steady auras of greens and golds and browns.

"Lovely," the hunter breathed.

Evin stiffened. He had almost forgotten she was there. But in his world, calm flowed around him again and he began to relax. "They are nothing to the gardens of the inner worlds. Our gardener is skilled, but he is a craftsman, not an artist."

A flicker of yellow—surprise?—showed in the hunter's aura. "You do not tend the gardens yourself?"

"I have my work," Evin said. And the work his father set to him. Second heir he might be, but the earl insisted he know the running of things. "The beauty you see comes not from the design but from the glowworms and the species of plants that are native to this world. Our plants and invertebrates are mostly symbiotic, and few can be transplanted elsewhere."

"I have heard that, yes. But whether this is the work of an artist or of nature, it is beauty enough. And I can't believe that you have had no hand in this garden's keeping."

Evin shrugged. "Enough of a hand." And he steered the hunter toward a fork in the path.

Ahead, trees parted and the glowworms lit up in a rush of blue and white.

The hunter inhaled sharply. "*The Waterfall.*" She watched as the glowworms rippled colors across the deliberate branches, cascading like water. The light sparked in her eyes. Her aura, which had stayed that steady violet-gray with only the occasional flicker, now steeped in a deepening gold.

Evin looked down.

"It's grown," she said. "It's different from the hologram."

Evin brushed his hand against the ends of the branches, making the glowworms ripple faster. "It's a living sculpture, one of my first. I have coaxed its branches for the last four years. It is quite different now than when I first allowed it to be finished."

The hunter circled *The Waterfall*, studying the sculpture with the same intensity as she had first studied him. Evin watched her warily. Could she see the most recent coaxings, far more honed and organic than the rest?

The hunter looked up at him, her eyes still glowing. "May I see the tiger?"

Evin stared back. News of his latest sculpture would have leaked. It always did.

"It's not finished," he said. And it wasn't. He had not yet found the adequate shape of its tail, and he was only now coaxing the left front paw into just the right arc. But that wasn't the point. The tiger was the first sculpture he had brought to full coaxing with the new senses of his second soul. He had found angles of growth he would never have used before, had set the glowworms into patterns he would not have thought possible two months ago.

"I haven't seen any holograms of it, if that's what you are wondering," the hunter said, her tone wry. "A rumor only. But your next project is truly a tiger?" And then she hesitated, her aura flickering something Evin didn't recognize. "I would like to see it, finished or not, if you will let me. That is, if you let anyone see your sculptures before they are completely finished."

Evin let out his breath. "It is nearly finished," he said. She would see it anyway, when it was scanned next month and released to the public. He couldn't hide anything then, and he doubted he could hide anything now. She was too keenly aware.

Evin wondered why he was taking her through the winding paths, deeper into the place where the older trees held glowworms higher overhead and bushes grew out over the path as it turned from flagstone to gravel. He never showed an unfinished piece to anyone. How much of his doubt showed in his aura, and what did the hunter make of it? Was this coercion on her part, to see the tiger? But he did not, for all the stories of the soul hunters, think she could change his thoughts. He certainly did not have that ability.

"Are you also an artist?" Evin asked. The question had been growing the whole evening. She wasn't a scholar, and she was more than an enthusiast, with her intensity and technical awareness.

She stopped. The path was darker here, and her silver hair glinted pink, then red from the glowworms high overhead. She was the predator again, still and waiting. Her aura did not so much as flicker.

"No," she said finally. "That is not a luxury afforded to the second-souled." She turned and picked up her pace on the path.

After a breath, Evin hurried to take the lead again. The tiger was not far.

He reached the mouth of the clearing, and the glowworms of the tiger lit up. The hunter barked an oath and crouched back. Above them, the tiger bared its teeth and extended its claws. Glowworms rippled in orange and white along its hide, the release of readied muscles.

The hunter let out a hissing breath. "That," she said emphatically, "is a tiger."

Evin coughed a laugh and pulled his gaze away from the pouncing tiger to see jagged green fear fading from the hunter's aura. He was going to say the sculpture wasn't done yet, but he stopped and absorbed the awe on the hunter's face. Nothing studied or calculating.

Evin closed his mouth and looked back up at his tiger.

The next morning, Evin rose before dawn, shaved his head and face and arms—anywhere the silver might be visible—and dressed in a plain white shirt and tan trousers. He carried his boots in hand and wove through the lightening house, adding his tuneless hum to the distant clatter from the kitchen and the hushed steps of servants preparing for the day.

Outside, the air was fresh with dew. Birds called across the garden, the morning music. He picked out each call and knew its source. Closing his eyes, he let the birds show him the path to the greenhouse and his waiting tools. He felt the souls of life all around him, better seen without sight, and changed his hum to a whistle.

Gravel crunched on the path behind him and he turned, opening his eyes. The hunter.

Evin rooted himself to the steadying earth and waited for her approach. He had not forgotten her, but he'd hoped to put her out of his mind for just this morning, at least. No one from the courts of the inner worlds rose before whatever sun they lived under neared its zenith. Still, he wasn't sure why he'd expected these rules to apply to her.

She smiled and made a slight bow. "Good morning, Lord Evin. Yes, I do rise early—this day, at least. The ships do their best to synchronize to a local time, but I'm afraid the majority of passengers were bound for the capital to the west." She grimaced, and Evin laughed despite himself.

"Tourists," he said. "There are always tourists this time of year, no matter that the capital is more a steam bath than a city. But it's when the gardens are flowering and at their greenest."

"Then I am surprised that you do not work your sculptures there."

"Oh, I give my father an excuse to escape to the country." Evin looked out over his own gardens, the balmy air settling heavier on his skin with the sun now edging the tops of the trees. "The glowworms are less judicious in the capital. My finer work is much more suited to this temperate clime."

"Are you working in the greenhouse today?" the hunter asked.

Evin turned back to her, feeling the loss of his guard and pulling it back up again. "No. It's where I store my tools."

"Ah. And will you be working on the tiger? May I watch you work?"

"No," he said. He never let anyone watch him work, and he was certainly not going to let her watch him work on the tiger.

He took a breath. Maybe he could ignore his senses for one day. He could prove to her he was normal. "I'm working on the hummingbirds today. Some of the branches need more coaxing back into alignment. The sculptures are living, you know."

But she did know that, and beyond all technical expertise, he'd told her again the night before. Evin looked down and tried to sort what to say next.

"Oh, the hummingbirds," the hunter said. He heard the disappointment in her voice, but he didn't feel any triumph in it. "We didn't see that one last night. But if you are sure you do not mind—"

"It's fine," he said, and turned to resume his walk to the greenhouse. At least she would be where he could see her and not wandering around, inspecting the coaxings on his tiger.

Evin collected his tools and wound through the garden pathways. In his bucket, pruning shears rattled against wire and the dented metal side—a familiar, calming rhythm. *Three Hummingbirds, Playing* was an older sculpture, set closer to the house, and as he approached its clearing, he was already planning which branches he would shift into the new pattern to keep its growth in shape.

Evin set down his bucket and unfolded his stool, pointing to a place a few feet away where the hunter would be in his line of sight but shadowed by the surrounding bushes and trees. She unfolded her own stool and sat, smiling when he glanced at her. "You'll forget that I'm here."

He doubted that. At least it would be a reminder for him to be careful. He couldn't make his coaxings by reading the plants' auras today.

Evin sat down, rolled up and pinned his sleeves, and absently flicked at the locks on his platinum talisman cuff as his eyes roamed the shapes of the hummingbird in front of him. The locks clicked open, and he let the cuff slide off his wrist, bending to set it on the edge of the root basin. Then he realized what he was doing.

He looked up at the hunter. She looked back at him from the tree's shade.

"Do you always remove your talisman when you work?" she asked, her tone conversational. "I wasn't aware they could be removed."

Evin thought of putting the cuff back on, but she'd already seen him take it off. He let it drop with a clink to the basin edge, pushing it beneath a branch so it wouldn't catch the sunlight.

"It makes a glare," he said. "I modified it so it can come off when I work." He reached inside his shirt and pulled out the simpler talisman, the soul symbol carved into a lightly polished disk of wood. A commoner's talisman. "I have this."

The hunter leaned forward to look. "Effective, and yet easily misplaced."

Yes, like two months ago when he'd got into the habit of taking off his cuff and got out of the habit of putting on the common talisman in the morning. No one knew why in the outsourcing process a soul would sometimes stray from the path the priests defined for it, but everyone wore their talismans to ward against receiving such a soul. Evin had thought that here, on a planet far from the inner worlds where few attempted to outsource their souls, the risk was minimal. He had been wrong.

"It has served me well enough," Evin said, and drew his shears from the bucket, setting his attention firmly back on the sculpture tree.

For a while, Evin worked to the sounds of the garden. He ran his hands across the branches, letting the subtle wills of the tree and the symbiotic glowworms guide where he pruned back, and where wire should be added or adjusted to coax the branches into the shape mutually desired. He was not trying to read their auras, but it had become part of his process.

"It is not often I enjoy my assignments away from my Lord Jerain's court," the hunter said softly.

Evin snipped a branch too far.

"My profession is not a pleasant one," the hunter continued. "If I'm not bullying a noble into doing Lord Jerain's will, then I am in the slums of our world watching our family's second-souled, making sure they keep to their places. Sometimes I am sent to find a soul that has gone astray."

Evin made his hands keep working, his attention so tight on the signals of the sculpture that the input was painful. It was like that day two months ago, when the branches beneath his hands had exploded into too much texture, too much color, the world into too much sound and soul. His hands trembled, and he eased his focus, the pain of the input fading.

"Those who receive a second soul are always carefully chosen. It's a permanent process, after all. We don't take volunteers; they are too eager for the abilities a second soul can bring, though most don't know that we can't kill with a glance, or read minds, or any of the other attributes the rumors give us. What we *can* do requires training, and we take special care the candidates do not have the discipline to achieve a competency that might pose a problem. Above all, the candidates must be miserable. Because that is how it works. A noble doesn't gain the desired bliss by sourcing out his soul. A noble is only as happy as his second-souled is miserable."

Evin looked up. Was she miserable?

The hunter's lips quirked. "I do not have it so bad. Soul hunters are chosen and paired for their neutrality."

She tilted her head. "You aren't afraid of me."

Evin cleared his throat, but she waved her hand.

"No, I know you fear what I am, that's not what I mean. You all fear that, though your father disguises it well enough."

"My father forgot you were anything but a courtier last night," Evin said.

"And that is a mistake. You didn't. But neither do you push me away. And you are not particularly polite."

Evin snorted, but he felt the blood rush to his face. "If I have given offense—"

"You have not," the hunter said, and smiled.

E vin found himself drawn into the dinner conversation that evening as the hunter burst fully into life, hands waving, anecdotes shot out with court precision. His father roared with laughter, the earl's great voice booming throughout the hall, and Evin struggled to keep some sense of decorum as the hunter mercilessly timed her punch lines to the moment he took a sip of wine. He told one of his favorite stories of the inner-world duchess who had come to see his sculptures, asked what all the infestation of vermin was on their branches, and then had been enraged to discover that the glowworms were what produced the whole effect.

He didn't time it completely right, but the hunter at least had to cover her mouth after taking a bite of the seasoned crab.

His father chimed in. "And do you remember when . . . ?"

Evin kept his eyes on the hunter. Her aura had been dancing with color throughout the meal, more color and variation than he had yet seen from her. She gave him a small smile, then turned back to his father and laughed as he built up to the conclusion of another episode of court intrigue. Her aura glowed with purples and reds, a close echo of his father's amusement.

And then she steered the conversation into more serious matters. Evin was less interested in these, but he tracked her aura, comparing it to his father's and what he had already learned of the colors in relation to the emotions and moods they represented. The discussion moved swiftly, turning from one aspect of a subject to another with specific responses: anger, annoyance, determination, satisfaction. He heard all these and recognized them in his father's voice, and saw their colors steady and unnaturally clear in the hunter's aura.

She was teaching him. This was a teaching pattern.

Evin held his fork halfway to his mouth for a long moment. His father looked at him, annoyance flaring in streaks of yellow-orange, the emotion heightened, clarified, in the hunter's aura. But it was not what she actually felt. Now Evin could see the deep violet of her aura beneath. None of these things were actually what she felt, not fully.

Why was she doing this? He had no secret any longer, and what did hunters do to those found with a soul that had gone astray? He had grown up with the stories—people taken by the hunters and later seen as raving mad, or never heard from again. The metal of his talisman cuff clinked as he set his hand back on the table.

He made himself take another bite, and then another. He forced himself to hold the conversation, and contribute where he had anything to contribute. The hunter brought the talk back to the gardens, and then he could speak more freely. She wanted him to relax. Like the moth-spider lulling its prey before it killed?

Evin watched her cycle through her teaching pattern, then relaxed a bit more as her aura smoothed back into only violet-gray, though she carried on with outward animation. He could see the strain in the set of her shoulders, the tightness around her lips when she paused between speaking.

She knew he was watching. She knew he was seeing her as human.

* * *

Hunter Mira Tran stayed for three more days, walking the gardens with Evin at night, staying with him as he worked, this time on the tiger. He didn't hold back any of his new senses or his ability to use them as he coaxed the front paw into its final shape. That would be pointless now. The hunter mostly sat on her stool, just watching.

Occasionally, Evin would glance over to see her leaning against a tree, face tilted upward to catch the patches of sun that filtered through the branches. Sometimes it was Evin who would talk, explaining an arc he had put into a group of branches and how it would form a stronger growth. He did not need to explain how he knew this, for she would see the same auras of the plant and leaves and glowworms once he had shown her what he was doing. She ran light fingers over the ends of the branches, and then drew back as if she had just touched someone else's lover.

She led him through teaching patterns at dinner every night until he began to know not only the boldest colors, but how to read variations in color patterns and frequencies of vibrations. He could read his father with a precision that felt intrusive. Subtle patterns in the plants that he had not seen before became clearer, and he honed further.

And then came the day when Mira had to leave.

"It was an unexpected pleasure," Evin's father said, bowing as he took her hands in a grip he reserved for friends. "Please feel free to visit again if you are ever on our world. You would be most welcome—indeed, I would insist."

Mira smiled. "I would insist as well." She glanced at Evin. "And now I must be going."

"I will walk you to the car," Evin said, with his own stiff bow. He didn't offer his hand, and she didn't offer hers.

Evin led the way down the marble entry steps and to the path that led to the mews where he could hear the soft whine of her waiting car. But he stopped when the hedge hid them from the house, and he pulled Mira out of sight of the driver. He stared at her, and she at him.

"What will you do?" Evin asked. He felt his throat tighten around the next words. "I have one of your family's—"

Green fear flickered around the edges of her aura. "Sometimes a soul truly does get lost. I am the only one who can find my Lord Jerain's soul; I will board my ship and continue my search."

Evin coughed. He had wondered just whose soul he had been given. What did she risk to do this for him?

Mira reached for his left hand and gripped the talisman cuff. "Don't take it off," she said. "I know it glares. Don't ever take it off."

She couldn't do this. Evin opened his mouth.

"I am valuable," she said. "So are you. *Live*, Evin Arduay. Make your waterfalls and your tigers; be happy." Her aura wavered. "Give us a voice."

Evin's hand twitched toward her, but then the whine of the car engine shifted pitch. The driver had seen them coming and was readying to go.

Evin cleared his throat. "May you travel safe, Ms. Tran."

She hesitated only a moment before nodding. Then she turned and strode for the waiting car.

Evin went to the clearing with the tiger, but he could not work. He paced, his boots tearing ruts in the grass.

Damn them all. Damn the nobles and their outsourced souls. And damn Lord Jerain most of all—

Pain clenched Evin's chest, and he gasped, leaning over. He couldn't damn that soul. It was inside him.

He looked up at his tiger and felt the aura of the trees and the glowworms, the honing and the calling to hone more. This was what he was. He hadn't wanted another's soul, but it was his now. He would not give it up if he could.

Evin grabbed his shears, pressed his hands to the leaves on the ends of the branches, and closed his eyes. He let the tiger's aura seep into his fingertips and into his souls.

He heard the tiger's voice and lent his own.

He let her roar.

# SABBATH WINE

### *Barbara Krasnoff*

"My name's Malka Hirsch," the girl said. "I'm nine."

"I'm David Richards," the boy said. "I'm almost thirteen."

The two kids were sitting on the bottom step of a run-down brownstone at the edge of the Brooklyn neighborhood of Brownsville. It was late on a hot summer afternoon, and people were just starting to drift home from work, lingering on stoops and fire escapes to catch any hint of a breeze before going up to their stifling flats.

Malka and David had been sitting there companionably for a while, listening to a chorus of gospel singers practicing in the first floor front apartment at the top of the stairs. Occasionally, the music paused as a male voice offered instructions and encouragement; it was during one of those pauses that the kids introduced themselves to each other.

Malka looked up at her new friend doubtfully. "You don't mind talking to me?" she asked. "Most big boys don't like talking to girls my age. My cousin Shlomo, he only wanted to talk to the older girl who lived down the street and who wore short skirts and a scarf around her neck."

"I don't mind," said David. "I like kids. And anyway, I'm dead, so I guess that makes a difference."

Above them, the enthusiastic chorus started again. As a soprano wailed a high lament, she shivered in delight. "I wish I could sing like that."

158

"It's called 'Ride Up in the Chariot,'" said David. "When I was little, my mama used to sing it when she washed the white folks' laundry. She told me my great-grandma sang it when she stole away from slavery."

"It's nice," Malka said. She had short, dark brown hair that just reached her shoulders and straight bangs that touched her eyebrows. She had pulled her rather dirty knees up and was resting her chin on them, her arms wrapped around her legs. "I've heard that one before, but I didn't know what it was called. They practice every Thursday, and I come here to listen."

"Why don't you go in?" asked David. He was just at that stage of adolescence where the body seemed to be growing too fast; his long legs stretched out in front of him while he leaned back on his elbows. He had a thin, cheerful face set off by bright, intelligent eyes and hair cropped so close to his skull that it looked almost painted on. "I'm sure they wouldn't mind, and you could hear better."

Malka grinned and pointed to the sign just above the front-door bell that read CORNERSTONE BAPTIST CHURCH. "My papa would mind," she said. "He'd mind plenty. He'd think I was going to get converted or something."

"No wonder I never seen you before," said the boy. "I usually just come on Sundays. Other days, I . . ." He paused. "Well, I usually just come on Sundays."

The music continued against a background of voices from the people around them. A couple of floors above, a baby cried, and two man argued in sharp, dangerous tones; down on the ground, a gang of boys ran past, laughing, ignoring the two kids sitting outside the brownstone. A man sat on a cart laden with what looked like a family's possessions. Obviously in no hurry, he let the horse take its time as it proceeded down the cobblestone street.

The song ended, and a sudden clatter of chairs and conversation indicated that the rehearsal was over. The two kids stood and moved to a nearby streetlamp so they wouldn't get in the way of the congregation leaving the brownstone in twos and threes.

Malka looked at David. "Wait a minute," she said. "Did you say you were dead?"

"Uh-huh," he said. "Well, at least, that's what my daddy told me."

She frowned. "You ain't," she said and then, when he didn't say anything, "Really?"

He nodded affably. She reached out and poked him in the arm. "You ain't," she repeated. "If you were a ghost or something, I couldn't touch you."

He shrugged and stared down at the street. Unwilling to lose her new friend, Malka quickly added, "It don't matter. If you wanna be dead, that's okay with me."

"I don't *want* to be dead," said David. "I don't even know if I really am. It's just what Daddy told me."

"Okay," Malka said.

She swung slowly around the pole, holding on with one hand, while David stood patiently, his hands in the pockets of his worn pants.

Something caught his attention and he grinned. "Bet I know what he's got under his coat," he said, and pointed at a tall man hurrying down the street, his jacket carefully covering a package.

"It's a bottle!" said Malka scornfully. "That's obvious."

"It's moonshine," said David, laughing.

"How do you know?" asked Malka, peering at the man.

"My daddy sells the stuff," said David. "Out of a candy store over on Dumont Street."

Malka was impressed. "Is he a gangster? I saw a movie about a gangster once."

David grinned again. "Naw," he said. "Just a low-rent bootlegger. If my mama ever heard about it, she'd come back here and make him stop in a hurry, you bet."

"My mama's dead," Malka said. "Where is yours?"

David shrugged. "Don't know," he said. "She left one day and never came back." He paused, then asked curiously, "You all don't go to church, right?"

"Nope."

"Well, what do you do?"

Malka smiled and tossed her hair back. "I'll show you," she said. "Would you like to come to a Sabbath dinner?"

M alka and her father lived in the top floor of a modern five-story apartment building about six blocks from the brownstone church. Somewhere between there and home, David had gone his own way, Malka didn't quite remember when. It didn't matter much, she decided. She had a plan, and she could tell David about it later.

She stood in the main room that acted as parlor, dining room, and kitchen. It was sparsely but comfortably furnished: besides a small wooden table that sat by the open window, there was a coal oven, a sink with cold running water, a cupboard over against one wall, and an overloaded bookcase against another. A faded flower-print rug covered the floor; it had obviously seen several tenants come and go.

Malka's father sat at the table reading a newspaper by the slowly waning light, his elbow on the windowsill, his head leaning on his hand. A small plate with the remains of his supper sat nearby. He hadn't shaved for a while; a short, dark beard covered his face.

"Papa," said Malka.

Her father winced as though something hurt him, but he didn't take his eyes from the book. "Yes, Malka?" he asked.

"Papa, today is Thursday, isn't it?"

He raised his head and looked at her. Perhaps it was the beard, or because he worked so hard at the furrier's where he spent his days curing animal pelts, but his face seemed more worn and sad than ever.

"Yes, daughter," he said quietly. "Today is Thursday."

She sat opposite him and folded her hands neatly in front of her. "Which means that tomorrow is Friday. And tomorrow night is the Sabbath."

He smiled. "Now, Malka, when was the last time you saw your papa in a synagogue, rocking and mumbling useless prayers with the old men? This isn't how I brought you up. You know I won't participate in any—"

"—bourgeois religious ceremonies," she finished with him. "Yes, I know. But I was thinking, Papa, that I would like to have a real Sabbath. The kind that you used to have with Mama. Just once. As . . ." Her face brightened. "As an educational experience."

Her father sighed and closed his book. "An educational experience, hah?" he asked. "I see. How about this: If you want, on Saturday, we can go to Prospect Park. We'll sit by the lake and feed the swans. Would you like that?"

"That would be nice," said Malka. "But it's not the same thing, is it?"

He shrugged. "No, Malka. You're right. It isn't."

Across the alley, a clothesline squeaked as somebody pulled on it, an infant cried, and somebody cursed in a loud combination of Russian and Yiddish.

"And what brought on this sudden religious fervor?" her father asked. "You're not going to start demanding I grow my beard to my knees and read nothing but holy books, are you?"

"Oh, Papa," Malka said, exasperated. "Nothing like that. I made friends with this boy today, named David. He's older than I am—over twelve—and his father also doesn't approve of religion, but his mama used to sing the same songs they sing in the church down the street. We listened to them today, and I thought maybe I could invite him here and show him what we do . . ." Her voice trailed off as she saw her father's face.

"You were at a church?" her father asked, a little tensely. "And you went in and listened?"

"No, of course not. We sat outside. It's the church on the first floor of that house on Remsen Avenue. The one where they sing all those wonderful songs."

"Ah!" her father said, enlightened, and shook his head. "Well, and I shouldn't be pigheaded about this. Your mama always said I could be very pigheaded about my political convictions. You are a separate individual, and deserve to make up your own mind."

"And it's really for educating David," said Malka eagerly.

Her father smiled. "Would that make you happy, Malka?" he asked. "To have a Sabbath dinner for you and your friend? Just this once?"

"Yes, just this once," she said, bouncing on her toes. "With everything that goes with it."

"Of course," her father said. "I did a little overtime this week. I can ask Sarah who works over at the delicatessen for a couple pieces chicken, a loaf of bread, and maybe some soup and noodles, and I know we have some candles put by."

"And you have Grandpa's old prayer book," she encouraged.

"Yes, I have that."

"So all we need is the wine!" Malka said triumphantly.

Her father's face fell. "So all we need is the wine." He thought for a moment, then nodded. "Moshe will know. He knows everybody in the neighborhood; if anyone has any wine to sell, he'll know about it."

"It's going to get dark soon," said Malka. "Is it too late to ask?"

Her father smiled and stood. "Not too late at all. He's probably in the park."

"So, Abe," Moshe said to Malka's father, frowning, "you are going to betray your ideals and kowtow to the religious authorities? You, who were nearly sent to Siberia for writing articles linking religion to the consistent poverty of the masses? You, who were carried bodily out of your father's synagogue for refusing to wear a hat at your brother's wedding?"

Abe had immediately spotted Moshe, an older, slightly overweight man with thinning hair, on the well-worn bench where he habitually spent each summer evening. But after trying to explain what he needed only to be interrupted by Moshe's irritable rant, Abe finally shrugged and walked a few steps away. Malka followed.

"There are some boys playing baseball over there," he told her. "Why don't you go enjoy the game and let me talk to Moshe by myself?"

"Okay, Papa," Malka said, and ran off. Abe watched her for a moment, and then looked around. The small city park was full of people driven out of their apartments by the heat. Kids ran through screaming, taking advantage of the fact that their mothers were still cleaning up after dinner and therefore not looking out for misbehavior. Occasionally, one of the men who occupied the benches near the small plot of brown grass would stand and yell, "Sammy! Stop fighting with that boy!" Then, content to have done his duty by his offspring, he would sit down, and the kids would proceed as though nothing had happened.

Abe walked back to the bench and sat next to his friend, who now sat disconsolately batting a newspaper against his knee. "Moshe, just listen for a minute—"

But before he could finish, Moshe handed him his newspaper, climbed onto the bench, and pointed an accusing finger at a thin man who had just lit a cigarette two benches over.

"You!" Moshe yelled. "Harry! I have a bone to pick with you! What the hell were you doing writing that drek about the Pennsylvania steel strike? How dare you use racialism to try to cover up the crimes of the AFL in subverting the strike?"

"They were scabs!" the little man yelled back, gesturing with his cigarette. "The fact that they were Negroes is not an excuse!"

"They were workers who were trying to feed their families in the face of overwhelming oppression!" Moshe called back. "If the AFL had any respect for the people they were trying to organize, they could have brought all the workers into the union, and the bosses wouldn't have been able to break the strike!"

"You ignore the social and cultural problems!" yelled Harry.

"You ignore the fact that you're a schmuck!" roared Moshe.

"Will you get down and act like a human being for a minute?" asked Abe, hitting his friend with the newspaper. "I have a problem!"

Moshe shrugged and climbed down. At the other bench, Harry made an obscene gesture and went back to dourly sucking on his cigarette.

"Okay, I'm down," said Moshe. "So tell me, what's your problem?"

"Like I was saying," said Abe, "I'm going to have a Sabbath meal."

Moshe squinted at him. "Nu?" he asked. "You've got yourself a girlfriend finally?"

Abe shook his head irritably. "No, I don't have a girlfriend."

"Too bad," his friend said, crossing his legs and surveying the park around him. "You can only mourn so long, you know. A young man like you, he shouldn't be alone like some alter kocker like me."

Abe smiled despite himself. "No, I just . . ." He looked for a moment to where Malka stood with a boy just a little taller than her, both watching the baseball game. That must be her new friend, he thought, probably from the next neighborhood over. His clothes seemed a bit too small for his growing frame; Abe wondered whether he had parents and, if so, whether they couldn't afford to dress their child properly.

"It's just this once," he finally said. "A gift for a child."

"Okay," said Moshe. "So what do you want from me? Absolution for abrogating your political ideals?"

"I want wine."

"Ah." Moshe turned and looked at Abe. "I see. You've got the prayer book, you've got the candles, you've got the challah. But the alcohol, that's another thing. You couldn't have come up with this idea last year, before the geniuses in Washington gave us the gift of Prohibition?"

"I want to do it right," said Abe. "No grape juice and nothing made in somebody's bathtub. And nothing illegal—I don't want to make the gangsters any richer than they are."

"Well . . ." Moshe shrugged. "If you're going to make this an ethical issue, then I can't help."

"Oh, come on," Abe said impatiently. "It's only been a few months since Prohibition went into effect. I'm sure somebody's got to have a few bottles of wine stashed away."

"I'm sure they do," Moshe said. "But they're not going to give them to you. And don't look at me," he added quickly. "What I got stashed away isn't what you drink at the Sabbath table."

"Hell." Abe stood and shook his head. "I made a promise. You got a cigarette?"

Moshe handed him one and then, as Abe lit a match, said, "Hey, why don't you go find a rabbi?"

Abe blew out some smoke. "I said I wanted to make one Sabbath meal. I didn't say I wanted to attend services."

Moshe laughed. "No, I mean for your wine. When Congress passed Prohibition, the rabbis and priests and other religious big shots, they put up a fuss, so now they get to buy a certain amount for their congregations. You want some booze? Go to a rabbi."

Abe stared at him. "You're joking, right?"

Moshe continued to grin. "Truth. I heard it from a Chassidic friend of mine. We get together, play a little chess, argue. He told me that he had to go with his reb to the authorities because the old man can't speak English, so they could sign the papers and prove he was a real rabbi. Now he's got the right to buy a few cases a year so the families can say the blessing on the Sabbath and get drunk on Passover."

Abe nodded, amused. "Figures." He thought for a moment. "There's a shul over on Livonia Avenue where my friend's son had his bar mitzvah. Maybe I should try there."

"If you've got a friend who goes there," Moshe suggested, "why not simply get the wine from him?"

Abe took a long drag on his cigarette and shook his head. "No, I don't want to get him in trouble with his rabbi. I'll go ask myself. Thanks, Moshe."

"Think nothing of it." Suddenly Moshe's eyes narrowed, and he jumped up onto the bench again, yelling to a man entering the park,

"Joe, you capitalist sonovabitch! I saw that letter you wrote in the *Daily Forward . . .*"

Abe walked over to his daughter. "You heard?" he asked quietly. "We'll go over to the synagogue right now and see what the rabbi can do for us."

"Yes, Papa," Malka said, and added, "This is David. He's my new friend that I told you about. David, this is my father."

"How do you do, Mr. Hirsch?" asked David politely.

"How do you do, David?" replied Abe. "It's nice to meet you. I'm glad Malka has made a new friend."

"Mr. Hirsch," said David, "you don't have to go to that rabbi if you don't want to. I heard my father say that he and his business partners got some Jewish wine that he bought from a rabbi who didn't need it all, and I'm sure he could sell you a bottle."

Abe smiled. "Thank you, David. But as I told my friend, I'd rather not get involved in something illegal. You understand," he added, "I do not mean to insult your father."

"That's okay," David said. He turned and whispered to Malka, "You go ahead with your daddy. I'll go find mine; you come get me if you need me for anything. He's usually at the candy store on the corner of Dumont and Saratoga."

"Okay," Malka whispered back. "And if we do get wine, I'll come get you, and you can come to our Sabbath dinner."

Abe stared at the two children for a moment, then pulled the cigarette out of his mouth, tossed it away, and began walking. Malka waved at David and followed her father out of the park.

The synagogue was located in a small storefront; the large glass windows had been papered over for privacy. CONGREGATION ANSHE EMET was painted in careful Hebrew lettering on the front door. Evening services were obviously over; two elderly men were hobbling out of the store, arguing loudly in Yiddish. Abe waited until they had passed, took a deep breath, and walked in, followed by Malka.

The whitewashed room was taken up by several rows of folding chairs, some wooden bookcases at the back, and a large cabinet covered by a beautifully embroidered cloth. A powerfully built man with a long, white-streaked black beard was collecting books from some of the chairs.

While Malka went to the front to admire the embroidery, Abe walked over the man. "Rabbi," he said tentatively.

The rabbi turned and straightened. He stared at Abe doubtfully. "Do I know you?"

"I was here for Jacob Bernstein's son Maxie's bar mitzvah two months ago," said Abe. "You probably don't remember me."

The rabbi examined him for a minute or two more, then nodded. "No, I do remember you. You sat in a corner with your arms folded and glowered like the Angel of Death when the boy sang his Torah portion."

Abe shrugged. "I promised his father I'd attend. I didn't promise I'd participate."

"So," said the rabbi, "you are one of those new radicals. The ones who are too smart to believe in the Almighty."

"I simply believe that we have to save ourselves rather than wait for the Almighty to do it for us," Abe rejoined.

"And so," said the rabbi, "since you obviously have no respect for the beliefs of your fathers, why are you here?"

Abe bit his lip, ready to turn and leave.

A small voice next to him asked, "Papa? Is it safe here?"

He looked down. Malka was standing next to him, looking troubled and a little frightened. "One moment," he said to the rabbi and walked to the door, which was open to let the little available air in.

"Of course it's safe, daughter," he said quietly. "Why wouldn't it be?"

"Well," she began, "it's just . . . there isn't a good place to hide. I thought synagogues had to have good hiding places."

His hand went out to touch her hair, to reassure her, but then stopped. "Malkele," he whispered, "you run outside and play. You let your papa take care of this. Don't worry about anything—it will all turn out fine."

Her face cleared, as though whatever evil thoughts had troubled her had completely disappeared. "Okay, Papa!" she said, and left.

Abe took a breath and went back into the room, where the rabbi was waiting. "This is the story," he said. "My little girl is . . . Well, she wants a Sabbath meal."

The rabbi cocked his head. "So, nu? Your child has more sense than you do. So have the Sabbath meal."

"For a Sabbath meal," said Abe. "I need wine." He paused and added. "I would be . . . grateful if you would help me with this."

"I see." The rabbi smiled ironically. "In other words, you want to make a party, maybe, for a few of your radical friends, and you thought, 'The rabbi is allowed to get wine for his congregation for the Sabbath and for the Holy Days, and if I tell him I want it for my little girl . . .'"

Abe took a step forward, furious.

"You have the gall to call me a liar?" he growled. "You religious fanatics are all alike. I come to you with a simple request, a little wine so that I can make a Friday night blessing for my little girl, and what do you do? You spit in my face!"

"You spit on your people and your religion," said the rabbi, his voice rising as well. "You come here because you can't get drunk legally anymore, so you think you'll maybe come and take advantage of the stupid, unworldly rabbi?" He also took a step forward, so that he was almost nose-to-nose with Abe. "You think I am some kind of idiot?"

Abe didn't retreat. "I know you get more wine than you need," he shouted. "I know how this goes. The authorities give you so much per person, so maybe you exaggerate the size of your congregation just a bit, hah? And sell the rest?"

The rabbi shrugged. "And what if I do?" he said. "Does this look like the shul of a rich bootlegger? I have greenhorns fresh off the boat who are trying to support large families, men who are trying to get their wives and children here, boys whose families can't afford to buy them a prayer book for their bar mitzvah. And you, the radical, somebody who makes speeches about the rights of poor people, you would criticize me for selling a few extra bottles of wine?"

"And so if you're willing to sell wine," yelled Abe, "why not sell it to me, a fellow Jew, rather than some goyishe bootlegger?"

There was a pause, and both men stared at each other, breathing hard. "Because he doesn't know any better," the rabbi finally said. "You should. Now get out of my shul."

Abe strode out, muttering, and headed down the block. After about five blocks, he had walked off his anger, and he slowed down, finally sitting heavily on the steps of a nearby stoop. "I'm sorry, Malka," he said. "Maybe I can go find the people that the rabbi sells to . . ."

"But David said his father could get us the wine," said Malka, sitting next to him. "David said that his father and his friends, they have a drugstore where they sell hooch to people who want them. Lots of hooch," she repeated the word, seeming pleased at its grown-up sound.

Abe grinned. "Malka, my sweet little girl," he said, "do you know what your mother would have done to me had she known that her baby was dealing in illegal alcohol? And by the way, I like your friend David. Very polite child."

"He's not a child," Malka objected. "He's almost thirteen!"

"Ah. Practically a man," said Abe, stroking his chin. "So. And his father, the bootlegger—he would sell to someone not of his race?"

"Well, of course," said Malka, a little unsure herself. The question hadn't occurred to her. "David said that they were looking for somebody to buy the kosher wine, and who else to sell it to but somebody who can really use it?"

Even from the outside, the candy store didn't look promising—or even open. The windows were pasted over with ads, some of which were peeling off; when Malka and her father looked through the glass, shading their eyes with one hand, it was too dark inside to see much.

"You stay out here," her father finally said. "This is not a place for little girls." He took a breath and pushed the door open. A tiny bell tinkled as he stepped through; Malka, too curious to obey, quietly went in after him and stood by the door, trying to make herself as small as possible.

The store looked as unfriendly inside as it did out. A long counter, which had obviously once been used to serve sodas and ice cream, ran along the right wall of the store; it was empty and streaked with dust, and the shelves behind it were bare except for a few glasses. At the back of the store, there was a display case in which a few cans and dry-looking cakes sat.

The rest of the small space was taken up by several round tables. Only one was occupied, and it was partially obscured by a haze of cigarette smoke. Malka squinted: Three men sat there, playing cards. One was short and fat, with the darkest skin Malka had ever seen; he scowled at the cards while a cigarette hung from the corner of his mouth. A second, much younger and slimmer, was carefully dressed in a brown suit with a red tie; he had a thin mustache, and his hair was slicked back so that it looked, Malka thought, like it was always wet.

The third man, she decided, must be David's father. He had David's long, thin face and slight build, but the humor that was always dancing in David's wide eyes had long ago disappeared from his. A long, pale scar ran from his left eye to the corner of his mouth, intensifying his look of a man who wasn't to be trifled with. As she watched, he reached into his pocket and pulled out a small flask. He took a pull and replaced it without taking his eyes off his cards.

Malka's father waited for a minute or two, and then cleared his throat.

None of the three looked up. "I think you're in the wrong store, white man," the fat man said.

Malka's father put his hands in his pockets. "I was told that I could purchase a bottle or two of wine here."

"You a Fed?" asked the man with slicked-back hair. "Only a Fed would be stupid enough to walk in here by himself."

"Ain't no Fed," the fat man said. "Listen to him. He's a Jew. Ain't no Fed Jews."

"There's Izzy Einstein," said the man with the hair. "He arrested three guys in Coney just yesterday. I read it in the paper."

"Too skinny to be Izzy Einstein," said the fat man. "Nah, he's just your everyday, ordinary white man who's looking for some cheap booze."

"I was told I could buy wine here," repeated Malka's father calmly, although Malka could see that his hands, which he kept in his pockets, were trembling. "I was told you had kosher wine."

The man with the scar stood and came over as the other two watched. Now Malka could see that his suit was worn and not as clean as it could be;

he walked slowly, carefully, as though he knew he wasn't sober and didn't want to give it away. When he reached Malka's father, he stopped and waited. He didn't acknowledge the boy who followed him solicitously, as though ready to catch his father should he fall.

Malka grinned and waved. "Hi, David," she said, and then, aware that she might be calling attention to herself, whispered, "I didn't see you before."

David put his finger to his lips and shook his head.

"So?" Malka's father asked. "You have wine for sale?"

"My landlord is a Jew," said David's father, challenging.

"So's mine. And I'll bet they're both sons of bitches."

There was a moment of silence. Malka held her breath. And then one corner of the man's mouth twitched. "Okay," he said. "Maybe we can do business." His two colleagues relaxed; the man with the hair swept up the cards and began shuffling them. "Where did you hear about me?"

"Your son David, here," said Malka's father. "He suggested I contact you."

"My son David told you," the man repeated, his eyes narrowing.

"Yes," Malka's father said, sounding puzzled. "Earlier today. Is there a problem?"

There was a pause, and then the man shook his head. "No, no problem. Yeah, I've got some of that kosher wine you were talking about. I can give you two bottles for three dollars each."

Malka's father took a breath. "That's expensive."

"Those are the prices." The man shrugged. "Hard to get specialized product these days."

David stood on his toes and whispered up at his father. The man didn't look down at the boy, but bit his lip, then said, "Okay. I can give you the two bottles for five dollars. And that's because you come with a—a family recommendation."

"Done," said Malka's father. He put out a hand. "Abe Hirsch."

David's father took his hand. "Sam Richards," he said. "You want to pick your merchandise up in the morning?"

Abe shook his head. "I've got to work early," he said. "Can I pick it up after work?"

"Done," Sam said.

Malka's father turned and walked toward the door, then turned back. "I apologize," he said, shaking his head. "I am an idiot. David, your son, has been invited to my house for dinner tomorrow night, and I have not asked his father's permission. And of course, you are also invited as well."

Sam stared at him. "You invited my son to your house for dinner?"

Abe shrugged.

"Hey, Sam," called the well-dressed man, "you can't go nowhere tomorrow night. We've got some business to take care of uptown at the Sugar Cane."

Sam ignored his friend and looked at Malka, who stood next to her father, scratching an itch on her leg and grinning at the success of her plan. "This your little girl?"

It was Abe's turn to stare. He looked down at Malka, who was nodding wildly, delighted at the idea of another guest at their Sabbath meal. He then looked back at Sam.

"Okay," said Sam. "What time?"

"Around five P.M.," Abe said, and gave the address.

"We don't have to be uptown until nine," Sam said to his friend. "Plenty of time."

He turned back to Malka's father. "Okay. I'll bring the wine with me. But you make sure you have the money. Just because you're feeding me—us— dinner don't mean the drinks come free."

"Of course," said Abe.

At five P.M. the next evening, everything was ready. The table had been pulled away from the window and decorated with a white tablecloth (from the same woman who'd sold Abe a boiled chicken and a carrot tsimmes), settings for four, two extra chairs (borrowed from the carpenter who lived across the hall), two candles, and, at Abe's place, his father's old prayer book.

Abe, wearing his good jacket despite the heat, and with a borrowed yarmulke perched on his head, surveyed the scene. "Well, Malka?" he asked. "How does that look?"

"It's perfect!" said Malka, running from one end of the room to the other to admire the table from different perspectives.

Almost on cue, somebody knocked on the door. "It's David!" Malka yelled. "David, just a minute!"

"I'm sure he heard you," said Abe, smiling. "The super in the basement probably heard you." He walked over and opened the door.

Sam stood there, a small suitcase in his hand. He had obviously made some efforts toward improving his personal appearance: he was freshly shaven, wore a clean shirt, and had a spit-polish on his shoes.

David dashed out from behind his father. "You see!" he told Malka. "Everything worked out. My daddy brought the wine like he said, and I made him dress up, because I said it was going to be religious, and Mama wouldn't have let him come to church all messed up. Right, Daddy?"

"You sure did, David," said Sam, smiling. "Even made me wash behind my ears." He then raised his eyes and looked hard at Abe, as if waiting to be challenged.

But Abe only nodded.

"Please sit down," he said. "Be comfortable. Malka, stop dancing around like that; you're making me dizzy."

Malka obediently stopped twirling, but she still bounced a bit in place. "David, guess what? There's a lady who lives across the alley from us who, when it's hot, walks around all day in a man's T-shirt and shorts. You can see her when she's in the kitchen. It's really funny. You want to come out on the fire escape and watch?"

David suddenly looked troubled and stared up at his father. "Is it okay, Daddy?" he asked. His lower lip trembled. "I don't want to get anyone mad at me."

Sam took a breath and, with an obvious effort, smiled at his son. "It's okay," he said. "I'll be right here, keeping an eye on you. Nothing bad will happen."

David's face brightened, and he turned to Malka. "Let's go," he said. The two children ran to the window and clambered noisily onto the fire escape.

Sam put the suitcase on one of the chairs, opened it, and took out two bottles of wine. "Here they are," he said. "Certified kosher, according to the man I got it from. You got the five bucks?"

Abe handed Sam five crumpled dollars. "Here you are," he said, "as promised. You want a drink before we start?"

Sam nodded.

Abe picked up one of the bottles, looked at it for a moment, and then shook his head, exasperated. "Look at me, the genius," he said. "I never thought about a corkscrew."

Sam shrugged, took a small pocketknife out of his pocket, cut off the top of the cork, and pushed the rest into the bottle with his thumb. Abe took the bottle and poured generous helpings for both of them.

They each took a drink and looked outside, where Malka and David sat on the edge of the fire escape, her legs dangling over the side, his legs folded. A dirty pigeon fluttered down onto the railing and stared at the children, obviously hoping for a stray crumb. When none came, it started to clean itself.

David pointed to a window. "No, that's not her," said Malka. "That's the man who lives next door to her. He has two dogs, and he's not supposed to have any pets, so he's always yelling at the dogs to stop barking, or he'll get kicked out." The children laughed. Startled, the bird flew away.

"So," said Abe.

"Yeah," said Sam.

"What happened?"

Sam took a breath, drained his glass, and poured another. "He had gone out to shoot rabbits," he said slowly. "I had just got home from the trenches.

We were living with my wife's family in Alabama, and we were making plans to move up north to Chicago, where I could get work and David could get schooled better. He was sitting on the porch reading, and I got mad and told him not to be so lazy, get out there and shoot us some meat for dinner. When he wasn't home by supper, I figured he got himself lost—he was always going off exploring and forgetting about what he was supposed to do."

He looked off into the distance. "After dark, the preacher from my wife's church came by and said that there had been trouble. A white woman over in the next county had complained that somebody had looked in her window when she was undressed. A lynch mob went out, and David saw them, got scared and ran. He wasn't doing anything wrong, but he was a Negro boy with a gun, and they caught him and . . ."

He choked for a moment, then reached for his glass and swallowed the entire thing at a gulp. Wordlessly, Abe refilled it.

"My wife and her sister and the other women, they went and took him down and brought him home. He was . . . They had cut him and burned him and . . . My boy. My baby."

A single tear slowly made its way down Sam's cheek, tracing the path of the scar.

"My wife and I—we didn't get along so good after that. After a while I cut and run, came up here. And David, he came with me."

For a moment, they just sat.

"We lived in Odessa," said Abe, and, when Sam looked confused, added, "That's a city in the Ukraine, near Russia. I moved there with the baby after my wife died. It was 1905, and there was a lot of unrest. Strikes, riots, people being shot down in the streets. Many people were angry. And when people get angry, they blame the Jews."

He smiled sourly. "I and my friends, we were young and strong and rebellious. We were different from the generations before us. We weren't going to sit around like the old men and wait to be slaughtered. I sent Malka to the synagogue with other children. There were hiding places there; they would be safe. And I went to help defend our homes."

"At least you had that," Sam said bitterly.

Abe shook his head. "We were idiots. We had no idea how many there would be, how organized. Hundreds were hurt and killed, my neighbors, my friends. Somebody hit me, I don't know who or with what. I don't remember what happened after that. I . . ."

He paused. "I do remember screaming and shouting all around me, houses burning, but it didn't seem real, didn't seem possible. I ran to the synagogue. I was going to get Malka, and we would leave this madness, go to America where people were sane, and children were safe."

"Safe," repeated Sam softly. The two men looked at each other with tired recognition.

"But when I got there, they wouldn't let me in. The rabbi had hidden the children behind the bima, the place where the Torah was kept, but . . . They said I shouldn't see what had been done to her, that she had been . . . She was only nine years old." Abe's voice trailed away.

The children out on the fire escape had become bored with the neighbors. "Do you know how to play Rock, Paper, Scissors?" David asked. "Here, we have to face each other. Now there are three ways you can hold your hand . . ."

"Does she know?" asked Sam.

"No," said Abe. "And I don't have the heart to tell her."

"David knows," said Sam. "At least, I told him. I thought maybe if he knew, he'd be at rest. But I don't think he believed me. And—well, I'm sort of glad. Because it means . . ."

"He is still here. With you."

"Yes," Sam whispered.

The two men sat and drank while they watched their murdered children play in the fading sunlight.

# THE TRINITITE GOLEM

## Sonya Taaffe

It is easy to destroy a life. Take thirteen and a half pounds of $\delta$-phase plutonium-239, stabilized by alloying with gallium at three percent molar weight and hot-pressed into solid hemispheres of slightly more than nine centimeters in diameter; electroplate with galvanic silver to reduce chemical reactivity and encase within a seven-centimeter tamper of neutron-reflecting uranium-238. Enclose within another spherical shell, a shock reflector of aluminum eleven and a half centimeters thick—some admixture of boron prevents the scattering of spontaneous fission neutrons from the tamper back into the pit. Place the whole assembly at the center of thirty-two hexagonal and pentagonal lenses of high explosive, tripartite blocks interlocking in the pattern of a soccer ball—each two-thirds high-velocity Composition B and one-third slower Baratol—and ring with explosive-bridgewire detonators whose shockwave converging on the plutonium pit will compress it, crushing the fragile gold-and-nickel urchin of the neutron initiator at its center and releasing, from the instantaneous mixing of polonium-210 and beryllium-9 and the bombardment of the latter's atoms by the alpha particles of the former, the nanosecond-pouring stream of neutrons that will trigger a chain reaction in the supercritical plutonium. Thirty meters over the sands of the Jornada del Muerto, the fireball ruptures the sky like a second sun. Five hundred meters above wood-framed houses, cathedral spires, cloud-covered steep hills, only shadows remain.

\* \* \*

174

It is easy to destroy a life. Take one theoretical physicist who has not published a paper in four years, who a dozen years ago made himself over into a director and administrator as thoroughly and ruthlessly as he once metamorphosed a misfit rock collector from Riverside Drive into a mesmerizing polymath with quotations in nine languages at his Chesterfield-callused fingertips, the benefit being the A-bomb, the cost being all the rest of his concentration, and then in open court and the public eye strip him of all authority and trust. A brilliant and distractable, self-despairing and ambitious man, tailor his cross-examination to his frailties and insecurities, his fracturing discomfort in his own taut skin: show him that he is unreliable, unstable, artificial, found out, no better for marriage and the Manhattan Project and all those covers of *Time* and *Life* and *Physics Today* than the tightly strung student his friends used to find collapsed in a depressive heap on Cambridge floors, and when he falls back on the pose of a victim, make all of the helplessness and none of the sympathy stick. It is not as clean-cut as martyrdom, Galileo-like though he will look. He was important, inventing the atomic age, arrogant with his creation as well as appalled; he gave up names to the same McCarthyist frenzy that now sweeps him over. Revoke his security clearance. The process will take about four weeks. For thirteen years after, he will speak about nuclear proliferation and write on science and ethics and oversee the researches of others at the Institute for Advanced Study, he will receive medals from two presidents, he will sail the peacock-bright waters of Hawksnest Bay and recite the *Odyssey* softly to the night, and contemporaries and historians will agree that something broke in him that spring of 1954, beyond healing or repair; he will not fight back. He will die of diffidence and five packs a day, a thin spiral of sand-white smoke finally burning out.

For some weeks after the hearing, he had known he was being followed. He was not surprised; he knew the joke about paranoia. Letters had been pouring in for days, some spiteful and vindictive, others aghast and supportive, the rare handful from friends that he was glad to read and the phone ringing off the hook until he hoped it was still tapped and giving someone in the FBI a headache. Surveillance swirled around him like a cloud of ash, a soft stain on the fingers of anyone who touched him. He watched the slight figure in the trenchcoat hanging back from the students on the station platform and the maple-lined bricks of Fuld Hall and did not wonder if it was a reporter or a gawker or a G-2 man; he could not see what difference it could make anymore, the last aftershock of plaster rattling down after the building's collapse. There were no more guards outside his office door like angels at the gates of knowledge, no more Washington on the line, no more classified papers and no more safe to store them in. He chain-smoked, read *Newsweek*, thought about St. Croix. If the watcher followed him home, down the dawning summer shade of Olden Lane to solemn-eyed Toni and Peter with his chalk-scrawling protests and fierce, brittle Kitty turning a martini glass between her hands as though it were just the strength of Teller's neck, he did not see it.

He saw it in late June, standing quietly in his office where the half-raised blinds made white cross-hatches of the morning light. At first he wondered if he was seeing some kind of eccentric prank, a coat rack from another office or a mannequin from some department store in town scarecrow-dressed in a tightly belted trenchcoat and a soft hat pulled down far enough to camouflage its absence of face, but he could not imagine who at the Institute would try something so pointless and juvenile, or to what end. He was a restless man, nerves ticking in the absentminded click of teeth or cigarette-worrying fingers; he was not given to jumping at shadows or unwanted guests, only the inside of his own head. He said sharply, "Are you here to audition for a part in this farce?"

In the silence, he heard for the first time the faint turntable hiss, the staticky nail-scratch of a Geiger counter registering only a little more radiation in the room than the background presence of a sleeping body. He could not hear breathing. The pulse in his wrists was suddenly quick as the blood in his ears, a clear cold shock that was not surprise. The figure by the window, as haloed by summer haze as a gunman by shadows in a gangster film, said, "I have been a long time looking for you."

If it had spoken in any language other than English, or sounded anything other than tired and a little like some of the voices he had known as a child at the Ethical Culture School, he thought afterward that he might have left the room then, as carefully and steadily as a man who knows he is undergoing a breakdown, picked up his hat and walked out across the lawns until either the trees or a passing scholar stopped him; he would have had no idea what to say. If he had seen, as it raised its face to him, the charred blood of Nagasaki ground zero or the throat of Shiva Nīlakaṇtha, poison-blue as a cloudless New Mexico sky—if it had been his own face, heavy-lidded, tight-haired, its fragile ascetic look aged as sharply as radiation sickness under the comfortable brown brim of his pork-pie hat. He saw a human face in glass as green and foamy as a breaking wave, hollowing the light against itself like jade. It was no one's he recognized, Pompeii-cast from the melted sands; its owner shifted its weight a little in the slatted light, the first unconscious movement he had seen it make, and he saw a hard-traveled man with quick dark brows, a mouth that might have been humorous if it had not held itself in so hard, eyes as green as the rim of a bottle of Coca-Cola.

Yiddish, he thought, as forthright Rabi, who had once asked him *why not the Talmud?* with all the argumentative assurance of an atheist from the Lower East Side who could nevertheless call a row of Orthodox men at prayer *my people* and introduce himself in prewar Germany with the unflinching *ich bin ein Aus-Jude*, and he knew then what his visitor was.

The golem said in its unremarkable voice, "Undo me."

He was neither mad nor dreaming, the desk under his hand as real as the cigarette forgotten between his fingers and the phantom of a Geiger–Müller tube still crackling its faint caution. Oppenheimer said, "I can't."

"None of the others can. That leaves you." He saw the burnt desert flicker again as the golem smiled, a sunset-green flash. It reminded him a little of Feynman, except that it did not, at all. Its voice was light with irony: "Destroyer of worlds."

He could smile a little himself, thinly. "At present, the world appears to be surviving me."

"Yes." The golem, taking one step forward, was abruptly on the other side of his desk, swift as a shockwave; its hands were still in its pockets, its hat pushed back only enough to see. "So. Don't let me."

The plaster falling, which was the last weight of the building after all. As suddenly and hopelessly as nausea, he wanted never again to be asked for anything, names or dates, admissions, miracles, unless it was Peter for some electrical gimmick or Toni for a hug, no accountabilities, no decisions, nothing. Carefully, steadily as he had imagined himself walking out of his life, he said, "It can't be done. Any more than the bomb can be un-dropped, or the atom un-split." He could not swear it was the truth, if he could take five minutes with a rock hammer and reduce an existential dilemma to a janitor's problem, put a green-eyed man on the next train to Nevada to wait for the countdown at Yucca Flats, but in Washington he had grown tired of talk of genies and bottles; he was thinking of the sky boiling at five-thirty in the morning, Bainbridge's handshake. *Now we are all sons of bitches.* He would not ask if the golem had pulled itself out of the glittering crater that night or some day long after, where it had learned to look as human as anything else born in the fallout age; he saw it riding the rails, Geiger-clicking its nights away in bus stations and hotel lobbies, one more drifter in the bright streets of tomorrow. His shoulders were stiff and slumped as if he sat on the old leather couch in Room 2022, waiting to be told how he had lied. He could take nothing back. He said softly, "I am afraid that kind of thing is out of my pay grade just now," and remembered to brush the ash from his cigarette just before it scarred the wood.

The golem said above him, "You don't have to go on living."

Automatically and testily as if it had said something idiotic about Sanskrit or Baudelaire, he snapped back, "Of course I do."

He was quiet, then. He had not thought it was true.

There was a breeze beyond the windows, ruffling the last of the dogwood blossom. The golem must have made another one of its fast-tracked, soundless movements; he registered that it had taken a cigarette from the half-empty pack on his desk, but by the time he reached instinctively for his lighter, it was already exhaling smoke. He thought of a hot white spark burning in its palm like the smallest of suns, but then he would have been dead already, like Slotin with his screwdriver, the sour taste of hard radiation in his mouth.

"You have that choice," it said gently. "I wasn't asked."

He could say nothing to the golem. He did not want to claim its existence or its undoing; he was not Rabi or even Einstein and had never known, never wanted to know the mysticism his parents' generation had shed long before they spoke more French at home than German and named their son for a father still alive. Prometheus was one thing, Rabbi Loew another. *This thing of darkness*—but Prospero had broken his staff of his own free will.

When he met the golem's eyes again, they were brighter than he had thought: copper salts in a flame test, a smoked-glass sunrise. Its cigarette was half gone, smoke curling about its shoulders like winter steam. He did not want to ask the question. He did not think it would lie to him.

"Why?"

As if it were taking polite leave of a colleague, the golem tipped its hat.

He saw its springing dark hair, as brushy as his own in the Trinity days; he thought, as distantly as if it mattered, that it looked younger, hatless, and more Jewish, and less like anyone he had ever known. He saw the letters on its forehead, torch-cuts of white fire writing מת, מת, and nowhere to smear out death or write the truth back in. He could not hear the noise of the Geiger counter anymore, only a dull roar billowing like the backwash of a vast tide and small popping clinks that might have been falling metal, broken blown glass, and he was less afraid than he had been every day of April in Building T-3, because the damage was already done, and more than the day after Trinity, because he had not known what it would be. There were cities burning, but he had known about those; islands, forests, children. The golem walked through blackened landscapes, carrying nothing, saving no one. It sat in hospital waiting rooms, its hat on its knee, as gravely speaking doctors passed charts and X-rays back and forth. It stood on a catwalk, looking down into a silvery plutonium swirl. It stood in the high cold air of a mesa, watching the silent fusion of the stars.

Undeniable as atoms, a pillar of sea-green glinting Alamogordo glass, the golem replaced its hat. Something in the room went out.

It was quiet in his office, at ten o'clock on a morning in June; it was not empty, with his books and letters and the sounds of mathematical conversation passing his door, and he heard a great silent space in between every heartbeat, after every breath. His throat was burning, as if he had breathed in a desert-blast of heat; his fingers, too, as if he had tried after all to write something in that glassy fire; when he reached for the half-cigarette smoldering in the ashtray, he found himself staring at his hand, thin muscles and wire-tendons, nails bitten down to their nicotine stains, frail as a shadow on the tabletop. It opened and tensed, aging, alive. After a moment, he used it to pick up the cigarette, and then a pen. He wondered what the FBI would make of the conversation—the disgraced scientist answering himself like a vaudeville act, or the soft white silence of blank tape, unspooling inch after inch of empty air until some bored G-man wondered if the microphone was broke? Or just a voice, weary and audible and mostly New York, just as they might see a slight man in a trenchcoat walking down Einstein Drive, waiting for the Dinky at the Princeton stop with his hands in his pockets, the sun in his sand-bright eyes. He would not see his golem again, he thought. It is easy to destroy a life; it is the things that come of living that are harder to kill.


We have an A-bomb and a whole series of it, and what more do you want, mermaids?
    —Isidor Isaac Rabi (1954)

# TWO BRIGHT VENUSES

## *Alex Dally MacFarlane*

**Year 1 inferior Venus sets on Shabatu 15 and after three days rises on Shabatu 18.**

Inferior Irunn sent the first transcription of inferior Venus's voice to superior Irunn a week after launch, adding, "It gets louder every day. What do you hear?"

The reply wasn't immediate.

Inferior Irunn sat strapped into the console chair of her spacecraft, watching inferior Venus. It grew in her screen. Overlaid data on the left and right sides of the screen showed her craft's speed (as expected), trajectory (on target), summary updates on superior Irunn's craft (on target to superior Venus), solar panel status (powering well), life-support system status (no surprises), summary readouts from the fifteen instruments already examining inferior Venus (steadily collecting data), transmissions from ground control (none new), global news updates (she had stopped caring as soon as she launched and her ears filled with inferior Venus). In the centre: inferior Venus as seen by the naked eye. The screen allowed her to enhance it, to see the planet up close across the electromagnetic spectrum. She preferred to wait.

It shone bigger and brighter than in any terrestrial sighting, but it was not yet a planet, not yet filling her screen.

To be the first to see its size, its white-yellow skies—

180

Inferior Irunn slept every night-cycle in her chair, closed her eyes in the console lights and drifted into dreams, and woke to that bright, glowing light.

The reply from superior Irunn arrived. "How did you write it? I tried—it falls apart; I can't use words for it." And an admission: "I'm glad it's not just me. I started worrying . . ."

Inferior Irunn paused, unsure, before replying, "I listened. I wrote. I—it felt like Venus wrote, like my hand was its input screen." Saying it frightened her.

It took a long time, far longer than the currently tiny time lag in transmissions between their two spacecraft, for superior Irunn's reply: "I don't think I want to try writing it again."

"I don't think," inferior Irunn said, "I can *not* write it. It fills me." She stopped.

Silence from superior Irunn.

Inferior Irunn left her chair to do the day's exercises, to eat, to manually check the algae banks that extended the oxygen tanks' lifespan, to look at Earth through a small screen. It was pretty. Inferior Venus sang in her ears.

### Year 5 superior Venus vanishes E on Kislimu 27 and after two months, three days appears W on Shabatu 30.

Two spacecraft, two trajectories to two bright Venuses.

Superior Irunn remembered being Irunn and drinking the air of the two Venuses in a two-chambered, two-tongued bottle, hearing a voice like yellow clouds as she swallowed.

Two pilots, precisely paired like the planets.

The Babylonian astrologers had thought they observed one planet when they wrote their observations about superior and inferior Venus in the reign of King Ammisaduqa in the seventeenth century BCE. The Greeks had been less sure. Only the work of Arab scholars in Aleppo and Baghdad had determined the true nature of Venus: two Venuses sharing the same orbit, two worlds of identical size. The astrolabes of the legendary Mariam Al-Ijliya in the tenth century CE were the first to depict the two Venuses in solid gold and gilt, bright as those bodies in the sunrise and sunset skies. The names superior Venus and inferior Venus were taken from the ancient Babylonian tablets excavated and translated by Baghdad scholars. It took centuries of fine-tuning to understand the co-orbital configuration of the Venuses. It took the entire nineteenth and twentieth centuries to determine how to send a crewed mission. Probes sent alone and to only one planet stopped functioning at the exosphere. Distant flybys sent back inconsistent data. Hao Yiting, a scientist in Shanghai, had a theory. At the height of its funding in the first half of the twentieth century, the Chinese Space Agency sent two probes, superior Dongfang Shuo and inferior Dongfang Shuo, coordinated to arrive at the two Venuses at the same time. Hao Yiting's theory proved true: the probes collected data and samples of the Venusian air. Together, the space agencies of China and Baghdad created the crewed mission.

Creating paired people took years.

To drink the air of two Venuses, to split into two people—that was successful. To stay sane was not. Irunn was the first.

Superior Irunn reread inferior Irunn's transcription: *yellow low in leaving skies, your—*

She swiped the screen empty. It unsettled her. It was wrong: What she heard was not words, not translatable, not even transcribable unless she wrote a series of sounds unlike any language she knew—not the Norwegian of her first years, not the Shanghainese and Mandarin she had learned to live with her Chinese relatives in Shanghai and get sex reassignment surgery there, not the Arabic she had learned in the Chinese Space Agency astronaut program. The sound of superior Venus filled her ears, as constant as the whirs and clicks of the spacecraft. She could try to learn it. She shuddered.

"This is what destroyed the first probes," she said to herself, staring at the transmit icon. She should talk to inferior Irunn. She should talk to ground control. "This is what made even the Dongfang Shuo data difficult."

She wanted to see Venus. She always had—she had joined the astronaut program to walk on another world, any world, anything to get to space—and now superior Venus sang her to it. Ground control might recall the mission if they feared for her survival.

She stayed silent.

The growing glow of superior Venus lit her as she slept.

**Year 9 inferior Venus sets on Adar 12 and after two days rises on Adar 14.**

"What worries me," superior Irunn said, unexpectedly, "is that we're hearing different songs or sounds or—"

Inferior Irunn looked up from her fourth transcription, her longest yet: started as six lines that repeated at least hourly. It had developed over the week. Only a week? Inferior Irunn glanced at the date on her left screen. A week and a day. Superior Irunn's face overlaid the date. It had been six days since they spoke of anything other than the standard updates.

"What do you hear?" inferior Irunn asked.

"Sounds." Distress folded superior Irunn's mouth. "I can't write it! It's like—"

Over a hundred and sixty lines now. Inferior Irunn wondered where to stop it. The six lines repeated throughout the transcription, ordering the other lines. Some of those were starting to repeat.

"That's the problem," superior Irunn said, calmer. "It's like no noise I've heard. It's too—you know how when a noise is so loud, you *feel* it? Your whole body feels the vibrations in your bones?"

"Yes."

"I feel that, but far more complex than someone playing a song too loud. How can you write a sound like that?"

"It's not—"

If inferior Irunn wrote a thousand lines, would she be close to seeing the full pattern? She swiped it aside to think about what superior Irunn had said.

"It's not like that for me," she said. "I don't feel it in my bones."

"I feel it on my skin, too," superior Irunn said. "I feel like I'm an instrument, being played."

"Like I'm keys," inferior Irunn said, "or an old brush being used to write. You know how writing is very visual? Beautiful writing, that is, not briefing lists or tests. The best poetry uses the right words and multiple meanings and builds it up into imagery, yes, and it uses the image, the shape of the poem. Seeing the shape of what I'm writing is making me understand it better. I think."

"Huh."

"Maybe," inferior Irunn said after a pause, "you need to dance what you're hearing."

"In zero gravity?" superior Irunn asked, grinning. "I'm not good even on the ground." They laughed as close together as the time lag allowed.

The grin gave inferior Irunn a feeling of discomfort at seeing herself, but not herself. It quickly slid away.

"I'm not a poet," she said. *I'm. We're.* "I can constantly see it, sort of. My eyesight is fine"—one of the numerous tests they had been subjected to after swallowing the air of the Venuses, after splitting—"but how I hear it is shaped."

"This is strange," superior Irunn said, and the grin was gone. "The Venuses sound different, but—" She looked at something on one of her screens. "The Venuses *are* different. We know that. We know their topography is different, with the same types of features—farra, novae, coronae, and a few craters— in unique arrangements." Inferior Irunn remembered the images from the Dongfang Shuo mission. "Their atmospheres contain the same gases and the same layers, but their cloud formations vary. If life evolved on both Venuses—" Superior Irunn's mouth closed like a door.

Inferior Irunn hadn't considered that she was transcribing the transmissions of Venusian life.

"When do we tell ground control about this?" superior Irunn asked.

"When we're there," inferior Irunn said, thinking of being ordered to return—of being unable to hear Venus. "When we know if it's life or, well, the planet?" It sounded laughable to say it, but superior Irunn only smiled in soft understanding.

"Or both," superior Irunn said. Then, after silence stretched between them like a beam of light, "Look, let's record some of this now, both of us, your transcriptions and both of our thoughts, and if something happens to us, if the computers register our vital signs stopping, it's automatically sent to Baghdad and Beijing?"

"Yes," inferior Irunn said after only a few seconds' thought.

The inter-craft channel went quiet.

As inferior Irunn created a potentially public packet of ideas and transcription copies, the song swelled. She wrote, *flee farra-floor flood, dry drowning, dead-free.* Frowned. No. Perhaps: *dead-free: fled dry drowning, farra-floor flood.* No.


### Year 10 superior Venus vanishes E on Arahsamnu 17 and after one month, twenty-five days appears W on Tebetu 12.

"The data your craft have taken on your approaches match in broad strokes the data from the Dongfang Shuo mission," ground control said. "We are therefore most interested in your mission's primary objective: to send you into the atmospheres and, ultimately, to the surfaces." A thrill lingered on superior Irunn's spine like superior Venus's song. "We are in agreement that you should follow the descent plan to arrive at a distant orbit of your Venus, establish continued complete operation of your spacecraft, and, if it is safe, descend to the lower mesosphere." The technical details of the descent plan appeared beside the small faces of ground control on the transmit screen: calculated projections of altitudes, wind speeds, spacecraft speeds, engine use, fuel consumption.

The word *safe* fell like acid from the transmit screen.

The sound of Venus stratiformed over superior Irunn's fingers. "Yes," she said. "I can confirm the descent plan."

After the time lag she heard inferior Irunn say the same.

"Thank you for your regular reports," ground control said. With friendly smiles: "Doing well up there?"

Venus cumuliforming across her chest—

"Oh, you know," she said, cheerful, "it's all the same: every day I do my exercises, look at the data, watch superior Venus get bigger." Venus a virga over her vertebrae— "I'm looking forward to getting a look under its clouds."

Inferior Irunn said, time-lagged, "I spend a lot of time looking at inferior Venus. It's very . . . I'm glad we're going straight in. I want to see it."

Ground control signed off soon afterwards. Superior Irunn sat in her chair, song-struck. Venus on her bones. Venus a non-cessation of clouds, a memory of movement across its surface—on her skin—and gases falling into space like hair's straggling stream in zero gravity. Heat rising like last breaths. Bones like powder on her cheeks.

Superior Irunn drifted in dream and dead-falling, with the weight of superior Venus's memories around her waist.

Waking, she accessed paper after paper on the possibilities of life on the Venuses. Extremophile single-celled or simple multicellular organisms on the dry surface. Acidophiles in the sulphuric acid clouds. Life absorbing ultraviolet light. Life beyond current scientific comprehension. Love poetry from seventeenth-century Damascus described the lakes on the Venuses, the lovers swimming in each: superior lover and inferior lover, gazing into the cloud-parted sky at the other Venus, longing to swim-cross the space between them. Clouds on superior Irunn's clenched fists—

She gasped into the ebbing silence of her spacecraft.


**Year 11 inferior Venus sets on Illulu 25 and after sixteen days rises on II Illulu 11.**

Inferior Irunn wrote,

> *drift in no-dark, no-depth, forever falling: dead-free*
> *fled dry drowning, farra-floor flood: dead-falling*

She slid the sentences to one side. She wrote,

> *dead-falling, dead-free:*
> *drift free of old farra, old forms*

The paired lines, plausible and inaccurate all at once, confused her. She had heard both. Neither looked true.

Her transcription had stalled at six hundred lines.

Patterns spread through it like pulses of sound, like a sculpture of precise peaks—then it fell apart. It failed to convey what she heard. Discarded sentences could fill a whole screen. Her confidence sagged. Perhaps the sounds of inferior Venus were changing as she got closer to it, perhaps the sounds were damaging her ears—or her sight—and affecting what she wrote. Tests, however, suggested it wasn't that.

"Perhaps the chaos is the point now," she said, just to hear a different sound.

The discarded sentences, gathered together, looked like tearing. Part of an atmosphere dispersing into space. Inferior Irunn arranged and rearranged until her eyes hurt.

She appended the repeating six lines to this section, rewriting rather than copying. She needed a rest.

She couldn't stop the sounds: *old sounds, old song-grounds—*

When inferior Irunn woke, she reread her work. She compared the repeating six lines to earlier copies, just to check, and gaped: they differed. Subtly, in two words. She knew those words, knew them like her console's curve, couldn't write them wrong, and she had heard them before she rewrote them. Heard them as she had immediately written them. Hadn't she? It had to be a copyist's error—

Couldn't it *all* be a copyist's error?

Inferior Irunn stared at that growing yellow-tinged sphere and swiped all her transcriptions into storage.

"Exactly six days until we arrive," she said to superior Irunn, who—some minutes later—replied that her screen told her the same.

### Year 15 superior Venus vanishes E on Abu 26 and after two months appears W on Tashritu 26.

Superior Venus glowed. Superior Irunn watched clouds move across its high atmosphere: swirling pale, swift patterns. The sounds of superior Venus played across her skin.

"Exactly one Earth day until we arrive," inferior Irunn said.

Together they ran checks. Outer shielding: still intact, self-repairs of micrometeorite damage successfully completed, safe to enter the hot, churning, acidic atmosphere of Venus. Radiation levels: safely low. Oxygen: the tanks, accounting for ongoing algae oxygen-production, were still supplied for a month on Venus and the return to Earth. Fuel: no unexpected adjustments en route had ensured the tanks held enough fuel to control the crafts' movements in Venus's atmosphere, escape its gravity well multiple times and return to Earth. Water and food: sufficient supply remaining. Instruments: all reading and recording accurately.

"We're going to see under Venus's clouds," inferior Irunn said.

"And hear," superior Irunn said.

"Yes." A pained look.

"We should record it," superior Irunn said, surprising even herself by voicing a thought she had found too uncomfortable to hold for long.

Inferior Irunn's face shifted into surprise minutes later. Their conversations went slowly now, with the increased time lag. By the time inferior Irunn spoke, superior Irunn still didn't regret speaking.

"Record the sounds? Transcribe? Or—dance?"

"Record with our instruments, if they detect anything," superior Irunn said. So far what she understood of their data hadn't matched what she heard, what she felt on her body, cumulonimbiforms on her back— "And us, yes, we should write or say what we experience."

"Yes," inferior Irunn said, taking longer than the time lag.

Superior Irunn finished her checks. Superior Venus grew perceptively in that time. Less than a day. Superior Irunn slept intermittently, skin-sung awake by the sounds of that brilliant ball filling her screens.


### Year 16 inferior Venus sets on Dumuzi 5 and after sixteen days rises on Dumuzi 21.

Inferior Irunn descended past the exosphere and through the thermosphere into the mesosphere on the dayside of inferior Venus at fifty degrees latitude in the northern hemisphere. Atmospheric pressure and temperature climbed. Warnings, but within parameters, accompanied her craft along the wind's current. Clouds climbed closer. Winds wrote.

Gale-glib winds, white-gleaming and gifting words.

The craft descended along its planned route into the lower mesosphere, as deep as they intended to go on this first attempt.

Clouds cover it, compass it, carry it and cry cacophony-cantos.

Inferior Irunn tried to transcribe them, but it took too long: her hands, her voice too slow for inferior Venus's song. Her body shook. Her eyes saw sounds, her ears heard none of her craft's updates. Too much. She tried to say what she felt: the pain, the planet-touched perspectives. She managed:

> Day 1 inferior Irunn: words yellow in my ears like pleas, I cannot taste what they touch, I—

Superior Irunn's screams interrupted inferior Irunn's shaking, halting speech.

The craft's computer registered superior Irunn's notation:

*Day 1 superior Irunn: arahhhh aaaa.*

Fly farra-round routes. Wind-whipped on. Sulphur sings up inferior Irunn's spine in screamed ecstasy, contorts her, cuneiform-carves her carpus. Words flow across inferior Irunn's tongue, but she cannot write. She cries. What wasted words: sounds senseless. Venus vents! Its stories remain unknown.

## Year 16 superior Venus vanishes E on Adar 24 and after two months, fifteen days appears W on Simanu 9.

Superior Irunn screams, skin sculpted into stories too topographical to tell. Mountains at her midriff. Plains at her pelvis. Arachnoids in her arching, her coronae contortions: gripped in gravity and ground, pestle-pained, into ink. Her body writes no stories. Clouds climb her collarbones, virga-vertiginous. Her screams fill the log file. Her agony an aria, a failed folksong. Venus vents! Its stories remain unknown.

The spacecraft computers communicated. Corrected.

## Year 17 inferior Venus sets on Adar 8 and after three days rises on Adar 11.

Inferior Irunn woke on the wall of her spacecraft, held in place by straps. Blood hung in perfect spheres. Sweat spheres, too. Urine? Her body hurt. Her throat felt wind-scoured. Scream-torn. Her ears registered a faint moaning: not hers. Superior Irunn. The transmit icon shone like superior Venus, a bright dot on one of her screens, and inferior Irunn groaned gently, closing her eyes. She wanted to sleep, sleep it away, sleep until the singing stopped and the wind—

"It's stopped," superior Irunn's shattered voice said. A cough. A cry. "I can think." Not stopped, but not the screaming immersion of inferior Venus's atmosphere. "I can hear other things, not just Venus. The computer. You— are you?"

Inferior Irunn opened her eyes, released the straps, and manoeuvred herself into her chair, wincing. Moving in zero gravity had never made her wince. The computer's additions to the screen resolved. The computers had communicated, superior with inferior, and coordinated both spacecraft into identical locations flying far above the north poles of both Venuses: far from its winds and clouds.

"I'm here," inferior Irunn said.

After the time lag said superior Irunn, "It hurts."

Inferior Irunn read and reread the data on her screen. Superior Irunn stared into the transmit screen, stared at inferior Irunn.

"We were down there for two hours," inferior Irunn said. Every word hurt. "It didn't feel like that. It felt—" She shook her head, reread the vital signs data. "I was conscious for an hour. How?"

"I saw the surface of Venus," superior Irunn said with eyes like farra formations: round and flat.

Inferior Irunn reread the data for superior Irunn's craft and saw that it hadn't descended into the troposphere, hadn't seen the surface in the visual spectrum. Other instruments had pierced the clouds beneath the craft, but not superior Irunn's eyes. "How?"

"All over my body."

"How?" Inferior Irunn knew that she might as well ask herself how it felt to be full of inferior Venus's voice—but she wanted an answer, wanted an explanation that amounted to more than the two Venuses on—in—their bodies.

"I know it."

"Come on, that's senseless." Like her own experience.

"I want to see it again."

Inferior Irunn felt her heart stutter at superior Irunn's words. "We need to decide what to do next. We need to talk to ground control—they'll have seen our vitals data, they'll know we went unconscious. We need to decide what to tell them. I don't know about you, but I need to clean up in here, wash, hydrate, eat."

Minutes later, superior Irunn nodded and said that they should tend to themselves and their craft, then discuss their reports. Inferior Irunn forced herself to move. Her craft's computer was already managing the airflow to process the waste. The medical unit told her that she had bruises and shallow cuts, and gave her the right patches to soothe and heal. She washed, changed into a new suit, drank, ate, thought—*yellow lowing cloud-loud, crying, dry clod-dying*—only of inferior Venus: the cacophony of sounds.

The disappointment.

At the console, she read the data again.

"Ground control will tell us to return," superior Irunn said. Disappointment gusted in her voice like the clouds of the Venuses.

"We can't ignore them," inferior Irunn said.

"We can. We're millions of kilometres away, and they can't remotely control our craft, not while we're conscious." She added, before inferior

Irunn's reply—saying almost the same—reached her, "Well, I suppose they could do it, if they overrode the computer. I'm sure they can."

"They would do it if they considered us insane," inferior Irunn also said.

"We have to report. And then—" They both wanted it. "Then we descend again."

"Yes," superior Irunn breathed.

Unsaid: descend even if ground control ordered them not to.

The data had told inferior Irunn that it wasn't enough to arrive at each planet—inferior Irunn for inferior Venus, superior Irunn for superior Venus—in one mission. "If we do it together," she said, "precisely together— if our computers coordinate the timing of the descent—we could survive it." Precisely paired like the planets. "We could see Venus, all of it, and fulfil our mission." To see it. To take samples. "We arrived one and a half minutes apart, our computers calculate. Too much. This time, we'll descend together."

To hear the songs underneath the sky. What sounds were there on the ground? Fear twisted inferior Irunn's stomach.

"If we go down and we go into that—that state—the computers will bring us back up," superior Irunn said. "The second we go unconscious, we return to where we are now."

"Yes."

"I want to see it. We're the first people to see Venus, and barely!"

"Then we go home," inferior Irunn said. "We don't try again. That's it."

To descend.

"Yes."

"Let's rest for at least ten hours. Then write our reports—they have the data already; they'll have plenty to analyse—then—" Half fear, half excitement. "Let's try this again."


### Year 18 superior Venus vanishes E on Arahsamnu 13 and after one month, twenty-five days appears W on Tebetu 8.

Their computers coordinated a synchronous descent through the thermosphere and the mesosphere down to the troposphere. Superior Irunn monitored the state of her spacecraft. It followed its course stably, remaining within safe operational parameters. The transmit icon blinked: ground control. The clouds climbed. Parted. Superior Irunn gasped at the ground.

Sulphur turns to bone: ghost writing in a language that the winds wend into Irunn's fingers.

Precisely paired, superior Irunn and inferior Irunn transcribed together:

*Superior Irunn: The dead are planted pelvis-deep in the plains of Venus, growing memories*

*Inferior Irunn: that seek the sky and its stars scattered overhead like ossicles, awaiting*

*Superior Irunn: our scream*

*Inferior Irunn: our scream*

*Superior Irunn: cloud-caught cantos-screaming*

*Inferior Irunn: I walked on webs braid-bonded to bridges over waters burn-bright and I was bold, bold—I died— we died—billions of years before your bones built you—we dream—Venus alive!—overhead a veil-sky vestment-kind, soft-voiced, killing slowly—if farra-found life plied far from its plain it perished—novae-novices broken navicular-bold, newly burning, betrayed—coronae circles cuneiform-boned by burnt brethren—we died by*

*Superior Irunn: Venus suffocating, sky hating, stars fading*

*Inferior Irunn: listen, legends-long songs glisten*

Days flew by.

Megabytes accreted.

In a still moment, superior Irunn said, "Venus wants us to tell it." Its history inking her bones. "It wants to share its stories with us, with life."

"Ghosts," inferior Irunn gasped. "Lonely."

Death-dreaming through depths of time.

"They died when the atmosphere changed," superior Irunn said, as if making a report, "when the oxygen dispersed into space. They couldn't adapt to the increasing temperatures."

*Superior Irunn: I screamed my scraping, scour-breaking, bones scattered in the wind!—I dried out!—I weakened, I wept!—I heard scream-hearses as I scraped life, I heard shout-shrouds, I heard final-fires, pitiful pyre-pants on the plains, palimpsests of dead: dead on dead on dead, I died on them!*

*Inferior Irunn: I shrine-shouted my death, dry-drowned in a
far farra!*

*Superior Irunn: shout, shout*

*Inferior Irunn: listen, listen*

A different day—days, superior Irunn saw, days were passing every time
she looked at her screen—inferior Irunn asked, "Is it possible they're alive?
Microbial life in the more temperate parts of the atmosphere, extremophiles
on the surface—something?"

"Soaking up ghost memories like us and passing them on? Nothing's
normal, Irunn."

"Telling stories. Inventions, not memories."

"Microbes don't do that!"

"Not on Earth, but we're not on Earth!"

"It's ghosts!" superior Irunn shouted. "Old, old ghosts and now they've
got us, trapped here like ear-bones transmitting to Earth, and it's beautiful—"

*Superior Irunn: I gripped ground long-gone, I long*

*Inferior Irunn: for far-flung farra full of life*

Superior Irunn saw the attempts by ground control to override her
spacecraft's computer. Saw the error messages. Saw soft-boned, beatific bodies
body-singing to her. The computer had extended a tube to her, to hydrate and
feed. Saw parabola-buried predators parading on her pelvis. Transmissions
from Baghdad and Beijing didn't reach her craft—or the sound didn't reach
her ears. Venus-drowned.

Transmissions from her craft reached Earth. She saw that.

Every time she thought of manually overriding the computer to lift her
from the planet's atmosphere and return—

*Superior Irunn: I long!*

*Inferior Irunn: I remember—radial fractures forming in my
family-farra, ground grinding open—breathing—breeding—
bones memory-modified in bright memorials—caressed, curve-
covered, breeding bone-bright—swift swimming-songs fought for
in filled farra, cracked coronae—rain—lost—I ate, I mated, I
made bone-life bright—life on life—lost—I want*

*Superior Irunn: memorial-life*

*Inferior Irunn: not no-life*

*Superior Irunn: not no-life*

*Inferior Irunn: shrine-shout memorial-life!*

Warnings of low oxygen went unheeded. Alarms screamed. Winds screamed. Superior Irunn screamed, and inferior Irunn gasped, empty-lunged—and eventually both went still.

Bones on both superior Venus and inferior Venus sing of her childhood as Irunn, sing of her splitting into superior Irunn and inferior Irunn—seeing herself, touching palm to palm and smiling, pride-flushed with the success of sanity—sing of her journey to Venus, sing of her work recording the memorial-life, the not no-life, of long-dead life.

Are singing still.

# BY THREAD OF NIGHT
# AND STARLIGHT NEEDLE

### Shveta Thakrar

S he gave me the moon.
I gave her the stars.

She let her gaze drift wearily over my gift, over the glitter and glitz, the shine and shimmer of silver fire. Sighing, she shook her head. "You always have to outdo me, don't you?"

"Yes," I said, seeing no reason to lie. "It's what I do."

My sister leaped at me then, fangs bared and flashing. I reached out to meet her, my claws bursting forth, eager to rend flesh from bone.

Once we were done tearing each other to shreds, all that remained was a black space encompassing everything, a void lit only by the luminous gifts we'd cast aside in our hunger to win. If you're feeling poetic, you might even call it the first sky.

It's my favorite love story.

ↄ

W hen nothing is left but the skin you have cast off, be it serpent or selkie, when you don and doff lives like ill-fitting dresses, when you twine the hearts of those you love 'round your wrists while allowing your own to wane, when at last you, too, learn the cost and promise of your blood, that is when you will be ready.

At least, so claimed the old woman who shamelessly sported a sheer fuchsia sari with gold embroidery instead of proper modest cotton. She

194

perched on the edge of her counter and sipped wine, a black like opal and just as iridescent. Kiran had never seen anything so odd.

"Bug wings," mouthed her brother Sanjay. For a second, Kiran imagined the old woman distilling molten moths, and she nearly gagged.

She frowned at Sanjay, then took another swig of her tea, a sparkling snow-blue beverage that tasted of nothing so much as candy and forbidden dreams. If the old woman was indeed a sorceress, as her reputation implied, perhaps she would have some advice for them. "Grandmother, we've come far to avail ourselves of your renowned wisdom."

The old woman let out a snort. "Just because I'm advanced in years, as they say, and indulge in a fine tea or two, I must be a witch?"

"Well, what do you expect when you keep drinks like those around?" asked Sanjay, who'd never been one for social niceties. Kiran kicked him under the marble tabletop.

"Young people are too self-absorbed to listen to the world around them," the old woman said. "All the answers are already there. And I'm hardly your grandmother, so 'Rekha' will do just fine."

"Well, then, Rekha," Kiran said, squeezing her mug harder so no one would see her hands tremble, "what is it we should be listening to?"

Rekha shrugged. She picked up the bottle of black wine. "Everything wants to be consumed, even stones. Even bugs that struggle to fly away. Everything longs to be part of something else." Before Kiran could argue, she laughed. "Yes, everything. Even you, or you wouldn't be here."

Kiran exchanged a horrified glance for Sanjay's amused one. Old women were supposed to wear white and be solemn in the twilight of their years, not drape themselves in garish colors and cackle about eating people. Maybe they were wrong to have come here.

She had just risen when Rekha spoke again. "Are young people really so easily scandalized these days? No wonder you know nothing!"

The irritation in her voice sparked a fire in Kiran's chest. She took her seat again. "I came here hoping you would help us, but I see there's no chance of that happening."

"Spit it out, girl," snapped Rekha. "How am I supposed to help you if I don't know what you want?"

"I want to know how to make wine like that," announced Sanjay.

Normally Kiran enjoyed Sanjay's quirky commentary, but right now, she could only curse the gods for his lack of decorum. "No!" she put in. "I—we—need to know how to—how to . . ."

The words failed her. She'd come for such a simple thing, but suddenly she didn't care. Not about that, anyway.

Now she just wanted . . . what?

"She wants to know how to create a bucketful of gold coins," Sanjay said in a bored voice. "She wants you to show us how to get rich. Me, I just want to drink that wine."

"Peace, boy," the old woman ordered, motioning for him to shut his mouth. His eyebrows raised, Sanjay did so. "Now, girl," said Rekha, her tone prickly as a thistle, "what do you want? Why are you really here?"

*જ*

See us now, stitched together,
Skin to unscarred skin,
By thread of night looped through
The eye of a starlight needle,
The eye, the eye,
The all-seeing eye.
We are bound for all time,
Brother and sister,
Kith and kin,
Hand in hand against
The relentless dark.

—from "Ballad of the Star-Stitched Siblings"

*જ*

Bindul held tightly to his sister's hand as they wandered through the market. It was a hot day, the kind where dust nestled into every crevice and spiced every breath with grit. Using the back of his free hand, he impatiently swiped at the stray lock of hair dancing into his face.

"I'm hungry," Sri complained. She was small, only reaching his knee, and Bindul knew it fell to him to keep her fed. She gazed up at him with large, innocent eyes. "I want a laddoo."

Bindul had no money, and his own stomach rumbled. He'd have to be quick. If anyone caught him stealing, he'd be separated from Sri, and likely tossed into a beggars' orphanage. The idea of her alone and at a slaver's mercy, cruelly maimed so she would bring in more coins from pitying tourists—it made his scratchy eyes sting.

So many vivid colors, so many lush fabrics, so many rich and sumptuous foods on display, and not a one was intended for them. This world hadn't realized the two of them even existed. For a moment, especially with his leg still bruised from the last near-capture, he felt so slight. So weak. He coughed, and his throat was as dry and shriveled as his hope.

But the tiny hand clutching his did so with such trust that of course he would try again.

Bindul found a nook between stalls and, after making sure no one was watching, lodged Sri into it. "Wait here," he said, "and don't let anyone see you. I'll be back as soon as I can."

☙

Sanjay was an elephant handler. He trained the strongest, most intelligent bulls and cows for the raja's and rani's army, and Kiran assisted him. Her favorite things were stroking the animals' trunks when feeding them and playing with their large, floppy ears. Yet the thought of the animals going to war—of Sanjay going with them—sickened her. She would do anything to keep him safe.

"I—I just wanted to find a way to . . ." She'd thought asking the witch for riches would be sensible, a guaranteed way to ensure a life of comfort and freedom from worry.

But the words stuck like burrs in her throat. Something inside her quavered, shaking loose in an avalanche of buried thoughts. They threatened to smother her, and at the heart of each was a single word: *alone.*

Though she didn't know what that meant, it made her skin hurt. She didn't understand; she'd crawled out of the womb followed by her brother. Her twin. They'd always been together. Even when she thought of marrying, she knew she would pick no man Sanjay did not approve of, any more than he would choose a wife without consulting her. It was unthinkable.

Rekha turned a razor-quick gaze on her. "You wear a strange skin," she said, "doubled." And then she spoke the words Kiran was certain were not for her. *When nothing is left . . .*

So she pushed them away. "I want security and safety. I want to know how to make the right decisions, the ones that will keep us from harm. You've lived a long time; surely you can teach me that?"

The old woman burst into rude, raucous laughter. "Is that really a thing you think you can solve with magic?" She glowered at the elaborate mosaic-tile ceiling, all reds and golds and blues. "Why is it only fools who seek my knowledge? No one can escape making mistakes. How do you expect to learn when you don't even know the right questions to ask?"

While she spoke, Sanjay stood and poured himself a goblet of the ebony wine. He sipped it, and something in his expression shifted. "This," he said, coughing. "Whatever it is, it's strong."

Rekha watched him, her eyes all keen interest. "Yes, it is."

Still smarting from the old woman's comments, Kiran watched him, too. Her thoughts refused to come together, coy as a house cat that yowled for affection until it was offered, then hissed in offense.

Claws. All claws, sheathed until they weren't.

Whatever Sanjay was about to say would draw blood. She could feel it.

Something kindled within him, turning his dark brown eyes bright. "I want to stay here." He looked at the old woman. "I want to learn from you. Really."

Now Kiran jumped to her feet. "No!" That wasn't the way it was supposed to go. He was supposed to stay still while she obtained the information, the magic spell she needed to keep him out of danger. What he was *not* supposed to do was get strange ideas about staying with the witch.

And if he did, what about her? Where was she to go?

༄

Dear Ketanbhai,
     There's a black forest in the world of stories. It could be across the planet; it could be just in your backyard. But one thing is for certain: it lives deep within you, its twisted roots intertwined with the shadows in your thoughts.

Did you know narwhals and unicorns share the same horn? It's called an alicorn, and maybe *share* is not the right word. Once we pushed unicorns from fact into the black forest, where all myths go once we think we've outgrown them, narwhals inherited the horn[*]. So you might say they're the unicorns of the water, down in the depths where it's black, except they grant no wishes and have no particular use for virgin women. Is that really the world you want to inhabit? Be honest, big brother.

You like to eat Black Forest cake. Did you know it's called *Schwarzwaldkuchen* in German, named for the Schwarzwald, the spooky forested mountains where wolves eat people in fairy tales? Well, it is. Think about it—you are what you eat, right?

Black forests are everywhere. I found one in India, just at the border of Nepal. You'd think it would contain bamboo. You'd be right. But would you think it would have a yaksha riding a unicorn? Because it didn't have that. I did see a yaksha[†], though. He seemed a little perturbed and offered me a wish if I'd go away. Maybe one day I'll tell you what I plan to wish. Maybe if you're nice to me, I might even share the wish with you.

What would *you* wish for, brother dearest?

Love always,

Your adoring and most devoted sister Jyoti

P.S. Are you ever coming home?

P.P.S. Do you still look for me in the stars?

*As per Dr. M. P. Bhatt's *Bestiary of the Dark Dreaming.* (No, I didn't make that up. Go do some research if you don't believe me.)

†He had your face. And your weird string-bean body. And that stupid smile you get when you think you've done something clever.‡

‡Was it you? Are you really a yaksha? You can tell me.§ Or maybe you're a bhoot. Your hair's certainly ragged enough. Do you ever wash it?

§Seriously, are you ever coming home?

℘

Sanjay didn't look at Kiran but instead at the bottle of black wine. "You're not the only one who wants something else."

"But—" Kiran began, not certain what it was she protested. She *did* want something else, it was true. Just perhaps not the same thing he wanted?

Rekha observed them, her head cocked at an angle like a bird's. A bird of prey, thought Kiran, quills taut with the same undisguised predacious glee. "You still have not told me what you truly want of me," Rekha nearly purred.

Kiran took another sip of tea, grateful for the few seconds the act bought her. "I could stay here, too," she said at last, each syllable as false as the cheer with which she imbued it.

"But you don't want to," Rekha pressed.

"No," Kiran admitted. No, she didn't.

"And I don't want you to, either," Sanjay said. "Really, it's all right." He poured himself another glass of the prismatic black wine. "Beetle wings."

"You have a decent eye," Rekha said, nodding.

Was she saying the wine really was made of insect bits? How?

Kiran chided herself. None of that mattered. "What—what will I tell the elephants?"

"They'll still have you," Sanjay said. "It'll be fine." He picked up another bottle, one filled with flickering orange flame, and began to question Rekha about the contents.

"What are you so afraid of?" Rekha murmured so only Kiran could hear.

The word came back to her in a flurry of whispers: *alone. Alone, alone, alone.* She had never been alone, not really. Not in any way that counted.

Kiran didn't reply. Why waste her breath when Rekha already knew the answer?

℘

Bindul hung his head and tried not to make eye contact with any of the customers he passed. He'd failed. He'd failed to distract even a single vendor long enough to snatch a laddoo or a samosa or, at worst, an unripe mango. He'd always been a mediocre thief, and today, with his leg still sprained and tender to the touch, it was a wonder he'd escaped without notice.

When he neared the nook where his sister waited, his cheeks flamed, and his heart spasmed painfully. How could he have failed her?

Resentment burned in him. He didn't want this responsibility! Wasn't it bad enough to have been cast out by his parents without another person to worry about, too?

But the image of Sri's round, happy face, her eyes lively even through the haze of sand, beckoned.

They would find something, he told himself. They had to.

Sri hopped out of the space then, throwing herself at him. "Look what I have!" she sang. Little fingers pushed a greasy bundle into his.

"I told you to stay put," Bindul said, but he couldn't really be mad.

"I was hungry. I told you," she said, blithe as ever. "I already ate two of the laddoos."

Taking care that no one was watching, Bindul loosened the rag. There, hastily wrapped and somewhat flavored with sand, were three crushed samosas, four soft yellow laddoos, and a heaping handful of saffron pulao, the grains of rice mashed together.

"I can take care of us, too," Sri informed him, earnest.

"I guess you can at that," said Bindul, trying not to laugh. Who was the burden now?

℘

> Skin torn from unscarred skin,
> Wounds weeping,
> O brother, you swore it,
> You said you would stay
> For always.
> Yet under the million-eyed
> Gaze of the star-flecked sky
> Unstitched, ripped asunder,
> By thread of night looped through
> The eye of a starlight needle,
> The eye, the eye,
> The unseeing eye,

We are unbound for all time,
Brother and sister,
Kith and kin,
Alone against the relentless dark.

—from "The Star-Crossed Sister's Lament"

✂

Sanjay had chosen, and now Kiran scowled at him. "All the things you could have asked for, and you wanted to get away from me?"

"Yes," he said, his jaw clenched. "It feels like you're always there, always in my face. When I turn around, there you are. It's as if we were sewn together at birth, and I can't breathe."

The remark slashed at her like teeth. How could he even suggest that?

Kiran growled. "You're lucky you have me to keep you from messing up." How many hasty barters had she saved him from? How many unwanted suitors had she chased off? And this was how he thanked her?

"You two are linked in time and space and destiny," said Rekha, with a firm shake of her head. "I could no more separate you than rob the moon of his starry consorts."

Instead, she offered another wish. "Choose."

Kiran shoved a fist against her quaking lips. She thought of all the times when no one watched, all the myriad ways to be invisible. She felt frail as the cosmos newly born, still cradled in the gods' arms and suckling the sweet Ocean of Milk.

"You don't need me," Sanjay insisted. "Not like this." Then he pinched the bridge of his nose. "I'm tired. Aren't you?"

She pretended not to feel his gaze on her, but of course she did. Of course she felt the link between them. It was far older than they were.

"This is not your first birth," Rekha muttered, her eyes narrowed to slits of focus. "Nor, if you do not act, will it be your last."

Memories rushed through Kiran, of other lives, other loves. Of the dark thread and shining needle that trussed two siblings together.

*Cut the cord.*

If she did that, she would be alone, truly alone once and for all. In the dark. Adrift.

She couldn't even imagine life severed. How would she breathe? No Sanjay to bring her sun-ripened bananas straight from the tree. No Sanjay to spin her stories about fools whose sloth and stupidity won the day as reasons why he shouldn't do his half of their chores. No Sanjay to comfort when the woman he fancied chose someone else. No Sanjay, no Sanjay, no Sanjay. It felt like drowning in the beetle wine, black and heavy as ink.

It felt like sticky gray spider silk enveloping her in a cocoon, with nothing and no one else to hold her up when she stumbled, unable to see. Kiran didn't know if her legs could bear her own weight.

She couldn't cut the cord. She couldn't. No Sanjay meant no home, no place that was hers. *Alone.*

But if she didn't, Sanjay would hate her. His eyes would go dark again and turn from her. And she would lose all those things, anyway.

"Scissors," said Kiran at last, rubbing her temples. "Where are the scissors that could cut the cord?"

Rekha reached behind the counter. "I'm certain I can find a pair that will do."

The gleaming copper grip could have been forged for Kiran's fingers, it fit so well. She opened and closed the crystal blades. Open, shut. Open, shut. They reminded her of beetle wings unfurling. She despised them.

Then the cord, too, was in her hand, thread black as wine, black as night, stitching her heart to Sanjay's.

The scissors glinted. All it would take was one snip. Just one.

*I can't.*

"Do it," whispered Sanjay. He swallowed so hard, she could see it. Rekha merely smiled.

Kiran ignored them both. He was hers! *Her* brother.

"Please," Sanjay added, and the cord shivered.

Kiran looked at him, from his pleading face to the cord joining them and finally to the pair of scissors, its blades opening like jagged wings in flight.

☙

I leaped at him then, fangs bared and flashing. My brother reached out to meet me, his claws bursting forth, eager to rend flesh from bone.

Once we were done tearing each other to shreds, all that remained was a black space encompassing everything, a void lit only by the luminous gifts we'd cast aside in our hunger to win. If you're feeling poetic, you might even call it the first sky.

I made a wish aloud never to be alone. What use to me was the sticky gray spider's web of solitude in a universe of never-ending black?

"Yes," he said, seeing no reason to lie. "I'll be by your side always."

And so he gave me the stars.

And I, I gave him the moon.

It's my favorite love story.

# THE GAMES WE PLAY

### *Cassandra Khaw*

The Dog-King is not quite what Yavena expects.

He is physically imposing, of course, military upbringing exposed in the thickness of his musculature, the midnight fur sliced close to his hide.

The other Ovia in Yavena's court speak of the Dog-King as a monster among Gaks, a fearsome legend. But where Yavena anticipated the flatness of a killer's regard, there is a penetrating curiosity instead. A scholarliness amplified by his chosen garb—the earthy, flowing raiment of an academic—and the small amber glasses crouched precariously atop his muzzle.

Nothing Hahvah prepared her for.

"Ah." His voice is warm and younger than the striations of white in his pelt suggest, boyishly pleased. The Dog-King slinks away from a desk piled high with official-looking documentation. "Yavena, was it? We're charmed."

Yavena traps fist against open palm, bows almost low enough to tempt accusations of impudence. Beside him, her sponsor—Hahvah, the little Gak with a wailing laugh—crumples into an exaggerated kowtow.

"This one is honored you recognize her face," declares Yavena, her command of the Gak's growling, liquid language impeccable. With monarchs, subservience is never inappropriate. "This one begs an audience from the Scourge of Kyonadrila Valley, the Conqueror of the Ten Thousand Colors, the Lord-General of the Gak, the—"

"'This one'"—a youthful playfulness thrusts through the Dog-King's voice—"is overwhelmingly polite. We're amazed that you resisted the temptation to call us the Dog-King. After all, is it not our name among those of the Ten Thousand Colors, our most treasured of vassals?"

Yavena snaps her head up, guilt blooming. Words can be schooled, but thoughts have always enjoyed a rebellious autonomy in her head. "This one would not dare! This one—"

"We would have you address us as peers, Yavena."

A beat. "My lord."

"Good enough, we suppose." A broad hand, caged in iron rings and steel-grey bangles, is flapped delicately.

Yavena unbends but finds herself unable to loosen the knot of tension crushing her lungs. She is disarmed, robbed of equilibrium by the Dog-King's frictionless affability. She folds her arms behind her, adopts the posture of a soldier at rest. As she does so, she captures the sliver of a smile on the Dog-King's mien, its meaning impenetrable.

Unbidden, her gaze jumps back to Hahvak next, but she finds no reassurance there, only slyness, a wheedling humor. Yavena stiffens further, elegant in defiance.

"So," the Dog-King begins as he mounts the steps to his throne. It is an intimidating structure, mythic in proportion, cobbled together from the bones of a thousand devoured Mothers. "What is it that you wish to ask from us, Yavena?"

"This one—" She stumbles, words snagging on ceremony. "I mean, I wish to play a game with you."

The Dog-King laughs loudly. "Cordial and learned! Trust the Ten Thousand Colors to know the ten thousand desires that lurk in the living heart. Tell us the desire that beats at the core of that most sacred organ."

The massive Gak monarch slouches onto his seat, elbow propped on an armrest, muzzle cupped in a broad paw. A hush glides over the dignitaries in the audience chamber, tautening muscles and attention. Dark eyes anchor on Yavena. They wait. Watch.

The Ovia inhales thinly, exhales her entreaty in a measured torrent.

"As per custom, I have won all of the Supplicant's Challenges." Here pride burgeons for an instant. "I have beaten all your Overseers. I have earned innumerable favors, six guild recruitments, three requests to join a noble's entourage, and . . . one slightly drunken marriage proposal."

Silence. The Gak are barely respiring, their bodies statue still. Only the Dog-King alters expression, smile broadening. In the background, Hahvah's slithering giggles. "Small little thing? Carmine fur? Pompadour? Speaks like he swallowed a flute?"

Yavena nods, expression grave.

"Avah has always enjoyed unusual tastes." A chuckle that spreads like an infection through the courtiers. "We apologize for the interruption. Continue."

The Ovia swallows her apprehension and resumes as instructed, voice held steady through the application of will. "I wish . . . I wish to claim my right to challenge you to a game of your design. If I win, return Iraline of the Ten Thousand Colors, Mother of the Dead and beloved brood-sister. If I lose—"

Ventricles strain against the onset of terror. Yavena's pulse hammers like fists. The audacity of her coming revelation is not lost upon her, and like the wail of a wolf pack, it bleeds her spirit of courage.

"—return Iraline to the Ten Thousand Colors and let me take her place instead. She is soft. I am muscled. Larger, better suited for your banquet hall, my plumage more impressive. I—"

Shocked noises detonate in the hall. In between, a strange, shrill laugh. Hahvak.

The Dog-King maintains his genteel smile. "Correct us if we are mistaken. But do you not belong to the Court of the Living?"

"I do." It is too late for retreat.

"And does not the duty of feeding the Gak belong to the Court of the Dead?"

"It does."

The monarch leans forward, eyes hooded, lamplight-gold. "Tell us, then: why would you have us risk political unrest between our kingdoms? Do we not have a treaty? Do my packs not watch the mountains of your nests? Do we not feed you as you feed us? Do we not have a deal?"

Yavena can scarcely breathe. "We do."

"Then tell us *why* we should grant you this boon."

*Because of love*, Yavena thinks. But what she tells him is, "But you are the greatest mind among the Gak. You would win. I'm sure of it, and you would have stories to tell of my insolence. Is that not worth the infinitesimally small chance of loss?"

"Your confidence in your deliciousness is appreciated." A slight, slow inclination of the head. The Dog-King shifts in his seat and rests his jaw atop steepled claws.

Yavena spreads her hands and advances a step, no longer willing to divide decorum from desire. After enduring so many trials, so many weeks of combat, has she not earned the liberty of uncensored expression? She is pleading now, openly. "Iraline deserves more years to her life. She is an accomplished artist, a masterful poet, a historian of unparalleled accuracy. I know there is no honor greater for one belonging to the Court of the Dead than to appear on your table, but give her back to me, Lord-General.

"Please." Ragged, that final word, like a belly slit open. "Give my nest-sister back."

The Dog-King says nothing for long minutes. Seconds lengthen, viscera thick, suturing together into a wait that might as well have been eternity. Around Yavena, silence descends in waves, until there is only the sound of a hundred lungs in harmonious palpitation.

Then at last: "We see merit in your suggestion."

Yavena waits, shoulders knotting. The Dog-King's easy acquiescence inspires suspicion. Triumph is never this faultless, this clean. Something is amiss. A heartbeat's worth of quiet, then Yavena cautiously supplies, "My lord."

Neither agreement nor displeasure, a neutral postponement of opinion.

"Mm." Equally ambiguous the Dog-King's response. "We agree to your terms, but we will set the structure of the game."

"I would desire nothing more."

The Dog-King's muzzle wrenches into something like a grin, feral in timbre. "So pliable. We would almost think you were born into the wrong court. Very well. This is our decision. This is what we require. Ask Iraline to leave of her own free will. Fail, and you shall have a fortnight to help prepare your own feast."

Confusion yields a thoughtless exclamation. "M-my lord? I don't understand. How is that even a game? That doesn't—"

Yavena's protest is slaughtered like a lamb, dismissed by a wave of the Dog-King's hand. "It makes every iota of sense if you have the right scales to weigh it. You simply need to adopt the correct perspective. Iraline is in the kitchens. We will have someone escort you. Our game begins now."

"My lord." There is nothing else she can say.

"Wrong, Scahul." A gentle rebuke, feather soft as it floats down the shadowed corridor. "It's a basic error, however. Many presume that the Ten Thousand Colors have a united physiology, a uniformed distribution of collagen in their muscle fibres. But we do not. Our muscular composition differs from—"

Yavena accelerates. Her steps lengthen. It is all she can do to resist breaking into a lope. She crosses the threshold into the kitchen, her voice hoarse when it escapes. "Iraline?"

She interrupts the scene: a kitchen vast enough to contain hundreds, a fragrant landscape of gleaming steel, threaded with spice and carnivore predilections. An Ovia stretched provocatively over a broad wooden table, posture relaxed, expression inviting. She is tattooed with ink, limbs separated by lines, her most delectable regions marked for easy identification. A quill—lime-green; it is from her own person—dangles from her claws.

Around her, a battalion of Gak, their hands crowded with notepads. One clutches an inkwell.

"Yavena?" The Ovia rights herself. Her manner is delicate, fertile with confidence. Every motion is an expression of art. "Yavena! What are you doing here?"

"Iraline—" Now Yavena's voice weakens, pales to a whisper. An avalanche of memories—Iraline at her Naming; Iraline's exhausted mien as she clutches her firstborn; Iraline and she as nestlings; Iraline, her sister of the spirit, her saviour, her sacrifice—chokes Yavena. Her knees sag. "Ira—"

"You've said my name twice already, you know?" A fluting laugh. "No need for the third, little sister."

"I'm sorry." Yavena's head lowers for an instant before she adopts a semblance of propriety, her smile ambassadorial smooth. "It's just been—I've—"

"It was you who caused all that commotion, wasn't it? Winning game after game, the Ovia foreigner, beating all the Gak at their own tricks. I'm so proud," Iraline says, excitement gleaming silver in her voice. She flutters a hand at the waiting mob of Gak who disperse after sketching respectful half-bows, their faces unreadable. Chattering softly among themselves, they slink back to their duties, the sounds of culinary effort rising like a war chant. "Did you kill anyone?"

"Yes. I—"

Iraline turns smoothly, an arm draping around Yavena, dominance claimed with a flippancy even kings would envy. "Well, finally. You were long overdue. Who ever heard of a Bloodless Keeper? You have no idea how many times I had to defend you among the other Mothers, who all thought you were a little . . . off your game, to borrow from the locals. Too kind to be a killer. Too—"

"Motherly?"

A jolt of remembered grief, and Yavena shrugs free of Iraline's grip. She was never meant to be Keeper. Iraline was. It was Yavena who was meant to bear a hundred eggs to a hundred strangers. Yavena who was meant to waste her last days in the kitchens of their benefactors, their masters.

"You said it, not I."

Yavena shrugs. She is too grateful for Iraline's presence, too enraptured by the scent of her—milk and vanilla, with a dusting of talcum—to consider offense. "I'm happy you're alive, Iraline."

The answering smile is halfway between ruefulness and pleasure, an expression glazed with sadness. "And I'm happy that you have an impeccable sense of timing. Just a little longer, and you'd need a necromancer."

Before Yavena can answer, Iraline interrupts her own non sequitur, laughter dazzling as a mouthful of stars. "A little joke, my beloved. Don't look at me that way. A Mother is allowed humour."

Iraline preserves eye contact for a moment longer before flouncing away towards a stove, unoccupied save for an earthen kettle. She pours herself a cup of something warm. Yavena follows, leaning over just enough to be able to inspect the contents—a decadent creaminess redolent of mugwort and blackberries.

"Are you here to rescue me?" Iraline asks over the rim of her drink.

"That was the plan."

More silence. Yavena already knows the answer, is already cogitating on solutions when Iraline concedes a reply, her voice weighted with a long, drawn-out sigh.

"Little sister, you know as well as anyone else that no one forced me here. I have no more eggs to give the Court. And so it is time to give my flesh."

Yavena's thoughts catch on a slurry of unwanted images, but she shoves them aside, hands balling into fists.

"You're lying." She spits out syllables that are broken-glass sharp, razored despite her attempts at congeniality. "You're too young to be barren. You have time. Years, Ira. You have years still. Why, why are you doing this? Iraline, come back with me. *Please.*"

Now the ambient bustle shrinks. Now it condenses to pinpoints of noise as the Gak slide curious glances over wide, dark shoulders.

"You're being unreasonable," Iraline retorts, tone reasonable as always.

"It should have been me."

Light drains from Iraline's stare. She puts her mug aside, face collapsing into quiet horror. "Yavena—"

"You. You're the one who belonged to the Court of the Living. Everyone knew it. All the fortune-singers, all the officials. They knew it. They knew you gave it all away for me." Yavena jerks backwards, all pretenses of composure forgotten, all poise submerged in that seething guilt which rises thick as tar, clogging her throat. She swallows and swallows, unable to dislodge the marrow-deep agony. "You could have been Keeper. You could have been happy. You should have been. I was supposed to be a Mother, Ira. Not you."

She freezes as long arms envelop her, warm with affection. "Oh, Yavena. You're being blind. In your Court, I would have been always afraid, always wanting, always desperate to hoard those few decades I owned, to pretend that seconds could be made to accumulate interest. This sacrifice is a small price to pay for the years of fire."

"I don't want you to die."

Iraline welds them cheek to cheek. Sighs. Her pulse reassures with its steadiness, appalls with its indifference. "We all die, little sister. Sooner or later."

Yavena pushes her away. "Yes, but one is preferable to the other."

The moment is broken. The Gak return to their toil. Iraline retreats to her drink, coiling catlike atop a counter, while Yavena glowers out a window. The light of the city has stained the night a seamless indigo, unscarred by constellations.

"If you're going to be maudlin, you should go home," Iraline declares finally, the music of her voice only slightly marred by petulance.

"I can't." Yavena folds her arms. "You know that. I'm playing a game with the Lord-General, and you're the prize."

The mug shatters in Iraline's grip, spilling blood and ceramic.

"You've always been a selfish child, haven't you?" Iraline remarks, tone mild despite the injuries that striate her hands. Legs cross. Iraline makes no move to bind her wounds, only stares beyond the horizon of Yavena's silhouette, features locked in grim contemplation.

"I'm only trying to—"

"Get out."

Yavena feels a weight descend upon a shoulder and turns to find a heavyset Gak behind her, somehow still menacing despite the ridiculousness of its kitchen accoutrements. "I'll see you tomorrow."

"Go." Soft, so soft, too soft, Iraline's repudiation, like the last gasp of a broken heart.

Footsteps like drumbeats, slow but nuanced, pregnant with meaning. "Ah, Yavena." The Dog-King manifests from around a corner, silhouette turned monstrous by the chiaroscuro of his lamp. "We were just thinking about you."

The Ovia inclines her head in answer, silent and resentful. It has been hours since Iraline banished her from her company. Hours spent prowling the periphery of the kitchen, seeking entrance, seeking escape from the automata that dog Yavena's every step. Her simulacra escorts, draped in gauze and off-white silks, still their twitching as the Dog-King approaches, their clockwork eyes whirling.

"How goes your onslaught on the walls of Fort Iraline?"

Yavena shrugs. As one, the automata return their attention to her, talons clicking. "Poorly."

"We see." The Dog-King lowers his lamp and pinches the space between his eyes. In the penumbra of the corridor, his features seem softer—the face of an everyman, rather than a monarch. "Well. You still have a few more days before the weekend arrives."

Bitterness knifes through Yavena's terse response. "As you say, Lord-General."

The Dog-King chuckles. A ripple of fingers causes the automata to erupt into movement again. Expressionless, and without so much as a backward glance at Yavena or the Dog-King, the animated corpses melt back into the shadows.

"There. Some privacy. Walk with us, Ovia."

Silence tightens its stranglehold over the environment, a hush Yavena is reluctant to break. It is only when it becomes evident the Dog-King requires that transgression that Yavena offers a quiet, "Some privacy for what, my lord?"

"Ah, Yavena. So diplomatic, yet so direct." The Dog-King makes a tutting noise, restarts his languid walk. The oil lamp keeps time with his stride. "To talk, of course."

The Ovia falls into lockstep, careful to remain a dagger's width behind him. "There's really nothing to talk about."

Cheerily, like someone recapturing the thread of an interesting conversation, the Dog-King says, "Individuality, you know, is sacrosanct among the Gak. We pride ourselves on nuance, on building a legacy that is absolutely unique."

Yavena cannot resist. "Does it gall you to use the majestic pronoun, then?"

They round a corner. The corridor swells into a massive hall, its walls fleshed with tapestries and naval charts. The Dog-King halts. His laughter, abrupt as thunder, ricochets through the space, unself-conscious, the merriment of someone unweighted by a crown. "Immensely. But we must make sacrifices for what we love."

"And that love of yours is power?"

"Power is a supplementary bonus," the Dog-King counters easily, as though debating the price of herbs rather than ownership of a country. "We do not love it. We appreciate it exists. What we do love is our people, our nation. We are enamored of them. Enough to allow our identity to be subsumed by our duty, to stop existing as 'I' but instead as the collective power of the throne. Surely you, of all people, can appreciate that—the desire to give oneself up for the sake of others."

Yavena says nothing, throat clotted with ruminations.

An interruption: "Tell me, Yavena, why do the Ten Thousand Colors lack family names?"

"Because we are merely feathers on a wing," Yavena recites, rhythmic, the words as familiar as breath.

The Dog-King cocks his head, ears pricking forward. "We know the propaganda. Tell us what your people think. Tell us if this ideology pleases you, if it appalls you, if you have secret names among yourselves—"

Memories spasm like birth contractions, like the convulsions of death; snatches of anguish and half-remembered diatribes, a swarm of faces and secrets, but Yavena wrestles it all down. She smiles instead, bows her head low. "Forgive me, Lord-General. But the hare does not trade gossip with the hawk."

Another explosion of laughter, rich and wild. "If you will not educate us about your people, tell us instead why you are violating the edicts of your twin Courts. Iraline comes to us with all her papers in order."

"Because—" Yavena enlarges her stance, prepares to author a lie that even the Gak cannot scale, only to crumple, stooping under her own exhaustion. "Because this is my fault. She wouldn't be in this situation if I hadn't—"

"If you hadn't what?" The prompt arrives in an inquisitive whine, scandalously bestial.

"Been a coward," Yavena finishes. It is, as far as she is concerned, an accurate summarization of the situation.

"You love her spectacularly."

Yavena trains her gaze on nothing and everything, expression abstracted by a morass of emotions. "More than breath and bone and hope."

"That is good." The Dog-King nods. "Devotion wins wars."

"Perhaps," Yavena replies, not wanting to allow him access into her private concerns. She bows during the lull in dialogue. "If the Lord-General no longer requires my presence, I should find my rest. I only have days to ask a mountain to weep blood."

"Find it, Yavena. Our apologies for keeping you. But a word of advice before you leave: Rules are meant to be domesticated, not regarded as apex predators. The best players are those who can make the guidelines play fetch."

Yavena does not sleep. She cannot.

Serpent-silent, she pads through the hallways of the complex, hounded by a tempest of what-ifs. She knows Iraline. There will be no persuading her, not when her mind has settled into its chosen configuration. But there are other ways to win a game, are there not?

"Ira?" A puff of sound, kept low to circumvent detection. No one has explicitly forbidden nocturnal expeditions, but Yavena has learned to guard against risk.

"Yavena?" A sleep-hazed answer as the door creaks open.

No response, save for her entrance. Yavena leans back, feels the wood click shut behind her. A swallowed breath to steady herself. She arches her head.

Iraline stands before her, tiger-striped by moonlight and carelessly dressed in a white cotton shift. "What are you doing here?" Iraline whispers as she rubs the sleep from her eyes.

"I came to talk." Yavena slumps onto the edge of Iraline's cot. "Why are you doing this?"

"Doing what?"

"This. This . . . *dying* you're planning on." Yavena spits the words, the taste of them like poison on the tongue.

"Because I belong to the Court of the Dead," Iraline replies, slouching against a wall, arms crossed. Outside, the night is silent, heavy with anticipation. Tropical heat steams through the iron slats of Iraline's window. "Why else?"

"You're a Mother. A *fertile* Mother. You have decades before you even need to—"

Iraline palms her face, nodding, her answering smile taut. "Oh, sweetmeat. I—do you want the truth? The truth is, I am tired. Tired of watching children die, of raising other people's children to watch them die, of feeding bright-eyed innocents—"

"Everyone gives of themselves willingly, don't they?" Yavena cannot contain the slither of petty viciousness.

"Yes. No. We are taught to forsake self, you know. What matter is one life when it can purchase happiness for so many?" Iraline chuckles, wan. "Not all of us are strong enough for this duty."

The moonlight bleaches the color from her feathers, turns the glow of her eyes feral and strange. "It doesn't matter. Go home, Yavena. I'll talk to the Lord-General. He'll let you forfeit without repercussion, I'm sure of it. He's a kind one, if nothing else. Go."

"I promised I would always take care of you, sister," Yavena answers, loathing the petulance that worms through her voice.

The older Ovia lowers herself to her knees. Their hands interlock, her touch edged with a gentleness that makes Yavena ache. "I know. But this is—I have my reasons for courting the Black Hound, beloved. Now go."

Yavena considers the puzzle of their lives, the parameters of love. She strokes her claws over Iraline's own, measuring the topography of knuckles, the texture of her palms, the width of their lives. She nods once. "Not without you."

No Ovia is harmless. Each and every one of the Ten Thousand Colors is taught the balletic elegance of the kris, the soft places common to all sapient life. But Iraline is only a Mother, and Yavena a Keeper whetted on desperation. She strikes before Iraline can protest: a needle plunged into a vein.

Betrayal widens Iraline's gaze for a heartbeat before she collapses into a boneless heap, inert and unfeeling. Yavena gathers her sister's form and pads towards the door. The Dog-King had only said to win Iraline from herself, had not he not? Not how it needed to be accomplished. He would appreciate this, certainly. More importantly, he would understand.

She steps into the hallway. It is time for a different game.

This is a dance: a ballon of escape, arabesques performed on razor-point steeples, entrechat between battlements, Iraline's weight on her shoulder like a lifetime of guilt.

Yavena doesn't stop, doesn't pause, doesn't think. Every breath is a transaction paid with someone else's blood. Knife and kris glimmer, a charnel duet, keeping counterpoint with an orchestra of split viscera, opened lung.

Time empties of meaning. Yavena's world contracts into muscle memory and offal, to reptilian instinct, to a single demand hammering between spasming ventricles. *Out, out, out.*

Around her, the Gak begin to howl.

*Out, out, out.*

Yavena traverses arrows and closing gates, past an artillery of talons and physiques made monstrous without the frame of protocol. Who knew, she pants in the red-black dark behind her eyelids, that the Gak could be so terrifying?

*Out, out, out.*

The howling deafens.

*Release.* Somewhere between impossibilities, Yavena crosses the final gate and hurtles into the blackness, her lungs boiling. She is barely Ovia at this point, only impulse and the appetite of survival, her body latticed with a thousand red scars. Into the jungle she flings herself, Iraline secure against her spine, and the last thought Yavena births before the Gak's fortress becomes a memory is this:

Why do the warning horns sound so much like pleasure?

The Dog-King looks up from his chess table, smile light.

"Aaaah, Hahvah, you were right," he breathes, attention swinging back to the smaller Gak sitting opposite the game board, face shadowed by a ludicrous cap. "Yavena is a runner."

"I get to marry your brother now." The little Gak relocates a bishop, his answering grin gleaming with teeth. "Your move, your lordship."

"So many deaths just because you wouldn't court him in public? Oh, the games we play, Hahvah. The games we play."

Hahvah's eyes are tar black, marrow sweet. "Checkmate. Do we have a deal, your lordship?"

"Of course. Set the board, will you? The new round awaits."

\* \* \*

She runs.

For weeks, for hours, for amoebic eternities, Yavena runs. Until her breath is splinters and her muscles rot. There is no respite, only shards of unconsciousness interlaced with days that will not end and ceaseless nights spent staring into the jungle's teeth.

The journey is complicated by Iraline's refusal of her rescue. The first time she wakes, the older Ovia screams, a thunder of rage and grief so loud that Yavena, desperate to circumvent discovery, poisons her with sleep. The second time, Iraline does not cry out, only flees. It is circumstance alone that allows Yavena to retrieve her, weeping, from the dark, Iraline's ankle a mess of broken bone.

"You need to return me, sister," Iraline hisses between gasps of pain.

"No."

"Yavena. *Please.*" Iraline traps Yavena's wrist in fingers made iron from desperation. "Please. You need to take me back. You can't—the Dog-King. He will not forgive this."

"No," Yavena repeats and squeezes Iraline's flesh, an exact application of cruelty that immediately robs the latter of her senses.

There is no third confrontation. Yavena does not permit it. She keeps Iraline docile with venom, her mind chemical-slurred, her movements leaden with toxins. Yavena's actions are a betrayal, she knows this, a blasphemy of trust, but there is no other hope, no way to go but forward. When they at last they reach the courts of the Ten Thousand Colors, absolution will surely be found.

There is no absolution, only fire.

"What—"

Yavena's eyes map the labyrinth of the Ovia capital, warped by destruction, its sunset-clasped minarets and aqueducts reduced to a memory. Smoke haunts rubble-licked streets, thick as lies, as anguish.

In the distance, knotting with the funeral hymns of the Ovia, the voice of the Gak, triumphant.

"No." Yavena exhales, fear congealing in her throat. She staggers through the archway into the main pavilion, now a landscape of broken bodies, whimpering survivors, and ravaged architecture. "Nononono."

Iraline, fingers crusted with the grime of the road, says nothing, only slumps to her knees as Yavena releases her.

"No," Yavena says again, as though the word could subvert the truth of a thousand half-eaten corpses. "How could this—"

Even as the question unspools, an answer decants itself into her mind, a taste like salt, like a sister's desperation.

*You did this.*

It is hours before Yavena submits to this knowledge, to the horror of her actions. Hours before she collapses in an alley, her face in her arms, and wails for forgiveness from a city of indifferent ghosts.

The Dog-King is not what Yavena remembers. He is colossal, primordial, a nightmare made fur and sickle-moon snarl. Where Yavena remembered a scholar's inquisitiveness, a boyishness of conduct, there is only a predator's stare, hard and flat and golden behind small amber glasses.

"Why?" It is the only word that Yavena can find.

"Because you betrayed your end of the bargain."

Yavena jolts forward, one wincing step at a time, back held straight despite the agony that oozes between every vertebra. She can barely feel her left arm, can barely register the connection between tendon and nerve, the muscles flayed almost to ribbons. With a grunt, Yavena transfers her kris to her right hand, her weight to her left foot. Her grip tightens. After all that has happened, she will not bow, will not bend till she carves absolution from the ribs of the king.

"It was one Mother," she whispers between a mouthful of blood.

The Dog-King bares an indolent smile. "One Mother. One bargain. One treaty."

"You tricked us—"

"We gave you every opportunity to perform as you should have, and you *failed.*"

"You *used* me!" she screams, limping closer, closer to where the Dog-King sits draped over his throne of dead Mothers.

"Perhaps," replies the Dog-King as he studies a fan of claws. "Perhaps we decided to use you in a stupid little bet with a stupid little mutt, but then thought, 'Ah! This could be so much more.' Perhaps we then decided that the Gak required a new world order, one where our pups would know the hunt as our ancestors did, and our meals were taut-muscled and not limp from a lifetime of coddling. Perhaps this was all our fault, but the hawk never discusses business with the hare."

"I'm going to kill you."

"Really."

Yavena squares her stance, swallows copper and bile, tries not to sway even as her head swims with grief and the ice-water fury of those without anything to lose. "I've killed everyone else. All of your guards, all of your soldiers. None of them could stop me. I—"

"Yes." The Dog-King grins, unfolding like the death of nations. "Tell me, little Ovia, why do you think that is?"

# THE ROAD, AND THE VALLEY, AND THE BEASTS

## *Keffy R. M. Kehrli*

The valley of my home is long and crooked and narrow, cut into the landscape like a knife wound. A river runs along the bottom, flooding often through the spring, drying to a barest trickle in late summer, and freezing in winter. Shadowing the river is the great old road, a broad expanse of weeds and cracked bricks that were laid by hands long since forgotten.

As a rule, we do not travel the road, as it is not ours to use.

Our town has no official name. It is merely a collection of houses rough-hewn from tree and stone for those of us who find ourselves here. There are never any visitors, and none of us ever leave, not by road, nor by river, and certainly never in the baskets of the dead. Perhaps the town had a name once, and the people who lived here before us decided that there was no need to keep a name if there was no one to speak with. Would we have names, ourselves, if there were never anyone to introduce ourselves to?

We are not born here, but here we die, and our bodies are buried in the cemetery tucked up against the eastern wall of the valley. There we rest with all those who lived here before, whether they gave the town a name or no, their own names obscured by lichens and mosses and worn away by the callused hands of time.

Why is there a road if it is not used? Ah, but it *is* used, frequently—only never by any of us.

There is a procession of giant Beasts that travels the great road past us twice a day, in the morning traveling upriver and in the evening traveling down. In the dim light of early dawn, the Beasts walk hunched and weary, their backs laden with baskets full of the newly dead, whose eyes stare and gleam in the dark, legs and arms limp or stiff depending on how long they've been dead. In the evenings, the Beasts pass us again, looking strong and refreshed, their baskets hanging limp and empty. Sometimes at dusk they whistle while they travel, the fluting sounds echoing down the valley for hours.

Somewhere, far away, there is a land where we are born. Somewhere, far away, there is a land where people are not buried when they die, but are taken upriver by the Beasts.

I dream of that land almost every day, whether I'm weeding the garden that my adoptive mothers have planted, or baking bread, or washing the clothes in a shallow section of the river. There are so many dead in the baskets of the Beasts each morning that this land they come from must be full of people, more people even than are buried in our cemetery, more than have ever existed in our small town. I wonder what things they have built, towers of marble, cathedrals of glass, bridges of gold that gleam red in the sunset . . .

My dearest love is a girl named Ria, who was given a boy's name when she first came here but let her adoptive father know that he was wrong as soon as she could speak. Although nearly adults, we two are the youngest living in the town, as it has been one of the longest stretches between new arrivals that anyone can remember.

In the evenings, Ria sits with me under the apple trees in my mothers' orchard, nibbling at my ears when she thinks that I have paid too much attention to the Beasts passing us by, holding my hands against her chest when I try to cup them behind my ears to hear the Beasts' strangely soft footfalls.

I prefer to watch them in the evening. They look happier, their burdens left behind them. Their springy coils of metallic hair bounce with each step. The lightened baskets swing down along their sides, empty and free. Their arms pump the air, all sinew and skin, and their long, long fingers snap quiet rhythms.

"Ria," I whisper into her ear, resting my forehead against her kinky black hair, "someday I will follow them home, back to where we came from, and I will find out why we were sent away, and how, and by whom, and then we will know who we really are."

She shakes her head, reaches behind us for a freshly wind-felled apple, and takes a bite before offering it to me. "Why should we care about who we used to be, or who we would have been, or those who never wanted us to begin with?"

The apple's flesh is crisp and cool and sweet between my teeth. "Aren't you curious?"

She rolls her eyes and runs her fingers through her hair. "Not about who I used to be, no."

"But what if . . . ?"

"No."

"We could be princes, or kings, or queens, or long-lost siblings to an emperor, or . . ."

"Or babies too strange to ever be wanted, people with no past worth speaking of or remembering."

She takes the apple back, and I say, "I don't understand why you don't even want to know."

"You won't go, anyway," she says. "You've been telling me the same thing, making plans like wisps of clouds, since we were children."

"Someday," I insist. "When I'm ready."

Ria shakes her head, and she pulls me down beside her on the grass, staring up at the leaves and branches and softly reddening apples. Above our farms and the trees, the walls of the valley ascend far into the clouds on most days, so high that nothing can grow in the thinned air. We are ringed around by jagged black teeth, as though we rest in the back of a mouth tipped to the sky.

It is later, after we have made up, and kissed again, and reached gentle fingers under clothes and into all our favorite places, that I realize my mistake. It is not that Ria is not curious. It is that she prefers the morning Beasts, prefers waking before dawn, alone, and watching them walk.

In the mornings, their backs are stooped under the weight of all the dead. In the mornings, they walk like dead things themselves, their eyes tired and pained, their fingers not snapping, but instead dangling near to the cracked road beneath their feet. They do not whistle on their travels upriver, but instead they sometimes hum a dirge, a lullaby, for the dead they carry.

I do not always wake to watch the Beasts pass us in the morning, but I know that Ria does, so I crawl from the warmth of my sheets an hour before dawn, too early, too early, the exhaustion making my skin feel tight and achy. I wash my face in the basin of cold water, trying to bring myself to wakefulness, then grab two rolls left over from dinner the night before and slip out the door quietly enough that my mothers will not wake.

Ria is not by the trees in the orchard, nor is she on the hill beside the river, but when I climb that hill, I do see her sitting on a large stone next to the great road. I sprint to her, nearly dropping our breakfast.

"Ria!" I say, starting to feel the soft, shuffling footfalls of the Beasts upon the earth. They are so near, so near, just around the bend of the river and road. "Ria, what are you doing?"

"Shh," she says. "They don't mind if you sit so close to watch them, as long as you are quiet."

"But . . ."

"Come and sit with me," she says, "or go back to bed."

I climb up to sit next to her on the stone, and hand her one of the rolls. She sniffs it, smiles, and then puts it inside a small canvas bag she has slung over one shoulder.

"You spend so much time thinking about the land we've come from," she says. "Do you ever think about what might be further on down the road?"

I frown, my fingers tearing into the roll I have kept for myself. Crumbs fall to the road, and a quick and fearless crow grabs them before the Beasts round the corner.

They are as heavily laden this morning as they ever are. I have never sat so close to watch the dead. I recoil slightly, but Ria grabs my arm and steadies me. The dead are old and young and in between. Some look peaceful as they gaze out at the valley. Others are weeping tears of blood, or holding together grievous injuries with pale, bloodless fingers.

The Beasts ignore us, ignore the valley, pay no attention to anything around them, until suddenly Ria jumps down from the stone and dashes onto the road, dancing around the feet of the Beasts in the front until she is standing before the last of them.

I cannot breathe, and I cannot move, and I cannot save her.

The Beast stops, its feet slowing to a shuffle and I see that Ria is barely as tall as half its shin. It stares down at her, long fingers straying up to scratch the curly hairs on its chest.

"I wish to go with you," Ria says.

The Beast looks over her to the others in its procession, passing the orchard and the hill, and soon to be out of our town altogether.

Its voice rumbles in its chest, and I think that it is about to talk, but it does not. It hums to itself quietly, thoughtfully, and then reaches behind to the baskets on its shoulders. It palms something, and then holds out a hand the size of a small house to Ria. A child sits there, eyes wide and frightened, not looking nearly as dead as the others.

"Stay here," the Beast says, its voice like rolling thunder. "Safe, here."

Ria looks for a moment like she will argue. But the Beast is as tall and implacable as a mountain. Her shoulders slump as she accepts the refusal. She reaches out, and the child slides down off the Beast's great hand to stand with her on the road.

The Beast considers them for a moment, rubs Ria's hair gently with a single fingertip, and then steps over them, walking a touch faster than usual so that it can catch up to its fellows.

# INNUMERABLE GLIMMERING LIGHTS

## *Rich Larson*

At the roof of the world, the Drill churned and churned. Four Warm Currents watched with eyes and mouth, overlaying the engine's silhouette with quicksilver sketches of sonar. Long, twisting shards of ice bloomed from the metal bit to float back along the carved tunnel. Workers with skin glowing acid yellow, hazard visibility, jetted out to meet the debris and clear it safely to the sides. Others monitored the mesh of machinery that turned the bit, smoothing contact points, spinning cogs. The whole thing was beautiful, efficient, and made Four Warm Currents secrete anticipation in a flavored cloud.

A sudden needle of sonar, pitched high enough to sting, but not so high that it couldn't be passed off as accidental. Four Warm Currents knew it was Nine Brittle Spines before even tasting the name in the water.

"Does it move faster with you staring at it?" Nine Brittle Spines signed, tentacles languid with humor-not-humor.

"No faster, no slower," Four Warm Currents replied, forcing two tentacles into a curled smile. "The Drill is as inexorable as our dedication to its task."

"Dedication is admirable, as said the ocean's vast cold to one volcano's spewing heat." Nine Brittle Spines's pebbly skin illustrated, flashing red for a brief instant before regaining a dark cobalt hue.

"You are still skeptical." Four Warm Currents clenched tight to keep distaste from inking the space between them. Nine Brittle Spines was a council member, and not one to risk offending. "But the ice's composition

**221**

is changing, as I reported. The bit shears easier with every turn. We're approaching the other side."

"So it thins, and so it will thicken again." Nine Brittle Spines wriggled dismissal. "The other side is a deep dream, Four Warm Currents. Your machine is approaching more ice."

"The calculations," Four Warm Currents protested. "The sounding. If you would read the theorems—"

Nine Brittle Spines hooked an interrupting tentacle through the thicket of movement. "No need for your indignation. I have no quarrel with the Drill. It's a useful sideshow, after all. It keeps the eyes and mouths of the colony fixated while the council slides its decisions past unhindered."

"If you have no quarrel, then why do you come here?" Four Warm Currents couldn't suck back the words, or the single droplet of ichor that suddenly wobbled into the water between them. It blossomed there into a ghostly black wreath. Four Warm Currents raked a hasty tentacle through to disperse it, but the councillor was already tasting the chemical, slowly, pensively.

"I have no quarrel, Four Warm Currents, but others do." Nine Brittle Spines swirled the bitter emission around one tentacle tip, as if it were a pheromone poem or something else to be savored. Four Warm Currents, mortified, could do nothing but turn an apologetic mottled blue, almost too distracted to process what the councillor signed next.

"While the general opinion is that you have gone mad, and your project is a hilariously inept allocation of time and resources based only on your former contributions, theories do run the full gamut. Some believe the Drill is seeking mineral deposits in the ice. Others believe the Drill will be repurposed as a weapon, to crack through the fortified cities of the vent-dwelling colonies." Nine Brittle Spines shaped a derisive laugh. "And there is even a small but growing tangent who believe in your theorems. Who believe that you are fast approaching the mythic other side, and that our ocean will seep out of the puncture like the viscera from a torn egg, dooming us all."

"The weight of the ocean will hold it where it is," Four Warm Currents signed, a sequence by now rote to the tentacles. "The law of sink and rise is one you've surely studied."

"Once again, my opinion is irrelevant to the matter," Nine Brittle Spines replied. "I am here because this radical tangent is believed to be targeting your project for sabotage. The council wishes to protect its investment." Tentacles pinwheeled in a slight hesitation then: "You yourself may be in danger as well. The council advises you to keep a low profile. Perhaps change your name taste."

"I am not afraid for my life." Four Warm Currents signed it firmly and honestly. The project was more important than survival. More important than anything.

"Then fear, perhaps, for your mate's children."

Four Warm Currents flashed hot orange shock, bright enough for the foreman to glance over, concerned. "What?"

Nine Brittle Spines held up the tentacle tip that had tasted Four Warm Currents's anger. "Traces of ingested birth mucus. Elevated hormones. You should demonstrate more self-control, Four Warm Currents. You give away all sorts of secrets."

The councillor gave a lazy salute, then jetted off into the gloom, joined at a distance by two bodyguards with barbed tentacles. Four Warm Currents watched them vanish down the tunnel, then slowly turned back toward the Drill. The bit churned and churned. Four Warm Currents's mind churned with it.

When the work cycle closed, the Drill was tugged back down the tunnel and tethered in a hard shell still fresh enough to glisten. A corkscrewing skiff arrived to unload the guard detail, three young bloods with enough hormone-stoked muscle to overlook the still-transparent patches on their skin. They inked their names so loudly Four Warm Currents could taste them before even jetting over.

"There's been a threat of sorts," Four Warm Currents signed, secreting a small dark privacy cloud to shade the conversation from workers filing onto the now-empty skiff. "Against the project. Radicals who may attempt sabotage."

"We know," signed the guard, whose name was a pungent Two Sinking Corpses. "The councillor told us. That's why we have these." Two Sinking Corpses hefted a conical weapon Four Warm Currents dimly recognized as a screamer, built to amplify a sonar burst to lethal strength. Nine Brittle Spines had not exaggerated the seriousness of the situation.

"Pray to the Leviathans you don't have to use them," Four Warm Currents signed, then joined the workers embarking on the skiff, tasting familiar names, slinging tentacles over knotted muscles, adding to a multilayered scent joke involving an aging councillor and a frost shark. Spirits were high. The Drill was cutting smoothly. They were approaching the other side, and though for some that only meant the end of contract and full payment, others had also been infected by Four Warm Currents's fervor.

"What will we see?" a worker signed. "Souls of the dead? The Leviathans themselves?"

"Nothing outside the physical laws," Four Warm Currents replied, but then, sensing the disappointment: "But nothing like we have ever seen before. It will be unimaginable. Wondrous. And they'll soak our names all through the memory sponges, to remember the brave explorers who first broke the ice."

A mass of tentacles waved in approval of the idea. Four Warm Currents settled back as the skiff began to move and a wave of new debates sprang up.

The City of Bone was roughly spherical, a beautiful lattice of ancient skeleton swathed in sponge and cultivated coral, glowing ethereal blue with bioluminescence. It was older than any councillor, a relic of the dim past before the archives: a Leviathan skeleton dredged from the seafloor with buoyant coral, built up and around until it could float unsupported, tethered in place above the jagged rock bed.

Devotees believed the Leviathans had sacrificed their corporeal forms to leave city husks behind; Four Warm Currents shared the more heretical view that the Leviathans were extinct, and for all their size might have been no more intelligent than the living algae feeders that still hauled their bulk along the seafloor. It was not a theory to divulge in polite discourse. Drilling through the roof of the world was agitator enough on its own.

As the skiff passed the City of Bone's carved sentinels, workers began to jet off to their respective housing blocks. Four Warm Currents was one of the last to disembark, having been afforded, as one of the council's foremost engineers, an artful gray-and-purple spire in the city center. Of course, that was before the Drill. Nine Brittle Spines's desire for a "sideshow" aside, Four Warm Currents felt the daily loss of council approval like the descending cold of a crevice. Relocation was not out of the realm of possibility.

For now, though, the house's main door shuttered open at a touch, and, more importantly, Four Warm Currents's mates were inside. Six Bubbling Thermals, sleek and swollen with eggs, drizzling ribbons of birth mucus like a halo, but with eyes still bright and darting. Three Jagged Reefs, lean and long, skin stained from a heavy work cycle in the smelting vents, submitting to a massage. Their taste made Four Warm Currents ache, deep and deeper.

"So our heroic third returns," Six Bubbling Thermals signed, interrupting the massage and prompting a ruffle of protest.

"Have you ended the world yet?" Three Jagged Reefs added. "Don't stop, Six. I'm nearly loose enough to slough."

"Nearly," Four Warm Currents signed. "I blacked a councillor. Badly."

Both mates guffawed, though Six Bubbling Thermals's had a nervous shiver to it.

"From how far?" Three Jagged Reefs demanded. "Could they tell it was yours?"

"From not even a tentacle away," Four Warm Currents admitted. "We were in conversation."

Three Jagged Reefs laughed again, the reckless, waving laugh that had made Four Warm Currents fall in love, but their other mate did not.

"Conversation about what?" Six Bubbling Thermals signed.

Four Warm Currents hesitated, tasting around to make sure a strong emotion hadn't slipped the gland again, but the water was clear and cold and anxiety-free. "Nine Brittle Spines is a skeptic of the worst kind. Intelligent, but refusing to self-educate."

"Did you not explain the density calculation?" Three Jagged Reefs signed plaintively.

Four Warm Currents moved to reply, then recognized a familiar mocking tilt in Three Jagged Reefs's tentacles and turned the answer into a crude "floating feces" gesticulation.

"Tell us the mathematics again," Three Jagged Reefs teased. "Nothing slicks me better for sex, Four. All those beautiful variables."

Six Bubbling Thermals smiled at the back-and-forth, but was still lightly spackled with mauve worry. The birth mucus spiralling out in all directions made for an easy distraction.

"We need to collect again," Four Warm Currents signed, gesturing to the trembling ribbons. "Or you'll bury us in our sleep."

"And then I'll finally have the house all to my own," Six Bubbling Thermals signed, cloying. But the mauve worry dissolved into flushed healthy pink as they all began coiling the mucus and storing it in coral tubing. Four Warm Currents stroked the egg sacs gently as they worked, imagining each one hatching into an altered world.

After they finished with the birth mucus and pricked themselves with a recreational skimmer venom, Three Jagged Reefs made them sample a truly terrible pheromone poem composed at the smelting vents between geysers. The recitation was quickly cancelled in favor of hallucination-laced sex in which they all slid over and around Six Bubbling Thermals's swollen mantle, probing and pulping, and afterward the three of them drifted in the artificial current, slowly revolving as they discussed anything and everything:

Colony annexation, the validity of aesthetic tentacle removal, the new eatery that served everything dead and frozen with frescoes carved into the flesh, So-and-So's scent change, the best birthing tanks, the after-ache they'd had the last time they used skimmer venom. Anything and everything except for the Drill.

Much later, when the other two had slipped into a sleeping harness, Four Warm Currents jetted upward to the top of their gray-and-purple spire, coiling there to look out over the City of Bone. Revelers jetted back and forth in the distance, visible by blots of blue-green excitement and arousal. Some were workers from the Drill, Four Warm Currents knew, celebrating the end of a successful work cycle.

Four Warm Currents's namesake parent had been a laborer of the same sort. A laborer who came home to cramped quarters and hungry children, but was never too exhausted to spin them a story, tentacles whirling and flourishing like a true bard. Four Warm Currents had been a logical child, always finding gaps in the tall tales of Leviathans and heroes and oceans beyond their own. But still, the stories had sunk in deep. Enough so that Four Warm Currents might be able to sign them to the children growing in Six Bubbling Thermals's egg sacs.

There was no need for Nine Brittle Spines or the council to know it was those stories that had ignited Four Warm Currents's curiosity for the roof of the world in the first place. Soon there would be new stories to tell. In seven, maybe eight more work cycles, they would break through.

After such a long percolation, the idea was dizzying. Four Warm Currents didn't know what awaited on the other side. There were theories, of course. Many theories. Four Warm Currents had studied gas bubbles and knew that whatever substance lay beyond the ice was not water as they knew it, not nearly so heavy. It could very well be deadly. Four Warm Currents would take precautions, but—

The brush of a tentacle tip, a familiar taste. Six Bubbling Thermals had ballooned up to join the stillness. Four Warm Currents extended a welcoming clasp, and the rasp of skin on skin was a comforting one. Calming.

"Someone almost started a riot in the plaza today," Six Bubbling Thermals signed.

The calm was gone. "Over what? Over the project?"

"Yes." Six Bubbling Thermals stared out across the city with a long clicking burst, then turned to face Four Warm Currents. "They had artificial panic. In storage globes. Broke them wide open right as the market peaked. It was . . ." Tentacles wove in and out, searching for a descriptor. "Chaos."

"Are you all right?" Four Warm Currents signed hard. "You should have told me. You're birthing."

Six Bubbling Thermals waved a quick-dying laugh. "I'm still bigger than you are. And I told Three Jagged Reefs. We agreed it would be best not to add to your stress. But I've never kept secrets well, have I?"

Another stare, longer this time. Four Warm Currents joined in, scraping sound across the architecture of the city, mapping curves and crevices, spars and spires.

"Before they were dragged off, they dropped one last globe," Six Bubbling Thermals signed. "It was your name, fresh, mixed with a decay scent. They said you're a monster, and if nobody stops you, you'll end the world."

Four Warm Currents shivered, clenched hard against the noxious fear threatening to tendril into the water. "Fresh?"

"Yes."

Who had it been? Four Warm Currents thought of the many workers and observers jetting up and down the tunnel, bringing status reports, complaints, updates. Any one of them could have come close enough to coax their chief engineer's name taste into a concealed globe. With a start, Four Warm Currents realized Six Bubbling Thermals was not gazing pensively over the city, but keeping watch.

"I know you won't consider halting the project," Six Bubbling Thermals signed. "But you need to be careful. Promise me that much."

Four Warm Currents remembered the councillor's warning and stroked Six Bubbling Thermals's egg sacs with a trembling tentacle. "I'll be careful. And when we break through, this will all go away. They'll see there's no danger."

"And when will that be?" The mauve worry was creeping back across Six Bubbling Thermals's skin.

"Soon," Four Warm Currents signed. "Seven work cycles."

They enmeshed their tentacles and curled against each other, bobbing there in silence as the City of Bone's ghostly blue guide lights began to blink out one by one.


The first attack came three cycles later, after shift. A pair of free-swimmers, with their skins pumped pitch-black and a sonar cloak in tow, managed to bore halfway through the Drill's protective shell before the guards spotted them and chased them off. The news came by a messenger whom Three Jagged Reefs, unhappily awoken, nearly eviscerated. Bare moments later, Four Warm Currents stroked goodbyes to both mates and took the skiff to the project site, tentacles heavy from sleep but hearts thrumming electric.

Nine Brittle Spines somehow contrived to arrive first.

"Four Warm Currents, it is a pleasure to see you so well rested." The councillor's tentacles moved as smoothly and blandly as ever, but Four Warm Currents could see the faintest of trembling at their tips. Mortal after all.

"I came as quickly as I was able," Four Warm Currents signed, not rising to the barb. "Were either of the perpetrators identified?"

"No." Nine Brittle Spines gave the word a twist of annoyance. "Assumedly they were two of yours. They knew the thinnest point of the shell and left behind a project-tagged auger." One tentacle produced the spiral tool and set it drifting between them. It was a miniature cousin to the behemoth Drill, used to sample ice consistency.

Four Warm Currents inspected the implement. "I'll speak with inventory, but I imagine it was taken without their knowledge."

"Do that," Nine Brittle Spines signed. "In the meanwhile, security will be increased. We'll have guards at all times from now on. Body searches for workers."

Four Warm Currents waved a vague agreement, staring up at the burnished armor shell, the hole scored in its underbelly. The workers would not be happy, but they were so close now, too close to let anything derail the project. Four Warm Currents would agree to anything, so long as the Drill was safe.

Tension became a sharp, sooty tang overlaying every conversation, so much so that Four Warm Currents was given council approval for a globe of artificially mixed happiness to waft around the tunnel entrance. It ended being mostly sucked up by the guards, who were happy enough already to swagger around with screamers and combat hooks bristling in their tentacles, interrogating any particularly worry-spackled worker who happened to look their way.

Four Warm Currents complained to the councillor, but was soundly ignored, told only that the guards had been instructed to treat the project site and its crew with the utmost respect. Enthusiasm was now a thing of the past. Workers spoke rarely and with short tempers, and every time the Drill slowed or an error was found in its calibration, the possibility of sabotage hung in the tunnel like a decay scent. Four Warm Currents found a slip in the most recent density calculation that promised to put things back a full work cycle, but still the Drill churned.

At home, they began receiving death threats. Six Bubbling Thermals found the first, a tiny automaton that waved its stiff tentacles in a prerecorded message: "We won't need a drill to puncture your eyes and every one of your eggs." Three Jagged Reefs shredded it to pieces. Four Warm Currents gave the pieces to the council's investigator.

Then, two cycles before breakthrough, black globes of artificial malice were slicked to their spire with adhesive and timed to burst while they slept. Only one went off, but it was enough to necessitate a pore-cleanse for Six Bubbling Thermals and a dedicated surveillance detail for the house.

Three Jagged Reefs fumed and fumed. "After the Drill breaks through, you'll let me borrow it, won't you?" The demand was jittery with skimmer venom, and made only once Six Bubbling Thermals, finally returned from the cleansing tanks, was out of sight range. "I'm going to find the shit-eater who blacked Six and stick them on the bit gland first."

Three Jagged Reefs had been pulled from smelting after an incidence of "hazardously elevated emotions," in which a copper-worker trilling about the impending end of the world had their tentacle held over a geyser until it turned to pulp. Staying in the house full cycle, under the watchful eyes and mouths of council surveillance, was not an easy transition. Not even stocked with high-quality venom.

"It'll all be over soon," Four Warm Current signed, mind half-filled, as was now the norm, with figures from the latest density calculation. One final cycle.

"Tell it to Six," Three Jagged Reefs signed back, short and clipped, and turned away.

Four Warm Currents swam into the next room, to where their mate was adrift in the sleeping harness. The egg sacs were bulging now, slick with the constant emission of birth mucus, bearing no trace of black ichor stains. The cleansing tanks had reported no permanent damage. Four Warm Currents sent a gentle prod of sonar and elicited a twitch.

"I'm awake," Six Bubbling Thermals signed, languid. "I'd sleep better with you two around me."

"They'll catch the lunatics who planted that globe," Four Warm Currents signed back.

Six Bubbling Thermals signed nothing for a long moment, then waved a sad laugh. "I don't think it's lunatics. Not anymore. A lot of people are saying the same thing, you know."

"Saying what?"

"You spend all of your time at the Drill, even when you're here with us." The accusation was soft, but it stung. "You haven't been paying attention. The transit currents are full of devotees calling you a blasphemer. Saying you think yourself a Leviathan. Unbounded. The whole city is frightened."

"Then it's a city of idiots," Four Warm Currents signed abruptly.

"I'm frightened. I have no shame admitting it. I'm frightened for our children. For them to have two parents only. One parent only. None. For them to never even hatch. Who knows?" Six Bubbling Thermals raised a shaky smile. "Maybe the idiot is the one who isn't frightened."

"But I'm going to give them an altered world, a new world . . ." Four Warm Currents's words blurred as Six Bubbling Thermals stilled two waving tentacles.

"I don't give a floating shit about a new world if it's one where you take a hook in the back," Six Bubbling Thermals signed back, slow and clear. "Don't go to the Drill tomorrow. They'll send for you when it breaks the ice."

At first, Four Warm Currents didn't even comprehend the words. After spending a third of a lifespan planning, building, lobbying, watching, the idea of not being there to witness the final churn, the final crack and squeal of ice giving away, was dizzying. Nauseating.

"If you go, I think you'll be dead before you come home," Six Bubbling Thermals signed. "You're worth more to us alive for one more cycle than as a name taste wafting through the archives for all eternity."

"I've watched it from the very start." Four Warm Currents tried not to tremble. "Every turn. Every single turn."

"And without you it moves no faster, no slower," Six Bubbling Thermals replied. "Isn't that what you say?"

"I have to be there."

"You don't." Six Bubbling Thermals gave a weary shudder. "Is it a new world for our children, or only for you?"

Four Warm Currents's tentacles went slack, adrift. The two of them stared at each other in the gloom, until, suddenly, something stirred in the egg sacs. The motion repeated, a faint but mesmerizing ripple. Six Bubbling Thermals gave a slight wriggle of pain.

Four Warm Currents climbed into the harness, turning acid blue in an apology that could not have been properly signed. "I'll stay. I'll stay, I'll stay."

They folded against each other and spoke of other things, of the strange currents that had brought them together, the future looming in the birthing tanks. Then they slept, deeply, even when Three Jagged Reefs wobbled in to join them much later, nearly unhooking the harness with chemical-clumsy tentacles.

Four Warm Currents dreamt of ending the world, the Drill shearing through its final stretch of pale ice, and from the gaping wound in the roof of the world, a Leviathan lowering its head, eyes glittering, to swallow the engine and its workers and their blasphemous chief engineer whole, pulling its bulk back into the world it once abandoned, sliding through blackness toward the City of Bone, ready to reclaim its scattered body, to devour all light, to unmake everything that had ever been made.

Four Warm Currents awoke to stinging sonar and the silhouette of a familiar councillor drifting before the sleeping harness, flanked by two long-limbed guards.

"Wake your mates," Nine Brittle Spines signed, with a taut urgency Four Warm Currents had never seen before. "All three of you have to leave."

"What's happening?"

"You'll see."

Four Warm Currents rolled, body heavy with sleep, and stroked each mate awake in turn. Three Jagged Reefs refused to rise until Six Bubbling Thermals furiously shook the harness, a flash of the old pre-birthing strength.

"Someone come to murder us?" Three Jagged Reefs asked calmly, once toppled free.

"You wouldn't feel a thing with all that venom in you," Four Warm Currents replied, less calmly.

"I barely pricked."

"As said the Drill to the roof of the world," Six Bubbling Thermals interjected.

Nine Brittle Spines flashed authoritative indigo, cutting the conversation short. "We have a skiff outside. Your discussions can wait."

The three of them followed the councillor out of the house, trailing long, sticky strands of Six Bubbling Thermals's replenished birth mucus. Once they exited the shutter and were no longer filtered, a faint acrid flavor seeped to them through the water. The City of Bone tasted bitter with fear. Anger.

And that wasn't all.

In the distance, Four Warm Currents could see free-swimmers moving as a mob, jetting back and forth through the city spires, carrying homegrown phosphorescent lamps and scent bombs. Several descended on a council-funded sculpture, smearing the stone with webbed black-and-red rage. Most continued on, heading directly for the city center. For their housing block, Four Warm Currents realized with a sick jolt.

"The radical tangent has grown," Nine Brittle Spines signed. "Considerably."

"So many?" Four Warm Currents was stunned.

"Only thing people love more than a festival is a doomsday," Three Jagged Reefs signed bitterly.

"Indeed. Your decriers have found support in many places, I'm afraid." Nine Brittle Spines bent a grimace as they swam toward the waiting skiff, a closed and armored craft marked with an official sigil. "Including the council."

Four Warm Currents stopped dead in the water. "But the Drill is still under guard."

"The Drill is currently being converged upon by a mob twice this size," Nine Brittle Spines signed. "Even without sympathizers in the security ranks, it would be futile to try to protect it. The council's official position, as of this moment, is that your project has been terminated to save costs."

Four Warm Currents realized, dimly, that both mates were holding tentacles back to prevent an incidence of hazardously elevated emotions. Searing orange desperation had spewed into the water around them. Nine Brittle Spines made no remarks about self-control, only flashed, for the briefest instant, a pale blue regret.

"But we're nearly through," Four Warm Currents signed, trembling all over. Three Jagged Reefs and Six Bubbling Thermals now slowly slid off, eager for the safety of the skiff. Drifting away when they were needed most.

"Perhaps you are," Nine Brittle Spines admitted. "Perhaps your theorems are sound. But stability is, at the present moment, more important than discovery."

"If we go to the Drill." Four Warm Currents shuddered to a pause. "If we go to the Drill, if we go now, we can stop them. I can explain to them. I can convince them."

"You know better than that, Four Warm Currents. In fact—"

Whatever Nine Brittle Spines planned to say next was guillotined as Six Bubbling Thermals surged from behind, wrapping the councillor in full grip. In the same instant, Three Jagged Reefs yanked the skiff's shutter open. Four Warm Currents stared at the writhing councillor, then at each mate in turn.

"Get on with it, Four," Three Jagged Reefs signed. "Go and try."

Six Bubbling Thermals was unable to sign, tentacles taut as a vice around Nine Brittle Spines, but the misty red cloud billowing into the water was the fiercest and most pungent love Four Warm Currents could remember tasting.

"Oh, wait." Three Jagged Reefs glanced between them. "Six wanted to know if you have any necessary names."

"None," Four Warm Currents signed shakily. "So long as there are Thermals and Reefs."

"Well, of course." Three Jagged Reefs waved a haughty laugh that speared Four Warm Currents's hearts all over again. The councillor had finally stopped struggling in Six Bubbling Thermals's embrace and now watched the proceedings with an air of resignation. Four Warm Currents flashed a respectful pale blue, then turned and swam for the skiff.

They were hauling the Drill out of its carapace with hooks and bare tentacles, clouding the water with rage, excitement, amber-streaked triumph. Four Warm Currents abandoned the skiff for the final stretch, sucking back hard, jetting harder. The mob milled around the engine in a frenzy, too caught up to notice one late arrival.

Four Warm Currents screamed, dragging sonar across the crowd, but in the mess of motion and chemicals nobody felt the hard clicks. They'd brought a coring charge, one of the spiky half-spheres designed for blasting through solid rock bed to the nickel veins beneath. Four Warm Currents had shut down a foreman's lobby for such explosives during a particularly slow stretch of drilling. Too volatile, too much blowback in a confined space. But now it was here, and it was going to shred the Drill to pieces.

Four Warm Currents jetted higher, above the chaos, nearly to the mouth of the tunnel. No eyes followed. Everyone was intent on the Drill and on the coring charge being shuffled toward it, tentacle by tentacle.

Four Warm Currents sucked back, angled, and dove. The free-swimmers towing the coring charge didn't see the interloper until it was too late, until Four Warm Currents slid two tentacles deep into the detonation triggers and clung hard.

"Get away from me! Get away or I'll trigger right here!"

The crowd turned to a fresco of frozen tentacles, momentarily speechless. Then:

"Blasphemer," signed the closest free-swimmer. "Blasphemer."

The word caught and rippled across the mob, becoming a synchronized wave of short, chopping motions.

"The Drill is not going to end the world," Four Warm Currents signed desperately, puffing up over the crowd, hauling the coring charge along. "It's going to break us into a brand-new one. One we'll visit at our choosing. The deep ocean will stay deep ocean. The Leviathans will stay skeletons. Our cities will stay safe."

Something struck like a spar of bone, sending Four Warm Currents reeling. The conical head of a screamer poked out from the crowd, held by a young guard whose skin was no longer inked with the council's sigil. The name came dimly to memory: Two Sinking Corpses. An unfamiliar taste was clouding into the water. It took a moment for Four Warm Currents to realize it was blood, blue and hot and saline.

"Listen to me!"

The plea was answered by another blast of deadly sound, this one misaimed, clipping a tentacle. Four Warm Currents nearly lost grip on the coring charge. The mob roiled below, waving curses, mottled black and orange with fury. There would be no listening.

"Stay away from me or I'll trigger it," Four Warm Currents warned once more, then jetted hard for the mouth of the tunnel. The renewed threat of detonation bought a few still seconds. Then the mob realized where the coring charge was headed, and the sleekest and fastest of them tore away in pursuit.

Four Warm Currents hurled up the dark tunnel, sucking back water in searing cold gulps and flushing faster and harder with each. Familiar grooves in the ice jumped out with a smatter of sonar, etchings warning against unauthorized entry. Four Warm Currents blew past with tentacles straight back, trailing the coring charge directly behind, gambling nobody would risk hitting it with a screamer.

A familiar bend loomed in the dark, one of the myriad small adjustments to course, and beyond it, the service lights, bundles of bioluminescent algae set along the walls, began blooming to life, painting the tunnel an eerie blue-green, casting a long-limbed shadow on the wall. Four Warm Currents chanced a look down and saw three free-swimmers, young and strong and gaining.

"Drop it!" one took the opportunity to sign. "Drop it and you'll live!"

Four Warm Currents used a tentacle to sign back one of Three Jagged Reefs's favorite gestures, reflecting that it was a bad idea when the young-blood's skin flashed with rage and all three of them put on speed. The head start was waning, the coring charge was heavy, the screamer wound was dribbling blood.

But Four Warm Currents knew the anatomy of the tunnel better than anyone, better than even the foreman. The three pursuers lost valuable time picking their way through a thicket of free-floating equipment knocked from the wall, then more again deliberating where the tunnel branched, stubby memento of a calculation error.

Four Warm Currents's hearts were wailing for rest as the final stretch appeared. The coring charge felt like lead. A boiling shadow swooped past, and Four Warm Currents realized they'd fired another screamer, one risk now outweighing the other. The roof of the world, stretched thin like a membrane, marred with the Drill's final twist, loomed above.

Another blast of sonar, this one closer. Four Warm Currents throttled out a cloak of black ink, hoping to obscure the next shot, too exhausted to try to dodge. Too exhausted to do anything now but churn warm water, drag slowly, too slowly, toward the top.

The screamer's next burst was half-deflected by the coring charge, but still managed to make every single tentacle spasm. Four Warm Currents felt the cargo slipping and tried desperately to regain purchase on its slick metal. So close, now, so close to the end of the world. Roof of the world. Either. Thoughts blurred and collided in Four Warm Currents's bruised brain. More blood was pumping out, bright blue, foul-tasting. Four Warm Currents tried to hold onto the exact taste of Six Bubbling Thermals's love.

One tentacle stopped working. Four Warm Currents compensated with the others, shifting weight as another lance of sound missed narrowly to the side. The ice was almost within reach now, cold, scarred, layered with frost. With one final, tendon-snapping surge, Four Warm Currents heaved the coring charge upward, slapping the detonation trigger as it went. The spiked device crunched into the ice and clung. Four Warm Currents tasted something new mixing into the blood, reaching amber tendrils through the leaking blue. Triumph.

"Get out," Four Warm Currents signed, clumsily, slowly. "It's too late now."

The pursuers stared for a moment, adrift, then turned and shot back down the tunnel, howling a sonar warning to the others coming behind. Four Warm Currents's tentacles were going numb. Every body part ached or seared or felt like it was splitting apart. There would be no high-speed exit down the tunnel. Maybe no exit at all.

As the coring charge signed out its detonation sequence with mechanical tendrils, Four Warm Currents swam, slowly, to the side wall. A deep crevice ran along the length. Maybe deep enough. Four Warm Currents squeezed, twisted, contorted, tucking inside the shelter bit by bit. It was an excruciating fit. Even a child would have preferred a wider fissure. Four Warm Currents's eyes squeezed shut and saw Six Bubbling Thermals smiling, saw the egg sacs glossy and bright.

The coring charge went off like a volcano erupting. Such devices were designed, in theory, to deliver all but a small fraction of the explosive yield forward. The tiny fraction of blowback was still enough to shatter cracks through the tunnel walls and send a sonic boom rippling down its depth, an expanding globe of boiling water that scalded Four Warm Currents's exposed skin. The tentacle that hadn't managed to fit inside was turned to mush in an instant, spewing denatured flesh and blood in a hot cloud. All of Four Warm Currents's senses sang with the explosion, tasting the fierce chemicals, feeling the heat, seeing with sonar the flayed ice crumbling all around.

Then, at last, it was over. Four Warm Currents slithered out of the crack, sloughing skin on its edges, and drifted slowly upward. It was a maelstrom of shredded ice and swirling gases, bubbles twisting in furious wreaths. Four Warm Currents floated up through the vortex, numb to the stinging debris and swathes of scalding water. The roof of the world was gone, leaving a jagged dark hole in the ice, a void that had been a dream and a nightmare for cycles and cycles. Four Warm Currents rose to it, entranced.

One trembling tentacle reached upward and across the rubicon. The sensation was indescribable. Four Warm Currents pulled the tentacle back, stared with bleary eyes, and found it still intact. The other side was scorching cold, a thousand tingling pinpricks, a gauze of gas like nothing below. Nothing Four Warm Currents had ever dreamed or imagined.

The chief engineer bobbed and bled, then finally gathered the strength for one last push, breaking the surface of the water completely. The feel of gas on skin was gasping, shivering. Four Warm Currents craned slowly backward, turning to face the void, and looked up. Another ocean, far deeper and vaster than theirs, but not empty. Not dark. Not at all. Maybe it was a beautiful hallucination, brought about by the creeping failure of sense organs. Maybe it wasn't.

Four Warm Currents watched the new world with eyes and mouth, secreting final messages down into the water, love for Six Bubbling Thermals, for Three Jagged Reefs, for the children who would sign softly but laugh wildly, and then, as numbing darkness began to seep across blurring eyes, under peeling skin, a sole suggestion for a necessary name.

# THE SOULS OF HORSES

### *Beth Cato*

Ilsa knew the souls of horses, how they twined between her fingers as silky and strong as strands of mane, how even in death they ached to gallop across fields or melt lumps of sugar upon their tongues.

Few men could understand them as she did.

"Sweet Jesus, are those the flying horses?" asked Lieutenant Dennis.

Ilsa granted him a curt nod. Captain Mayfair and more soldiers waited in her house, and she didn't know what they wanted of her. Only that she must pack her necessities and best tools and leave promptly.

Her barn held a fully assembled flying-horse carousel. A dozen horses dangled from a wooden canopy that could be dismantled to fit in a large wagon. For many years she had traveled summers and worked fairs from Virginia to Connecticut. Cannon fire at Fort Sumter had ended that.

"Pardon my blasphemy, ma'am. I've never seen the like before. Is it steam-run?"

"Yes." She eyed the Confederate officer. He couldn't be older than twenty. His gray uniform draped from his reedy frame.

He frowned as he circled a piebald Arabian mix. "Why carousel horses? Why would dying horses even want this . . . existence?"

"The Captain said you were a cavalry unit, correct? I assume you know horses well?"

"Yes, ma'am. My mama had me on a horse when I could scarcely walk, and my father breeds racing stock."

Ilsa had no desire to get chatty with a soldier, much less one who intended to drag her from her home, but this was a horseman. "Then you understand that horses know what they want. Like a person, they hate some tasks and love others. These horses love people, being ridden, and don't want to lose that joy. I show them what awaits, and they make this choice."

"They really have a choice?"

She stiffened. "Of course. An unwilling soul can't be bound. A horse might lose its body, but it doesn't lose its kick."

"If they are a different sort of horse, one that wouldn't like a carousel, what happens?"

"They float away." She left it at that.

Her papa had been a transferor, too. He had staunchly believed that since a dying horse's soul drifted upward, it must travel to heaven. When Ilsa was a child first witnessing those tendrils of escaping souls, such a thought had been of great comfort and joy.

It had been a long time since she was a child.

Ilsa rested her hand against the smooth paint of a mare's neck. Beneath her touch, the soul stirred. The mare was strong, even after death; Ilsa needed that same resilience.

The officer darted out a hand to touch the mare's blaze. Astonishment brightened his face. "It . . . quivered?"

Lieutenant Dennis *was* a special sort of horseman to sense that. "Souls can only inhabit something that once carried life. Wood works well. The carousel grants them some locomotion, too. They miss the ability to move."

"I'm glad this horse can move then, be happy. What about that horse figure in the house, ma'am? That one—I stared at it, and it stared straight back. Gave me chills. That horse wasn't the sort for a carousel?"

"No. Some aren't content to spin in circles. Bucephalus . . . he's the kind of horse who would unlatch his stall and that of every other horse in the barn, and kick his heels like a colt afterward."

Lieutenant Dennis burst out laughing. "I've known the very sort, ma'am. He's named after Alexander the Great's warhorse?"

"The same."

"We could use more horses like old Alexander's." His expression sobered as he looked to his pocket watch. "We must go, ma'am. The Captain's waiting."

Ilsa looked to her tools again, remembering why she was there, who she was with. She hefted a skew gouger in her palm, the handle's patina dark. These tools had been brand-new when she bought them in New York City twenty years before. They had aged with more grace than her.

She found Captain Mayfair in her parlor. He scowled and motioned her to the door. She looked to her mantle.

Bucephalus was carved in pale butternut and no larger than a grown man's hand. Three hooves were grounded, the muscles of his hindquarters tensed as if ready to rear. Ilsa wanted to plead for a few moments of privacy with her horse, to say farewell, but she had no desire to show any weakness to these men.

She turned away and blinked back tears to find Captain Mayfair gazing past her to Bucephalus, his grizzled features softened with wonder.

They arrived at the encampment of the newly formed Confederate Independent Provisional Cavalry, and Ilsa was escorted straight to a makeshift foundry. Men talked in the shadows, metal clanging, their furnaces like blood aglow in the weak evening light.

"Captain Mayfair, why am I here? You do know I can't transfer into metal?"

"Yes."

Ilsa opened her mouth to scold him, to demand answers as they entered a dim room. Light slanted down from a high window, as if in a cathedral, and illuminated a gleaming horse. She gasped.

Silver skin flowed with the ripple of muscles, highlighting an arched neck and strong hindquarters. It stood fifteen hands tall, the same as an average horse. Black orbs for eyes had the dull sheen of rocks worn smooth in a river. This was no crude machine. It was a sculpture, a masterpiece.

"What is this?" she whispered.

"The auquine, the automatic horse," said Captain Mayfair. Lieutenant Dennis stood beside him. "This is our prototype. Steam-run in part, but requires the motivation of a soul."

"I already told you, I cannot—"

"You will carve the wooden heart. Its nervous system consists of vine coated with gutta-percha. The soul will have room to expand, control the limbs."

Ilsa knew the relentless, unfilled ache to truly *move* that irritated every horse bound to the carousel. "The engine and soul together. It could work."

*Bucephalus would love such a body, but he's no warhorse, nor could I steal a creation like this. There would be no way to keep such a thing a secret.*

Dennis cleared his throat. "It has worked, ma'am, in Britain. They're readying cavalry units for India."

"People with your skills are scarce, Mrs. Klein," said Captain Mayfair. "We're in dire need of horses."

She looked between the metal horse and the soldiers. A horse's soul—one suited to be a warhorse—would delight in this new form, so much closer to its original. She touched the metal neck, almost expecting the lurch of life that pulsed within her own carvings. "Who made this?"

"Culver," said Captain Mayfair.

She wondered if she should recognize the name, but a shadow shifted behind the horse, and she realized it had been a summons.

The Negro looked of age with her, his white hair bound in a queue at his neck. He was clean-shaven, his clothes tidy despite their extreme wear.

"Culver's from my father's plantation. No one knows horses and metal like him," said Lieutenant Dennis with obvious pride.

"Impressive," Ilsa murmured. Impressive that a slave had been granted such a role in this army.

"Master Dennis." Culver bowed, the motion slow and heavy like an old oak bent by a fierce wind.

"Sir! Captain Mayfair!" Another soldier strode in. "An urgent telegraph from General Lee, sir."

"Culver will show you how the auquine works, Mrs. Klein." Captain Mayfair exited. With a bright smile for both her and Culver, Lieutenant Dennis departed as well.

Ilsa considered the craftsman. "Is everyone in the forge working on these . . . auquines?"

"Yes'm. This's the first one done, 'bout twenty more juss 'bout there, and salvage aplenty for makin' more."

Her hands traced the seams of metal, the large eyes. "You modeled this on a Morgan."

"Y'know your horses, missus."

Her voice lowered. "Metal is soulless, dead, but this—this *works*. You know horses' souls."

"Slave's not supposed to know 'bout such things, missus."

"Neither are women."

"God's truth, missus."

"How do you open up the horse?"

Culver crouched down. His leg wobbled, and he landed on all fours with a grunt.

"Are you well?" Ilsa lay a hand on his shoulder. Through the worn fabric, she felt the ridged scars of the lash—layers, mottled like cold candle wax.

Equine memories flashed in her mind. Agonized neighs. The fall of the whip, the fierce sting, the heat of weeping blood.

"I'm sorry," she said, recoiling, and knew he wouldn't grasp the full meaning.

"Body don't work like it used to." He trembled as he leaned on the auquine.

She shivered, too, willing away the shadowed pain of other souls. Culver was property, same as a horse.

Ilsa made herself focus on the task at hand as he opened a hatch in the auquine's chest to show her the fundamentals of its design.

Lieutenant Dennis beamed with pride as he reentered the room. "The auquine's a beauty, isn't he?"

She liked the boy, his enthusiasm for horses. *He's of attitude and age to be my son.* The thought provoked a twinge of grief that hadn't stirred in years.

"Yes. I should speak to Captain Mayfair again, if you please." With a nod to Culver, she followed Dennis into the brisk evening air.

Captain Mayfair stood beside a campfire with a group of soldiers. "Mrs. Klein. What did you think?"

She took a deep breath. "This man Culver's work reminds me of the high craftsmanship I saw as a girl in Germany. Extraordinary."

"Yes. He's a peculiar Negro."

"That said, Captain, my carousel brings joy to my horses and riders, especially children. Working on warhorses like this . . . it's not right for me."

"I was afraid you might be reluctant." Captain Mayfair nodded to a soldier beside him. The man folded down a burlap bag between his feet. There, wadded in wrinkles of coarse cloth, stood Bucephalus.

Ilsa couldn't hold back a gasp, her hand flying to her mouth. Lieutenant Dennis shuffled his feet in clear discomfort.

The captain kept his focus on her. "This horse is special to you. People talk of him. I understood why once I entered your home."

Ilsa shivered in rage. These soldiers took her as they took so many horses, supplies, even homes. If she fled north, she couldn't expect any better. The Yanks would be constructing their own horses soon enough. They'd be no kinder in their pillaging of property or people.

But maybe the Yanks wouldn't stoop this low.

"How dare you, Captain?" she whispered.

Captain Mayfair glanced at the fire behind him. "It's my understanding that nothing binds as well as an original body. You must be very close to catch a soul, correct?"

She barely managed a nod. *For Bucephalus's soul, I would brave the fire. A strong soul like his can be transferred several times. I could make him a new body.*

"We need horses, Mrs. Klein. We'll house you well. My men will not harass you."

She ached to bolt, to make for the road, to fly from this place. She looked at Bucephalus and shuddered. "If I am to—to help, then I must say straight out that I won't abide with any horse being killed without need."

Captain Mayfair motioned, and Bucephalus was gently wrapped up again. "Horses are dear to us. We have no desire—no capacity—to replace them completely. And it's not as though we lack in dying horses." Sadness curved his mustache.

"Yet you threaten to burn mine."

"Is he a horse anymore?" The captain sounded curious rather than facetious. "How long has this Bucephalus been bound by wood?"

"Twenty years."

"As long as you've been in America, then." The man had done his research. "Lieutenant Dennis will show you your quarters and your workshop."

"You want me to start now? Tonight?"

"Yes. The Union's building pontoons to cross the river. Soon there'll be plenty of horses in need of new bodies."

Smoke veiled the furrows as if attempting to hide the mangled blue and gray bodies in the mud. The air of the place—of so many distended souls—weighed on Ilsa like a hundred winter coats.

Lieutenant Dennis helped her down from a buckboard wagon loaded with rattling wooden equine hearts. "Ma'am, I'm sorry. This is no place for a lady."

"It's not a place for anyone," she whispered.

Never before had she sensed the presence of human souls, much as she had tried. God, had she tried. She couldn't see them, but there were so many here that her head felt as afloat as a hot air balloon.

"There's a horse over here!" called a soldier.

She stumbled over roots and rocks and things her gaze slid across but could not comprehend, and then she came to the horse.

The air shimmied as the stallion struggled against death. He stubbornly stood on all four legs even as his ribs—and more—were bared to the air.

"There, there," Ilsa crooned, focusing on him. "Good boy."

His eyes were glazed over with pain, but she saw beyond that. He was a horse as described in the Book of Job, all flaring nostrils and eagerness at the herald of a trumpet.

Like men, some horses were born fools.

"Fine lines," murmured Dennis. "Some Thoroughbred to him."

Ilsa brought her face so close that vapors of soul caressed her like steam. "Do you want this?" she whispered. She exhaled an image of what awaited the horse: a new body, built strong; how the hooves would clatter; how he might miss the taste of oats, but he would still know the joy of a gallop.

Even in agony, his ears perked up. His soul gushed outward, eager to move on.

"His body's pain needs to end," she said.

A soldier aimed a gun barrel between the stallion's eyes. At Ilsa's nod, the gun fired. Even expecting the noise, she flinched. The horse collapsed.

She grabbed hold of the soul as it drifted out from his eyes. The effervescent strands were strong, testing her as if straining against a bit.

"I need cherrywood." A strong wood, bold as the horse. A soldier dashed off for the wagon. "Shh, shh, easy there," she whispered. She plaited the soul with her deft fingers, forming a loop to confine its essence.

She pressed the soul into the wooden heart as she took it in her hands, patting the ventricles the way a person molds clay, and after a few minutes, she nodded. The soldier took the heart away.

"I wish I could see and feel what you do, ma'am," said Dennis, voice softened in awe.

"No, you don't, lieutenant."

Ilsa rubbed her torso, reminding herself that there was no pain, no blood. Impressions from the dying horse glistened across her mind's eye. Green fields, contentment. The good man who smelled of leather and damp wool, how they rode into battle together—excitement—hoofbeats—wind—galloping, galloping—and then a lightened load. Many others had sat on his back since. Where was the good man?

She shivered out of the reverie. At least she had granted this horse's soul some extra time on earth, doing something he would love. For the first time, this enterprise felt worthwhile.

Though given her druthers, she would still grab Bucephalus and run.

"There's another horse over here, sir! Ma'am!"

The dying mare lay on her side. Her ribs heaved like bellows, breaths wheezing through bloodied nostrils. Wisps of her soul clouded the air and Ilsa's consciousness. A child's laugh. A hand at her mane, a kiss at her muzzle. The girl's wails as the horse was ridden away. The mare kept turning to look toward home, toward the girl. Reins jerked her head straight.

Home. Where the girl waited along the split-rail fence.

"What sort of wood?" Dennis's voice shattered the image.

"No." Ilsa gasped. "Not a warhorse. She should never have been here. She needs . . . I need . . ."

Children. Soft hands. Bouncy, light bodies within the sway of her back.

"Mrs. Klein, I'm sorry. We can't fill a heart we can't use."

"I just need one!"

"Will there be only one like this here?"

This soul wasn't as strong as Bucephalus. It couldn't transfer more than once. Nor could she hold more than one soul at a time as she journeyed across the battlefield, but she wanted to, she needed to. This mare belonged in the carousel. Ilsa couldn't bring forth the same girl, but there'd be others. She clawed for the dissipating strands of the horse's soul. The bellows of breaths softened, the horse's gaze distant.

The last vapors vanished against a sunbeam.

*Gone. Not human, not saved by baptism. Lost, like the soul of the unchristened stillborn babe, born in an outhouse behind a Berlin carousel shop.*

Ilsa would grab all the souls if she could. She would be the leaden weight to anchor them to earth.

"Ma'am?" Lieutenant Dennis whispered. "I'm sorry to put you through this, but—"

"I came to America to start my life again. I'm in the same place, but this is no longer America." Her voice rasped like that of an old woman. She *was* an old woman.

She stumbled onward, eyes blinded by tears, guided only by the tendrils of another agonized equine soul.

Confederate commanders encased her in a gray ring. They murmured excitedly, buzzing like machinery.

Culver waited by the first empty auquine, the prototype. "Pay them men no heed."

"If this fails—"

"Ain't gonna fail, missus. You know what you doing. You know these horses."

She thought of Bucephalus, the horse she knew best of all, then looked to the heaping basket of wooden hearts beside her. The harvest of the battlefield. Days had passed, and her agony had turned to numbness.

*Do the job. Give these souls a home. Let some good come of this.*

She touched a knob of smoothed walnut, then delved deeper to find cherry. The heart pulsed in her hand, quickening. In her mind, she retraced the metal body before her, showed it to the soul the way she would once have extended a palm of oats.

As she knelt before the auquine's chest, the murmurs behind her ceased. The horse's chest compartment opened on hinges to show the vascular chamber. Stroking the heart, she murmured wordless assurances as she set the wood within its new cradle.

*Death is rife with pain. So is rebirth.*

Ilsa stabbed sharpened wood connectors into the heart. At each strike, the soul shivered as it spilled through the puncture wounds to explore gutta-percha veins. The auquine rumbled as the engine started.

She sealed the body shut. A hoof tentatively stomped on the dirt. At the auquine's head, Culver made shushing noises, stroking along the silver muzzle. Ears pivoted on their roller joints, head lifting as if to sniff. The commanders broke out in applause.

"There, there. You mighty fine. You doing good, girl."

Culver wasn't whispering to the horse.

Ilsa moved on to the next auquine in the long row.

"Y ou'll look after Culver for me, won't you, ma'am?" Dennis asked. Dawn had yet to pierce the oil slick of the sky, yet the camp bustled.

"Lieutenant, he's as old as I am. I think he can look after himself." Ilsa softened the words with a faint smile, her eyes on the auquines. Her horses, their silver and copper hides dull by firelight.

The Provisional Cavalry had practiced in the valley for weeks to acclimate the horses' souls to their new, stronger bodies. Now their orders had come in.

"Well, I-I suppose so." Dennis stooped in a way that reminded her of Culver, an invisible yoke heavy on his shoulders.

"Lieutenant Dennis. Mrs. Klein." Captain Mayfair granted Ilsa a tip of his hat. "It's time to mount up."

"Yes, sir," said Dennis, snapping out of his salute. He cast Ilsa a nod and joined the rest of the horsemen.

"I have been meaning to speak to you, Mrs. Klein," Captain Mayfair said, "on the matter of that horse of yours."

*Bucephalus.* The name pained her. "What of him, Captain?"

"He has a strong soul, doesn't he?"

"Yes."

"Could he be transferred to an auquine?"

She looked at the men—boys, really—and their metal horses. All of them giddy in anticipation of what was to come. These horses would truly die if their wooden hearts were pierced or their veins too badly mangled. *Their souls escaping into nothingness.* Ilsa couldn't follow the cavalry and save them.

"You'd put Bucephalus in front of cannons?" she asked. "Why not just drop him in the campfire, then? It's faster."

It was selfish of her, she knew, to value his soul more than the rest, but Bucephalus had been her constant companion for decades. She had twined his soul and kept it warm beside her own heartbeat. She spent weeks carving his new body in butternut. They traveled the seaboard with her carousel until the war started. She talked to him; he listened.

"A great deal depends on this unit and its success, Mrs. Klein. These auquines could turn the course of the war. They could end it." The captain was silent for a long minute. "I met my wife when I was at West Point. At the start of the war, she went back to New York to be with her parents on the farm. I would very much like to see her again."

"My horse will not change that."

"Smaller pebbles have changed the world, but that's not my point. My inquiry is not about Bucephalus now, but for when the war is done. I own property in the Low Country down near Charleston. There'd be a place for him there. I would like to see him in action as he really is."

"Captain," said a soldier. He passed over an auquine's reins.

Captain Mayfair swung himself into the saddle. "It's something to keep in mind while we're away, Mrs. Klein. Farewell." He rode to join his men.

"Bucephalus is my horse," she whispered to the dust. "Not yours. You *stole* him."

Ilsa retreated to her room and listened to the soft thuds of hoofbeats as they faded away. The walls boxed her in like a stall, the ropes that bound her invisible yet strong.

The knife was a familiar weight in Ilsa's hand. She inhaled the heady scent of wood so fresh it almost cleared her senses, her memories. A gas lamp cast the workshop in an orange glow.

Beyond the thin walls, men cheered. The first mission of the Provisional Cavalry had been a grand success. Their two-day pursuit of the Yanks had resulted in a decisive victory and the acquisition of a Union quartermaster's wagon loaded with honest-to-God coffee beans.

"We couldn't have achieved this victory without you," Captain Mayfair had said. As if she needed the reminder.

She also did not need anyone to do the mathematics for her. Five horses gone. She did not count the men.

Ilsa didn't look up when the door opened. As had become their ritual over the past month, Culver sat down on the lopped-off stump across from her. She was so used to working and talking aloud to Bucephalus that it felt peculiar to share her space with someone who replied. Peculiar in a pleasant way.

Culver opened a toolbox and began busywork with wires and bolts and fingernail-size scraps of metal. The soldiers in the foundry knew their jobs well by now, and he wasn't required there anymore. He mostly acted as manservant for Lieutenant Dennis.

A fiddle whined outside, and voices arose in chorus:

"Jeff Davis is our President,

Lincoln is a Fool!

Jeff Davis rides a white—horse—auquine!"

The song broke off at the overlapped words. The men cheered again.

"They better be glad Cap'n said they sleep late tomorrow," said Culver. "Gonna be a long train ride down to Alabama in three days."

Alabama. Deeper south, deeper into this whole mess, and this time Ilsa was to come along. More horses would die. Dozens heaped together in a day, their memories blurred like hummingbird wings.

"How do you stand it?" She clenched the handle. "Knowing that if you headed north a ways, you could be free. That every time you build a horse, you're building something that keeps you a slave."

"I been free."

"What?"

"I been free. When I's a young man, I ran north, to New York. What a place, what a place." Culver shook his head, still marveling. "Got me a 'prenticeship and a girl and a baby girl-child. And then blackbirders came, trussed me up, and hauled me back to Georgia."

"My God," she whispered. "I lived in New York back then—twenty years ago, was it?" Culver nodded. "I heard about those men, that they even dragged free-born Negroes south and into slavery. Your family—what happened?"

"Don't know. But I had my family down in Georgia, too. Lord be praised for that. Got to see my boy grow up." The curve of his smiling cheeks reminded her of Lieutenant Dennis, how he looked at the auquines.

*My boy never grew up. He never even breathed.* She was ashamed of herself for envying Culver in such a way when he had lost so much more.

"To be free and captured again . . ."

"Didn't lose all my freedom." He tightened a bolt.

"How is that?"

"When you carvin' those carousel horses, what's it do for your soul?" An oddly blunt thing for Culver to ask.

Ilsa stroked the half-carved heart in her hands. "Years ago, I had a small boy ride the carousel time and again. He told me he'd truly been riding a mustang to California. He said the horse knew right where to go. That's how I feel when I carve, when I see the carousel horses in their new bodies. That I'm going the right way. Escaping without escaping."

"Mustangs. I heard 'bout them, out west. Crazy place, all dirt far's the eye can see."

"We should go there." She set the knife on her lap. "The two of us. Forget this fools' war."

"Aw, Missus Klein. I'm too old to go off somewhere new. Maybe you can, your skin. Anyone take one look at me, they know where I come from, know right where I go. Blackbirders did."

"I knew a horse like you once." She resumed carving in furious strokes. "He had known freedom. He had known love. He was a bit Arab, a bit Thoroughbred, a bit of everything. He could race—Lord, could he race. His mind, it was faster than any whip. But then he was hurt and sold, and spent his last year pulling a glueman's wagon down the cobbles in New York City. He pulled it like a royal chariot, awful as its load was, piled with dead of his own kind."

"This that horse of yours? The one Cap'n has?"

She nodded, not trusting herself to speak.

The two of them worked in silence as her mind untangled frustration and fear and the need to do something for Culver, for Bucephalus, for herself. She thought of her carousel horses and mustangs.

"I'm going to ask the captain for a last trip to my shop for supplies." Ilsa smiled at Culver. "I don't suppose you've ever been on a flying-horse carousel?"

"I'll need a few minutes to start up the steam engine." Ilsa scurried about the old barn, connecting the engine and walking the long length of the cord, checking for rust or rat's nests.

"Can I be of help, ma'am?" asked Dennis, their guard for the foray into town. He had seemed especially weary in recent days. She didn't think he was too happy about the cavalry moving south. Maybe it brought the war too close to home.

"I know my own rig best," Ilsa said. To his credit, Dennis let her be.

A neighbor had kept an eye on the place these past few months, but that did nothing to ward away dust, or to fill that empty place on her mantle. Walking through her parlor just about broke her heart, especially as she'd seen Bucephalus that morning for the first time in weeks.

The wooden horse sat on the corner of Captain Mayfair's desk in the command house. Bucephalus had a window view of soldiers drilling on newly transferred auquines.

Captain Mayfair didn't seem worried that Ilsa would try to escape on her trip into Richmond. He had Bucephalus, after all.

She had noted that not a speck of dust was to be found on the carved horse, not even in the delicate whorls of his mane. In truth, he looked . . . loved.

That pleased her and vexed her all at once.

Her fingers had brushed his back. If Bucephalus had been of flesh, he would have scarcely flicked an ear her way. He was fixated on the auquines in the yard with an intensity she hadn't seen in years, not since they traveled the coast with the carousel.

*Bucephalus is mine. He should be home. I could move him from the mantle, give him a better vantage of the street.*

She directed her frustration into the carousel's crank. She could already feel the wood-bound horses' anticipation. They stewed with restlessness, just as they had in life at the first hints of spring.

"Choose your horse and mount up," she called.

Culver ambled around the carousel. He stopped at the most ornately carved of the lot, a white stallion on the outside ring. The lead horse. Ilsa had designed the horse's colorful barding like that of a medieval charger straight out of *Ivanhoe*. Culver tried to lift his foot to the stirrup and staggered backward.

"Here, old man," Dennis said as he gave him a boost.

"Thanks to you, master."

The two men shared like smiles. It made Ilsa grin, too, to see how Dennis doted on Culver. "What about you?" she asked Dennis as he joined her in the center. He shook his head.

Ilsa released the brake lever. The canopy shuddered as the mechanism activated. Slowly, the horses began to move.

Culver gripped the red pole and looked to either side of his horse as it swayed. "This horse. It different."

"It's a rare breed from Austria, called Lipizzaner. They're taught to dance."

"Fancy that!" Culver's eyes shone as he passed by.

"Thank you for letting him do this, lieutenant," she murmured.

Dennis was quiet for a long moment, watching the horses spin. "One of my first memories is Culver standing alongside Mama, both of them holding me on a horse." He sighed heavily. "I didn't just bring him to Virginia because he's the best artist with metal. I wanted to save his life."

"Save his life? By bringing him into the middle of a war?"

"Safer than being near Papa. He's never treated Culver well, and in recent years . . ."

Ilsa thought of Culver's escape, his layers of scars. The horses picked up speed as centrifugal forces began to pull them outward at an angle. Culver passed by, his gap-toothed grin brilliant. He circled again, and this time, his arms were flung wide, his eyes closed.

"These are very different horses than the auquines, ma'am, and I don't mean the contrast of metal and wood." Dennis shook his head. "These horses—there's a particular kind of happiness. Like foals in a meadow."

Proof again that the lieutenant had an extra sense of horses' souls. Ilsa wondered who it carried through in his family.

"You understand, then, why I told the captain I shouldn't be making warhorses." She paused. "I think you understood from the very start. Since you first saw my carousel."

He said nothing for a time, watching Culver. "You know, ma'am, things will get terribly confusing as we ship south. People might go missing."

Her breath caught. "The soldier in charge of those people might get in awful trouble."

"You're set to ride on a civilian train part of the way. No guards. The captain believes Bucephalus is all the motivation you need to come along. I think that's because he'd do as much for that horse. Captain even talks to him, there in his office."

The words hurt. "I used to do the same."

"What if I can steal the horse?"

"I'm afraid to ask too much, lieutenant."

"What if you only took his soul, and left the carving behind? The captain wouldn't know until he unpacked Bucephalus down in Alabama."

Tears of hope made Ilsa's eyes smart as she nodded.

Culver flew by, laughing. His eyes were still shut, his arms still out like wings.

"I don't think I've ever heard him make such a sound." Dennis's voice was soft with awe. "You know what, ma'am? I changed my mind. I think I do want to ride."

As the horses slowed, Culver opened his eyes, his arms dropping to his sides. The carousel rocked to a stop.

"Missus Klein, never in my life I had an experience like that." He made to stand up, but she waved him down.

"Sit. You get another round, and this time you won't be alone. Lieutenant, mount up."

Culver craned around. "Master, you can't be back there, you—"

"I'm fine here. You lead me like when I was a boy." Lieutenant Dennis took the horse directly behind Culver. It was a red unicorn with a gold-leaf horn. A goofy grin lit the officer's whole face. "Mrs. Klein, don't tell me this holds a unicorn's soul."

"Why don't you tell me once you've had a go?" Ilsa started the machine.

She leaned against the central pillar and closed her eyes as the men laughed and whooped and eventually turned silent as midnight mice. Beneath the engine's rumble, she heard the echo of hoofbeats.

Ilsa waited in a shed adjacent to the rail yard, her satchel at her feet. The gray blurs of soldiers constantly passed the window. The Provisional Cavalry was mustering a quarter mile away to load up for their journey south.

The clock tolled eight times. Lieutenant Dennis was now late.

Ilsa's stomach twisted in knots, her fingers clenched with the need to hold Bucephalus again.

A knock shuddered through the door. She gasped, a hand at her anxious heart.

Lieutenant Dennis entered, Culver in his wake. "I got him, ma'am."

The lieutenant motioned to Culver, who held a worn leather bag. Ilsa reached inside and found those curves and nicks made by her own hand. She knew Bucephalus's alarm—his frustration—at being in the bag, at this change.

"It's me," she murmured. Her fingernail found the soft juncture where his left foreleg met his body. She pressed in just enough to know the heat of his soul there, lingering beneath the surface.

Ilsa let her joys and hope flow through to him—how she would braid his soul and hold it close as she traveled, how she would carve him a new and even more beautiful body, how they would explore the frontier west together.

He balked. His soul dug itself deeper into its wooden body.

"Bucephalus?" she whispered.

He told her without words, showing her the coziness of a body that he had known for twenty years, far longer than he had ever known flesh. He showed her the view from Captain Mayfair's window, the auquines engaged in their drills. He knew they were horses—he recognized the scent and presence of like souls. Bucephalus was not a warhorse, but the bustle of the encampment made him feel *alive* again, even as a statue. He didn't comprehend that he was stolen; all he knew was that he was in good care and stimulating company. Bucephalus, in life, knew how to work a stall clasp open with his lips so he could get to an oat bucket. Now he saw something else he wanted that was just out of reach.

*He wants to stay with Captain Mayfair, not me.* The betrayal stung her. He hadn't even thought of the captain, not directly, but the implication was there. She gripped the wooden horse as if she could convince him to leave through sheer will.

Bucephalus coiled within his shell, alarmed. Afraid of her.

*What am I doing?* Ilsa knew the feel of spurs and the lash. She would not—could not—be like that.

Her son's invisible soul had once slipped away. Now Bucephalus had escaped her, too, but only in part. He was still on earth. He had not dissipated. *He is not lost.*

"I understand. I don't like it, but I understand," she said to the horse then looked to Culver. "Bucephalus wants to stay in this body." Tears streaked down her cheeks. Culver nodded, expression thoughtful as he secured the horse in the bag again. "Captain Mayfair will take good care of him. So will you, lieutenant."

Dennis looked genuinely confused. "I—of course, ma'am. I just didn't expect . . . Well, this will be a trade, then." He pulled a stack of tri-folded sheets from his jacket and passed them to Ilsa. "Those are Culver's papers. Take him with you."

"Master Dennis?" Culver blinked rapidly.

"I gave her your papers, old man. You're going west." Dennis took the bag from Culver.

Shock filtered over Culver's face, then joy, then anger. "Master, no, I am not. I cannot."

"You must. Captain Mayfair's sending you back to the plantation." Dennis's voice cracked. "You know how Papa is since Mama passed. I won't be there to protect you, I . . ."

Ilsa looked between them and thought on their like recognition of equine souls, their uncommon closeness, the similarity in their smiles. Their skins were of different shades, true—Culver's dark as ebony, and the lieutenant's the deep walnut tone of a man who lived in the sun—but their bearings would have established their disparate roles even if they stood in silhouette. Culver's back was bowed by a life of hardship, whereas Dennis was the epitome of a Confederate officer, his posture ramrod straight and ready for a parade. *They're slave and master by reality. Father and son by blood.*

She took a steadying breath to hold back a new wave of sorrow.

"You never ask me nothing, Master Dennis. You never ask me where I wanna go, what I wanna do."

Frustration twisted Lieutenant Dennis's face. "Then what do you want?"

"If I'm a-going anywhere, I'm going north. Got family I'd like to find again, if they livin'."

Dennis clearly tried to act stoic even as he blinked back tears.

Ilsa tucked the papers into her bag and pried out stationery and a pencil. "I can smuggle him north." Smuggle herself, too, so the Union wouldn't use her as the Confederates did. "I know New York."

"Missus, you already gave me freedom on them horses the other day. I don't ask for more than that."

"You shouldn't just get one or two chances at such a thing, Culver. I promise I will do everything I can to help you find your daughter." Ilsa scribbled words onto a piece of paper.

"New York City." Culver said the words like a prayer.

"Thank you," Lieutenant Dennis whispered, his voice breaking.

A train whistle pierced the air.

The two men stared at each other, saying everything in nothing. Culver brushed a gnarled hand against Lieutenant Dennis's gray sleeve, then turned away, trembling.

Ilsa steadied him. Even through layers of cloth, the scars on his back were hard lumps. "You'll need to carry my bag for appearances."

"Of course, missus. Of course."

Ilsa sealed the paper into an envelope addressed to Captain Mayfair and passed it to Dennis. "When the war is done, Captain Mayfair is to expect company in the Low Country. I told him this is no giveaway. An old woman might be asking for room and board as part of the deal." Culver opened the door.

"I'll tell him you left behind this letter," Lieutenant Dennis said, his voice thick. "And ma'am?"

She looked back. He cradled the bag with Bucephalus as if he held a newborn baby. "It really was a unicorn I rode, wasn't it?"

Ilsa smiled. She turned away again, her gaze already northward.

# PINIONS

## *The Authors*

**Jason Kimble** left the tornadoes of Michigan for the hurricanes of Florida, because spinning air is better when it's warm. He lives there with his finally legal husband. Other stories set in the world of "The Wind at His Back" have appeared in *The Sockdolager* and the anthology *Twice Upon A Time: Fairytale, Folklore, & Myth. Reimagined & Remastered.* Other recent work appears or is forthcoming in *Betwixt* magazine and *Escape Pod.* You can find more of his nattering at http://processwonk.wordpress.com or by following @jkasonetc on Twitter.

About "The Wind at His Back," he had this to share: "While nosing about for folklore to play with, the 'tall tale' struck me as something that might be interesting fodder. It was littered with giants: Paul Bunyan and Joe Magarac and Old Stormalong come to mind. It posited a world where a man could ride a tornado, or could blanket the countryside with fruit trees while protected by nothing more than a tin pot on his head. It populated the wilds with whiskey-drinking jackalopes and snakes that could put themselves back together if you cut them in half. Just how wild might the West have been, I wondered, if none of that was an exaggeration?

"The tall tale, however, is pretty exclusively white, and even more exclusively straight. Anyone who doesn't fit that model is either there to motivate or juxtapose with the awesomeness of the White Straight Dude The Story Is Really About.

"*Oh,* screw *that,* I thought.

"At the very least, I wanted to create a haven where those restrictions didn't apply. Westerns have no end of little utopias, after all. Quaint little towns where Everyone Thrives. This is one of them, where Benito Guzman Aguilar sheriffs when he isn't spending time with Casey, the warm-hearted farmer he fell in love with. Of course, this is a utopia in the center of a world with tornado wranglers and giants and supernatural critters and magic fruit trees, some or all of whom may already be part of the town. Besides, the thing about Western utopian settlements is, there is always, always trouble on the horizon. And it's almost always personal.

"In that respect, at least, 'The Wind at His Back' is no exception."

**Rachael K. Jones** grew up in various cities across Europe and North America, picked up (and mostly forgot) six languages, an addiction to running, and a couple degrees. Now she writes speculative fiction in Athens, Georgia, where she lives with her husband. A winner of *Writers of the Future*, her work has appeared or is forthcoming in many venues, including *Shimmer, Lightspeed, Accessing the Future, Strange Horizons, Escape Pod, Crossed Genres, Diabolical Plots, InterGalactic Medicine Show, Fantastic Stories of the Imagination, The Drabblecast,* and *Daily Science Fiction.* She is the coeditor of *PodCastle,* a SFWA member, and a secret android. Follow her on Twitter @RachaelKJones.

About "The Fall Shall Further the Flight in Me," she writes, "What do you do when your whole worldview comes undone in a moment because you met someone who made you question the path you'd tried so hard to stay on your whole life? We don't like unexpected detours, but in my experience, the straightest, quickest line to your destination doesn't always bring happiness. Life's about the surprises, the adventures, the unexpected friends you make along the way. This story celebrates finding what you really needed instead of what you sought. Because sometimes when faith shatters, it hatches love; and when you search for heaven, you arrive home; and when you fall, you fly."

**Patricia Russo**'s stories can be found in many places, including *Daily SF, The Dark, Not One of Us,* Rich Horton's *Year's Best Science Fiction and Fantasy 2015, Clockwork Phoenix 4,* and the collection *Shiny Thing,* published by Papaveria Press. She adds, "This is not an exhaustive list . . . ☺"

About "The Perfect Happy Family," here's what she had to share: "My favorite band is New Model Army. They have been my favorite band ever since I came across an EP of theirs in the early eighties at the Tower Records on East Fourth Street in NYC, a store which ceased to exist a very long time ago. New Model Army, however, carries on. One of their songs includes the line 'looking for family, looking for tribe.' I think I had this line in my mind when I was writing 'The Perfect Happy Family.' Other elements come from previous stories of mine (the six-sided world, the City of New Unity City), folklore, and the mysterious depths of my notebooks, the handwriting in which even I can't read sometimes."

**Marie Brennan** is the World Fantasy Award–nominated author of several fantasy series, including the Memoirs of Lady Trent, the Onyx Court, the Wilders series, and the Doppelganger duology, as well as more than forty short stories. More information can be found at http://www.swantower.com.

About "The Mirror-City," she shares that "this idea sat around in my head for the better part of a decade before finally getting written. The starting concept was simple—too simple. 'What if there was a city like Venice, and its reflection in the canals was another city?' The problem with that is, it has no plot. I don't know why it took me so many years to figure out what story I wanted to tell in that setting . . . but once I did, the words flowed like water."

**Benjanun Sriduangkaew** writes love letters to strange cities, beautiful bugs, and the future. Her work has appeared in *Tor.com, Beneath Ceaseless Skies, Clarkesworld,* and *Year's Best* anthologies. She has been shortlisted for the Campbell Award for Best New Writer, and her debut novella *Scale-Bright* has been nominated for the British SF Association Award.

She tells us that "The Finch's Wedding and the Hive That Sings" is "one of my first stories where I overtly bring together the military and the domestic, a direct negotiation between war and relationship. I also wanted to see if I could put together fairly complex political intrigue in a short story, where every character has their own motive and each of whom is very intelligent, and I'm happy with the result. The bees are, naturally, practically a prerequisite. You always make room for bees."

**Rob Cameron** is an ESL teacher in Brooklyn. When he's not writing stories, planning events for the Brooklyn Speculative Fiction Writers, or producing the *Kaleidocast*, he finds time to climb large objects, race dragon boats, fight ninjas, and pity fools. His e-mail address is cpr.words@gmail.com, and he blogs at http://rob-cameron.com.

Cameron tells us he wrote "Squeeze" while road-tripping from New York City to Burlington, Massachusetts, on the way to Readercon.

**A. C. Wise**'s short fiction can be found in publications such as *Clarkesworld, Shimmer, Uncanny,* and *Clockwork Phoenix 4,* among other places. Her debut collection, *The Ultra Fabulous Glitter Squadron Saves the World Again,* was published by Lethe Press in October 2015. In addition to her fiction, she coedits *Unlikely Story* and contributes a monthly "Women to Read: Where to Start" column to *SF Signal*. Find her online at http://www.acwise.net.

She writes that "'A Guide to Birds by Song (After Death)' started with the image of whale bones in the desert. There really are whale bones in the desert—Wadi al-Hitan (the Valley of the Whales) was first discovered in the Egyptian Sahara Desert in 1902. Of course, the whale bones in my story look nothing like the real thing, and my story has nothing to do with Egypt, because that's the way writer brains work, right? We fix on an irresistible image or idea, and twist it around and make it our own. Birds tend to show up in my fiction quite a bit; there's something eerie about them, maybe because they never forgot how it felt when they were dinosaurs. Somehow it seemed natural to pair birds with the themes of love, loss, and death, and that's how this story came to be."

**Gray Rinehart** is the only person to have commanded an Air Force tracking station, written speeches for Presidential appointees, had music on "The Dr. Demento Show," and been nominated for a literary award.

Gray's fiction has appeared in *Analog Science Fiction and Fact*, *Asimov's Science Fiction*, *Orson Scott Card's Intergalactic Medicine Show*, and elsewhere. His story, "Ashes to Ashes, Dust to Dust, Earth to Alluvium," was a finalist for the 2015 Hugo Award for Best Novelette. He is also a singer/songwriter with two albums of mostly science-fiction-and-fantasy-inspired songs.

Before becoming a Contributing Editor (the "Slushmaster General") for Baen Books, Gray fought rocket propellant fires, refurbished space launch facilities, commanded the Air Force's largest satellite tracking station, and did other interesting things during his rather odd United States Air Force career. Gray's alter ego is the Gray Man, one of several famed ghosts of South Carolina's Grand Strand, and his website is http://www.graymanwrites.com.

About "The Sorcerer of Etah," he writes, "I walked some of the frozen terrain in this story when I was stationed at Thule Air Base in Greenland. It is stark, forbidding, but often beautiful, and the Inuit who live in the local towns and villages are friendly, resourceful, and imaginative. I hope I did them, their language, and their legends justice, and that readers find it hard to tell where my fiction ends and the struggle for life on the edge of the ice cap begins."

**Sam Fleming** is a writer and scientist living in northeast Scotland with an artistic spouse and the correct number of bicycles, that being more than most people think sensible and still not enough. Her work has appeared in *Black Static*, the Dagan Books anthology *Fish*, the NewCon Press anthology *Looking Landwards*, and most recently in *Apex* magazine and the *Best of Apex Volume 1*. Find her at http://ravenbait.com and http://ravenfamily.org/sam.

About "The Prime Importance of a Happy Number," she had this to share: "I had a dream about a fragile but extraordinarily strong woman hurling objects across a table at a powerful young man who wanted to rule the world, trying to make him *see* her. The young man forced himself to be polite to the old man with her, only because the people he wanted to join were always polite, not because he understood why, or had any intention of remaining polite once he had what he wanted, which interested me. I see that a lot: women's roles undervalued, and politeness used as a disguise in order to get something, rather than out of respect for others as human beings. It's irksome. Incidentally, I laughed like a drain on discovering shrinking the Eiffel Tower by that prime number resulted in an approximation of pi, and matching word count to prime number tables wasn't as hard as I expected. I like Audrey. I hope to see more of her."

**Sunil Patel** is a Bay Area fiction writer and playwright who has written about everything from ghostly cows to talking beer. His plays have been performed at San Francisco Theater Pub and San Francisco Olympians Festival, and his fiction has appeared in *Fireside Magazine, Orson Scott Card's Intergalactic Medicine Show, Flash Fiction Online, The Book Smugglers, Fantastic Stories of the Imagination*, and *Asimov's Science Fiction*, among others. Plus he reviews books for *Lightspeed* and is Assistant Editor of *Mothership Zeta*. His favorite things to consume include nachos, milkshakes, and narrative. Find out more at http://ghostwritingcow.com, where you can watch his plays, or follow him @ghostwritingcow. His Twitter has been described as "engaging," "exclamatory," and "crispy, crunchy, peanut buttery."

About "Social Visiting," he shared that "growing up, I rarely enjoyed social visiting, the tedious and repetitive process of visiting various aunties and uncles. Yes, it was an important part of keeping in touch with my extended family—which, in Indian culture, is as close as direct family—but let's face it, it was boring. What if it wasn't, though? What if there was something secretly magical about it all? This story was my attempt to inject some beautiful strangeness into a common Indian teen experience."

By day, **Carlos Hernandez** is a CUNY Associate Professor of English, with appointments at BMCC and the CUNY Graduate Center. He is the author of over thirty short stories, mostly SF/F, as well as SF/F drama and poetry. His first collection of short stories, *The Assimilated Cuban's Guide to Quantum Santeria*, was published in January 2016. Find out more at http://quantumsanteria.com.

**C. S. E. Cooney** lives and writes in a well-appointed Rhode Island garret, across from a Victorian strolling park. She is an audiobook narrator for Tantor

Media, a performance poet, and the singer-songwriter Brimstone Rhine. Her poetry collection *How to Flirt in Faerieland and Other Wild Rhymes,* her *Dark Breaker* series, and her novellas *Jack o' the Hills* and *The Witch in the Almond Tree* are available on Amazon. In 2011, she won the Rhysling Award for her story-poem "The Sea King's Second Bride." Her first short fiction collection *Bone Swans* (Mythic Delirium 2015) has garnered starred reviews from *Publishers Weekly* and *Library Journal.* Keep up with Claire at http://csecooney.com.

Together they had this to say about "The Book of May": "We have entered a new Golden Age of epistolaries. In the age of the telephone, many lamented the lost art of letter writing. But now it's back: e-mail, texting, voice-to-text, e-invites, Facebook status updates, Tweets. We are, as a culture, rediscovering our textual selves. *Some of us still write snail mail, too. We read Flaubert's letters at an influential age, and all we ever want to do is send our friends miniature novels in stamped and sealed envelopes. We know they're our friends, of course, if they take time to decipher our execrable handwriting. That said, whether scribbling our innermost thoughts in peacock-blue ink on illuminated vellum or knocking off an e-mail at forty-five words a minute, there is something so intimate, so revealing in a letter unique to that medium.* The people we are when we write are both idealized and inadvertently exhibitionist. After all, we can edit, rewrite, delete, and trash—we can try again. But at the same time, writing reveals how unaware we can be, how casually and blithely we expose our ugliest prejudices to the world. *And the insights, hopes, terrors, raptures, and kindnesses we didn't even know we had. Like wrapping up an exposed nerve still singing and stinging and raw from its contact with the ravages of the world and posting it in trust to the person at the other end of the line/signal/private message box/USPS delivery service.* That's what's strangest about writing, finally, how ghost-laden it is, how queerly capable concatenated strings of ink or pixels are at rendering the human mind. *And the ghost is, in the end, all that remains of us.* —CAPH, *CSEC*"

**Holly Heisey** launched her writing career in sixth grade when she wrote her class play, a medieval fantasy. It was love at first dragon. Since then, her short fiction has appeared in *Orson Scott Card's InterGalactic Medicine Show* and *Escape Pod,* and she is a multiple finalist in the Writers of the Future Contest. A freelance designer by day, Holly lives in Pennsylvania with Larry and Moe, her two pet cacti, and she is currently at work on a science fantasy epic. You can find her online at http://hollyheisey.com.

About "The Tiger's Silent Roar," she writes, "I have never known a line between science fiction and fantasy. I grew up on Madeleine L'Engle's genre-bending Time Quintet, and in my teenage years devoured *Dune*. For me, the beauty of speculative fiction is that there are no lines, no limits to the possibilities of what you can do with story.

"With 'The Tiger's Silent Roar,' I wanted to explore a world that held both the familiar—corruption, passion, and self-sacrificing love—and the wondrous. Today we outsource our companies; is it so implausible that one day we might outsource our happiness? As for myself, I want to embrace the world with my senses wide open. I want to experience the trees and birds and insects as the grand system they are, and view the people around me with a whole new level of wonder. There might be tragedy and tyranny in the world, but if there's one thing I learned from those Madeleine L'Engle books growing up, it's that love and beauty will always win in the end."

**Barbara Krasnoff**'s short fiction can be found in a wide variety of anthologies, most notably (of course) *Clockwork Phoenix 2* and *Clockwork Phoenix 4*. Others (many with very long names) include *Menial: Skilled Labor in Science Fiction, Fat Girls in a Strange Land, Subversion: Science Fiction & Fantasy Tales of Challenging the Norm, Broken Time Blues: Fantastic Tales in the Roaring '20s, Such a Pretty Face: Tales of Power and Abundance*, and *Memories and Visions: Women's Fantasy & Science Fiction*.

Her work has also appeared in a number of online and print magazines, including *Mythic Delirium, Triptych Tales, Crossed Genres, Perihelion, Space and Time, Abyss & Apex, Electric Velocipede, Apex, Weird Tales, Lady Churchill's Rosebud Wristlet*, and *Amazing Stories*. She is a member of the Tabula Rasa writers group and attended the 2015 Starry Coast workshop.

When not writing fiction, Barbara works as Sr. Reviews Editor for the tech publication *Computerworld*. She lives in Brooklyn, New York with her partner Jim Freund and lots of toy penguins. Her website can be found at http://brooklynwriter.com.

She writes that "the origin of 'Sabbath Wine' stems from a variety of inspirations. They include three books: *Jews and Booze: Becoming American in the Age of Prohibition* by Marni Davis, *Last Call: The Rise and Fall of Prohibition* by Daniel Okrent, and *Without Sanctuary: Photographs and Postcards of Lynching in America*, from the collection of James Allen and John Littlefield. And, not least, stories from my family—especially my mother, who as a little girl would sit outside a storefront church and listen to the gospel music."

**Sonya Taaffe**'s short fiction and poetry can be found in the collections *Ghost Signs* (Aqueduct Press), *A Mayse-Bikhl* (Papaveria Press), *Postcards from the Province of Hyphens* (Prime Books), and *Singing Innocence and Experience* (Prime Books), and in various anthologies including *The Humanity of Monsters, Genius Loci: Tales of the Spirit of Place*, and *Dreams from the Witch*

*House: Female Voices of Lovecraftian Horror.* She is currently senior poetry editor at *Strange Horizons*; she holds master's degrees in Classics from Brandeis and Yale and once named a Kuiper belt object. She lives in Somerville with her husband and two cats.

She tells us that "'The Trinitite Golem' occurred to me first as a title in the summer of 2013. By the following February, I thought it was going to be a poem. A week-long writing blitz that concluded in early March disproved this notion. As with almost all of my historical fiction, I did a bibliography's worth of research for a couple of thousand words. My primary biographical source for Oppenheimer was Kai Bird and Martin J. Sherwin's *American Prometheus: The Triumph and Tragedy of J. Robert Oppenheimer* (2006). My primary source for nuclear physics was Robert Serber's *The Los Alamos Primer: The First Lectures on How to Build an Atomic Bomb* (1992). Rabi is only a walk-on in this story, but I recommend John S. Rigden's *Rabi, Scientist & Citizen* (2000) if you're interested in him: at the 1954 hearing, he was the one person besides Kitty Oppenheimer who spoke out openly against the House Un-American Activities Committee and the Atomic Energy Commission. The epigraph is from his testimony. I did not know until I had finished the story that 'Oppenheimer' is a name associated with a branch of the descendants of Rabbi Judah Loew ben Bezalel, the Mahara"l, the creator of the Golem of Prague, but that's all right; I don't imagine Oppie knew, either. This story appears with thanks to my father, Jaime Taaffe, who never thought I couldn't do the math."

**Alex Dally MacFarlane** is a writer, editor, and historian. When not translating from Classical Armenian or researching narrative maps in the legendary traditions of Alexander III of Macedon, Alex writes stories, found in *Clarkesworld Magazine, Phantasm Japan, Solaris Rising 3, Gigantic Worlds,* and *The Year's Best Science Fiction & Fantasy: 2014.* Alex is the editor of *Aliens: Recent Encounters* (2013) and *The Mammoth Book of SF Stories by Women* (2014), and in 2015 joined Sofia Samatar as coeditor of nonfiction and poetry for *Interfictions Online.* Follow @foxvertebrae on Twitter for more.

About "Two Bright Venuses," they write that the story "belongs to a framework set out in another story, 'Pocket Atlas of Planets,' published in *Interfictions Online.* It combines two of my favourite things: the wonders of space and the possibilities of gender beyond the binary. I wanted to expand on parts of that story in longer pieces, and this is the Venus section. When I originally wrote the short Venus section, I found (on Wikipedia) a translation of the 'Venus tablet of Ammisaduqa': a record of astronomical observations of Venus most likely made in the reign of King Ammisaduqa in the seventeenth century BCE. It describes the rising and setting of superior and inferior Venus, reflecting the different positions of Venus in Earth's sky, which led some to believe that there were two separate stars. That was the seed for this story. I'm currently working on a novella set on an alternate Mars, bringing in a lot of the non-binary gender considerations I want to explore further (which 'Two Bright Venuses' doesn't contain) as well as more space and alien life."

**Shveta Thakrar** is a writer of South Asian–flavored fantasy, social justice activist, and part-time nagini. Her work has appeared in *Interfictions Online, Mythic Delirium, Uncanny, Faerie, Strange Horizons, Kaleidoscope: Diverse YA Science Fiction and Fantasy Stories*, and *Steam-Powered 2: More Lesbian Steampunk Stories*. When not spinning stories about spider silk and shadows, magic and marauders, and courageous girls illuminated by dancing rainbow flames, Shveta crafts, devours books, daydreams, draws, travels, bakes, and occasionally even practices her harp. Find out more at http://shvetathakrar. com or follow her on Twitter @ShvetaThakrar.

As for "By Thread of Night and Starlight Needle," she had these thoughts to share: "Kill your darlings, they say, unless you can find a way to make them add to the story.

"What often goes unmentioned, however, is that sometimes a single line or paragraph, a glittering idea you really love, might come to you in your current manuscript but be destined for a different project. Then it's not a question of wrong text so much as of the wrong time, of not killing your darling so much as cutting it out of the false home and stitching it into the true one.

"This happened to me; a bit I cut from my novel in progress helped spark a new story, the one you can read in this anthology. I began to play with structure and metanarrative and attachments literal and figurative, and quickly realized the snippet I'd set aside would fit right into the burgeoning tale. So in it went, and if you'll forgive me the extended metaphor, I used my sharpest needle to sew it to the newer scraps of text.

"The result? A crazy quilt of witchy old ladies, bewildering beverages, and the question of just what, exactly, siblings owe each other. Oh, and seams. Lots and lots of seams."

**Cassandra Khaw** is a London-based writer with roots in Southeast Asia. She works as a business developer for Ysbryd Games, has published an e-novella with Abaddon Books, and writes a lot about fantastical creatures like old women with a sense of agency. When not otherwise doing all manner of other things, she practices Muay Thai and dance.

She writes that "'The Games We Play' came from a world I built when I was in college, about a dog-people and a bird-people who had, at some point in history, learned to coexist in a horrible way. The bird-people tithed about half their population to the dog-people, who gave them military support and whatnot in exchange. I never did anything with the world, but the idea of it stuck. And 'The Games We Play' kinda came about because of it, and because of thoughts about how we sometimes help continue systemic abuse without realizing it. But mostly, it comes from rage. Rage at people who will abuse the weak, who will manipulate them for the sake of simple, stupid games. Rage that may never find resolution, but a powerful rage all the same."

**Keffy R. M. Kehrli** is a science fiction and fantasy writer currently living on Long Island in New York. When he's not writing, he's busy working on his PhD, doing science, or editing *GlitterShip* (http://www.glittership.com). His own fiction has appeared in publications such as *Uncanny Magazine*, *Apex Magazine*, *Lightspeed Magazine*, and *Clockwork Phoenix 5*, among others.

About "The Road, and the Valley, and the Beasts," he writes, "The core of this story has hopefully ended up being the characters and how they deal with living in a mostly unknowable world. However, it started with the image of an old, mysterious road and the beings that use that road. A lot of fantasy deals with ancient architecture that has survived to the 'present day' of the story, and that's something which has always fascinated me."

**Rich Larson** was born in West Africa, has studied in Rhode Island, and worked in Spain, and at twenty-three now writes in Edmonton, Alberta. His short work has been nominated for the Theodore Sturgeon Award and appears in multiple *Year's Best* anthologies as well as in magazines such as *Asimov's*, *Analog*, *Clarkesworld*, *Fantasy & Science Fiction*, *Interzone*, *Strange Horizons*, *Lightspeed*, and *Apex Magazine*. Find him at http://richwlarson.tumblr.com.

He tells us, "I was inspired to write 'Innumerable Glimmering Lights' after reading about liquid oceans under Europa's ice crust. The idea of sapient life evolving in a similar situation, underneath a physical barrier that blocked out the sky and stars, was really interesting to me. It might be a huge turning point for an aquatic civilization to become aware of outer space for the first time. Four Warm Currents was conceived as a sort of Copernicus figure in that way, permanently reordering their known universe."

**Beth Cato** hails from Hanford, California, but currently writes and bakes cookies in a lair west of Phoenix, Arizona. She shares the household with a hockey-loving husband, a numbers-obsessed son, and a cat the size of a canned ham. She's the author of *The Clockwork Dagger* (a finalist for the 2015 Locus Award for Best First Novel) and *The Clockwork Crown* from Harper Voyager. Follow her at http://bethcato.com and on Twitter at @BethCato.

About "The Souls of Horses," she had this to share: "When I was in fifth grade, I won a school district library essay contest by saying I wanted to write books about the Civil War and horses, maybe even from the horse's point of view. Here I am, almost twenty-five years later. I feel like 'The Souls of Horses' is the story I have been waiting for all this time. It took me that long to know how to tell it. I think my inner child is pleased."

On weekdays, **Mike Allen** writes the arts column for the daily newspaper in Roanoke, Virginia. Most of the rest of his time he devotes to writing, editing, and publishing. He's the editor of *Mythic Delirium* magazine and the *Clockwork Phoenix* anthologies, and the author of the novel *The Black Fire Concerto* as well as the short story collections *Unseaming* and *The Spider Tapestries*. He has been a Nebula Award and Shirley Jackson Award finalist, and has won three Rhysling Awards for poetry.

If you read Mike's introduction, you may recall him mentioning that he likes to hide things in his bio notes at the back of the *Clockwork Phoenix* books. Yet this time he did nothing of the sort. He left not a hint that the *Clockwork Phoenix* series might be his bid to recreate or even improve on the fantasy compilations that blew his mind open when he was just a kid, Terry Carr's and Martin H. Greenberg's *A Treasury of Modern Fantasy* being the most guilty of all culprits. Nor did he suggest that *Clockwork Phoenix* could simply be viewed as the prose version of the offbeat, theme-linked mix of provocatively crafted words he and his coeditor Anita Allen had already been assembling for years in the form of their poetry journal, *Mythic Delirium*. (Now that *Mythic Delirium* also includes prose, the metaphor no longer smoothly maps.) It certainly never crossed his mind to reveal the delight he's taken over the years in the various expressions of puzzlement he's read as readers and reviewers have pondered what makes a story right for *Clockwork Phoenix*.

(He does know what makes a clockwork phoenix tick, but he'll never tell.)

Mike did include that he still can't believe how lucky he is, that his particular variety of artistic weirdness connects so strongly with so many. He's also bloody lucky to have such a beautiful and creative soulmate in his artist wife Anita. (And he concedes that the entertainment provided by mutt Loki and felines Persephone and Pandora also constitutes a form of luck.)

You can follow Mike's exploits as a writer at http://descentintolight.com, as an editor at http://mythicdelirium.com, and all at once on Twitter at @mythicdelirium. You can also register for his newsletter, "Memos from the Abattoir," at http://tinyurl.com/abattoir-memos.

# ACKNOWLEDGMENTS

The campaign to create *Clockwork Phoenix 5* easily constitutes the most ambitious and complicated project I have ever tackled. Individual projects that were in themselves laborious and time-consuming doubled as sprockets fitted into the workings of the beast, interlocking to animate a greater whole. With so much to keep track of, I'd best just apologize up front to anyone I unintentionally leave out.

Thanks first and foremost must go to Anita Allen, my wife and cocreator, who (as she has done with every volume) arranged the stories in the order they appear in this book. She helped me sort through more than 1,300 submissions, both by reading stories as they came in over the transom and offering feedback on the finalists. She also made jewelry, etched tumblers, and even canned jars of jam to broaden the range of rewards we could offer in our Kickstarter campaign to fund this book. She used her editorial eye to arrange the stories in several of the other books put up as rewards, such as *Mythic Delirium* volumes one and two, my collections *Unseaming* and *The Spider Tapestries*, and C. S. E. Cooney's collection *Bone Swans*. Finally, she supplied treasured advice, sanity, support, and love every single step of the way.

Thanks to Paula Arwen Owen for her gorgeous cover art for this book, for the new *Clockwork Phoenix* emblem, and for coming up with rewards of her own to help bring the anthology into being, such as decals and signed prints; and more thanks to her and her husband Kevin for their unflagging shows of support. (I think as the Kickstarter campaign came down to the wire, Paula and Kevin were at least as stressed as Anita and I were.)

I must shower gratitude on my nagini liege, Shveta Thakrar, for the amazing job she did copyediting this anthology on short notice, and for the many evenings she lent this editor an understanding ear. She received help with the former task from Francesca Forrest, whom I also owe a huge debt of thanks, not just for offering her novel *Pen Pal* and hand-decorated bottles as bounty for Kickstarter backers, but also for helping me keep my digital magazine *Mythic Delirium* running (more or less) without a hitch in her capacity as the 'zine's copyeditor.

On the *Clockwork Phoenix* side, my assistant editors Cathy Reniere, Sally Brackett Robertson, and Sabrina West, all veterans of volumes past, helped me stem the relentless tide of story submissions. Meanwhile, Christina Sng, my new assistant digital editor for *Mythic Delirium*, provided invaluable and timely help producing the magazine amidst the tumult.

Catherynne M. Valente, Laird Barron, C. S. E. Cooney, and Paul Dellinger all graciously agreed to let me offer their fiction as special rewards. In addition, several more accomplished wordsmiths stepped up during the campaign to add to the goodies: Nicole Kornher-Stace, Rachel Swirsky, Marie Brennan, John Grant, and Patty Templeton. Ken Schneyer proffered sage advice and his skills as a critiquer, plus the chance to get tuckerized in one of his deftly written stories. Thanks, too, to Neil Gaiman, both for signing his poem in the tenth-anniversary *Mythic Delirium* issue and for sharing that special issue's availability as a prize with his fans.

A shout-out goes to Carlos Hernandez for organizing a Reddit Ask Me Anything promotion with practically no lead time, with additional tips of the hat to Benjanun Sriduangkaew for explaining the lay of the land and to Claire Cooney, Francesca Forrest, Margo Lea-Hurwicz, and Paul Barnett for getting the conversation started.

Alex Shvartsman, Lynne and Michael Thomas, Bill Campbell, C. S. E. Cooney, and Rose Lemberg were all kind enough to suggest to the backers of their own worthy projects that they should take a gander at mine. Jeremy Holmes set aside a precious chunk of time from family and gaming to co-script and shoot the campaign's video, and Dan Stace provided timely and vital technical wizardry on multiple occasions.

I don't know how I could have gotten through this without the cheerful signal boosting of the many contributors to the first four books in the *Clockwork Phoenix* series and the new incarnation of *Mythic Delirium*, not to mention previous subscribers and Kickstarter backers. Here's where I'll single out Rose Lemberg again, whose incredibly creative suggestions made during our very first Kickstarter are still paying dividends the third time around.

Let me also bow in awe and appreciation to a special muse whose contribution is one of the most crucial of all. You know who you are. We'll do dinner soon.

And now a curtain call, the other person who gets the award for both "Most Giving" and "Most Crucial": Elizabeth Campbell. None of the wonderful things that have happened in my writing, editing, and publishing career over the past five years could have happened without her.

Finally, my everlasting gratitude to the backers of the *Clockwork Phoenix 5* Kickstarter campaign, both to those few who have chosen to remain anonymous and the many fine folks whose names are listed below.

Danny Adams
Seth Alcorn
Cristina Alves
Jenise Aminoff
Erik Amundsen
Scott H. Andrews
Anonymous
Eagle Archambeault
Asymptotic Binary
Daniel Ausema
Ashley M Baldon
Rayne Banneck
Barbara Barnett-Stewart
Andrew Barton

Robin Bayless
Bec
beentsy
Chris Bekofske
Beth Bernobich
Martin Bernstein
Deborah Biancotti
Edith Hope Bishop
Carina Bissett
Chris Bissette
Chad Bowden
Lisa M. Bradley
Kelly Braun
Romy Brizak

Samantha Brock
Cathy Brown
Terri Bruce
D Burkett
Charlie Byrd
Elizabeth Cady
Patrick Cahn
Dan Campbell
Autumn Canter
Anthony R. Cardno
Paul Cardullo
Castle KleinHouser
CGJulian
Carolyn Charron
Matthew Cheney
Neal Chuang
Ian Chung
Sara Cleto
Jessica Cohen
Alicia Cole
C.S.E. Cooney
Fred Coppersmith
Cathy Cordes
Aleph Craven
Jennifer Crow
Vida Cruz
Dana
Sean Dannenfeldt
Jeanne Davidson
Rob Davies
David Davis
DB
DeadWriter
Benet Devereux
Alexandra Dimou
Zach Drager
B L Draper

Shana DuBois
Jeff Eaton
David Edelstein
Hisham El-Far
EnricoB
Gary Every
Lennhoff Family
Matthew Farrer
Joanna Fay
C.C. Finlay
Ellen Fleischer
Sam Fleming (ravenbait)
Kori Flint
Victoria Sandbrook Flynn
Francesca Forrest
M. J. Francis
D Franklin
Alis Franklin
Dina G.
Ken Gagne
Joanna Galbraith
Kurt C. Garcia
Gwynne Garfinkle
Gavran
M. E. Gibbs
Andrew Gilstrap
The Goblin Queen to Whom
Mike Allen Owes Fealty
Brady Golden
Richard Gombert
Jeremy M. Gottwig
Jenny Graver
Alicia Graves
Cathy Green
Arthur Green
A. T. Greenblatt
Liz Grzyb

Carol J. Guess
Stephanie Gunn
Amy Gwiazdowski
Daniel P. Haeusser
Kathleen T Hanrahan
AJ Harm
C.R. Harper
Benjamin Hausman
Edie Hawthorne
Kate Heartfield
Bran Heatherby
Andy Heckroth
Samantha Henderson
Michael L. Hicks
Cameron Higby-Naquin
Woodrow "asim" Hill
Erin Hoffman-John
Joseph Hoopman
Simon Horn
Lauren Hougen
Margo-Lea Hurwicz
J.M.
Izlinda Jamaluddin
Shawna Jaquez
Paul y cod asyn Jarman
Arun Jiwa
John Philip Johnson
Glenn A Jones
Michael M. Jones
Jules Jones
Rachael K. Jones
Melanie Joy
Ranti Junus
Max Kaehn
Andrew Kaye
Keffy R. M. Kehrli
Brian Kitchell

Jeremy T Kizer
Yoshio Kobayashi
Jeanne Kramer-Smyth
Barbara Krasnoff
Matthew Kressel
Lace
Nat Lanza
lauowolf
Shiyiya LeCompte
Yin Harn Lee
Y. K. Lee
Sandi Leibowitz
Zoe Lewycky
Joanna Lowenstein
C.S. MacCath
Alex Dally MacFarlane
S.M. Mack
Kate MacLeod
Alex de Jarem Mandarino
Tommi Mannila
Susana Marcelo
Kevin J. "Womzilla" Maroney
Arkady Martine
Michael J. Martinez
Robin L. Martinez
Melanie Marttila
Michelle Matel
D. Elan McAtee
Elizabeth R. McClellan
Lynne A. McCullough
Ian McFarlin
Ian McHugh
Lynette Mejia
Chris Mihal
Kara Miyasato
Virginia M Mohlere
Samuel Montgomery-Blinn

Diane Severson Mori
Brooks Moses
Andreas Muegge
Simo Muinonen
Vic & Zoe Munoz
Tricia Psarreas Murray
Paul Muse
Paul Nasrat
Craig Neumeier
Andrew Nicolle
Richard Novak
Victor Fernando R. Ocampo
Erica Pantel
Tiago Becerra Paolini
Dominik Parisien
Chuck Parker
Chelle Parker
Rhonda Parrish
Susan Patrick
Helene Pedot
David Perlmutter
Sasha Pixlee
Amanda Power
Sara Puls
Brian Quirt
rachaar
Rivqa Rafael
Adam Rains
Jeff Raymond
The Reinhardts
Catherine Reniere
Suzanne Reynolds-Alpert
Julia Rios
Aaron Roberts
Martin Roberts
S. Brackett Robertson
Karen Robinson

K.A. Rochnik
Lauren Roy
Anastasia Rudman
María Pilar San Román
Amy Scheiderman
Ken Schneyer
Rebecca Schwarz
Nick Scorza
Gopakumar Sethuraman
Katherine Shan
Patti Short
Sita
Mike Skolnik
S Sloyan
Charles Smith
Andrea Smith
Gregory P. Smith
Cat Sparks
Spidere
Mary Spila
Margaret St.John
April Steenburgh
Erica Stevenson
Ian Stockdale
Amy H. Sturgis
Robert E. Stutts
summervillain
Jonah Sutton-Morse
Rachel Swirsky
SwordFire
Tanbiere
Judith Tarr
Natalia Theodoridou
Dave Thompson
Tibicina
Tibs
Chris Tierney

Tiggerperson
Trentmw
John S. Troutman
Anne Tweed
amber van dyk
Dave Versace
Viktor With a K
Jetse de Vries
Ray Vukcevich
Lauren Wallace
Brittany Warman
James Weber
Sarah Lynn Weintraub
Eric Wells
Sabrina West
Tom Whiteley

Brontë Christopher Wieland
Tor André Wigmostad
Ollie Wild
Connie Wilkins
Meg Winikates
Cliff Winnig
A.C. Wise
Jessica Wolf
Navah Wolfe
Greer Woodward
Xewleer
Isabel Yap
Alan Yee
yo
Gretchen Zelle

# Copyright notices

Horsham Township Library

CPSIA information can be obtained at www.ICGtesting.com
Printed in the USA
LVOW07s2303300316

481511LV00006B/258/P

9 780988 912472